DEBBY HANDMAN

House on Sand

She did not know her house was built on sand until the storm hit.

This book was professionally typeset on Reedsy.
Find out more at reedsy.com

Foreword

Praise For *House on Sand:*

House on Sand taps emotions every woman can relate to feeling - heartbreak, questioning God with *"Why me?"*, and the deep joy of a circle of genuine, faithful friends while teaching us to apply a depth of love that enables forgiveness.

-*Kate Bowers Educator, Speaker and Author of Publicly Schooled*

In *House of Sand*, Debby Handman courageously tackles the issue of infidelity and the deep hurt, betrayal, and trial of faith that ensues. Handman shows us, through her courageous heroine, Ellie, that no matter what trials we face, God brings hope and healing—often in unexpected ways. The cast of characters in this heartfelt story will remind you of the importance of friendship, prayer, and beautiful second chances.

—*Melanie Campbell, Author of One Woman Falling and Winner of the 2020 Cascade Award*

Acknowledgement

To Seth and Isaac the most amazing sons a mother could have. You always remind me of God's goodness and grace. Thank you for being the kind of boys that let mom do her work without complaining and griping. You have been so patient with me. To my loving parents: Steve and Carol. Mom, thank you for proofreading. Dad, thank you for always believing in me and thinking I'm talented. This book would not exist it wasn't for my praying sisters and muses: Alesha, Heather, Ronda, and Sara. You add so much spice and joy to my life. Your prayers are nourishment to my soul. Melanie Campbell, your kindness and advice were a wonderful blessing and help to me. Kate Bowers, you have been an amazing inspiration. Thank you for helping me in learning the ins and outs of putting a book together. I am also thankful for all of my praying sisters: Shelly, Melissa, Jayme this means you too! Erica and Kyla, I didn't forget you. Thank you for the love, support, and laughter. Thank you to all my initial readers who believed in this story and worked alongside me to make this novel a reality. You believed in me even when I didn't believe in myself. Thank you to all of you who reached out with encouragement and who faithfully read my blog. You have encouraged me so much by letting me know my story resonates and provides help to you in your own life circumstances. I dedicate this book to my Aunt Julia, who was truly a woman of faith, a single mother like me who loved her two sons with her full heart. Like Ellie, she was brave and courageous. I am foremost thankful to God for transforming pain into hope. This is truly what it means to be victorious.

Chapter 1

Part I

Tremors

Whatever the natural cause, sin is the true cause of all earthquakes.

—John Wesley

Ellie Gold did not know her world was built on a fault line. She had grown accustomed to the tremors and learned to ignore them. It was easy to do. Small quakes are often imperceptible, a shift in the ground so slight, they can only be recorded by a seismograph machine in a scientist's lab. Large quakes, on the other hand, can't be ignored. They are deadly.

* * *

Her thoughts were interrupted by arguing from inside the house and then screaming. She followed the sound of wails to the living room where 8-year-old Miles howled on the couch, an accusing finger pointed at his 10-year-old brother. As crocodile tears fell from his cheeks, Ellie groaned inwardly. She could tell the difference between genuine injury and theatrics. Miles

1

was going for an academy award with this performance. Her older son's face was rigid with indifference as he ignored his brother's screams and continued to play on his game console. "Miles, what happened?"

"John hit me and called me stupid!"

"John, is that true?"

"No, I never touched him. He kept touching me and he hit me too."

"It's my turn to play the Switch and I'm not stupid!" Miles wailed.

Ellie fought for focus and went into mom mode. "John, hand me the game. Neither of you get to play for the rest of the day. I'm tired of this constant fighting. John, you've been playing that game for hours."

Before John could respond Miles flung his small fists at his brother behind Ellie's back. She turned and grabbed his waist, struggling to restrain his squirming body. "Miles! No! Stop! John, stop egging him on." Ellie felt anger rising to the surface. "You know what? Just stop. Both of you. I've had enough. Go to your rooms!"

John stared at Ellie with sheer hatred. "I didn't even do anything." He threw the console on the couch.

"Go." Ellie pointed to his room with an authoritative gesture she didn't feel.

The boys skulked to their corners. Ellie moved to the kitchen to prepare an afternoon snack of apples and peanut butter. "I can do anything through Him who gives me strength," she whispered as she consciously slowed her breathing to relax. Even as she repeated her go to scripture verse in her head, she doubted the veracity of the words. God had felt distant at best recently. She glanced at her watch. Davis was late. She bit her lip trying to hold back the litany of criticisms forming in the back of her mind. Lately when it came to Davis she felt a deepening frustration, but she could always rationalize away her worries. Tremors like these were common in any marriage, small lapses in communication. She was never one to make mountains out of mole hills. At that moment, the phone rang.

"Ellie, it's me."

"Nora?" Ellie had to pull the phone tighter to her ear to hear her older sister's reedy voice.

"Yeah, it's Nora. Look I'm sorry, but something's happened." Her voice was faint, birdlike.

"What Nora? You don't sound good, what's going on?"

"I had a little bit of an episode yesterday. My doctor prescribed me some new meds and well, I was thinking I could wait till I picked them up at the pharmacy and that was about three weeks ago."

She could not hide the strain in her voice. "Nora, are you trying to tell me that you're not on your meds?"

Nora's voice became softer. "They cost $400 and my insurance won't cover them. The old meds were about $100, but Dr. Wills said they weren't working as well as they should, and I oughta try this new one."

Ellie closed her eyes keeping her tone even, "Nora, your prescription should be covered by your OHP plan. Are you sure you ran the purchase through your insurance?"

Nora's voice turned strident. "Ellie, I don't even know. My mood swings have been crazy, and I have headaches all the time. I almost bit the head off of a client yesterday who was checking in and Dr. Mike had, well you know, *the talk* with me. He says if there's another episode like that one, he's going to let me go. I need the meds to work, Ellie. Look, I still have my job, but you know what I make never covers all the bills."

Ellie swallowed the lump forming in her throat. Nora had been working as a receptionist in a dental office. She was lucky to have the job and everyone in the family was just praying she'd keep it. Ellie's father had called in on every favor in the book to get her that job. She gripped the phone to her ear and forced herself to speak in a measured tone. "Okay, Nora. Look, I'll transfer you the money again."

"Oh, Ellie, Thank you. You know I'll pay you back or I'll do something for you. You always fix everything. I can always count on my little sis."
Did she detect a slight trace of resentment in her sister's voice?

"How are Lee and Mariah?" Ellie pressed.

"Lee's been pretty down. He hasn't found a job and he's been looking for months. I'm just afraid he's going to stop looking all together."

"Oh, Nora. I'm sorry to hear that. You know I'll keep my ear out for any jobs in his field. He's a great diesel mechanic and anyone needing his skills would be lucky to have him."

Ellie did not add that alcoholism made him unreliable. After all, she did not blame Lee. Loving Nora came at high cost literally and figuratively. She tried to keep her voice neutral. "And Mariah?"

"Oh, sis, I can't believe my little girl is starting college in the fall and at the University of Oregon. Did you know only ten percent of her senior class is moving on to four-year college? She was picking out her political science classes and everything. Ellie, she's doing everything I couldn't. She wants to be a lawyer, a lawyer!"

Ellie could hear the pride in Nora's voice. "Nora, that's wonderful. We're so proud of her too." The turn in conversation toward Mariah made Ellie realize she hadn't heard from Nora's daughter in a few months. The last time she spoke to her was when she helped Mariah with her University of Oregon application. Maybe things were turning around for Nora and her family. Ellie hoped the best for her sister.

Nora was still talking, "Ellie, you know how smart Mariah is? Right? She scored over 1200 on her SATS. She's going to take that college by storm."

"We're all so proud of her, Nora." Ellie needed to wrap up the conversation. "I'm going to have to go soon, but I'll send you the cash through the usual App."

"Thanks Ellie." Nora hesitated for a moment. "I know it's a lot to ask, but groceries have been a little tight too."

Ellie inadvertently rolled her eyes. "I'll put a little extra in okay?"

"Thank you. My little sis has really arrived in the world. You know I appreciate everything you do for me, right?"

"I know you do. It's okay. Goodbye Nora. Hopefully we'll get to see each other at Thanksgiving."

She pressed the end call icon on her screen and the phone went silent. Her stomach rose and fell uncomfortably. Whenever she gave Nora money it strained their relationship. Nora was supposed to be the older sister and Ellie felt the tension of displacing the order of things. Nora had once many years ago been the older sister Ellie looked up to, but when Nora was in high school the dynamic between them changed forever. They didn't know at the time that Nora had a chemical disorder, that her brain refused to process emotions in a rational way.

The blessed person has a Christian obligation to help the needy, Ellie heard her father's voice in her head. Wasn't Ellie's life filled with blessings? She had stability both in temperament and finances. Nora, in contrast, had neither. Her sister lived out her emotional life on a roller coaster.

Her mind drifted from Nora back to Davis and she wondered what was taking him so long. He had been gone constantly the last few months or so it seemed. Ellie had been trying very hard to be understanding and patient but Davis had changed.

When the phone rang, Ellie jumped. She was already tense from her call with Nora. She immediately picked up when she saw Davis' name appear on her screen. "Davis? Where are you?"

"Ell, Ellie! I can't hear you very well." His voice was muted by static. She could tell he was on the road, maybe on the edge of a mountain pass where phone service was patchy.

A desperate urge overcame her, to talk to him before she lost him again. "Davis, where are you? I haven't heard from you all day."

"I'm pulling over so I can talk." She heard the flick of the ignition as he turned off the engine. The static stopped abruptly, and Davis' voice was suddenly clear. "Ellie, I'm on my way from Bend. I had to go to Bear Mountain Bookstore to get the commentary I needed for Sunday's sermon."

The heat rose to her chest. "What? Davis, I wish you would have told me that. It means you won't be home for at least two more hours."

Davis' voice was tight and clipped. "Look, I'm sorry and I need a favor."

The tension traveled to her neck and shoulders, the knots in her stomach churning. "I'm about to start dinner for the boys. What is it?"

"Sally called me. The hospice nurse told Sally he may not make it through the night."

"Oh, Davis. That's awful. She doesn't have anyone. Poor woman. What does she need?"

"She was hoping I could come over and pray with her, but I'm just leaving

Bend now and I can't make it. I was hoping you could go."

Ellie paced back and forth as she grasped her cell tighter to her cheek. "I've got the boys. What about Walter or Bud?" The church elders would usually help Davis in a pinch.

Davis' voice was rushed, impatient. "Ellie, you know they've had to step up a lot lately. I don't want them to think I'm not doing my job."

Her meandering thoughts found focus on Davis' dilemma. Problem solving was one of her gifts. "I guess if I bring their DS devices, John can stay in the car and I could bring Miles in with me. They're pretty good boys when they're separated and busy. When we're done, I'll just take them to McDonalds or Taco Bell. Okay Davis, I think I can make it work. I just wish you would text me or let me know when you're not even in town. I mean what if something happened with the boys?"

"Yeah, I'm sorry Ell. I wouldn't have gone if it was something I could live without." In spite of the apology, he sounded angry.

Ellie swallowed her own anger and spoke to him as she would a wayward student, "Would you please text me and communicate a little better next time? I don't mind helping you, but I don't like being taken for granted."

Davis' voice lost its edge. "I will and I'm really sorry. You're saving my skin here. Okay, I gotta go, if I'm ever going to get home."

After the call went cold, Ellie closed her eyes remembering a time not so long ago when Davis could do no wrong in her eyes. As she washed her face with warm water and braided her hair, she realized she could not remember the last time she had heard him laugh. She could not remember the last time they had laughed together. Ellie felt the tremor, the strange sensation of the ground shifting beneath her feet.

She bribed the boys with McDonalds and ushered them towards the car with their game devices in tow. The sun was brilliant through the hazy skies of August even though it was past six in the evening. Ellie could taste smoke in the air, which was not unusual this time of year. Long gone were the rains which vitalized the Willamette Valley and fires now raged in forests across Oregon. Most of the year there was no more beautiful place on the planet than the Willamette Valley, but August was the one exception.

She pulled into the Pearson driveway and Ellie absorbed the vibe of their house. Although a solidly working-class neighborhood, their home was beautifully maintained with what HGTV would call curb appeal. The house was painted a dark blue but had a striking white door with jeweled mosaic glass inset in the shape of a dove. Sally and Gary in their retirement had both been obsessed with gardening and every available space on their property was claimed by flowers or plants. The artist in Ellie loved the clash of colors and she smiled as she traveled the walkway to their front door. Even game obsessed Miles looked up in awe at the magnificence of the Pearson sunflowers.

"Wow. Those are huge."

The flowers were as big as small trees and framed both sides of the house. Hiding between the sunflowers were stalks of corn and tomato plants. Orange, pink, and purple dahlias formed a colorful border around the entire house. The eclectic garden was a testament of the life the Pearson's built together, a marriage built on love.

She tapped on the glass mosaic. A diminutive and frail woman appeared at the door. Sally was in her 70's. Her hair was solid white and cut in a short, no nonsense pixie style. She had sharp features and piercing eyes that now looked red and swollen from crying. "Hi Sally. Davis called me and told me the news. I just wanted to come down and pray with you."

Sally reached out her arms to Ellie. "Thank you for coming sweet girl. I've just been sitting here listening to him breathe and I know the Lord's going to take him any moment. I can hardly stand it."

Sally was so thin Ellie could feel the protruding edges of her shoulder blades through the light fabric of her summer sweater. "I'm so sorry Sally. I've brought Miles. I couldn't get anyone to watch him on short notice. He's perfectly happy to sit in the kitchen and play his game while we visit. We won't stay too long."

"That's just fine, honey," Sally said as she pulled away from the hug. She smiled at Miles. "I have some cookies too."

Miles looked up from his game. "I love cookies."

Sally patted his head playfully. "You do? I thought you would. Come on in little gentleman."

Despite the stress Sally was enduring, her home was free of dust and smelled of cinnamon and brown sugar. Ellie loved her white and blue kitchen. Finely crafted open cabinets displayed China and knick-knacks including a decorative assortment of spoons and paddles, her Dutch heritage in proud display. Sally handed Ellie a cup of coffee.

"I know it's late for coffee, but I've been drinking it all day. It looks like you could use a cup too Ellie dear."

"Oh, Sally, that's lovely. Thank you. You don't have to play the host for me. I'm here for you, remember?"

"You don't know how much I appreciate it. I like keeping my mind on something else. You're a breath of fresh air."

They sat together at the table. Sally brought Miles a plate of chocolate chip cookies and a tall glass of milk. His eyes widened. "Thank you Mrs. Pearson."

"Miles, you know you can just call me Sally." She tousled his hair before sitting across from Ellie at the table.

Miles smiled and rammed a cookie in his mouth before returning to his video game.

Ellie placed her hand gently on Sally's. "Tell me how he's doing?"

Sally's lips tightened into a straight line as she allowed herself a moment to gather her thoughts. "Well, I'd call his breathing labored. That's what it is. He's in pain and hospice set him up with a morphine drip. He's just slowly drifting away." Sally's show of strength faltered as she choked back tears.

"I'm sorry," Ellie sighed. "Poor Gary, he's been in such pain. Has he been able to say anything?"

Sally's voice steadied. "Not much. He squeezes my hand. He knows I'm here and I know it's almost time. This pancreatic cancer has been nothing but pain and suffering for him. I just don't want him to suffer anymore."

"Sally, you've been such an amazing partner to Gary. Look at this house, the beautiful life you've built together. When he goes to Jesus, he's going to be free of all the pain and suffering, but it doesn't mean it's going to be easy to let him go."

Sally looked at Ellie through her tears. "I think I'm ready to let him go. I never would have said that a week ago, but the pain, Ellie, the pain. I just can't see him like that."

"Should we go in together?"

Sally led Ellie to the back of the house where the bedrooms were located. Ellie could hear Gary's ragged, erratic breathing before entering the room. She knew from the sound he did not have long.

In his full health Gary had been a large and rather imposing figure but lying in the hospice bed he looked frail and pallid. He was hunched over on his side in a fetal position, moaning between labored breaths as if bracing for the next wave of pain. The morphine drip and IV were set up, but other than that, the room was mostly spared of large medical equipment. Hospice had left for the day, but now it was a matter of time.

Ellie approached Gary gently and lay her hand on the coolness of his wrinkled shoulder left exposed by the loose fitting hospice gown. "Gary, it's Ellie. I'm here to pray with you. It's good to see you." She put gentle pressure on his shoulder and began to pray. "The Lord is my shepherd. I shall not want. He makes me lie down in green pastures. He leads me to still waters. He restores my soul. He leads me to paths of righteousness for his namesake. Even though I walk through the valley of the shadow of death, I will fear no evil. For you are with me." Ellie moved her hand from Gary's shoulder and held his hand. His palm felt clammy in hers and she tried to steady his frail trembling fingers by squeezing his hand.

"Gary, God is with us. He is with you!" She continued the recitation. "Your rod and your staff, they comfort me..." When she had finished the Psalm, she forged her own heartfelt prayer. "Lord, please welcome Gary into your Kingdom. We pray for his pain to end. We pray that he will have eternal life, peace, and joy. I pray also for Sally who he leaves behind. Please provide her with the peace that passes all understanding. Help her to know that Gary is with you and that he is safe." Sally lay her hand on her shoulder and Ellie sensed she wanted to pray.

"Lord, take this man, my husband. I give him to you. He's my everything, but I give him to you," she began to sob and could not finish. Ellie squeezed her hand tighter and felt the tears forming in her own eyes. When the prayer was finished, they sat together and listened to Gary's uneven breathing. Ellie excused herself from the room and took her phone out. She hurriedly texted Roberta, the leader of the South Hills Christian Women's Group.

Roberta,

I'm here with Sally Pearson. Gary does not have long. Please let our church people know to pray for them. Also, if any of our ladies would be willing to sit with Sally tonight, it would be a real blessing. Gary could pass at any time and Sally could use support and love.

Thanks,

Ellie.

Upon reentering the bedroom, she saw Sally stroking her husband's forehead with divine tenderness. Ellie watched silently for several moments.

"What is his favorite hymn?"

"In the Garden"

Ellie smiled. "Of course, it is. Should we sing it?"

Sally smiled down on her husband. "I think he would like that."

They sang together.

I come to the garden alone, while the dew is still on the roses.

And the voice I hear, falling on my ear, the son of God discloses.

And he walks with me, and he talks with me and he tells me I am his own.

And the joy we share, as we tarry there. None other has ever known.

Ellie left the room and went back to the kitchen. Miles had finished his cookies but was still furiously pressing buttons on his device. Her phone chimed, a text from Roberta.

We are praying. Maxine is on her way over.

A rush of air escaped her lips. Maxine was a wonderful prayer warrior, and she was also a good listener. She was the perfect person to minister to Sally, to comfort her during the difficult night to come.

They said their goodbyes to Sally at the front door. Ellie assured her the church was praying and that they were only a phone call away. Miles skipped ahead as they walked through the front yard back to the Ford

10

Explorer. John was lying down with his seat reclined all the way back and his feet propped against the window. The engine had been running the entire time to keep the A/C on.

"That took forever." John whined when Ellie opened the car door.

"This is from Mrs. Pearson." Ellie plopped a Ziploc bag into his lap.

"What is this?"

"They're like the most delicious chocolate cookies in the world," chimed in Miles. "Way better than Mom's."

"Oh, awesome! I like that lady," John said as he pulled the bag open.

"I like her too," Ellie agreed. "John, I really appreciate your patience." She stroked his cheek with gentle affection and then turned her focus to driving.

Since it was now 8 pm, the roads were relatively clear as they drove to McDonalds. Miles spoke from the backseat, "Mom, where did you learn all that stuff?"

"What stuff, Miles?"

"I don't know. Helping people like Sally."

Ellie smiled. She thought Miles was completely absorbed in his game, apparently not. "I learned it from Grandpa and Grandma mostly. You know Grandpa's been a pastor for nearly forty years. He's helped a lot of people. I got to see him pray and comfort people during their hard times a lot when I was a girl your age."

John interrupted. "Mom also went to school like Dad to be a pastor. It's where they met."

"Yes, that's true, John."

"Mom's good at that minister stuff," Miles said. "She got Mrs. Pearson to give us cookies and everything."

Ellie laughed. "I think Mrs. Pearson would have given you cookies anyway, Miles. She likes you, but you are sweet boys and I love you both."

They did not arrive home till about 9 p.m. Davis was still not home. "Miles, it's time to take a bath and then bed."

"Do I have to?"

"Yes, you have to. I don't want a stinky boy."

"Mom, I'm not a stinky boy."

"You will be if you don't take that bath."

John laughed, "Mom said you were stinky, oooh stinky Miles, stinky Miles!"

"You're stinky and you smell like poop!" yelled Miles.

"Stop both of you!" Ellie went to John and Mile's bathroom and started the water in the tub adding toys and bubble bath solution.

"John, don't forget to brush your teeth."

Miles took a quick bath and Ellie rushed through their bedtime routine, reading to Miles and praying with both boys. Her stomach was churning and her back and shoulders ached. *What if Davis was in an accident and needed help? What if he had hit a deer? Why didn't he call?* For a moment she remembered the panic her family experienced so many years ago when Nora went missing and they feared the worst. That fear had marked Ellie. No one could forget the fear even if they wanted to. Ellie suppressed the dark thoughts the best she could while cursing his thoughtlessness. Finally, she heard the key in the door.

"Sounds like Dad's home. He should be in to give you hugs before you're asleep, okay?"

She left Miles' door open just a crack and contemplated what strategy to take when seeing Davis for the first time that day. She felt a pressing need. *You've got to fix this, Ellie.* She forced a smile and raised her face to greet Davis. He shut the front door behind him and looked at her briefly. "Hey Ell, I'd like to see if I could just work about an hour on my sermon before going to bed."

Ellie hesitated before speaking, "I was hoping we could talk. You're so late. What took so long?"

Davis seemed oblivious to her concern. "I was behind a logging truck and there was an accident on the mountain. It took forever to get over the pass. You know there's no phone service up there. I'm exhausted and now I've got so much to do tomorrow, I don't know where to start."

She looked at him as if she was seeing him for the first time. He had lost nearly 30 pounds in the last few months. At first, everyone at church had given him compliments on his efforts to get healthier and shed those extra pounds. He really looked good and had seemed happier for a few months despite his long work hours. Now, Ellie felt he looked haggard, tired, and aged. She spoke carefully. "The boys are in their rooms. They're almost asleep, but probably not quite. They'd like to see you. They haven't seen you all day. We've missed you."

"Uh…okay, alright. I'll be with them soon. I'm just going to get a quick bite."

He moved past her and headed to the kitchen. Ellie noted that he could barely look her in the eye. The weight felt heavier than ever. She was certain. There was something wrong. *I'm in this marriage too. Do you see me?* Another voice inside her reproached such selfishness, *what kind of wife are you?*

Ellie swallowed hard as her mind went to even darker places, suspicious places. *Davis has been shutting you out. Something is very wrong. The marriage is crumbling. He won't talk to you.* Then, her more reasonable voice: *No, it's just a rough patch. All marriages go through hard times. He's having a hard time and it's your job to support him right now.*

"I visited Sally this evening. Gary's in bad shape. He won't last the night I'm afraid. I called the ladies and Maxine went over to stay with her. Sally's a pretty amazing woman, doing all this alone." As she jabbered, Davis seemed to stare through her. She did not feel like he was really listening. He was tired she supposed, but she was tired too.

"Uh huh…Thanks Ellie. Thanks for doing that. I'll stop and check in on her tomorrow. I just wish sometimes they could die at more convenient times. I've got a sermon to preach in two days. You're busy with the kids. It's just overwhelming for both of us."

Ellie's eyes narrowed. She couldn't hide her distaste. "Davis, people don't get to choose when they die. They aren't going to get sick around your schedule."

Davis' frown deepened. "Ellie, I've had a long day. Please lighten up. It's just a little gallows humor. I wasn't being serious."

The energy between them was tense with what was unspoken. In her heart she acknowledged the truth: The foundation of their marriage was on a fault line, but there would be time to talk it through. Two committed people who loved each other could fix whatever was broken. Davis left and went to his study. She heard him make the rounds to the boys' rooms to say goodnight. She was glad at least for that.

To settle her racing nerves she escaped to the shed, which also served as her art studio. She studied her current unfinished painting critically. She was working on a canvas inspired by a 1948 photo of her grandmother Lydia. Her grandmother had been a beautiful young woman, but Ellie had painted her in a way she wasn't sure she liked. She had captured her expression and her smooth pale skin, but her grandmother's gray eyes stared back at her from the unfinished portrait like they carried a secret, a terrible one. Ellie felt vulnerable and uneasy under their gaze. Painting usually brought her healing and peace, but tonight she felt like everything was about to come undone.

Chapter 2

⎯⎯⎯⎯❧❧⎯⎯⎯⎯

Quake

Ellie was staring at her feet. She heard the breakers and the seagulls and smelled the salt air. Her toes were curled in the sand and the receding waves cooled her feet. John and Miles played in front of her laughing. Miles held a sand bucket and shovel, and John was helping him put broken sand dollars and mussels in his pail. Ellie turned in search of Davis, longing to share this moment with him, a rare instant when the boys weren't fighting but genuinely enjoying one another's company. He was not behind her like she thought. She scanned the beach a slight feeling of panic rising in her gut. He had just been behind her not a moment ago, but now even as she scanned the open beach, he was nowhere to be seen.

Off in the distance she saw a figure walking, he was laughing talking to another figure, but she couldn't see clearly. "Davis!" she screamed. Her voice was buried in the sea wind. She looked at her feet now and noticed that the receding waves were no longer playing at her feet. The beach seemed strangely calm, barren and the waves had retreated far back into the sea. She sensed something amiss and peered directly at the ocean. She was unable to process what she saw, a towering mass of dark blue bearing down on them from a mile away.

She turned frantically toward Miles and John and screamed, "Run!" They were laughing and looking at her bemused. They did not understand her terror. They thought she was playing a game. She grabbed them roughly by the shoulders and pushed them toward the sandy dunes. John looked behind his shoulder and saw the fortress of water bearing down on them. His eyes reflected Ellie's terror. He reached his hand out to his brother and pulled him forward into a run. Miles stumbled forward crying and mumbling that he had dropped his pail. Ellie screamed, "Never mind. Just run!" Ellie followed them prepared to turn around and wrestle the wave down herself if she had to. Their feet hit the hard wet sand and they ran for their lives, but before they could make progress the water lifted them, swelled around them, and her little family was overcome. She woke in a panic.

Her eyes bolted open in terror as she scanned her bedroom, gasping for air. She processed the nightmare and sat back on the pillows to try to relax and steady her breathing. Davis was already sitting up watching her, his eyes deeply sad and his face etched with pain.

"You okay?" he asked, his voice strangely tender.

"Yeah, I had a nightmare," Ellie said as she tried to breathe through the panic. "Have you been up the whole time?"

Davis seemed to actually look at her for the first time in months. "I haven't been able to sleep for a few nights now. I've just been watching you sleep." The intensity of his stare unnerved her.

"Davis, what's going on? That's kind of creepy. You look terrible. Please tell me."

"God, Ellie, I don't know if I even know where to begin." He was wringing his hands again and swaying back and forth on the bed.

Ellie brought her hand to his wrist and traced her fingers lightly on his warm skin. "Davis, you've been acting like this for months now. You can't keep carrying this burden alone whatever it is? I'm listening."

"You'll never be able to look at me in the same way." His voice was tight.

"Davis, whatever it is, we can get through it, but there's no way forward if you don't talk to me."

"Mariah just called me."

Ellie was confused. "Mariah? Is she okay?"

"She's in downtown Eugene right now. She says she's planning to jump from the Autzen Bridge and kill herself."

"Oh my God! What? Davis, we have to go down there and stop her. What is going on? We need to call her parents immediately and…." Ellie was thrown for a loop by the calm in Davis' voice which did not coincide with the worry she felt they both should be feeling.

"Ellie, wait…we've been having an affair. She says if I don't leave you, she's going to kill herself."

Ellie's heart dropped to the pit of her stomach. She sat stunned. She heard the syllables but could not apply them to her experience. The force like lightning hitting a sparrow. Ellie waited for the emotion to flood her to feel pain and anger, but she was numb. All she could think was, *I must fix this.* A force possessed her. "Davis…We have to go."

"What?"

Ellie ran to her closet and threw on a sweatshirt and some old jeans. She ran a brush through her hair and tied it into a hasty bun. Davis' eyes trailed her movements, his mouth open. She left the bedroom without speaking and quietly snuck into John's room. Davis followed her from behind. She glanced at her watch. It was 1:30 a.m. in the morning.

"John, John. Sweetie. Wake up just for a little bit. Daddy and I have had a family emergency. It's okay, but we need to step out of the house for a little bit. You need to be in charge of your brother while we're gone."

"Ma, what's going on? What?" He rubbed his eyes and looked at her.

"We've just had a little family emergency and we have to go help someone. I need you to be in charge while we're gone. You can go back to sleep, but just look out for your brother. Use your phone and call us if there's any emergency okay? I'll make sure the house is all locked up and you're safe. If you wake up and I'm still not home, please remember to be kind to your brother."

"Yeah, okay Mom." He slumped back into his bed. Ellie kissed his forehead and smoothed the sandy hair away from his face. She hurried to check in on Miles. His soft breathing filled the room, and she could see his beautiful profile illuminated on the wall by his star shaped night light. He was at peace. She closed the door gently and faced Davis.

"Okay. I'm ready," she whispered. "Let's take the Subaru to Autzen Bridge."

"Ellie, Thank you. I don't know what to do with her. She's been threatening self-harm for months. She's insane. Help me."

Ellie bit her lip and waited till they were in the car driving. "So, you said months. How long has this affair been going on?"

Davis answered cautiously, "About eight months."

"Eight months!" Ellie felt the first real wave of anger move through her. He had been preaching, pretending to be her faithful husband, pretending to be a man of God for eight months. She choked back the wave of emotion allowing its force to recede deep inside of her. Abruptly the conversation halted. Ellie concentrated on a solution. "Do you think she'll do it?"

"God, I hope not, but Ellie, she really is insane."

"You know Davis, that's what happens when you sleep with a teenager, one who could be your daughter. You idiot!" she spat.

"Yeah, I know. I know. It was so stupid." He hit the dashboard for dramatic effect and sighed while burying his face in his hands. Turning his head, he looked at her, his eyes pleading. "So, what's the plan?"

The plan of action had come to Ellie as she went through the step-by-step instructions of how to get through a crisis in her mind, as if a solid plan could shelter her from reality, like she could pretend Davis and Mariah were just acquaintances that needed her help in an emergency. For some reason, thinking like that helped. "You talk her off the ledge, we call her parents, we get her therapy, which you're paying for. You let her know it was a mistake and you're a married man and this relationship is not okay. It's over. It has to be over. Davis, she's nineteen. You're forty-six. She's my niece. It's sick! Also, you quit the ministry. There's nothing more to say."

"Yeah, yeah, okay. I know you're right. I was just in such a dark place. I can't justify it."

"No, you can't!"

Davis maneuvered the car to public parking near the bridge. They got out. In summer, the evenings in the Willamette Valley could still be chilly and Ellie shivered even though it was August as she followed Davis. They spotted Mariah in the walkway when they were about 20 feet away. She was hunched over the railing of the pedestrian bridge and swaying back and forth like a drunk. Her long brown hair hung in ragged unwashed clumps.

She looked unkempt and half mad. Her beat up bicycle was balanced on the railing next to her. For a moment Ellie could only see her sister Nora in Mariah's disheveled form, like mother, like daughter.

The area was desolate. *Crazy kid. This wasn't a safe neighborhood at night. Mariah had no survival skills and seemed to have no thought for her own safety.* Ellie was unsure how she would feel when she saw this girl, this betrayer who she had welcomed into her own home. This girl was sleeping with her husband, but Ellie was unable to feel hatred when she looked at her. She felt distant from what she was witnessing, and the scene was just too pathetic. Maybe she just couldn't feel at all? Ellie could not imagine allowing herself to fall apart like this for a stupid man, especially a married one with children. Mariah was a hot mess, but Ellie knew from experience with her sister, she would use that to her advantage. There was a time she thought of Mariah like her own child. She had never been a stable person. Like Nora, she suffered from the manic personality. How could Davis cross the line with her own niece, a vulnerable and unstable child? He knew the difficult dynamics of Ellie's sister's marriage and all the borderline emotional abuse in that home. How could Davis, her Davis, succumb to an action so evil, so hurtful to both her and Mariah? They were supposed to be her refuge from a fallen world. His actions were a terrible abuse. He had undone all the work she had invested in trying to help Mariah. He had undone everything. Now all that was left was an irreparable disaster. She must be walking through someone else's life? Dr. Phil drama was not something that happened to Ellie. It wasn't her reality, except now it was.

Davis hesitated to go to Mariah. Ellie pushed him aside, disgusted, "You have got to be kidding me?" She looked at her husband in dismay with new eyes. She felt the last shred of respect for him wither and die.

Ellie moved toward Mariah. "Mariah. We're here. What's going on?"

"You brought her!" Mariah wailed. Her face was tear-stained. Mascara and dripping eyeliner ran down her cheeks. She looked like a crazed raccoon.

Davis' voice was calm and weary. "Mariah, I didn't know what else to do. You were threatening to kill yourself."

"Mariah, Davis has told me everything," Ellie said. "Regardless of all the terrible things that have happened, we both want you to be okay and we don't want you to hurt yourself."

Mariah looked pitifully at Ellie through tear-stained eyes. "Are you going to let him go? Are you going to take the kids from him?"

"Mariah, I don't know what Davis has been telling you. I just learned about what's been going on between the two of you an hour ago. We haven't had time to talk about the future. All I know is real love doesn't look like this. It doesn't lead to threatening to kill yourself in the middle of the night on a bridge in downtown Eugene. I'm just here to support you and we're both going to try to get you the help you need."

Mariah looked at Ellie with blind hatred, "Well aren't we just Miss America? He doesn't love you, you know. He told me he doesn't. He told me he never did."

Ellie was paralyzed. The warm heat of humiliation filled her body. *He had never loved her?* The hurt she felt was so staggering, she froze. She had never been anything but kind to Mariah. She had bought her clothes, taken her to concerts and events, spent hours talking and counseling her, and bought her thoughtful gifts for her birthday. She had tried to be the mother figure the girl never had. Despite all this Mariah hated her. And Davis... Davis had never loved her? 15 years and he had never loved her? Ellie closed her eyes and struggled to compose herself. She saw her mother and father back in her childhood home and she channeled them, their love for her, their belief in her the best she could. She redirected her thoughts to crisis training. She would remain calm, handle the crisis and deal with her own emotions later. "Mariah, I'm going to take your bicycle. Davis needs to talk to you alone. You can take the car. Davis, I'll meet you in fifteen minutes at the Starbucks near Mariah's apartment."

"Thanks Ell. I'm sorry. She doesn't mean it. She has manic swings. I'm so sorry." She could see in his shameful expression that he knew how much Mariah's words stung. "Mariah, come on. It's okay. We've got to talk."

Ellie watched as Davis led a crying Mariah to his white Subaru hatchback, his arm around her back in an intimate fashion that revealed a truth Ellie did not want to see. He wore an expensive leather jacket and looked striking next to his new car. Ellie tried to see Davis from Mariah's eyes. How she had craved a stable father figure, and he did look accomplished and successful with all the fruits of his mother's money.

Mariah's bike was old and rickety. It was the kind of bicycle that no one would want even if it was on the curb with a *For Free* sign attached. She was surprised that Davis with all his mother's money hadn't at least purchased the foolish girl a new bicycle or a car. It wasn't a safe mode of transportation for a college girl. If Davis had lavished gifts on Mariah, Ellie would never have suspected anything. She had always been so trusting in the marriage. Davis always handled his own finances. How could she be so stupid?

Ellie no longer had the figure she had when she first met Davis. She had put on about fifty pounds, thirty in the last year. As out of shape as she was, it took her a few minutes to find balance on the bike. *Divorce.* The word hit her like a ton of bricks. No one in her family got divorced; not even Nora, whose marriage was dysfunctional to say the least. Even Nora could make a marriage work, when she couldn't. Nora could make men love her. Apparently, Ellie with all her stability and Christian faith was the true failure. Her parents had been married over forty years. *Was Divorce inevitable now? Was this something she and Davis could work through and come out the other end?*

I can do anything through God who gives me strength. Ellie repeated the scripture several times in her mind, but she felt like someone had punched her in the gut. *I can't do this! There's only so much a person can take. Here I am helping my niece, my husband's mistress from taking her own life. When do I get to fall apart? Who will comfort me and put me back together?* As Ellie bicycled clumsily, she stopped to catch her breath. She wiped her eyes with her wrist and discovered her hand was completely wet with tears. She had been sobbing freely without even being aware she was crying. *Weird,* thought Ellie. Her body and mind were so disconnected. *I must be quite the sight.* She laughed hysterically out loud as she imagined the frightened passerbys of Eugene encountering this overweight sobbing woman on a wobbly bicycle in the middle of the night. She must look ridiculous and a bit terrifying.

Do not worry about tomorrow. Tomorrow will take care of itself. Do not be anxious about anything. The Sermon on the Mount was always Ellie's favorite. Davis loved the book of Mark, but she always loved Matthew. There were so many verses about relying on God rather than one's self. Ellie realized that she was too tired to even think about what tomorrow would hold. Her task now was to get this damn rickety bicycle to the damn Starbucks. *I hate bicycles and Starbucks,* she decided. It wasn't true. She loved Starbucks, but now she was sure the coffee would leave a bitter aftertaste probably forever. She had allowed her thoughts to ramble incoherently. She would give the rest to God, because what else could she do? She prayed. *Lord help me. I don't know what else.... I don't know what to think. I don't have words. I am completely overwhelmed. Who can I go to with this? I am embarrassed, ashamed, hurt, humiliated, betrayed. I have done nothing but give my best to this man and this is how he has repaid me? God...?*

When she reached the closed Starbucks, Davis was holding a sobbing Mariah. The spectacle sickened her. He motioned for Ellie to join them. She put the kickstand down on the bike. She wiped her eyes and found suddenly that an unworldly strength had overcome her, and she didn't know where it came from. *It must be adrenaline*, she thought, hormones coursing through her body, making her brave. Adrenaline can make you do amazing things, including confront your cheating husband and the niece he's been cheating on you with.

"Ellie's here now," Davis said patiently. The three of us need to talk. "What did we agree on, Mariah?"

Mariah looked up at Ellie like a petulant child, "It's over. We have to end it. But Davis, I can't even see you? I can't even call you? I won't be able to live without hearing your voice!" she wailed.

"We agreed our relationship isn't good for you or me. How is Ellie supposed to trust me, if we still have contact?"

"Okay. I'll just disappear forever. I don't want to be a bother to you."

"No Mariah. I made a mistake. It's not your fault, but surely you know this isn't right?"

She whined, "But you love me. You said you love me, and you don't love her."

"It's complicated Mariah. I have a family. I have kids."

Ellie felt uncomfortable speaking, but she knew she must. "Mariah, you've threatened your own life. We should call your parents."

"No!" she protested. "Don't call them."

"She's my sister. If you were my daughter, I would want to know what's going on."

"You also know, you're nothing like my mother. If she learns about this, she'll be shattered. She can't handle it."

Ellie was torn. Mariah wasn't wrong about her mother. Nora was fragile, both women beautiful, but unstable. A few months after the runaway incident, Nora had been diagnosed with bi-polar disorder and the family learned that even small things could send her into debilitating depression. There had been about two suicide attempts already in Nora's life that Ellie knew about, a drug overdose and like Mariah a threat to jump off a cliff. Lee had stayed with her, faithful through it all. He had succumbed to alcoholism, true, but his love for Nora could never be questioned. But now, Ellie was not sure how Lee was equipped to help Mariah since he had never been able to help her during any other period of her life.

Nora had been overwhelmed by life and parenting in particular. Ellie's family had stepped in to help. Mariah had spent so much time with the Golds and Ellie's parents because Nora was often completely overwhelmed by the task of parenting, especially any kind of discipline or maintaining of boundaries. Ellie knew Nora and Lee were not equipped to deal with Mariah. She wondered seriously if telling them would make things worse. Another part of her writhed in shame at the thought of revealing the affair and having her entire family know the truth about her marriage. Ellie did not like how this would reflect on her. They would see her stupidity, her naivete. They might think she had enabled Davis' sick behavior. The secret would be explosive and destructive. Ellie did not want her family destroyed and it was inevitable the whole family would know if the secret was shared beyond Davis, Mariah, and herself. She was not sure if she could step in the light and let her family see the truth. Ellie was a pastor's wife, and she had her Christian pride.

Ellie looked at Mariah with as much intensity as she could muster. "I won't tell your parents if you promise me you will see a counselor immediately and weekly. If you want, Davis can choose the therapist you end up seeing. We'll make the appointment for you, but you've got to go. If you don't go to those appointments, I will call your mom. You got it?"

Mariah nodded her head. "I'll go," she said. "But Davis needs to choose my therapist."

"Whatever, as long as you go," Ellie said.

"I'll choose the therapist, but Ellie will text the appointment and location to you. There's going to be no more contact between you and me."

Ellie could not stand the thought of prolonging the conversation another minute. "We've got to go, Davis. The kids are at home waiting. You going to be alright, Mariah? Can we call a friend to stay with you?"

"No. I'll be okay," Mariah said bitterly.

Mariah took her bike and they watched as she locked it in the bike rack and then walked up the stairs to her dingy apartment. Ellie realized with clarity that she did not believe that Mariah would take her life at all. The antics in the parking lot reminded her vaguely of Mile's crocodile teared tantrums at home, strategic manipulation. She was well familiar with the strategy from her experience as a middle school teacher. *I want what I want and I'm going to get it.* The car ride home was silent. Neither Davis nor Ellie knew what to say.

Finally, Ellie spoke, "Buy your stupid girlfriend a bike that works."

When they got home, it was around 5:00 a.m. Ellie poked her head in Miles' room and saw that he was still sleeping and then to John's room. Both boys were safe. She breathed a sigh of relief. She went back to their bedroom and Davis reached his arms out to hold her. "Ellie, I…"

Ellie was overcome with nausea. She rushed past him and ran to the bathroom to vomit. She threw up till there was nothing left in her system. When she finally stopped, she realized her whole body was shaking uncontrollably. She rested her knees on the hard tile floor and clung to the seat of the toilet till she was sure there was nothing left in her stomach to expunge. She grew too weak to hold herself up and lay down with her cheek on the cool tile and her knees pulled to her chest in the fetal position. She wondered if Gary Pearson was also taking his last breath.

Chapter 3

Aftershocks

Grief is like an earthquake,
The first one hits you and
The world falls apart.
Even after you put the world
Together again there are
aftershocks, and you never
really know when
those will come.
—Unknown

Two days of no sleep and no appetite! That's how long it takes for a lie to eat you up inside, she thought. Ellie wondered how she would face the day. August was coming to a close and orientation for teachers was starting at Fern Ridge Lake Middle School. She woke early to shower and prepare herself to meet the other staff and brace herself for the upcoming school year. Only briefly had she considered staying home and calling in sick. She knew hiding from her problems wouldn't help. They would always be there to greet her again in the morning. She needed to be busy. Time to think and ponder her life was the last thing she wanted. Routine for herself and the boys would help them heal and endure.

After an almost too hot shower, she stood in front of the steamy bathroom mirror and scrutinized her appearance. Her face was as pale as a radish root and the dark circles under her eyes made her look like a terminally ill patient. She wondered if her fellow teachers, the principal, and support staff would perceive that something was deeply wrong with her. Her face betrayed her, aging her several years in the span of hours. She patted her skin dry with a wash towel and reached for moisturizer and full coverage foundation and powder. *I never needed makeup more than today,* she thought. The drastic change in her appearance had really only taken two days to achieve. Two days ago, she had been a different person.

Davis had left even earlier than Ellie. The tension between them was almost unbearable. They had come to one agreement. He was going to the elders today to tender his resignation and give the church four more weeks of his time. Only then would they leave South Hills and make serious decisions about their future. Davis would cite stress and health as his reasons for stepping down.

"I can't hang them out to dry. They need at least four weeks to get an interim and make a plan."

"Davis, it will be four more weeks of this lie! I won't be able to look any of those people in the eye."

"Ellie, I've been living a lie for months. I finally see a way out. Four more weeks of being a hypocrite and then I'm out. We're out. I won't have to lie anymore. You won't have to lie."

"We'll work on the marriage and get therapy?" Ellie asked. "Is that what you want?"

"Yeah. We'll get therapy and decide what we need to do without the church breathing down our necks. It'll finally just be the two of us, figuring it out, working on the marriage."

Ellie tensed as she applied her makeup. The thoughts were racing through her head. *I'm not good at secrets,* she realized. There had always been confidantes, whether her mother or father, work buddies, or her women's

Bible study group at South Hills. What Davis had done with Mariah had effectively isolated her from talking to anyone about the most painful event that had ever happened in her life. She now knew what the expression meant to live with skeletons. The situation demanded secrecy that oppressed her like a weighted jacket.

Ellie reflected on the realities of her situation as she dabbed concealer under her eyes. There was no one she could talk to, not one person. She certainly couldn't talk to anyone at church. They would be horrified by what their pastor had done. She didn't want her little family to suffer. Her sons were innocent and did not need to share the punishment for their father's sins. Her own children would not be compromised. The scandal would blow up the church circuit in Eugene. Her boys would be followed by gossip and innuendo wherever they went. Worse than that, Davis' fall from grace would be an incredible disillusionment to all the Christians who had looked to him as a moral teacher and spiritual leader. They might believe their faith in Christ was fraudulent because of Davis' dual life. Ellie wanted to tell the truth, to come out clean, but how could she do it without hurting anyone? She couldn't.

The same dilemma loomed if she told her family. Her father would be heartbroken, devastated. Both of her parents would be so disgusted with Davis. In no future reality could she imagine they would be able to support Ellie with any attempts at reconciliation. They hated divorce, but this was beyond what they could be expected to forgive. The affair with Mariah was an attack on the family and they would be horrified by its perversion. Ellie was not sure she would be able to argue that they were wrong. She could not defend Davis's actions. Worse yet, they would lose respect for her. They would love her of course; she knew that, but she would live under the weight of their pity, a wounded fragile creature. Ellie did not want to be seen as a victim or to be viewed as a woman with severely impaired judgement. She wasn't Nora. Ellie was educated, independent, and grown up. She was the child who had her life together. She didn't want to be a mess.

Ellie decided to pass on applying mascara and reached for the eye shadow instead. Emotions she couldn't control might overcome her at work and she needed to be able to put herself together quickly. Mascara was not a good option today. As she thought about work, she reflected on whether she might confide in Melissa. Melissa Neilson was the 7th grade science teacher and her closest work friend. Ellie realized quickly that dragging Melissa into her problems would be a bad idea. Personal drama at work was never good. Work was now her safe place. Ellie had the reputation as an effective and competent teacher. She did not want to create any drama that would compromise her professional reputation. If anyone knew the awful truth, they might project that she wasn't able to handle her job. They might put her under unfair scrutiny. Ellie knew that she would never talk about Davis' affair at work, not with anyone. She also knew that Melissa would be appalled. Melissa was not a Christian and she didn't share Ellie's traditional values. She could not support Ellie's conviction to give one hundred percent commitment to her husband and marriage no matter what the circumstances. She would insist Ellie divorce Davis immediately and possibly lose respect for her if she didn't follow her advice.

Ellie knew the marriage was damaged beyond recognition, but she couldn't quite accept the avenue to move straight to divorce. She didn't believe in divorce. As a teacher, she was trained in statistics. She saw how it hurt children and their chances for a bright future. The shadow of a failed marriage followed a person and left its stigma imprinted on their lives, especially in a Christian community. Of course, she knew many divorced people and had divorced friends, but that wasn't supposed to be Ellie. She refused to accept that fate. She believed all marriages could succeed if you worked hard enough.

Nora's presence loomed over her, a dark shadow, her sister, whom she loved. How could they ever retain a normal sisterly bond after this? If Nora knew the truth, if she knew that Ellie had kept this secret from her, how could she forgive Ellie? She also feared her sister's delicate mental health. How would she deal with the truth about her daughter? Would it tip her over the edge and lead her into a spiral of depression, addiction, and another possible suicide attempt? Davis' transgression would leave its mark on their family and destroy it from the inside out like a malignant cancer. Ellie would be the gatekeeper to this destruction. She saw no way out, but to keep the secret, close the gate, but even in the best-case scenario she could not foresee a future in her mind where her world didn't fall apart. She could choose her marriage to Davis or her family. There was no smooth path forward. In light of the situation, the only person they could confide in was a therapist, a person paid and sworn to secrecy.

When she arrived at school, she greeted Melissa warmly and said hello to her colleagues without sharing many details of her summer. Ellie realized that social pleasantries in this setting were not much different from the church face she put on every Sunday. She was skilled in the role of pastor's wife. She remembered when the family dog, Crayola died two years ago. John had named him. He was a German Shepherd and when he got hit by a car, she was devastated. The whole family ravaged by grief, but Ellie had kept her pain away from her students and colleagues. No one knew of her loss. She had taught for two weeks while experiencing waves of wild grief that would hit suddenly without warning and yet, she was always able to recover, to keep that raw emotion concealed. The ability to continue to function when others would crumble in the same given situation, gave her a sense of pride. Other people did not need to be weighed down with your personal problems. As she touched base with the other teachers, she was able to deflect questions about how Davis was doing rather easily. Several colleagues engaged in the standard niceties and inquired politely after her family. Ellie shared how John and Miles had grown over the summer and how they had enjoyed the garden. No one seemed to notice anything amiss, except Melissa.

"You look a little tired, Ellie."

"Do I? It makes sense. I've been staying up so late during the summer and today I had to wake up so early. I'm all out of sorts."

"Isn't that the truth?" Melissa affirmed. She did not press but did reach out and give Ellie a squeeze as if she sensed that she was holding something back but was too good of a friend to press.

Orientation week was filled with meetings and conferences, trainings designed for professional development. *Teacher Strategies on Bullying* was the name of the morning's session. Gina Mattheson, an expert in Educational Sociology was the keynote speaker. All the teachers from the elementary, middle, and high schools were gathered in the auditorium. Ellie sat with Melissa and the rest of the middle school teachers listening to the cacophony of excited voices as the space filled with teachers fresh and rested from their summer break.

Gina was an older woman with a chin length gray bob and choppy bangs. She looked like the typical paid professional speaker in her black pantsuit and white collared blouse. Ellie always fought an inner distrust towards the type. She put on her teaching game face and tried to at least appear objective and receptive to the speaker's message.

"The bully…" Gina was saying "enjoys putting his or her victim in a corner. They have to make their victims feel alone and hopeless." Gina clicked on the next slide which pictured a young girl sitting next to her locker at school in the fetal position. Ellie winced when she saw the expression on the girl's face. She read the image with new clarity. The girl was not crying because she was sad. Her expression was one of shame, being caught and embarrassed because everyone else had realized what she had always suspected: she was worthless.

"This is why they must recruit witnesses." Gina continued. "These are the students who create an audience for the bully and yet are afraid to help the victim. They become tacit supporters of the bully and they help create the illusion that the victim is completely alienated. The victim, you see, begins to believe that they deserve the bullying, that they are defective in some way. Next slide."

Ellie knew how it felt to feel powerless, unable to reach out to anyone. She was sinking under its weight.

"Do you know what's interesting here though, folks? Do you know what ties the bully, the witnesses, and the victims all together?"

"Narcissism?" asked a teacher toward the front.

"Anger?" said another.

"Repression?" said yet another.

Gina smiled. "Those are all good guesses, but the true unifying trait is shame."

"Why would the bully be ashamed? They have all the power,"Melissa blurted.

"Do they?" Gina asked. "Don't we all feel basically inadequate? Consider all the time and effort we put into making it look like we have it all together. Don't even get me started on social media." The audience laughed. "Every form of bullying is a way of hiding an inadequacy. This includes the bully, the enablers, the witnesses, and the victim. Our whole social structure is based on concealing vulnerabilities. Imagine for a moment, the different world we would live in if everyone trusted each other enough to make themselves truly vulnerable. Bullying would cease to exist." Gina surveyed the crowd and her eyes locked with Ellie's. "When you look at your students, find their vulnerabilities and let them know they're okay that you accept and love them, just as they are."

Ellie took an uneven breath. She thought about Gina's statement. What was Davis ashamed of in his life? What was Mariah ashamed of? She knew what she was ashamed of, her failure to hold her marriage together, her inability to make even her own husband love her. How wonderful to be loved just for being yourself. Ellie had never felt that way with Davis.

Although difficult, Ellie was able to hold her emotions together and function through the day. It was more than she could have hoped for and she was relieved. *Would she pay a price, for holding so much pain inside?* When Crayola died, she had grieved and survived. Would she do that again? Ellie left as soon as the workday ended. She called Kid's Club, where Miles and John were in after school care. During orientation, Kim who ran the program would take care of all the teacher's kids for an extra fee. Ellie called her to make sure that she could continue watching the two boys for a couple more hours. Kim assured her it was no problem. Ellie had to meet Davis for their first therapy session.

Finding a therapist was nearly impossible short notice. Ellie had flagged down a therapist for Mariah first thing on Monday morning. Orientation didn't begin till Tuesday, so she had one day to set events into motion, to start the steps to fix what was broken. Davis had told Mariah he'd find a therapist for her, but he had not taken the initiative and Ellie wanted to follow through quickly on what she had promised Mariah on that awful night. Through the internet, she found a woman with an office walking distance from Mariah's apartment that specialized in bi-polar, autism, and depression and fortunately, she was taking clients, especially those willing to hire her with a $2000 retainer. The next priority was to hunt for a counselor for Davis and herself. She used the internet to help her trace the man they would be seeing. He was a licensed clinical social worker who specialized in marriage counseling. His name was Robert Hastings. She would have preferred a woman. Ellie did not know if he was good or if he came highly recommended by anyone or not. It was not like she could ask her friends for advice. She knew nothing about him, except the standard reviews on the internet. He was the tenth person she had called, and he agreed to see them because they were in crisis and he was taking new patients. She was happy to find someone who would take them on such short notice. The phone call itself was as pleasant to Ellie as biting down on a metal fork.

"Uh, I'm calling because my husband and I need to see a therapist," she choked out for the tenth time that day.

"Let me patch you into Robert. He's our one counselor seeing new patients." Ellie was placed on hold and listened to a strange rendition of Nirvana's *Smells like Teen Spirit* performed by what sounded like a high school orchestra.

"This is Robert. What can I do for you?"

"Uh, yeah. My husband and I need to see a therapist. Um… We're in crisis in our marriage and we need help. I don't know what else to do."

"Yeah, yeah, okay. Well, I'm looking at my calendar. I can see you Tuesday around four. What are your names?"

"I'm Ellie and my husband is named Davis."

"Okay. Davis and Ellie. Got it. Does four work for you? It's $150 per session and depending on your insurance, some of that usually gets covered."

"That would be good. Um, thanks."

"See you then. I'll patch you back to Felicia and she'll get your insurance information."

The phone clicked and Ellie tried to say a prayer. She wanted God to bless this man and help their therapy sessions be productive toward healing their marriage. Prayer was difficult recently. *How do you pray to a God you feel has abandoned you?*

The counselor's office in downtown Eugene was nothing special, an industrial looking grey building with sparse windows and a teal metal roof. Ellie saw Davis' white Subaru and was relieved that he had arrived first. She parked her Ford Explorer into the spot next to Davis' car. The parking lot was busy. She got out and walked to where he waited at the entrance.

Ellie recognized Davis' game face. He was determined, like her, to survive. "You ready for this?" Davis asked.

"As ready as I'll ever be. How did it go at church?"

"As good as can be expected. They're very sad I'm going, I mean we're going, but I told them about the panic attacks, high blood pressure, and the toll on my health and family, and they all said they understood. They're forming a minister search committee."

"Good, good. Anyone want more of an explanation?"

"No, not really. Walter said he had been sensing that I was under extreme pressure for months. He didn't really seem surprised."

"Well, I guess that's all we could hope for."

"It's the first step."

He let her take the lead into the office and placed his hand on the middle of her back. She felt her body shudder in distaste. He read her body language and removed his hand.

The waiting room was filled with clients of all walks of life including children, married couples, disabled vets, and the elderly. A harried receptionist, Felicia, Ellie presumed, took their names and told them Robert would be with them soon. There were several hallways behind the reception area. They branched in different directions. Each hallway contained several metal doors that opened into the counseling spaces. The metal doors and lack of windows insured privacy for the numerous clients, but not beauty.

The layout reminded Ellie of a factory—*assembly line therapy,* she thought. She told herself to force away negative thoughts. *No one in their right mind wanted to go to therapy.* It was normal to be fearful, but she needed to give it an honest try and reserve her impulse toward negative thinking.

They didn't wait long. An older man in his late fifties came out to greet them in the waiting room. He had a benign face and tired eyes. He held out a perfunctory hand to Davis and then to Ellie.

"Nice to meet you. We'll just head down the hall here and go ahead and take the second door on the left." He motioned with his hand for Ellie to take the lead. Ellie followed his gesture, Davis behind her. Robert's office was small, but cozy. There were no desks, but a cream coffee table with a large brown decorative plate in the center. The set up included a brown leather loveseat with red pillows, and two red armchairs. There were framed modernist paintings on the wall and a geometrically designed carpet under the coffee table. The room looked like it had been taken from the sales floor of Ashley Home Furniture and although cozy, felt a little impersonal. She waited for Robert to direct them where to sit.

"You can sit on the sofa if that's okay with you?"

Ellie took a ragged breath and sat on the left side of the couch as Davis took the right. Robert settled in one of the armchairs. As Ellie and Davis sat side by side, he reached out his hand to her and she took it. He gave her hand a gentle squeeze and he laced his warm fingers between hers.

"So, I understand we're having hard times. Why don't you go ahead and tell me why you're here?"

Ellie and Davis both hesitated. She felt overwhelmed by the task of articulating clearly the ordeal she had experienced for the last few days. The sheer enormity of it took her breath away. However, Ellie felt the energy in Davis' body shift.

"I've cheated on my wife. For eight months I've been sleeping with her niece, Mariah. She's nineteen-years-old."

"I see. Is it over with this young woman?" Robert asked.

"Yes. I ended it with her. We're just trying to see if there's a path forward for me and Ellie."

"Tough times, tough times," Robert said. "Well, there's no path forward with your wife, if you don't end it with this young woman, but it looks like you've taken the first steps to do that. Why don't you tell me a little about yourselves?"

Davis did. He told Robert about his childhood in New York, his mother Madeline's obsession with perfection and how much of a disappointment Davis had been to her. He shared about his father's sickness and death. He talked about his acting days in New York and the overwhelming sense of rejection he experienced. He then shared the same story Ellie had heard early in their relationship about how he had become a Christian and a pastor. Robert was captivated, so was Ellie. Somewhere in the middle of his autobiography he released Ellie's hand so he could gesticulate with more passion. No one could tell a story like Davis. The time passed quickly. Robert glanced at his watch. "I hate to cut this short, but we're out of time and I have my next client coming in soon. Ellie, I realize, we didn't get to hear much from you. Is there anything you wanted to say?"

Ellie felt confused. She had listened to Davis for over thirty minutes and had lost track of any semblance of coherent thought. "I didn't want this to happen," she finally said weakly. "I put everything into this marriage. I tried to give him everything he wanted. I don't know why this happened?"

Robert narrowed his eyes as he turned toward her. Ellie thought his face looked hard. "Ellie, I think you really do believe that, but sometimes we're not giving people what they truly need, even when we think we're doing things right. This week that's your homework okay? Reflect a little bit on what it is you really want in life and if you can get that moving forward together. That's for both of you, okay?"

When Ellie returned to the car, she could hardly breathe. She watched as Davis pulled out of the parking lot. She started the engine and let the A/C hit her face. She did not know how she could have loved Davis more or given any more of herself. She felt completely defeated.

The next four weeks settled into a kind of purgatorial rhythm, a strange terrain between marriage and divorce. Work, children, church, and therapy repeated in a tireless, endless circle. Ellie went through the motions at church and did her best to repeat Davis' story to anyone who asked why they were leaving. Ellie cried when she said goodbye to the kids in the youth group and the women in her small group Bible Study. She grieved like she would the death of a loved one.

She was thankful for work. She now had a new group of students and Ellie worked very hard to leave her personal drama at the door every time she entered the classroom. Kids need stability from adults; they feel so lost in the world. She could relate to that feeling. Ellie was committed to staying positive and to continue to laugh and play with her students. She immediately set them to work, creating art and her classroom was so busy, she had little time to wallow in despair.

At home, Ellie focused on her boys. She made dinner and helped Miles with his reading. John was at an age, almost eleven years old, where it was harder to relate to him. As a middle school teacher Ellie had experience with pre-teens. She prepared questions and topics in advance to ask him at the dinner table. John was obsessed with a Switch game called *Breath of the Wild*. Ellie discussed the game with her students at Fern Ridge and could usually come home with insightful comments or questions about the game. John's face transformed when he talked about his beloved video games, suddenly vibrant and animated. Davis was disengaged, going through the motions of dinner with family, his heart obviously somewhere else. She tried to engage him in the family conversation, but Davis was aloof. In fairness, he always had been, so it was not a new dynamic to the boys.

In the evenings after the boys went to sleep, Ellie tried to spend an hour or two in her art studio. She stared at the canvas for hours, but she was not productive. Her mind raced with thoughts of Davis. She would analyze his individual features, his voice, the way they engaged. In spite of the therapy and efforts to work on the marriage, she felt more distant from Davis than ever. Ellie wanted to forgive him, but she was hurt to the core. She didn't feel like he was really trying.

Ellie had spent almost every day reflecting on counselor Robert's home-work. *What did she really want?* She knew what she wanted. She wanted Davis to love her. It was really that simple. She wanted him to find her beautiful and sexy even at thirty-nine years old. She wanted to be enough. The idea that he had looked for sex with a nineteen-year-old outside of their marriage made Ellie feel like she was inadequate, *less* of a woman. Ellie realized she was shattered because Davis had made her feel like less. She remembered their wedding vows. *Do you promise to love and cherish this woman?* At the time, Davis and Ellie didn't really know what loving and cherishing meant. They had said *I do*, but they didn't understand the words they were saying. Ellie went to the cupboard behind the canvas and pulled out a worn Bible, she turned to the famous love chapter in 1 Corinthians 13, which her brother Andrew had read aloud at their wedding.

If I speak in the tongues of angels, but have not love, I am a noisy gong or clanging cymbal. If I have prophetic powers and understand all mysteries and all knowledge, and if I have all faith that I can move mountains, but do not love, I am nothing. And if I give away all my possessions and if I give over my body in order to boast, but do no love, I gain nothing.

Love is patient, love is kind. Love does not envy, is not boastful, is not arrogant, is not rude, is not self-seeking, is not irritable, and does not keep a record of wrongs. Love finds no joy in unrighteousness but rejoices in the truth. It bears all things, believes all things, hopes all things, endures all things.

The passage was poetic, one of the most beautiful in the New Testament. Ellie believed she had loved Davis with her whole self. She had tried to be patient and kind. She had certainly put Davis first in her life. There were times when they had both been arrogant, rude, and irritable, but those moments were not the norm in their marriage. *Why did it all go to hell?* Ellie thought. What did she do wrong that every other married couple was doing right? *Love finds no joy in unrighteousness, but rejoices in the truth...* These words struck her. How could one rejoice in the truth when it was so terrible, so hurtful?

Robert was looking at them both with his sad eyes again. "Okay, Let's talk about the homework. Go ahead Davis."

"I love Ellie. I do. She does everything. She works, takes care of the kids, the people at the church love her. She's always there kind of pushing us all forward."

"Okay and…"

"Well, it just begins to feel like it's not my idea anymore."

"Okay. Ellie are you hearing that?"

"I just felt trapped. It was different before the kids, but when the kids were born, she changed. I didn't feel like she was there for me in the same way."

"Davis, my priorities just shifted to the kids. They were babies. That's normal, right? I mean, you knew I still loved you."

"Ellie, try to let your partner speak without interrupting."

"Yeah, I knew you loved me, but the dynamics were different. You just begin to remind me of my mom rather than my wife. It was hard to be sexually attracted to you."

Ellie's stomach dropped. She felt sick. Her face flushed with warmth and she now recognized the feeling: humiliation. "Davis, just because I became a mom, I didn't become a different person. Is it because I gained weight? I thought we were raising a family together? But you just abandoned me! I know I got more structured and maybe nagged you a little more, but that's because I was being a mom by myself!"

"Yeah, and then you decided to have another one."

The words burned like flesh seared by an open flame. "I thought you wanted to be a family?"

"We should have talked about it, is all. You just tell me you're pregnant. What am I supposed to do?"

"I thought it was what we both wanted? Davis, I really didn't know you felt that way?"

"How could you not know? Do you remember how I reacted to the news you were pregnant? Most people act happy if it's something they want!"

Ellie did remember and the memory still pained her. Robert interrupted. "I know it's hard to believe, but this is really good work. We're getting to the heart of the problem. Davis has shared and he's been very brave, now what do you want, Ellie?"

She was still reeling from Davis' attack. "I thought we wanted the same thing. I just want to love each other. I… I just don't understand why Davis

39

is so angry at me? We met at Bible College. He knew who I was. He knew what I wanted. I didn't change."

Robert interrupted. "Your choice of words is interesting there. Why do you believe Davis is angry at you?"

Ellie struggled to express what she wanted to say. "Because of Mariah? Why Mariah? She's my niece. I put a lot of work into mentoring and helping her. I care about her. He knew. He knew everything. Why did he choose to sleep with her? It's like he wanted to hurt me."

"That's ridiculous! I didn't want to hurt you. It just happened."

"I think Ellie makes a good point, Davis. If you really wanted to send a message to Ellie and her entire family, you certainly sent it. Maybe Davis, you did want to hurt Ellie? Think on that. We have to be honest here about our true intentions toward each other. We've reached our time for today. You did good work today. We'll start again here next time."

After the session, Ellie sobbed alone in her car. Why did therapy sessions make her feel like she'd been cornered in an alley and beaten to a pulp?

Chapter 4

❧

Red-Tag

After a serious earthquake, city officials are required to assess buildings to make sure they are structurally sound. Construction experts appraise the structure and then classify the building with a color tag to represent its level of structural integrity. Green tagged structures are considered undamaged or superficially damaged. A yellow tagged structure has suffered moderate damage and will need renovations and structural support in order to avoid being red tagged. The red-tagged structure has suffered so much damage it is deemed uninhabitable. Red tagged structures are damaged beyond repair and slated for demolition.

* * *

Ellie stared at the painting above Robert's head, an obvious knock off of a Jackson Pollock. She realized with sudden intensity that she hated it. The painter, whoever it was, communicated nothing with the piece. Random splotches of red, orange, brown, and black filled the frame. *Maybe that painting was meant to represent the state of her marriage, and the marriages of Robert's other clients?*

"Ellie, do you think you can ever forgive Davis?" Her thoughts were interrupted by Robert's expectant stare.

She reflected on his words. "Yes…, I think I could. I want the marriage to work. I believe people can change, but there has to be a change."

"What kind of change?"

Ellie was slow and careful with her words as a knowledge began to surface from deep within. "That night, when I confronted Mariah. She said to me that Davis had told her he didn't love me. He never loved me."

"Come on Ellie! You know Mariah was speaking from a manic state. She didn't mean it."

"Davis, let her continue, please," Robert scolded.

"I guess I just thought, he would beg me for forgiveness. He would say that he had made the worst decision of his life and that everything in his heart was leading him back to me. He would tell me he loved me and that he would do anything to save the marriage. You know he would fight for me, for the marriage. He didn't do that."

"What do you think that means, Ellie?"

"I think it means Mariah was telling the truth."

"Ell, it's a lot more complicated than that. I do love you."

"Maybe, but you don't love me the way a man should love his wife."

"Ellie, you know I'm messed up. I can't just manufacture emotions to make you happy."

"That's probably true Davis, but I don't see where we go from here. Feelings and actions should go together. Don't you see that I feel broken too?" Ellie felt her words gaining steam. "I just feel like you don't care that I'm hurting. Where is there to go in this marriage if you're not really sorry for your actions and how they've hurt me, your wife? Aren't we supposed to be one flesh?"

"Of course, I'm sorry for what I did, Ellie."

"I know I can't see your heart, but I don't feel like you're sorry. I don't believe you. I just don't."

"How can I possibly be responsible for your feelings, Ellie?"

"You seem to feel responsible for Mariah's."

"That's not fair, Ell. She's not mature like you. She can't handle her emotions. You're so well adjusted, that nothing practically moves you at

42

all."

Ellie was stunned. "Of course, I'm moved, but when I married you and when I had the kids, I decided that you all were my everything. I would never even talk about suicide. Do you know why? Because I have kids, that's why? I would never let them live in fear that I was going to leave them or you. Do you know why? Because I'm a grown up! Davis, you would give up the kind of love that can move mountains for what? A fling with a completely selfish brat who hasn't reflected at all on how her actions hurt our children, our family. You have replaced diamonds, pearls, and rubies for costume jewelry, Davis. Don't you tell me that I'm not moved!" Ellie took a breath as Robert leaned in his chair to observe them like lab rats. Ellie felt waves of anger moving through her veins with each heartbeat. "Your actions hurt you, me, and our children. Don't you see that? Just because I don't run around threatening suicide like a hysterical teenager does not mean I don't hurt and bleed like everyone else. There's only one person in this marriage that has no clue what love really is and it's not me!"

Ellie could not take the sight of Davis' gawking face or Robert's tragic eyes for one more second. She had never bolted out of a room in anger in her life, but the pressure had risen to the boiling point. Robert called after her to stay, but Ellie did not like the feeling of being emotionally out of control. She was a loose cannon. "By the way, that painting is terrible, Robert!" She fled and did not look back.

* * *

Two weeks later she took her 8th graders on a field trip to the Jordan Schnitzer museum at the University of Oregon campus. Her students had an assignment: explore the museum and then select an artistic piece as inspiration. After their museum tour, two art professors from the University met with her students in a campus studio and helped them work on their own pieces. The day was sunny and beautiful. There was a crisp chill in the air and the students were eager and excited about both the trip and the assignment. Ellie was energized by their excitement. She had been planning this trip for months and everything was going well, a brief and wonderful escape from reality.

Around lunchtime, Ellie's phone beeped. She glanced down to find a message from her youngest brother Brian. *Ell, please call me when you get a chance. It's important.*

Ellie quickly texted back. *I'm on a field trip, but I will call you back as soon as I can talk. Maybe 6 pm?*

Brian didn't contact Ellie much. She was surprised to get a text from him. She loved him and they were close, but he was busy living his own life and rarely initiated conversation. Brian had married two years ago, and the family still considered him and his wife Maggie newlyweds. Shortly after the wedding he got a job working IT at Lane Community College. He was a wiz with computers, but he was new on the job and his work schedule was demanding to say the least. Brian and Maggie also lived in the Eugene area, but on the other side of town. Brian and Davis had never hit it off, which probably contributed to their less frequent meetups. Ellie tried to touch base with them about once a month, but this text from Brian was out of the norm. She felt worry building in the pit of her stomach. Something must be wrong. *Well, I'm not going to let it destroy this beautiful afternoon,* she decided. Ellie texted Davis.

I'm turning off my phone, so I won't be disturbed during the field trip. Please keep your phone on.

* * *

When Ellie arrived home after 6pm, she was tired. She entered the house through the garage and saw Davis sitting at the kitchen counter. His face sent a chill through her body, his expression sorrowful, and his eyes drooped with fatigue. He looked like a man about to be condemned. "Are the boys okay?" Ellie asked.

"Yeah, they're in the family room downstairs watching a movie. We got pizza."

"Good." Ellie opened the cabinet to get a glass and stepped back in surprise.

"What is this?"

"I thought the kitchen needed a few new things."

Ellie's eyes widened as she took in the brand-new teal Williams Sonoma plates. "These are beautiful! This is quite the surprise." She had been eyeing the plates for months. *Why would Davis buy them now?* Ellie grabbed a glass and filled it with ice water. She took her cell phone out of her purse and turned it back on. She heard several beeps and looked down to find that she had fifteen missed calls and several texts. Davis eyes followed her every move as she scanned through them. Two more texts from Brian. Five texts from her mother, and two texts from her father. She also had a text from her brother Andrew. All of the messages asked her to call immediately but didn't specify why.

"Who are the messages from?" Davis asked.

"My mom, dad, brothers…There's something wrong."

Davis sighed, "You should call them."

Ellie's eyes narrowed. "Davis, do you know something? You need to tell me if you do."

His voice was tense. "Just call them and you'll know."

Ellie's body temperature spiked and she felt the heat in her cheeks. "No! You tell me what you know. You're not going to let me walk into whatever this is blind."

Davis sighed. His eyes were set in a grim stare. "The affair, Ell. It didn't end. I wanted it to, but Mariah just kept calling me. She just really needs me."

Her voice trembled. "You got a new phone, a new number. You gave her your new number? My family knows this?"

"Your brother Brian may have seen us together at Lane Community College."

"You've been meeting in public places here in Eugene? Anyone could have seen you." Her voice now sounded raspy and foreign in her own ears.

"Mariah has episodes, and she threatens suicide if she doesn't see me."

Ellie rolled her eyes. She felt a raw cynicism take over her. "Oh, would you give me a break? Davis you promised me! You lied again!" Ellie felt numb, but her arms were shaking, her whole body shaking. "This is not okay. This is not okay!"

"Ell, I'm sorry."

"No Davis! Not again. You have to leave now!"

Davis stood up slowly and spoke wearily. "I know. I packed my things." Now that he was standing, she saw that he carried one small duffel bag. Ellie noted that the kitchen and living room looked neat and tidy; not like someone had packed in a hurry.

"Where are you going?"

Davis spoke quietly. "To my apartment."

Ellie's eyes widened. "You have an apartment?"

"Yeah."

"It takes weeks to find an apartment," she said slowly as the depth of his lies dawned on her.

"I've had it for some time." Davis could not look her fully in the eyes.

"How long?"

"Four months."

"I see." She let the information sink deep. "You need to leave now. It's over," she said with surprising control.

"I know. Ell, I really am sorry. It's not like I don't know how great you are. I mean, I'm giving up my home, my family, I just can't…"

"I can't either, Davis. Not anymore."

"Goodbye Ell."

She watched him leave through the garage door, his shoulders stooped and his posture weary. *He thinks he's the victim here,* she realized. The door closed with a soft thud. She thought he couldn't hurt her more, yet he could. She took a few breaths and went to the stairwell to listen for the boys. "You guys okay down there?"

"Yeah mom. We're watching Kung Fu Panda," yelled Miles.

"That's great! I'm going to make a few phone calls and then I'll join you." Ellie called Brian first.

"Brian?"

"Ell! How are you?"

"I've been better, Brian. I just kicked Davis out of the house!"

"Then you know?"

"I know he's cheating on me with Mariah."

"That bastard!" Brian's voice teemed with anger.

"How did you find out, Brian?"

"It's weird, Ell. I saw Davis and Mariah talking about two weeks ago on campus. I was going to say hey and approach them, but something about their body language was way off. I couldn't sleep that night. I talked to Maggie about talking to you. She said I should do some investigating before I said anything. So, I abused my position a little bit. You know Mariah takes a class here at Lane and I tracked her account. She has a couple fake social media accounts including one on Facebook."

"She's so stupid!"

"Yeah, and Davis too! Their whole affair documented on fake Facebook accounts: Mariah goes by Miranda Cohen and Davis by Marcus Duman."

"How bad is it?"

"There's pictures, Ell, of the two of them kissing and holding hands and some racy conversations. Looks like they hit some clubs together. Risky behavior for a minister."

The reality of their physical relationship hit her hard. "Everyone knows?"

"Everyone in the family. Ell, I'm sorry. I wanted to just talk to you, but I called Andrew and he went right to Mom and Dad. But, Ell, none of us are going to tell anyone else, okay?"

Ellie felt completely sick. "Did Andrew tell them about the affair or…"

"They've seen the Facebook accounts, Ell. They know everything."

"Oh God! What about Nora? Does she know?"

"I'm not sure, Ell. I didn't tell her, but I think Mom and Dad did. They thought she needed to know. It's okay if you want to take your time before you talk to her. Everyone understands."

"Does Nora understand?"

"I don't know, Ell. It's probably going to take some time."

"Brian, would you send me the pics. I need to see them myself."

"Ell, are you sure?"

"If you and Maggie and Andrew have seen them and Mom and Dad, then I need to see them too. I have to deal with this head on. Did you take screenshots?"

"I did, but Ell…"

"I'll be okay, Brian. I can't hide from the truth anymore."

"Okay. I will. But Ell, you know this isn't your fault, right?"

"Thanks Brian. I appreciate it."

"Ellie, I love you, sis. This should never have happened to you. You don't deserve this. You're the last person to deserve this."

She didn't know how to respond. "Hey Brian, could you tell Andrew you talked to me. I'm not going to have the energy to call him tonight."

"Yeah. I got you covered."

"Thanks Brian."

She terminated the call and then dialed her mom with clumsy fingers. She tried to steady her ragged breathing.

"Ellie is that you?" She could hear the worry in her voice.

"Yes, hi Mom."

"Thank God! Ellie, I don't know how to tell you…"

"You don't have to tell me anything, Mom. I know. I kicked Davis out today. I know everything."

"Oh Ellie! I'm so sorry. Is there anything we can do?"

"No, Mom. I'm just really tired." She was so tired. If only she could close her eyes and escape this nightmare.

"I'm so sorry. What can we do?"

"Mom, I don't know. I need to sort things out."

"Well, are you okay? Can your father and I come down and help you with the kids? Anything you need, you just ask."

"Thanks Mom. I'm okay. That would be a little overwhelming for me right now. I think I need a little time, but the boys are okay and I'm okay. Please don't worry."

"Ellie, you are the most wonderful girl. I'm just outraged. Oh wait, your dad wants to talk to you." Ellie heard commotion and shuffling and then her dad's voice.

"Ellie?"

"Yeah Dad. I'm here."

"I want you to know you're going to be okay. Please hear me."

Ellie felt the emotions overwhelm her when she heard her dad's voice. "I do, Dad. I just feel so ashamed!" Suddenly the tears she had worked so hard to keep at bay rose to the surface. "Dad, how could I be so stupid?"

"Ellie, hear your dad here. You are a beautiful creation of God. Never call yourself stupid because you had faith in someone's goodness. That is a wonderful quality. You are lovely and beautiful. Anyone who knows you sees this. This is not your fault, honey. If Davis cannot commit to the most wonderful young woman, then the hell with him. I know that God has something better in mind for you. Do you hear me?"

"Oh, Dad! I'm not so sure." Ellie choked. Then she laughed cynically, "Dad, I'm not young anymore. You know I'm thirty-nine years old, right?"

"You are young, beautiful, strong and you love your family fiercely."

"Thanks Dad, but I don't feel that way right now."

"I know, but it doesn't mean it isn't the truth. I've been ministering a long time, Ellie, and some people can't appreciate good things. They are poisoned by bitterness and anger. They've let their own disappointments destroy any of God's blessings. I don't want to speak hatefully of Davis, but you have to know that his sin is eating him from within. He is seeing through a glass darkly. As hard as it is, hold on to your faith and the beautiful hope and joy that you have. I love you. You have incredible strength. You have from the time you were a little girl."

"Thanks Dad. I hope you're right."

"I am. There are some things you know in your heart." Ellie tried to allow her father's words to sink in. He paused for a few seconds before speaking again and then said, "Okay, here's your mom."

"Bye Dad." Ellie felt a small sense of peace overcome her. How her dad always had that effect she would never know, but he made her feel better. She heard shuffling again as her father handed the phone back to her mother.

"Honey, we're here for you. You call okay? If you need anything?"

"I love you guys. I have to go, okay?"

She touched her screen to end the call before her mother could protest and dried her eyes on a rough dishtowel. In the den, she squeezed between the boys on the couch while they finished the last fifteen minutes of Kung Fu Panda. Miles squirmed as she held him tight. When the closing credits came on John asked, "Where's Dad?"

Ellie considered all the lies she could tell. She hated lies. What good did they ever do anyone? "Dad has an apartment. He's going to be staying there for a while. He loves you guys very much, but Dad and Mom aren't getting along right now." Ellie was surprised when neither boy seemed greatly surprised or upset by the news.

"Are we still going to see him?" John asked.

"Of course, John, as much as you want. Daddy and I both love you boys more than anything. Nothing will change that. But things might look a little different."

"Are you getting a divorce?" Miles asked.

Ellie was surprised her eight-year-old had even heard of a divorce. She looked at him with all the love she could give, hoping it would soften the blow of her words. "Yes. We are."

Miles took her hand. "Don't worry Mommy. It's okay. We love you."

"Oh Miles! I love you too. I'm sorry if Mommy and Daddy failed you both." She fought back the tears.

"Mom, you didn't fail us. We know you always do your best." John's eyes looked world weary like he knew the depths of the matter.

"How lucky both Daddy and I are to have you both. Come on guys, we need to get to bed." The boys went through their evening routine. They brushed their teeth and then headed to their bedrooms. She read Miles a story, prayed with him and kissed his forehead. When she reached John's bedroom she tapped on the door. Lights out at 10:00 okay?" She looked at her little boy who was now so close to being a teenager. She said a prayer in her heart. *Lord, help me teach my boys to love you with their full hearts. Help them to make good choices. Make them good husbands and good men.*

Once the house was quiet and the boys were asleep, Ellie took out her phone and opened the screenshots from Brian. *Lord, give me strength. I can do anything through Him who gives me strength.* She opened each photo that illustrated the narrative of her husband's sordid affair. She saw how Mariah had wooed him with salacious photos and how Davis had been more than receptive to each solicitation. He should have resisted. He should have been the grown up and loved her as a daughter, but his ego was flattered. Her sexual interest in him made him feel young and desired again. Hiding the affair from Ellie was almost a fun game for the two lovers. In that disconnected sense, Ellie was not completely without understanding. She knew the need to feel loved and desired. She had forgotten what it felt like to have someone make her feel the way Mariah made Davis feel. When she was finished, she deleted each photo. She would never look at any of them again.

Ellie made her way to the kitchen. She pulled out the beautiful Williams Sonoma plates and carried them to the second-floor deck that overlooked the backyard. She took a plate daintily in her hand. She scanned the yard. Her eyes locked on the tall Douglas fir in the middle of the yard. With deliberate aim, she threw the plate like a frisbee. Surprised by the velocity she was able to create, Ellie felt a stifled energy inside of her come to life with a flick of her wrist. She heard the plate shatter, and she could just make out pieces of glass gleaming in the porch light. She smiled. She released each plate into the sky and waited for the delicious sound of shattering glass. In her head she heard her father's voice. *You are worth so much more than designer plates.*

Chapter 5

Demolition

Gemini is characterized by the Twins, Castor and Pollux, and is known for having two different sides they can display to the world.
—horoscope.com

Even when she tried to sleep, her brain refused to settle. The Davis of Ellie's past and the Davis of her present could not be reconciled. She tried to understand how she could have fallen under his spell. Intelligent, educated, and accomplished as she was, she had been easily deceived by an easy smile and smooth words. Was Davis ever sincere? Or had he lost his faith along the way? Ellie would probably never know. She recalled their first real conversation over coffee. He revealed more of himself than he probably intended.

* * *

"Why do you want to be a pastor?" She sipped her latte, careful to avoid creating a cream mustache on her upper lip. The coffee shop was close to campus and not busy this late in the afternoon. Davis brought her here so they could really talk. Her body tensed with the excitement of a one-on-one uninterrupted conversation with the most exciting man on campus.

"It will sound odd if I tell you?"

"Odd? Really? That just makes me more curious."

"Well, you know, I didn't meet God till I was thirty. Not in the Christian sense anyway. A girlfriend at the time, took me to a Bible Study. I was pretty lost in my life."

"You weren't born into a Christian family?"

"Not at all. My mom, well, she wanted me to be a doctor, lawyer, or an accountant like my dad. I grew up hearing about the successes of every person in our social circle. Let's see… There was Michael Randolph. He was admitted into the John Hopkins internship program to study neurology. There was Susan Cohen, who passed the bar exam while also graduating cum laude from Harvard. My cousin Pete Simmons graduated from Northwestern with a degree in architectural engineering. He helped to design the 9-11 Memorial by the way. It was a list of ridiculously successful people. Anyway, you get the point. The bar was set very high in my family. I got to hear a lot about successful people and then I kept waiting for the other shoe to drop. You know…reading between the lines, it always came back to criticism toward me. So, Davis what are YOUR plans? Why aren't YOU at Harvard or making a billion dollars on Wall Street? I just didn't want any of it."

Ellie set her coffee mug down on the table, drawn in by his candor, his unique perspective. He was not a typical mid-western Christian farm boy. She leaned in, fully engaged. "Well, that's a lot to live up to. But… surely your mom is proud of you? I mean, hasn't she heard you speak? You're accomplished and talented. There's practically a waiting room to hear you whenever you're speaking in class. You've set the bar here at Blue Ridge."

"My mom will never see me that way. Blue Ridge isn't exactly the ivy leagues you know."

"And your dad?"

"He passed away when I was twenty. Heart failure."

"I'm sorry." She wasn't just saying the words to be polite. Ellie felt a genuine hurt in her heart at his loss.

"Oh, well I'm not sure he'd be too proud of me either."

"Why would you say that?"

"He was Jewish."

"You don't think he'd approve of the fact that you want to be a Christian minister?"

Davis lifted his eyes heavenward and rolled his eyes. "I think he'd be surprised to say the least. He paid a half fortune on my Bar Mitzvah. Well, I'm only half ethnically Jewish," Davis chuckled under his breath as he took a sip from his cup. "Mom was Irish Catholic, and Dad was Jewish really only in name. Neither faith would probably claim me. My dad wasn't super religious. He loved food, cigars, a hedonist in some respects. He worked all the time, but he was a good husband. He loved my mom."

Ellie reached over and squeezed his hand, surprised by its smooth unblemished texture. His eyes met hers and her heart quickened. "And I'm sure he loved you too. How could he not? Well, I can't imagine that they wouldn't be proud of you. I'm sorry your dad isn't here to see the amazing man you've become."

Davis's eyes brightened as he looked at her, taking her fully into his gaze. The intensity of his eyes was almost worshipful, like she was a goddess. He placed his other hand on top of hers and gently stroked the top of her hand. The electric warmth rushed through her again. In that moment she was determined she would help him find the acceptance that he had never experienced. She wanted to help him. Her eyes widened with interest and she hastened to continue the conversation.

"But back to the ministry. Why the decision to be a pastor?"

"It's a recent decision; my first career choice was to be an actor."

Her jaw dropped. "What? Really? That, I'm trying to picture. Okay, yes, I can see it."

Davis shrugged. "I didn't always make the greatest choices, but don't look so surprised. I even auditioned for a pretty famous movie my senior year of high school. Obviously, I didn't get the part, but yeah, I made it to the third audition. I didn't get the movie, but I did get the lead in my high school's production of Death of a Salesman."

"Very impressive." Ellie laughed. "I am in the presence of a star."

Davis' eyes shone with mischief. "I like to think so. I thought I might want to do something like that."

"And…"

"Well, I went to undergrad and trained as an actor at NYU, but if I thought my mom was superficial, the acting world was worse. I didn't finish the degree. Talk about politics. That program was ridiculous. Superficiality as a profession is all I can say. I got a little lost in that world for a while. It just made me feel… I don't know. There's just so many auditions and most of the time it doesn't work out."

"I can imagine," she sympathized.

He visibly winced before drawing focus back to her. "Anyway, a few years down the line, I'm trying to be a Broadway actor in New York, and I meet this girl in my acting class. She's a Christian, very young and attractive. Obviously, it didn't work out between us as you can tell, but she made me go to Bible Study with her. I thought it would be kind of a lark. At least I'd have a fun story to tell later to my friends. You know one of those I-met-one-of-those weird Christians kind of story. Well, she takes me to this brownstone out in Queens, takes us an hour to get there. This pastor guy and his wife and a few college kids and young career types are all there. Anyway, pastor Sam tells me we're studying the book of Mark and hands me a New Testament."

"Mark? The shortest and least quoted gospel. Interesting. The plot thickens."

"Well, I wanted to impress the girl, you know. I took the Bible home, and I memorized the entire first chapter of Mark, just like I was preparing for an audition. The next time I saw her, well, I recited it to her."

Ellie gasped in mock surprise. "The whole chapter?"

"Yeah, the whole chapter, with just a tinge of British accent."

"You didn't?" She laughed again.

"Oh, I did. Anyway, she's pretty impressed and we start getting a little more serious and I keep going to Bible study. But something happens?"

"What?"

"Well, they're just words at first, but then I start reciting Mark before I go to bed and then when I wake up in the morning in between brushing my teeth and showering. It's not just about impressing a girl anymore. It's about this man from 2000 years ago speaking words of such power and truth that I'm still reciting those words today. I feel their power too and for some reason, they make me feel better, peaceful. Verses like, 'The time is fulfilled, and the Kingdom of God is at hand, repent and believe in the gospel.' That's Mark 1:15."

Ellie's surprise was now real. "That's powerful."

Davis' voice sounded different, lower, more serious. He hunched forward and almost whispered. "And a little trippy. I've opened this door now and I can't close it, even if I want to. I've got to open it all the way and see what's on the other side."

"What's on the other side?"

He seemed to hesitate from the weight of his thoughts. "Pastor Sam says to me in Bible Study, 'What do you see in Jesus?' I say, I see my Savior. I don't even know what I'm saying, but I say it with complete conviction. I keep hearing that voice say *repent and believe in the gospel*. And then... I say, I want to be baptized. I want to be a different man. Sam just smiles and he takes me into the bathroom. The group fills the bathtub and Pastor Sam baptizes me right there. Do you accept Christ as your Living Savior? And I'm saying yes. Yes, I do, and you know what? I believe it."

"That is quite the testimony." She tried to sound nonchalant. "And the girlfriend?"

"We broke up two weeks later. She dumped me for an actor in a new play she got cast in and I didn't even care."

Ellie's shoulders relaxed. "And here you are now."

"Well, two years later, yes."

"New York to Blue Ridge? Why here?"

"Just so you know, I got a scholarship. Pastor Sam encouraged me to apply and told me about the school. Nothing was happening with my acting career and Sam kept saying God would open a door or a window. When I applied, I sent in my testimony video. Guess who called me two weeks later?"

"Who?"

"Northam."

"No?" Ellie couldn't contain her surprise. Professor Northam wasn't impressed easily.

"He says he wants to mentor me and that he's convinced the entire Blue Ridge Staff to give me a full ride scholarship. He sees my potential."

She was impressed. "Lovely! That's amazing and much deserved."

* * *

How naive and silly she had been to believe Davis' testimony. Was it possible, he was just playing a role, one that lasted 15 years? Actors on TV dramas did it all the time. They would play the same role for decades. Ellie wondered who this man was that she had married.

Despite a restless night, she woke early in the morning to clean up fragmented pieces of dinnerware from her backyard. Just as she suspected, her parents were unable to stay away. They arrived later that morning ignoring her requests for them to stay home. She felt frustrated at first by their arrival, but they came bearing gifts, including lunch for the boys. She knew they were motivated by concern.

On Saturdays, Ellie did not have work and a whole day alone with her thoughts was not desirable anyway. Ellie's mom, Sandra believed in a tidy house as therapy and she helped her daughter chemically clean every nook and cranny of the house. Richard cleaned the gutters and made outside repairs. She watched their silent teamwork with new respect. They loved each other and worked together even after forty years of marriage in a quiet harmony. Later in the afternoon, they all watched a movie while Sandra made her much loved banana pudding. After the movie was over, Richard took the boys to the park and played ball with them. Ellie realized that she was blessed to have them, even if they didn't always respect boundaries.

Before dinner time, Richard reminded Sandra that they had to get home soon. Sandra turned to Ellie, her body language cautious.

"So, Ellie, have you talked with Davis about the boys?" She tried to keep her face even, but Ellie could trace the concern in her voice.

Ellie responded with a hollow laugh that failed to reach her eyes. "Mom, do you think Davis will fight me for custody of the boys? The split just happened."

"Well, I don't know. That's why I'm asking you."

"I'm not even sure I'll see him again. The truth is, Mom, the one thing that I know is Davis Gold wants to be free as a bird. He doesn't want anything tying him down. He's not going to fight me for custody of the boys. If he had any interest in being a father he wouldn't have had an affair."

"You're sure?"

"I'm quite sure."

"All the same Ellie. You need a lawyer, and you will need to have everything legally arranged. Things can change on a dime." Her father's voice was soft, but persistent.

"Do you have someone in mind?"

He put a business card on the table. "Lyle Shepherd is a member of my church. He's a family lawyer and he already told me he'd help. He is a good lawyer. Lyle was an alcoholic for a number of years and lost his wife and family because of it. When he gave his life to Christ, he turned his life around. He told me he'd be happy to help you with the divorce paperwork and custody arrangements."

Ellie had not even thought to call a lawyer. "Thanks Dad! You're right. I've got to look out for the boys, and this will help." She felt an overwhelming weariness as she looked at Lyle's card. Paperwork and legal arrangements were as appealing to her as a root canal, but she knew they were necessary evils. She hugged them both. She asked the next question tentatively, "Mom, have you talked to Norah or Mariah?"

Her mother exhaled in relief. "Oh Ellie! I'm so glad you asked. Nora is taking the news better than we expected. She's terribly disappointed with Mariah. She's been afraid to tell Lee. Mariah isn't talking to anyone. I'm sure she's very ashamed of her behavior."

"Does Nora blame me?"

"Blame you? Honey, no! She blames herself. She feels like she did a poor job raising Mariah. You should call her? She's afraid to call you."

The characterization of Nora rang a little false to Ellie. Nora had been so proud of her daughter. She would not be able to adjust to the harsh reality that the daughter she was so proud of was in reality following in her mother's footsteps. Ellie was certainly struggling to accept the truth about Davis. "Mom, I just don't know. I feel so ashamed."

"Why do you feel ashamed?"

"He's my husband. I knew about it for some time and I didn't tell anyone. I didn't want my marriage to fail."

"Ellie, no one blames you or Nora. We women always feel responsible for everyone else's behavior. You couldn't control Davis; Nora couldn't control Mariah. As much as we wish we could, we don't get to control other people or make their decisions for them."

Ellie nodded in agreement, while biting her lip. Her shame wasn't the only barrier that was keeping her from calling Nora. She could not forget Mariah's face that night and its uncanny resemblance to her mother's. She did not want to acknowledge the passionate, uncontrolled, and unidentifiable emotion locked deep inside of her; the resentment she had buried toward her sister. She feared a conversation might unleash something monstrous. Ellie sought reassurance. "Do you think I'm a terrible person for marrying him in the first place?"

"Oh Ellie! How could your father and I think that? Look at your lovely boys. We are so grateful for them. Davis made mistakes, but it doesn't mean your life with him has been a mistake."

"Thanks Mom." Ellie gave her mom another hug and tried to hold back the tears. There was a sense of relief that she didn't have to keep the secret anymore.

"Ellie, we're only an hour away. You call us night or day," her dad reminded her as they left.

* * *

Thanksgiving was fast approaching. On good days, Ellie grieved the loss of her marriage. The feelings would overcome her often unexpectedly. As she made the bed, she realized she would never hear Davis' breathing next to her or feel his arms holding her when they slept. She would not laugh at his little jokes or tease him for putting on mismatched socks. As she organized the closet, she knew she would never choose his Sunday tie or listen to him prepare his sermons. She had enjoyed those things. A future of loneliness spread out before her with fatal determinism. She did not have a person, that special person who loved her. She was an orphan adrift in the world without protection.

On bad days, Ellie experienced waves of anger and humiliation. She imagined Davis and Mariah together in the heat of intimacy. The lovers of her imagination laughed at her, *Stupid Ellie. She thinks she's so smart and doesn't see what we're doing right under her nose.* She replayed conversations with Davis with the new realization that he had been lying through his teeth every time he had come home late or made an excuse. With each remembrance, the pain felt fresh, a punch to the gut. In unexpected moments, a thought could be so powerful, the images of his betrayal so real, they could debilitate her. She would have to step outside for air or excuse herself to the restroom to vomit.

A person changes after a traumatic event, she realized. Their life becomes defined by the Before and the After. In the After, Ellie did not paint anymore. Painting was painful now. The memory of her last painting now haunted her. A dark revelation came to her as she worked to finish the portrait of her grandmother Lydia. In her mind, Ellie knew she wanted to create a young and beautiful version of the elderly woman she vaguely remembered, to reimagine the matriarch in her prime of life, to capture the essence of a strong woman who had raised eight children. Ellie wanted to show that even in her youth and innocence, the promise of what she would become could be seen in her soulful grey eyes. The face emerged on the canvas, but as she fleshed out the piece with light and shadow, an old, shriveled woman appeared. Her eyes were small and tight, her mouth set in a hard grimace. They were not eyes of strength, but eyes of despair. Ellie gasped in shock when the truth of the painting revealed itself. The face was withered and broken, but through the dark lines and shadows she did not see her grandmother's face, but only her own. She did not need her fears coming to life, the fear that she would age bitter and alone. Ellie shredded the canvas with a paper cutter and decided to take a break from painting, maybe forever. She wasn't ready. She didn't have time to paint anyway. Her boys needed her.

Staying busy was Ellie's survival skill. She filled her school calendar with projects for her students and between planning lessons, gathering supplies, setting up art labs, and cleanup, she rarely had a spare moment. In the evenings, she focused on the boys. Several nights, they slept with her in the big king-sized bed after watching a movie. It was nice to not be alone. On Friday, she called her mom and asked if her parents would take the boys during the Thanksgiving holiday for a few days. Ellie realized that the toll of her dead marriage was catching up to her. She needed time to release her emotions and experience the sadness without the boys having to bear witness to their mother's emotional breakdown. She didn't want to frighten them.

"We don't mind taking the boys at all, but what about Thanksgiving? Are you coming? We're having the usual family gathering. They'll be turkey and my apple crisp."

"Yes, Mom. It's Thanksgiving. There's always turkey. I'm just not feeling up to it this year. I just can't give you a firm answer. I know I want the boys to have the family experience, but I'm not sure I'm going to feel like it—a big family gathering just feels kind of unpleasant to me right now. I know you understand."

"Of course, but it will be fun, and it might be good for you."

On Saturday morning they drove down and picked up the boys. Ellie opened two packages from Amazon that she ordered after they left: two sets of soft fleece pajamas. Her plan for the next four days was to live in those pajamas, watch TV, cry, or pray; do whatever she felt she needed to do. While the boys were in the house, Ellie needed to stay strong, but now that she was alone, she needed to face her emotions head on.

Without going into details, Ellie had told Melissa at work that she and Davis were splitting. Melissa knew Davis was a minister and she saw the shock in her eyes, but she did not pry. Melissa, having survived a divorce herself, recommended that Ellie take some time to process and heal. Melissa called it "quality self-care". Ellie liked to think of it as a first-rate pity party for one. *Only women schedule time for their emotional breakdowns*, she thought.

The first night alone, Ellie drank two glasses of wine and took two melatonin pills. Exhaustion caught up with her and she couldn't think clearly about Davis, her current situation, or her future. What she needed was sleep. She passed out at 7p.m. and didn't wake up till 10:00 a.m. the next morning. When she woke, she felt confused and out of sorts. The week had taken its toll on her. She didn't realize how much energy was spent in trying to pretend her life was normal and that she was okay.

After a cup of black coffee, Ellie perked up and decided to soak in the hot tub. She eased into the hot water and reclined into the frame of the tub. She no longer feared an interruption from the boys and the tears came on suddenly and easily. She washed them away by cupping the warm water and splashing her face. When her eyes were red and her tears spent, she rested her head gently on the edge of the spa. She tucked her legs beneath her in the water and sat still, listening to the birds and soaking in the warmth. Finally, she wrapped herself in a long kimono robe and hurried back into the house to avoid the chilly fall air. The refrigerator beckoned to her and she decided on moose tracks ice cream for breakfast. Without guilt, she surrendered to the temptation of chocolate syrup and whipped cream. The artist in her wished she had a maraschino cherry to put on top, just for optics. Dressed in new fleece pajamas, she watched a terrible Lifetime movie about a cheating husband while taking oversized bites of ice cream. The husband was righteously stalked and tormented by his faithful wife. *Good*, Ellie thought. Throughout the day alone, she allowed the waves of Davis' betrayal to hit her and she faced them instead of trying to push the feelings deep inside. She didn't feel good exactly, but just as she needed to look at the Facebook photos of Mariah and Davis straight on, Ellie realized that there was value in the truth plain and simple.

Davis had pretended to protect her by lying and Ellie now realized that the truth was a gift. Only the truth allowed you to move forward. No sound structure can be built on a lie. Davis had robbed her of the truth, the ability to make decisions for herself. He had treated her like an idiot. Ellie realized now that the hurt of betrayal was intrinsically connected to being thrown outside the circle of intimacy and truth. Mariah and Davis shared that intimacy now and she had been cast to the side. At the heart of her pain was the knowledge of the rejection and exclusion from the person she loved and trusted most. She grieved now over the loss of the husband she thought she had married and tried to come to terms with the unknown man Davis was. The path ahead was filled with tough choices. She had an opportunity now to build her life on something better, but where to begin?

Ellie called Lyle Shepherd that afternoon. He answered on the second ring, his voice rich with a slight country twang.

"This can be a very expensive process, Ellie. Most of it will depend on whether Davis will agree to your terms. Have you thought about what those terms should be?"

"The terms of the divorce? I'm thinking about that, Mr. Shepherd, but I don't know yet. There's a lot to consider."

"I understand. You should put a lot of thought into it. Do you know what your husband's assets are?"

A thought suddenly came to Ellie. She remembered that before Madeline had died, she had requested a sit down while Davis was out of the house, a heart to heart.

"Someday when I die, you and Davis will come into a lot of money,"

"Madeline, I don't want to talk about you dying…" She paused mid-thought as she stared at her mother in law's perfectly arched eyebrows.

"Listen to me. Davis is going to need your help. He will lose that money if he doesn't learn some management skills. Personally, I don't think he has it in him. I think you can help him." From her white alligator skin handbag she withdrew a small flash drive and placed it firmly in her palm. "This has my will and testament and all my financial records. You need to prepare and plan for this kind of money. Maintaining wealth is not the party people

63

think it is. You want to stay wealthy and see your investments grow? It takes work."

Ellie's mind drifted back to Lyle's question. "Actually, I do know all his assets."

"That's good. A lot of spouses don't know how much money is really there. When we meet, you should have a clear idea of what the terms of the divorce should be at least in your mind. You should know what you're asking for? Can we meet next week? Wednesday is looking good on my calendar."

"Would four work? I would like to not have to miss work if possible."

"Yeah. That's fine for me."

"Mr. Shepherd, I really appreciate that you would meet with me so quickly during the holidays and everything."

"Ellie, it is not a problem. Please call me Lyle. I owe a lot to your dad. I'd meet you on Christmas day if it was needed."

"Well, thank you and that won't be necessary, Lyle, but it's very kind."

She breathed a sigh of relief as she ended the call. With that one appointment now arranged, she felt the momentum of her life finally moving forward.

Ellie soaked in the hot tub again that evening. The sky hung heavy with mist, casting eerie shadows through the dim dusk light. She could just barely make out the shape of the Douglas fir only ten feet away. The sharp contrast of her wet face exposed to the cold November air and the rest of her body submerged in the heat of the tub, provided a curious sensation. She wondered what a life alone would look like going forward. The boys would eventually grow up. They would marry and move on with their lives. She had always envisioned having a big family like her parents. A profound emptiness filled her heart. She let tears fall freely. She was not sobbing or weeping, just grieving for her lost marriage and the lost vision of what she always believed her future would hold. Letting go of that future was a brutal exposure to the unknown. She was headed into the mist.

After another night of tossing and turning, Ellie finally drifted to sleep and woke the next morning relatively rested. She showered and dressed in the second pair of fleece pajamas. She felt stronger. She accepted the inevitability of divorce and she accepted that she did not have control of her life. She never did. Ellie looked at the Bible on her coffee table reproachfully. *Why God? Why did you let this happen to me? Why didn't you protect me?* When she was a young girl, she loved the story of the Prodigal son. She always rejoiced in the father's welcoming of his wayward boy. She now felt differently. *What about the older son?* He was faithful and true. The older son worked the land and supported his father. He made personal sacrifices for the good of his family and yet the reward? The feasting? The rejoicing? They all went to the younger son, the ungrateful brat who had done nothing but embrace sin, betray his father and disobey. Forgiveness was not justice, she decided.

In times of trial, Ellie's parents had taught her to go to the Word of God if she had any need or struggle in her life. She wasn't sure why she had been resistant up till now to open her Bible and meditate on the Word, but now she realized she had been avoiding it. In her Before, she always felt sure of her faith and trust in God's plan for her life, but now in the After, she no longer felt like she was in God's favor. Her failed marriage changed everything. *Okay God,* she thought. *I'm giving you a chance to say something to me. Something I need to hear to prove you're still out there and that you still know my name.* Ellie tried an old trick from her Christian camp days and closed her eyes. She opened the Bible randomly to a page and blindly placed her finger. She opened her eyes and read, *Cast all your cares on him because he cares for you. Be alert and of sober mind. Your enemy the devil prowls around like a roaring lion looking for someone to devour. Resist him, standing firm in the faith...* The verses were from 1 Peter 5:7-9.

The thought struck her powerfully. This was faith, to move forward without knowing if everything would be okay, relying on God, casting your cares. Davis had made decisions that impacted every member of her little family. Ellie had no say in the matter. She would never have chosen this, not any of it. Yet, she was left to pick up the pieces. She realized that when life was completely out of control, faith was really all a person had. And Satan? Was he prowling? Yes. Satan was the voice that told her Davis was right.

The voice that told her she was ugly, undesirable, and unwanted. *Maybe if you hadn't gained weight or tried to be sexier? Maybe then, he would have been satisfied with you. He would have loved you, if you had just tried a little harder.* Those thoughts were numerous and overwhelming. The voice that told her she wasn't worthy to be truly loved.

Davis had betrayed her with not just any woman, her niece. No one could tell her what she already knew. It was personal. He wanted her to hurt, to be in pain. Why? She didn't know why. She didn't care. She wanted him to feel pain too. Staring into the deep pool of Davis' betrayal, she did not believe forgiveness was possible.

She grabbed a notebook and a pen. *What do I want?* she wrote. She considered the question. Should she ask for half of Davis's estate? More? Should she keep the children from him? His behavior was awful, and Ellie believed all these moves would be justified. Melissa would certainly support her, especially if she knew everything. If Davis' behavior came out in family court, she couldn't imagine any judge looking favorably on him. Ellie had always been the stable and consistent parent for her boys. Davis had been a neglectful parent at best. Sleeping with his children's cousin certainly did not make him father of the year. She wanted Davis to suffer for the hurt and rejection she felt like a jagged spike moving in her heart.

But Ellie also heard the voice of God. His voice came from the place in her heart where she had accepted Jesus as her Lord and savior when she was only seven years old. That voice, which sounded a lot like her father's, reminded her that her boys needed their best mother and their best father.

By Tuesday, Ellie felt better. When her parents came home with the boys there was a surprise.

"Andrew?" Ellie exclaimed as she saw her brother towering over her parents from behind the open doorway.

"Mom, Mom!" screamed the boys.

She kissed and hugged them both. "I missed you two." They both spoke in rapid fire telling Ellie all they did at Grandma and Grandpas. Miles had made chocolate chip cookies with Grandma and John had gone fishing with Grandpa. "Thank you so much!" Ellie mouthed to her parents. The boys darted under her arms and ran to the backyard. "Andrew! What are you doing here?"

"Can't a brother stop by to see his favorite sister?"

"That's a little weird," Ellie joked.

"Ah good! She hasn't lost her sense of humor."

"Never. Where's Emily and the kids?" Andrew and his wife Emily had three little ones: Alex, Jane, and baby Isaiah.

"I made an escape and came alone. Emily's going to kill me," he laughed. "No, I just really wanted to see you."

"Come in, Come in." Ellie moved out of the way and ushered them in.

Her mother sounded almost out of breath as her voice dripped with forced enthusiasm. "Ellie, your dad brought some wood airplanes for the boys. We're going to go out to the yard and help them build and fly them. Why don't you and Andrew have a nice visit?"

"Yes. Very smooth, mom. Enjoy your airplane flying." Ellie rolled her eyes at her mother's attempt at subtlety. Richard shrugged apologetically and followed Sandra out to the yard. "They're quite the pair, aren't they?"

"Yes, they are. They're strange, but they're ours."

Ellie laughed. "You want some coffee?"

"That sounds great."

In her galley kitchen, Andrew stood like a colossus as Ellie opened a cabinet and selected two festive mugs. She hadn't seen Andrew since summer. When they were kids, he had been her closest sibling. Only two years separated them and as children they were playmates and confidantes. Andrew had a delicious sense of humor and between her brothers, he reminded her most of their father with his kind heart and wry humor.

Andrew followed her to the dining table with two steaming mugs of coffee. "So, I'm guessing Mom wants us to talk alone?"

"How did you guess? She's hoping I can convince you to come to Thanksgiving, you know, since I'm your favorite brother and everything."

"Oh Andrew. I don't know," Ellie sighed.

"Are you seriously thinking about spending Thanksgiving alone? Thanksgiving? Don't you think that would be kind of depressing?"

Ellie's laugh sounded hollow. "Totally depressing, but I think seeing Nora would be worse. It's just so awkward."

"Oh, you mean because your husband was sleeping with her daughter. Come on now it's a modern world. Get with the times. That's nothing!"

"Geez Andrew, don't joke! Saying it out loud didn't make it sound better."

Andrew's eyes searched her face. "It must seem to you like the worst thing in the world. I'm sure it does, and I get it, but you know families get over pretty unbelievable, terrible stuff all the time, right? It's what families are supposed to do."

"I'm not sure I'm over it, much less getting you all involved. Things are just weird with Nora and me."

"We're involved whether you like it or not and you know what? We're on your side. We're on Nora's side. We don't want our family hurt by what Davis and Mariah chose to do."

"You never liked Davis, did you?"

Andrew's mouth tightened at the edges. He shifted uncomfortably in his wooden chair and took a sip of coffee. "You know. You're right. I'm going to say this now because I can. I kind of hated the guy."

Ellie's eyes widened. "Hates a strong word. I could always tell that you didn't hit it off, but hate?"

"You're right. Hate is a strong word. I didn't hate the guy exactly, but I hated how he treated you."

"What? Really? How did you think he treated me?"

Andrew furrowed his eyebrows and leaned forward. "Ellie, I know you. When we were kids you used to go out in the yard and dig bear traps. Remember when you put the dog in the trap, and I thought poor Scout was a real bear? Or when we decorated cupcakes in the shape of planets, and you helped me get an A on my science project? We used to roll around in paint in the backyard, and grab bird feathers and make weird collages. You were the coolest and most fun person that I've ever really known. Ell, I mean you're the best. Davis never appreciated you. He was so self-absorbed and pretentious. He treated you like an accessory. I didn't like it and I'm not going to apologize for it."

Ellie was stunned. "I didn't know you felt that way." She smiled, "I hope Emily knows what a lucky girl she is."

"Well, right now at home with a baby, a toddler, and an escape artist, she's not feeling real lucky, but I'll let her know you said so."

"Why didn't you say anything?"

"People have to find things out in their own way. You would have been mad at me. You can't tell people the real truth till they're ready to hear it."

She frowned as she considered the revelation. "I suppose you're right."

"So, Thanksgiving?"

"Have you talked to Nora or Mariah?"

"Mariah has not talked to anyone in the family besides her parents. She won't be there. She says she's never planning to show her face to a family event ever again."

"That makes me sad, Andrew. I mean I guess I should hate her for sleeping with Davis, but I hate what this is doing to our family."

"She's made her choices, Ellie."

"And Nora?"

"She's like you. Doesn't want to come." Andrew's eyes studied her. "Ellie, someone's got to be the first person to reach out, the grown up so to speak. I'm thinking that's you."

"Thanks Andrew. No pressure." Ellie sipped her coffee as she thought. "I'm just feeling a little tired right now of always being the grownup."

"Blessed are the peacemakers."

Ellie thought for a moment. Andrew had taken time from his busy schedule to give her a pep talk. Her parents had taken the boys and given her time to sort through some of the pain. They were not asking for much. "Alright. I'll go."

Andrew smiled. "We could dig some bear traps in the backyard."

"That's where I'm putting your dead body."

Andrew grinned. "She's back."

Chapter 6

Cleanup

> *Sisters never quite forgive*
> *Each other for what happened*
> *when they were five.*
> —Pam Brown

Thanksgiving morning brought unseasonably cold temperatures to Oregon. Ellie bundled the boys in sweaters, gloves, and jackets and made the sixty-five-mile drive to her parents' house with care. As she drove, she realized that she hadn't thought about Davis. Usually, she was hyper aware of his absence from the moment she woke, but not today. Holidays had been difficult for him. Ellie dragged him annually to her parents' house for Thanksgiving and Christmas both. He hated it.

Ellie's family were a lively bunch and Davis felt overshadowed in their midst. Andrew would start telling stories from their childhood and the whole family would join in. Before long they would all be laughing in hysterics, even Maggie, Emily, and Lee, but not Davis. Ellie loved to laugh and reminisce, but Davis' moodiness cast a shadow. When they drove home, guilt would overcome her as Davis would check off his litany of complaints. Davis, after all, didn't have a lively fun-loving family. After his father died, he only had his mother. Their Thanksgivings before Ellie were quiet and civilized. On those drives home she reminded herself that a good wife needed to support her husband. Now, she knew better. If Davis loved her, he would have wanted her to enjoy Thanksgiving with her family. He wouldn't have tried to sabotage her joy or separate her from them.

The roads were slick, but fortunately not crowded on Thanksgiving Day. She was grateful that the boys were peaceful playing with their Nintendo DS devices. She pulled into the driveway of her parents' two-story brown craftsman house. The memories of her childhood home flooded her mind with memories, and she was filled with contentment.

Her brothers had not yet arrived and the house was almost eerily quiet when she opened the front door.

"Hey Mom? Dad? We're here."

"Come on in, Honey. I'm in the kitchen."

Ellie caught the fragrance of turkey with hints of rosemary and mint as she entered the house.

"Smells good, Mom."

"Have the boys go to the living room. We have some games set up and Grandpa's ready for them."

"You heard Grandma. Go ahead John. Be good to your brother. Your cousins will be here soon."

"They better get here soon, because Miles can't even roll dice without them going everywhere."

"That's not true! I can roll dice. It's just you distract me."

"Hush, that's enough. Play a game without dice. Don't give Grandpa a hard time."

The boys ran to the living room as Ellie entered the kitchen. "Hi Mom. Wow. You've been busy. Need some help?"

"Take a look at what's under the tin foil over there." Ellie sneaked a peek and saw a two-tiered chocolate raspberry cake. "It's all baked and cooled. I've created the canvas for my beautiful artist."

Ellie smiled. She loved cake decorating. She grabbed a bowl and some quick ingredients and began a chocolate ganache. "You got the fresh raspberries."

"They don't call me Betty Crocker for nothing."

"No one calls you Betty Crocker, Mom," Ellie kidded. "But if you want me to start, you could probably bribe me with babysitting."

"Honey, I'm always happy to take the boys. No bribery necessary."

"I know, Mom and you guys have really been great." Ellie hoped her mother did not really feel that she took them for granted. Without any more delay, she decided to acknowledge the elephant in the room. "So, what's the scoop? Who's going to be here today? It looks like the table's set for an army."

"Andrew and Emily and their kids of course. I can't wait to see that little Isaiah. Brian and Maggie of course and you and the boys."

She noted her mother's tactful omission of Davis' absence. "So, you weren't able to convince Nora and Lee, I take it?"

"I have table settings all ready to go, just in case."

"You're always hopeful, Mom."

"When it comes to my kids, you bet I am. There is nothing better than having all of you around the table together."

Ellie smiled. She loved how her mother's focus was always on family. Ellie had made a tradition to arrive first on holidays because she liked to help her mom in the kitchen and also have a little one on one time to talk and gossip. They were a great team because Sandra was an excellent cook. Ellie was no chef, but she could make any dish her mother made look beautiful. This year, based on the packed countertops, Sandra didn't need much help.

She put the ganache to the side of the stove to cool slightly and began to peek at the covered dishes and rearrange them for the best possible optics.

"You have such a gift, Ellie."

"Oh, I don't know. It doesn't take too much effort to make delicious food even more appealing."

"Well, you have the touch. So, what's your idea for the cake?"

"I'm thinking—raspberries used as flower petals. I'm going to shave some chocolate and use it to give some texture." She set to work starting with pouring the ganache over the cake and letting it cool. She set aside the decorating tools including just a small amount of fondant to provide some color contrast and a few bright green mint leaves as a garnish. Finally, she arranged the raspberries and chocolate shavings with her expert hand. "Voila. Perfection."

"There's our centerpiece," laughed Sandra.

"Team effort."

"It always is."

Richard entered the kitchen. "Ellie." He gave her a hug and kissed her forehead.

"Hey Dad,"

"Richard, don't you even dare think about poking your nose under any of these dishes!"

"I wouldn't dream of it, dear." He let Ellie see the slight roll of his eyes.

She laughed and secretly siphoned off the edge of a cinnamon roll and handed it to him. "Poor Dad. Mom, there's got to be some advantages to living in this house?"

"Oh, your father is already fully aware of the advantages of living in this house. Don't you poor Dad me." Sandra wagged her finger in mock discipline.

"Ellie, I'd like you to come with me on a little errand." He turned to Sandra. "Do you think you could spare our daughter for about an hour or so?"

Sandra stared at Richard, her eyes wide. "What possible errand would you have on Thanksgiving morning?"

"Oh, it's just a little something. You know I won't get in any trouble. Ellie will be with me, if you can spare her?"

"Well, I guess everything is mostly done. I've just got the turkey in the oven, so I can watch the boys, if it's just for an hour. Andrew and Brian should be here in about two hours or so. But where are you going?"

"We've been married a long time, Sandy. You know you just have to trust me sometimes."

Sandra wrinkled her nose. "If you're late for Thanksgiving dinner, you won't have a home to come home to."

Richard embraced and kissed her. "I would never jeopardize that!"

Sandra took the dish towel and swatted him. "Don't be long."

Ellie followed her dad to his blue Dodge Ram pickup, her curiosity stoked over what errand her dad could possibly need to run. The pick-up smelled of her father's Old Spice aftershave. There were tools scattered on the seat and Ellie tossed them to the back of the cab. Sitting in the large truck always made her feel like a little girl again. Richard turned the key and the engine roared to life. "Where are we going, Dad?"

"You'll see Ell." He drove his usual five miles below the speed limit as they drifted toward the highway.

"You know it's kind of gross how you and Mom still flirt," Ellie teased.

"Someday you will understand," he said.

"I'm not so sure I will."

"Oh, you will. There are always storms, but sometimes the most beautiful sights to see come after the storm. It's not like your mother and I have the perfect marriage, you know."

"You guys make it look easy."

"I know it might look that way, but that woman drives me half mad, most of the time. She's constantly pressuring me to be a better man and there are times I fight her. Most of us are pretty set in our ways."

Ellie's eyes widened in surprise as the pickup turned into the parking lot of the Salem IHOP. "Um, Dad? Are you afraid we don't have enough food for our Thanksgiving dinner? Are you feeling like pancakes?"

He smiled and raised his eyebrows. "You know there aren't a whole lot of places open on Thanksgiving."

Ellie was confused, but she followed him through the double glass doors. He nodded at a young server and walked past the foyer down the aisle to the back corner of the restaurant. Ellie saw Nora before she spotted them. "Dad, I don't think this is a good—"

"Nora. Happy Thanksgiving, sweetie." Nora stood from the table and hugged him. He kissed her on the forehead.

"Hi Dad, what did you want to see me about? You know I told Mom I wasn't com…" and then she saw Ellie. Her eyes opened wide and then hardened into tight slits. "Oh, I see…"

"Hi Nora. I didn't know you'd be here either." Ellie's tone was cautious.

"Girls, you have a lot to talk about. I'm going to wait out in the truck and give you sisters some time to talk things through." Before either of them could protest he was gone.

"So here we are," Ellie said uneasily.

"Yes, here we are," Nora's voice was cold.

Ellie put on her church face. *I can do anything through him who gives me strength.* With resignation, she hooked the strap of her purse to the back of the chair and took the space across from her sister. She remembered what Andrew said about being the adult. Nora looked different to her somehow, thin, almost waiflike with large brown doe eyes. She generally had the vulnerable female look perfected, but as she sat in the booth fidgeting with the table, she looked harder, angrier.

"Can I get you coffee or something to eat?" asked a young blonde server with a bouncing ponytail.

"I'd love a coffee, Ellie said. I won't need anything else. Thanks."

"You got it." She turned swiftly and headed toward the kitchen.

Ellie took a deep breath. "Nora. I'm really sorry I haven't called. I just didn't know what to say."

Nora stared at her and said nothing. Ellie felt awkward and deeply uncomfortable. "Did you know about it, Ellie? About the affair?" Nora blurted.

She was stunned by Nora's directness. She felt cornered. "Yes. There was a short period of time when I knew about the affair before everyone else," she admitted. Ponytail returned and set a black coffee on the table. Ellie took a clean spoon out of a napkin and began to stir cream into the cup and watched the server head to another table.

"How long?" Nora pressed.

"I've known since August," she said slowly. Davis told me he had ended the affair and we were in therapy. We were going to try to work on the marriage."

"I'm not interested in your marriage, Ellie. Did Mariah threaten to kill herself?" Nora's voice was quiet, but ominous.

"Davis told me she had threatened her own life. Yes. She told him she was going to jump off the Autzen Bridge. We went there in the middle of the night to take her home. That was the night I found out what had been going on."

"How could you not tell me, Ellie? I am her mother!" Nora snapped.

Ellie was on the defensive. "Nora, she begged me not to. She was afraid how you would take it and frankly, I was too."

"Here you are. Little miss perfect Ellie. You're everyone's favorite daughter and apparently that's not enough for you. You have to take my Mariah too!"

Ellie was floored and then something broke inside of her. "I didn't take Mariah from you! She's been running away from you from the time she was eight years old!" The dam that held Ellie's angst suddenly burst and the words gushed out of her with force. "And what exactly would you have done if I had called you? Because I can picture it. Your daughter is hysterical and threatening to jump off a bridge and we call you. You drive down and maybe you die because you're high on a substance while you're driving and crash, or you're so depressed you overdose on your meds, or you drive down all the way to Eugene and come running to the bridge more hysterical than your daughter. Guess what we have then? Two hysterical people threatening to jump off a bridge. Any way you look at it, when you're involved things get worse!"

Nora's eyes burned daggers. "Oh, yes. You're the perfect mother. You know what's best for everyone. You've got it all handled. No one else even gets a choice. I see now why your husband decided to stray. Who could stand being on that tight leash?"

Nora's words found their mark. Her stomach twisted in a painful knot. "Okay, you want to get dirty? You really want to go there?" Ellie was aware that other customers were now staring at them. "Let's talk about the inappropriate pictures your daughter sent to my husband before anything even started. Let's talk about what she learned from you, her own mother about what's right and what's wrong. Apparently, there's nothing off limits for that girl. I'm a teacher, remember? We all know where kids learn their

76

morality, from their parents. This is what you taught her! You're the one who taught her to take and take, to turn on people who've helped her like a snake. That was you, Nora! I did everything for that girl. Where were you? Where were you?"

Nora's eyes filled with tears and her words were choked. "No Ellie. You have all the advantages here. You had the money, the job, the perfect family. Everyone looks at you and thinks you're perfect. You and Davis have everything, and you decide it isn't enough. You take Mariah away from me and your husband, your husband…"

"I hate Davis for what he did, but they were both adults and Mariah made a choice too, the kind of choices people make when they are so selfish, they only care about themselves. That's the truth about Mariah and it's also true about you!

"I have a mental illness and it's real. What's your excuse?"

"I don't get an excuse, Nora. I just do the work. I don't get to break down or ask my sister for money or ask my dad to find me a job. I don't get to cry and have some man save me. I rely on myself and I do it by working hard. You should try it. At the end of the day let's not forget your daughter took my life from me, not the other way around." Ellie fought back tears. She got up from the booth abruptly and spilled coffee on her jeans and sweater. She didn't care. She ran out of the IHOP as customers gawked.

The freezing air cooled her hot tear-stained cheeks as she ran to her father's truck. The passenger door was locked. She banged desperately on the door. Startled, her father unlocked the door and Ellie jumped into the seat. "We gotta go. Please Dad, now!"

"What about Nora? Ellie, what's…" He looked at her face and understood. "You wait here, Ellie." He rushed from the truck into the restaurant to check on Nora. Ellie pressed her cheek on the cold passenger window and watched her breath fog the glass. Never in her entire life had she allowed herself an outburst in front of a crowd of strangers; never had she allowed herself to express her darkest and most hateful thoughts aloud. Her whole life she had been protecting and shielding her older sister and where had it gotten them? Nowhere. A horrifying revelation came to her. She did not feel guilty.

Ten minutes later Ellie and her father were on the road again. They sat in silence as Ellie listened to the Ram's engine purr. "I'm sorry Ellie." She turned from the window to look at her father. His eyes were furrowed with concentration on the road and his jaw tight. "I shouldn't have meddled. It was too soon. I expected too much from you both."

"Dad, I didn't know. I didn't know I was going to yell at her or react that way. I thought I was okay. I didn't even know how angry I was, how angry I am. I'm not even sure I know what I'm angry about. You shouldn't have surprised us. We weren't ready. I don't know if we ever will be."

"You're right. I let your mother push too much. She wants everyone to get along."

Ellie looked at her father with wide imploring eyes. "But Dad…I don't think that's what I want. I don't want everyone just to get along anymore. I just want people to be honest. If Davis had just been honest with me, it would have saved a lot of grief." In the moment, she made a promise to herself. She would not lie anymore. She would tell the truth if at all possible, even if it was difficult or awkward. *The truth will set you free,* she thought.

"Do you know why you're so angry with your sister?" Her father's voice interrupted her chain of thought.

"I think I've been holding some feelings inside, Dad. I think maybe I've been holding things in for a really long time. I'm not really sure I'm okay."

"You're okay. You will be okay Ellie."

"I hope so."

* * *

Wednesday dawned with the advance of a low-pressure weather system that brought rain and warmer temperatures. Ellie zipped her Columbia trench style rain jacket and darted across Willamette Street in downtown Eugene toward a three-story brick storefront. The first floor housed an artsy coffee shop with a bright yellow awning. She took in the scent of freshly roasted coffee beans and remembered visiting the shop during happier times. She recalled that she used to drink coffee with friends, laugh, and dish on the latest gossip. Now, those days seemed like another life.

She stood under the awning near the side entrance and read the information posted on a metal plaque: *Lyle Shepherd-Attorney-3rd Floor 302B.* She wrote the number on the back of her hand and opened the heavy wooden door to the stairwell. The building was old and smelled musty. There was no visible elevator, so Ellie took the stairs.

The third floor was desolate. Lyle's office was located in the far corner. There were several small offices for attorneys and one large office housing a taxidermist with the clever name *Living Dead* inscribed in bold white print on the glass door. The big glass window of the business displayed a myriad of stuffed dead animals. A cougar stared at Ellie with a ferocious glare, its wide mouth stretched back to reveal giant incisors that looked ready to devour her. *That's nice,* Ellie thought. *Hope it's not an omen of things to come.* She made an effort not to look at the cougar as she knocked on Mr. Shepherd's door.

"Come in," said a friendly voice.

Ellie opened the door and entered a small cluttered one room office. Lyle did not meet her expectation of what an attorney should look like. He wore jeans, cowboy boots, and a grey and black flannel shirt. He carried most of his weight in his belly and looked to be about in his mid-fifties.

"Hi. I'm Ellie."

"I assumed as much," Lyle said and reached out his hand. "Go ahead and have a seat. Did you get all the paperwork I sent?"

Ellie nodded and sat in a standard blue office chair and clasped her hands together. "I appreciate your time here."

"Not at all, Ellie. It's my pleasure. So, your husband sounds like quite the douche," Lyle's tone was light and conversational.

Ellie choked. "Uh… I don't know what to say." Suddenly she felt the release of something tightly bound inside of her and laughed. "Yes. He is quite the douche actually. Some might say a real douche bag."

"It's sometimes a good thing just to get that out right from the start," Lyle said with a chuckle. "Thanks for the files you sent me. I just need to know what you want to do. I'm going to take my direction from you. We can go light or aggressive, but I want you to be happy, okay?"

Ellie's eyes narrowed as she looked at Lyle. "He shouldn't be allowed to get away with this."

"I agree. Based on the files you sent me, I think you can take him for a lot. He has nearly two million dollars in assets. I think you could ask for half of that and for the house. That doesn't even include monthly child support. What about custody of the boys?"

"Davis was hardly a father. I always did ninety percent of the work in raising the boys even when I had the full-time job with the least flexible schedule."

"Full custody, then. Visitation?"

"I want the boys to have a father, but the idea of them spending time with him, especially if he's with my niece. No! Just No."

"Have you talked to him?"

"He hasn't called me. I haven't called either since I asked him to leave."

"That's okay. I can handle that for you if you need me to. Every case is different, but if you can work together and agree, the process will go much smoother. It will also be less expensive. You have the advantage here as the injured party. He might work with you. Guilt can be a powerful weapon."

"I just don't know, Mr. Shepherd, I mean Lyle. I don't have much faith in my ability to talk to people recently."

"Well, it looks like you know what you want. I'm going to get the divorce proceedings started. You've filled out all the paperwork. I'll keep you posted on the filing and where we are in the process. Your husband will get divorce papers served to him through the court once you've signed. He may call you. Be careful when you talk to him, if you talk to him. You can always just direct him to me. It might be safer. I don't know him, but he sounds like a manipulative son of a bitch."

Ellie smiled. "You know my dad from church?"

Lyle laughed. "I'm one of the rogue members, but Richard puts up with me and my colorful language."

Ellie took a deep breath as she put on her hood and walked out into the rain. The thought occurred to her that her life was her own again. She could make decisions for herself, plot out her own course. Her cell phone rang. She did not recognize the number. "Hello?"

"Ellie." Davis' voice was hesitant.

She held her breath and then slowly exhaled. "Yes Davis. It's me."

"I'd really like to see the boys. I miss them." Ellie felt a quiet anger burn.

"Davis. You're going to need to talk to my lawyer. I don't want to talk to you. I'll text you his number."

"Ellie, I—" She pressed the end call button before he continued. For a brief moment she had felt a sliver of peace and then it was gone the second she heard his voice. She felt raw. Would she ever be okay again?

Chapter 7

Part II

New Ground

Leave your native country, your relatives, and your father's family,
and go to the land that I will show you.
—*Genesis 12:1*

Since that fateful night at the bridge three turbulent seasons had passed. With her divorce to Davis now official, the summer season lay before her like an open canvas.

"Are you sure, Ellie? Is this the right one?" Ellie's father asked.

"Oh yes!" A slight breeze touched her face as she gazed at the ranch style farmhouse framed by an acre of orchards and pastureland. "Just look at it!" Her eyes moved to the red barn. "Can't you just see an art studio there? Look. The boys have so much room to run and just be boys. Apples, pears, cherry trees, I can even hear the water from the creek. It's just a dream."

Her father lifted his brows quizzically. "Ellie, it was built in 1945. Do you know what that means?"

"That this property has a classic style that will never go out of fashion?"

"No. It means that it will need lots of repairs. You're a single woman and

I don't mean to be offensive to you in the post women's liberation era, but you have no construction skills at all."

"Oh Dad. Don't be silly. I have you. You'll help me." She flashed her most charming smile.

"Honey, you are overestimating your old dad's skills. You are also 15 miles further away from your mother and me in this house. That's a long commute for your mom and me. It will be harder for us to help you out if you have an emergency with the kids. Are you sure you really want to sell?"

"Dad, I need to get out of Eugene. My job is here in Veneta and I'm only a few miles away, which is going to make my commute to work so much easier. This is going to be a fresh start. Besides, everything reminds me of Davis in that house. You know the house is already sold and I've already signed the papers. There's no turning back now."

"Oh Ellie, this is beautiful! Did you see the orchard? There are cherries almost ready to be picked," her mom yelled excitedly from the barn where she and the boys were exploring.

Richard rolled his eyes in defeat. "Like mother, like daughter. You and your mother are big picture people, but the details…You just figure they'll take care of themselves. "

"Dad, I know the house might take work, but it's going to be so worth it."

"That roof looks several years past its prime," he sighed with resignation and then grinned. "But it's a beautiful piece of land and that's God's honest truth."

"Dad, it's been a hard year for me and the boys, but the divorce has gone through. I have money from the house and the settlement. This is the time to do it."

"Be honest with me Ellie. Do you feel like this decision is God's leading or your own?"

"Oh Dad, I don't know. I'm taking a little hiatus from God for a while. I thought I was following his lead when I married Davis, so I'm not sure now that I have a functional God gauge."

"Well, your mother and I are praying for you and the boys and that's going to have to be enough for now, I guess."

"Thanks Dad." She kissed him on the cheek. "I think God listens to you more anyway."

* * *

Six weeks later Ellie parked the Ford Explorer in front of the yellow farmhouse. She held the keys in her hands savoring the feeling of owning her own home.

"I'm getting the biggest bedroom," taunted John.

"Mom, why does John get the biggest bedroom?"

"He doesn't Miles. I get the biggest bedroom because I'm the mom and you know what? I just bought this house."

"Way to go Mom." cheered Miles. "Can I have the next biggest room?"

"There are four bedrooms in this house. The next two bedrooms are the same size and the smallest one is going to be my office. You guys get to decide who wants the barn view and who wants a view of the orchards."

"I want to have the barn view."

"I want the orchards," John blurted at the same time.

"Well then it's settled. Everyone is getting what they want."

Ellie had to twist the key hard to turn the lock on the front door and use additional strength from her core muscles to push it forward. "Oh Wow!" Ellie exclaimed as she walked into the kitchen. The old laminate flooring was gone, replaced with light maple hardwood. The kitchen cabinets were painted white and the faded yellow Formica countertops replaced with white Silestone quartz. Her fingers lingered over the farmhouse double basin kitchen sink and the large wooden island. "Oh, it's better than I imagined it." The renovators were successful in bringing her vision to life. The walls were freshly painted in white and beige, the appliances replaced, and the bathrooms remodeled much like the kitchen. In the middle of the living room was an old-fashioned fireplace. She listened to the boys padding through the house as they yelled with excitement.

"This is my room!"

"Hey, this one's mine."

Ellie walked through the sliding glass doors to the back deck. The view of the river and the mountains far in the distance took her breath away. Her hot tub had been transported from the old house and Ellie looked forward to the evenings she would spend soaking after a hard day's work. The farmhouse may have been built in 1945, but the design now was modern and clean.

The moving van arrived fifteen minutes later. Andrew and Brian had volunteered to help her move, but this was something she wanted to do herself. She was the provider now. She needed to stand on her own two feet. The movers carried in her furniture and she began the arduous task of putting items away. Ellie was so involved in her work that she was startled when she saw movement from the corner of her eye. A young girl stood in the kitchen doorway. Her long brown hair hung in a side ponytail, a bit disheveled like a girl who spent her whole summer outside without shoes climbing trees.

"Hi," she said when Ellie met her eyes. "I'm Rae."

"Oh, hi there, Rae. I'm Ellie. Can I help you with something?"

Rae took a few steps forward into the kitchen. "It looks like maybe you and your husband have kids. Do you?"

Ellie smiled. "Well yes and no. There are kids, but no husband I'm afraid."

"Oh, I'm sorry," said Rae without sounding sorry at all.

"Oh, no reason to be sorry. Did you want to meet the boys?" Rae nodded. "John! Miles! Come down. I want to introduce you to someone." She turned her head back to the girl. "Do you live next door?"

"Yeah. I live in the blue house with my dad."

"Nice," said Ellie. This is our first day here. How old are you?"

"I'm twelve."

"Oh, John is eleven. Ah, here they are."

John and Miles stood in the kitchen and stared at Rae with a mixture of awe and fear. John finally broke the silence while still keeping his distance. "Hi. I'm John. I'm going into sixth grade."

Miles rushed forward with his hand out. "I'm Miles. I'm nine years old."

She smacked her gum to show her level of indifference and then shook

Miles' hand awkwardly. "I'm Rae. I'm going into seventh grade at Fern Ridge Middle."

"Really?" Ellie exclaimed. "You might be in my class next fall. I teach middle school art at Fern Ridge."

Rae looked unimpressed. "I thought you guys might want someone to show you around?"

"Can we, Mom?" John asked.

Ellie hesitated. "Yes, but only if you're very careful. Stay away from the river and watch for your brother. Keep your phone on you, okay? Rae, it's really nice of you to be so welcoming and show the boys around."

"Yeah, sure!" she said while popping another stick of gum in her mouth. Ellie was not sure she liked the look in her eye.

She was positioning furniture when she heard the screams. The sound of her children in distress made her hyper alert. She bolted toward the sound, running behind the house, toward the river.

"Miles, hang on! Hang on!" John was yelling from a large rock in the middle of the water. Ellie scanned the river and her eyes locked on Miles drifting downstream with the current, his arms flailing while he screamed in terror.

"Help! I can't swim. I can't..."

Terror struck her. "Miles! I'm coming!" She yelled even though she knew he couldn't hear her. With adrenaline pumping through her veins, she ran through a makeshift shortcut to the riverbed through blackberry bushes and brambles screaming his name. "I'm coming. I'm coming. Hold on!" On the other side of the river, she saw Rae also running and John now not far behind her. *Oh Lord. Don't take him. Don't take my son. He can't swim. She* pleaded with God as she ran.

Through the haze of panic, she saw a tall figure downstream from Miles making its way into the water. She forced herself to move faster. The figure pulled into focus at her approach. She could see him now, a man with a dark green jacket and grey khaki pants. He stood waist deep in the river and he moved swiftly, almost gracefully through the water to cross paths with her terrified son. Using his body, he blocked Miles from traveling any further with the current. He scooped her child into his arms and carried him towards the river shore. A cry of relief escape from her lips, "Thank you God!" Although she was exhausted and her muscles screamed with pain, she pushed herself by sheer will to Miles. When she reached him, she threw her arms around his shoulders in a bear hug and sobbed. "Oh God! I thought I had lost you."

"I'm okay. I'm okay Mom. You're choking me. Your bleeding, Mom. I'm alright."

"I don't care. I'm hugging you anyway." Her voice was raw and broken. Rae and John joined the stranger on the riverbank and watched Ellie cling to Miles in desperate relief.

The man finally spoke in a measured baritone. "How did he get in the river? He's not dressed for swimming that's for sure?" He wrung water calmly from his pant leg as he spoke.

Ellie looked up at him now and identified him as a police officer, a sheriff. He had a shiny brass star on his jacket. He was tall, rugged, and appeared to be in his mid-forties. Ellie immediately felt the authority of his office. "I'm not sure. This girl was taking my boys around while we were moving in and I heard screaming."

"You want to explain this to me, Rae?"

"We were just playing on the rocks. I told him not to go out too far, but he wouldn't listen and then splat, he was in the water. I didn't know he couldn't swim. Besides, the creek's only about waist deep. He wouldn't have drowned anyway. He's just scared of getting a little wet cuz he's a baby."

"I'm not a baby!" Miles glared.

"And you, what did you see?" the sheriff asked John.

"Well, Rae said only big kids could go out to the far rock. Miles wanted to show us he could do it, but then he just slipped. We tried to grab him, but the current already took him."

Ellie reached out her arms to John and held him and kissed his forehead. "I'm just so glad you're both okay." With the panic subsiding, Ellie felt a fierce indignation. "This girl's parents oughta know what she's been up to today. Something very serious could have happened and she's lucky I don't press charges."

An emotion Ellie could not read flashed in the sheriff's eyes. He looked at her intently. "You think we should tell her parents?"

"Well yes. Look at her? She's out here all alone leading children who are smaller and more susceptible into dangerous situations like jumping in the river. She looks like she hasn't had a shower in a week. Where are her shoes? She's obviously not getting the supervision and care she needs."

"Oh really? Do you agree with this lady's assessment Rae?"

"No. I think you take care of me just fine, Dad." Rae glared at Ellie, her expression openly hostile.

Ellie felt heat rise to her cheeks. "You're her dad?" Ellie was now sure she saw amusement in his eyes. "You're my new neighbor?"

"Yup."

"That's just wonderful." She could not keep the sarcasm out of her voice. This man was intimidating, but Ellie would never let a man bully her again. She had learned to speak her truth. "Okay. I'm going to start over again here. I'm Ellie. Now you've met John and Miles. I'm not happy that your daughter almost got my son killed, but I am very grateful that you came when you did and took him out of the water and saved his life. I am not planning on holding a grudge and I hope you won't either. Apparently, we're neighbors, and neighbors should be neighborly." Ellie held out her hand in what she hoped was a cordial gesture.

"Apparently," he said evenly. He stared at her with quiet intensity making her feel uncomfortable. Finally, he reached out his hand. "I'm Levi Monroe. I'm the sheriff here in Veneta as you probably guessed. As a friendly suggestion, people in this community generally keep their noses out of other people's business, but under the circumstances, I can see how scared you were for your boy and that's something I can understand. I also appreciate a young man who tells the truth." He nodded to John who nodded back. "You look like you need a little medical care there." He gestured towards her legs.

Ellie examined her arms and legs and realized she was covered in scratches and welts. Blood streamed down her legs and her arms were covered in angry red marks. "I didn't even notice."

88

"You better go take care of yourself," Levi nodded to Ellie. "Boys, I'm sure you learned a lesson today."

"Yeah. I need to learn how to swim," Miles said.

Levi smiled. "I was thinking maybe the lesson was to think for yourself and use good judgement. Did you think going out on those rocks might be dangerous?"

"Yeah. I was scared, but I didn't want them to say I was a baby."

Levi got down and rested on his knee so he could look Miles in the eye. "Next time, don't listen to them, okay?"

"I won't. I'm really glad you were in the water."

"Me too," he said and gave Miles a fist pump.

"Dad, we were just hanging out. It was an accident."

"Rae, we'll talk more when we get home. You have no idea how close you came to something you wouldn't be able to take back."

"I was having a good time till Miles fell in the water," John said. "I think we'll be here if you want to hang out tomorrow, Rae."

"We will see," Ellie said quickly. "We better go. Please say goodbye to Rae and Sheriff Monroe."

"Bye Sheriff."

"Goodbye Rae."

"Goodbye neighbors," Levi nodded. His voice made her shudder. She felt the flush of embarrassment heating her face all the way back to the house. *Great way to introduce yourself to the neighbors.*

After a busy day of moving and the trauma at the river, or creek as Rae called it, Ellie wanted to order take out for dinner. The short list that made up Veneta's restaurant offerings was less than desirable and there were few delivery options. *I guess a shortage of restaurants is to be expected in a town of 4800 people*, she thought. *I'm definitely going to need to be a better cook.* She opened her new refrigerator and grabbed eggs, bacon, and the Krusteaz buttermilk pancake mix she had just stashed away from the pantry. *There's nothing better than breakfast for dinner*, she thought.

"Boys! I have dinner." They met around the table.

"Yes." John exclaimed when he saw the bacon and eggs.

"I have pancakes too." Ellie placed a plate stacked with hotcakes on the table. The boys dove into the food like ravenous wolves. For a few minutes the only sound was chewing around the table.

"Mom, what did you think of Rae and Sheriff Monroe?" John asked.

Ellie bit her lower lip and allowed herself a few moments of think time before answering. "I am absolutely grateful that the sheriff was there when he was."

"Rae's kind of cool. I like her."

"Why do you like her, John?" Ellie did not want to admit that her first impression of Rae had not been positive.

"She showed us the coolest places. There's a spot near the river where there's these rocks that have big holes in them. She had some Indian arrowheads, old bullets and all these clear rocks that she's put in the holes. We found feathers, berries and old bottles and we put those in the shelves in the rock too. When we were out on the river, she had us pretending we were on a raft escaping from pirates. I don't know. It was just fun."

"Sounds like you guys were using your imagination. That's how we used to play before video games took over the planet," Ellie teased. "Do you like it here?"

"The house is cool, but…" Emotion clouded his features.

"What is it, John?"

"I miss my friends and I miss Dad."

"I miss Dad too," Miles said. Suddenly his eyes filled with tears and he began to bawl.

"Miles, what is it? What's wrong?"

"I think what happened today just kind of scared him," John said.

Ellie drew Miles into a full embrace. "You're okay. Everything's alright." She stroked his wispy hair and soothed him.

"When are we going to see Dad?" Miles asked.

"You get to see him on Fridays. Dad and I have agreed you should spend one night a week with him. You can do the fun Daddy things then, okay?"

"It's not really the same," John said. "It's not our family anymore." John's voice sounded strangely mature in her ears.

Ellie remembered the promise she had made to herself that she would not lie anymore. She would tell the truth even if it was difficult. "You're right John. It isn't the same. I'm sorry you're having to make all these adjustments. It isn't fair. You deserve a home where a mom and dad live together and love each other."

"Did the divorce happen because of what Dad did with Mariah?"

Ellie took in a rush of air and coughed. She felt the pain flare inside her again, almost take her breath away. "Miles, why don't you brush your teeth and head to bed."

"Do I have to?"

"If you want me to read to you, you do."

"Oh, okay, whatever." Miles scurried to the bathroom. She watched him turn the corner and head into the restroom.

"What is it you think your dad did?"

"He had an affair?"

"Have you talked to Dad about this?"

"No."

"Where did you hear this?"

"I saw it on Dad's phone."

Ellie tread carefully. "What did you see John?"

He was hesitant. "There was a message from Mariah. It said, *I love you* and some…well, some like sexy stuff."

"Oh God." Ellie dropped her face into her hands. "When was this, John?"

"It was a long time ago. When we all lived together in the other house, you know, a while before Dad left."

Ellie felt sick. *Was it possible her eleven-year-old son had known about his father's infidelity even before her?* She felt a wave of nausea. Rekindled rage seethed through her veins.

"Are you angry, Mom?"

She tried to control her breathing. "Yes. I'm angrier than I've ever been in my life, John, but I need you to know something."

"What?"

"I love you."

"I know, Mom."

She struggled to focus on John and his pain. She buried her own anger with the force of her will. "What are you feeling, John? Are you okay?"

"Mom, I know Dad hurt you, like really bad." He paused, afraid to continue.

"It's okay, John. I can handle whatever it is you want to say to me."

John looked up at her, his eyes glistening with tears. "Is it okay if I still love him?"

Ellie's heart tightened so hard in her chest, she winced with pain. "Oh John! Yes. Of course. You can love your dad. You should love your dad. I want you to love your dad."

"How can I love someone you hate?"

Ellie fought to control the quivering in her lips. "John, I don't know if I hate your dad. It's just really fresh, the hurt I feel right now. I don't know how long it's going to take for me to know how to feel about your dad, but I always want you and Miles to feel okay. That's more important to me than anything."

"I want you to be okay too, Mom."

Ellie wrapped John in her arms. "I am so incredibly lucky to have you."

Chapter 8

Excavation

So, he built an altar there and called upon the name of the Lord,
and pitched his tent there; and there Isaac's servants dug a well.
—*Genesis 26:25*

Ellie's heart beat erratically in her chest as she prepared for the first day of school. The orientation with teachers and administrators had come and gone with little variation from previous school years. It was good to catch up with Melissa, who thought she was insane for moving to Veneta. "You really want to live in the same town as the students? You're going to regret it, Ell. You'll be harassed by parents and kids everywhere you go." Ellie realized moving was a big decision, but she needed the change.

Only a year ago, her whole world had been in complete upheaval. She wasn't going to be the commuter teacher anymore, one of those teachers that drove into Veneta from Eugene and then drove away at the end of the school day. Veneta was her home now. She was a part of the community and for some reason the task of teaching felt weightier with that knowledge. She was committed to these students because they were now fixtures in her world. They would see her at the Grocery Outlet and the hardware store. She would meet their parents while running errands. Her children would go to school alongside her neighbors. The idea of having roots in a place that went deep into the soil comforted her. She braided her hair and applied make up carefully. *Here goes nothing.*

The Ford Explorer was spotless as Ellie and the boys climbed aboard for the drive to school. Every year she gave her SUV a thorough scrub down before the school year. If only the pieces of her life could be set into place as easily. She arranged her coffee in its Hydro Flask tumbler next to the driver's seat and checked to make sure both boys had fastened their seatbelts. The school bus would eventually pick up Miles to take him to the elementary school, but she wasn't ready for that separation yet. Life was already moving so fast. All she wanted was the extra time with both her boys when they could all be together. Time felt precious.

"You got everything Miles?" She smiled as he entered the backseat. He looked so grownup wearing a T-shirt, jeans, and a plain red Jansport backpack. Miles had declared his Spiderman backpack from last year too babyish and Ellie experienced a small heartbreak. He would not be her baby much longer. "Check your bag to make sure your lunch is in there, okay?"

"Okay, Mom. What's in the lunchbox?"

"Tuna fish and carrot sticks. Don't complain or you'll be making your own. There's also a bag of Doritos in there and maybe a bag of gummies."

"Tuna fish is okay, Mom." He gave her a thumbs up.

John looked at her from the passenger seat. "Do I have the same lunch?"

"Pretty much, except I gave you two sandwiches since you eat like a horse."

John laughed. "Thanks, Mom. Tuna fish is actually my favorite."

Recently he had been very kind to her, Ellie thought. "Miles, you'll go to Veneta Kids Club after school. The teacher should show you where to go when the school day ends. It's located in a pod on campus. Okay?

"Alright Mom"

"John, you'll be in the middle school club program. You'll have to take the school bus after school to Kid's Club. Come get me in my classroom if you have any problems, okay?"

"We got it, Mom. You worry too much. Miles and I have got this covered. You should concentrate on your own day."

Ellie laughed. He sounded so mature, like the man of the house. "Well, okay then. But it's normal to be nervous at a new school."

She dropped Miles off at the front of the elementary school and monitored his progress through the front doors, her heart beating nervously as she focused on his red backpack bobbing through the crowd of children.

"You shouldn't worry about him, Mom. He makes friends with everyone."

"Someday, you'll understand, John. When you're a parent." Ellie sighed. She navigated the SUV carefully out of the parking lot. "Do you have plans after school?"

"Yeah. Rae and I were going to hang out by the river when we all get home. Don't worry though. I'm not taking Miles."

Despite the year and a half age gap, John and Rae had become fast friends. They played together most afternoons and although Rae was never friendly to Ellie and rarely came into the house, she was glad for John to have a friend. His face lit up every time he saw her. When he recounted their adventures later at dinner his eyes danced. Ellie was grateful that John had found a distraction, one that kept him from fixating on the divorce and the sudden changes in all their lives.

"Just make sure you don't stay out too long and you're back at six for dinner. You might have homework tonight."

She pulled the car into the staff parking of Fern Ridge Middle School. Fern Ridge was where Ellie had taught for a few years now, even when she commuted from Eugene, but the school was all new to John. Because of their move to Veneta, the boys were new to the school district and he was transitioning to middle school. Ellie gave John an encouraging nod. "Do you want to walk in together or would you rather go alone?"

"I think alone is better. Thanks Mom." He made sure no one was looking and gave her a quick hug before opening the door and jumping out.

"Good luck." Ellie called as he ran toward the front entrance.

Blank faces stared up at her as she introduced herself as Ms. Gold. Many of her students were new, but the few who she had taught the previous year did not seem to notice the change from Mrs. to Ms. On the first day of class, Ellie liked to allow students to sit in whatever seat they wanted. She could observe their friend groups, identify the talkers and troublemakers, the highflyers, those that were shy and lacked confidence and kids with social emotional issues. A seating chart was inevitable in middle school, but she would put one together that she believed would set them up for the best success possible in her class.

She introduced herself and set them to work almost right away with the assignment of sketching a quick self-portrait. "Let me know what you think you look like or how you think others see you or better yet, how you truly see yourself. It can be realistic or completely symbolic. It's up to you to help me see you through your eyes."

Within the first fifteen minutes of class, Ellie identified a clique of popular 7th grade boys. Mason, a mature looking boy with the beginnings of manly facial stubble was the ringleader. He wore his red basketball jersey with the number seven emblazoned on the back proudly. Three boys served as his henchman. Taylor, Gabe, and Eric who were also athletes, but content to let Mason call the shots. They sat together and joked around, throwing paper across the room. Ellie sensed cruelty in their humor but had not yet seen evidence to confirm her suspicions. She would make sure they didn't sit together in the future.

There were other students who caught her eye. Natalie was a shy and withdrawn 7th grader. Even though the students could choose their own seats, she seemed to have no friends to commiserate with. As they sketched, Ellie approached her gently, "Are you new this year?"

"No. I've been here all my life." She looked at her shoes as she answered.

"I'm really glad you're in my class," Ellie said quietly. Natalie's self-portrait, which was really quite skilled for a young girl left an impression. She had sketched herself from the point of view of a bird or a tower looking down on herself. The viewer could only see the part in her long dark hair as they looked down on the subject from above. There was no face to be seen, but her jeans and Converse tennis shoes were visible on the grass and drawn with intricate detail. "That's so interesting," Ellie said. "I love how you did something unique and different with your point of view. You have an artist's eye. I can tell."

Natalie's face beamed as she looked up. "Thanks!"

"No. Thank you. It's going to be fun to have you and your perspective in this class," Ellie whispered.

Then there was Rae. Ellie called out her name at the beginning of class. Rachel?" Rachel? Is Rachel Monroe here?"

"It's Rae." Ellie spotted her in the left corner, her head down in her notebook with her usual sulky expression.

"Oh, hi Rae. I didn't realize you were a Rachel. Good to see you."

Rae did not acknowledge her but scribbled in her notebook. Ellie continued with attendance and as she introduced herself and went through her classroom expectations, Rae would occasionally raise her eyes above the rim of her notebook to glare at her. *If looks could kill*, thought Ellie. Like Natalie, she didn't seem to have any friends.

As her young artists labored over their self-portraits, Ellie surveyed the classroom and checked in with every student. She saved Rae for last. Her teacher instincts were on edge. This girl was planning to test her. As she suspected, Rae's self-portrait was completely blank. "Oh no, Rae. What happened?"

"This is how I see myself," she said. "I followed the assignment."

"You see yourself as a blank piece of paper?" Ellie tried to keep her voice objective. "Rae, can I talk to you out in the hall, just for a sec, and could you bring your notebook?"

Rae groaned audibly for the class to hear and rolled her eyes. "Do I have to?"

"Yes," Ellie said cheerfully as she walked toward the door and checked the hall to make sure the coast was clear. When they were in the hallway Rae slouched against a locker and held her notebook protectively to her chest.

"Do you really think you followed the assignment?"

From her slouched position, Rae narrowed her eyes and focused on Ellie with laser intensity. The hostile stare was a direct challenge. "Yeah. You said to draw how we see ourselves. I see myself as nothing so that's what I drew."

Ellie held her gaze, allowing the awkward exchange to grow even more uncomfortable. Gina Mattheson's presentation from a year ago suddenly popped into her mind. *When you look at your students, find their vulnerabilities and let them know they're okay that you accept and love them, just as they are.* "Rae," Ellie said sympathetically. "That really concerns me that you see so little in yourself. You know John can't say enough positive things about you. He thinks you're incredible. He says you're adventurous, imaginative, creative, and you make him laugh and have fun every day. I'm so grateful to you. I was so scared for John because he's new and he really needed a friend."

Rae's fierce stare softened. "It's no big deal," she muttered.

"Well, I see you've been sketching something in your notebook. Do you think I could take a look?" Rae hesitated while studying Ellie's face. She passed her notebook with unsteady fingers. Ellie's eyes lingered over the page. "Oh Wow! Rae." She traced her finger over the sketch of a brown bear eating a fish. "This must have taken you a long time. You can almost feel the texture of his fur and the scales on the fish, so detailed."

"Yeah. That took me like five hours," Rae said.

"Well, it's amazing. You have real talent. I think this could work for our assignment today. Your picture can be symbolic after all. It should just represent you in some way. Can you see anything in you that's like this bear? You're pretty strong like a bear. Do you see yourself that way?"

Rae looked upward and blinked. "I think I'm like a bear because I have to do a lot of things for myself. That's the way it's been since my mom died. Bears are alone a lot. They learn how to take care of themselves."

Ellie felt a wave of empathy rise from her gut. She gulped and swallowed her feelings. "I can see that. Please, Rae, you don't need to hide your talent from anyone. This is something to be proud of." She tried to meet Rae's eyes, but failed. "We better go back inside before there's mutiny in the classroom. Thanks Rae, for talking to me."

"It's okay." Rae said. She went back to her seat and buried her head back into her notebook. Ellie could only hope she had made a tiny break in Rae's defensive wall.

* * *

Friday arrived quickly and Ellie hurried to get the boys ready for their night with Davis. He had never been to the house in Veneta before and her nerves were rattled. Since their settlement, Ellie had been dropping the boys off at Davis' apartment. Most of her communication with him had been through Lyle, except for brief texts regarding the welfare of the boys. She and Lyle had both been surprised when Davis had agreed to most of Ellie's terms. He had not given them the fight that Lyle seemed to expect. "I think he just realizes that you could humiliate him before the judge. He must realize that even in his job, he relied on you to do the work." Ellie didn't fully buy Lyle's explanation. Asking for the house and monthly support were justified, she thought, but half his estate? She didn't really believe she had a claim on Madeline's money, but she had demanded it anyway. It served him right. Davis, however, had agreed to the terms. She assumed he was relieved that she wanted full custody of the kids. Davis could never handle the job of full-time parenting. *It's a quid pro quo. He doesn't want to raise the boys. This settlement is a way to pay me to do it,* Ellie thought. She had come to terms with the realization that she did not respect Davis as a man or father. For years she refused to acknowledge her true feelings.

Ellie heard tires on the gravel driveway. Glancing at her watch she realized he was about thirty minutes late. When they were still married, Ellie nudged and reminded him constantly to get to church on time and to make meetings. She felt physically drained as the memories overwhelmed her of all the times that on top of managing her own life and the boys' schedules, she had pushed Davis out the door to make the various meetings required for his job. He was like a third child. Without that push, he seemed to have settled into a pattern of perpetual tardiness. He pulled up in his white Subaru hatchback. She signaled to him from the kitchen window. "Boys! Your dad is here." She walked to the front porch and down the steps to the driveway. "Hi Davis. Did you find it okay?"

Davis ambled out of the car. He looked pale and exhausted. He needed a haircut and his shirt had small red splotches stained around the collar.

"Yeah, I got a little confused off of Territorial Highway, but I found it." He looked around vaguely. "It's nice. The kind of place you think kids should grow up."

Ellie ignored the comment. "I think the boys had a good week at school. John has a new friend, Rae, he can tell you about and Miles has several friends already. He seems to like his teacher."

Davis nodded his head. "Good, that's good. When are you picking them up?"

"I thought I'd drive by your place around 1:00 tomorrow afternoon? Does that give you enough time?"

"Yeah. I've really missed them. I haven't been able to find a job, you know. Ex-ministers don't have very many practical skills. We're not very employable. Sometimes I feel like I'm just staring at four walls every day."

"Do you want me to feel sorry for you?" Anger flashed in her voice. "I'm sure you can and have found ways to occupy yourself."

"Ellie, no." Davis' voice was strained and weary. "I'm just saying I'm glad to be with the boys."

Ellie took a deep breath and tried to dial back her tone. "Well, they're excited and they've missed you."

The boys came out the front door together and ran down the stairs. "Dad, Dad!" Miles yelled. Davis put his arms out and hugged Miles.

"I've missed you, Miles" He reached out his other arm and gave John a side hug. "You too, kid." They threw their bags into the trunk.

"Double check that you packed underwear, John. Please be safe, Davis. They're my everything."

Davis sat in the driver's seat with the car door open. "Ellie, you're not the only one who loves them. I love them too. I'm not going to let anything happen to them." He closed the car door and Ellie watched as they disappeared down the driveway.

* * *

Her little family had found its groove. The heat of the summer was fading, and she could feel the chill in the air, especially in the mornings and evenings. She reveled in wearing cardigans and replacing her sandals with boots. Fog would settle in the valley in the morning, but sometimes the sun would peek through a gap in the clouds and the whole world would glimmer as the sun visibly melted the mist away. Ellie was still driving both boys to school and John was packing his own lunch. She no longer had to remind them to grab their backpacks.

At school, when she met her students in the hallways, she could greet them by name and they would say, "Hi Ms. Gold." The rhythm of the school year was falling into place. Each face of her nearly eighty students told a different story, and she was learning to read their pain, their joy. She felt alive as the routine of each day settled under her skin. Last fall, Ellie's only goal had been to survive through the biggest crisis of her life. She had traveled through the school year like a drugged sleepwalker. An entire school year was lost to grief and she was determined to recapture what she had lost. Her favorite season of the year was fall and she vowed to appreciate each of its subtle changes. She planned to sip a pumpkin spice latte and actually taste it.

Melissa entered her classroom about thirty minutes before first period. "Ellie, I need your help. You have got to save me!"

Ellie laughed. "You are so dramatic Melissa."

"No, really. I'm in huge trouble."

"Okay. What is it?"

"The fall auction, the fall auction, Ellie! You know it's organized by the Veneta Historical Society, right?"

"Uh, I guess so," Ellie said, only half interested.

"Ellie, they're raising funds this year for the Science Department. My department! You know I've been complaining for months that all our lab equipment is busted to hell. The money is going to replace all my equipment. Can you imagine? Walking my students through a lab with functioning equipment?"

Ellie laughed. "Some things are much too good to be true. I don't think we should dare to dream so big."

"The point is, I need this to go off without a hitch and we've hit a hitch."

"What's the hitch?" Ellie asked suspiciously.

"Well, the society is run by a parent and they do the same thing every year, which I guess is just a big sensation and makes us tons of money. There's a write up in the paper and everything."

"What is it?"

"Local painters across the community paint each of the historical structures in town, you know, like the town hall, the covered bridge, and the library. They auction them off at the Thanksgiving fundraiser dinner and it's a huge tradition, important to the community, yada yada yada!"

"Okay? So, what's the favor?"

"We had a painter who was going to paint the historical church here in town and they've backed out for medical reasons. None of the other painters want to take it on with just a few weeks till the dinner. It also causes problems if we give any painter more than one job."

"And..."

"Well, I just thought... I have this friend and she's awesome, an amazing painter, and she always steps up to help a friend..."

"Melissa, I don't really do pastoral painting. I mostly paint portraits, faces." Ellie pointed to her own face like she was explaining herself to a non-English speaker.

"Ellie, I've seen your work. You can paint freakin' anything! You are my superstar. Please, please, please!"

"Well, since you put it that way. Yes. I'll do it," Ellie said with a sigh. "But you owe me, big. I'm talking like pumpkin spice lattes for the rest of the year kind of owe me."

Melissa blew her a kiss. "I love you. We need the painting in about six weeks." She breezed out of the room. Ellie shook her head and smiled.

* * *

As she introduced the new art project to her students, Ellie experienced one of her greatest joys as a teacher. Starting a class was always her favorite part of any lesson. She loved the expectant look on the faces of her students, the repeated cries of *What are we going to do today?* For that moment, the whole world hung in the balance as students anticipated what kind of art, they would get to create for fifty minutes in a middle school art room. Ellie could see that most of her students were excited about learning, even Rae who was very skilled at hiding her enthusiasm.

"We're bringing a cherished object from home tomorrow to class. Something that is special to you, represents you in some way. We're going to use watercolors to paint this object and you're going to bring it to life through your artist's eye." She could hear the bustle of excitement as students whispered what item they planned to bring. "It should be a small item. Something safe, obviously, and it should follow school rules. Okay. You've got the assignment. Meet in your planning groups and brainstorm." *Once you allow a child room to create, anything can happen,* Ellie thought.

Chapter 9

Blueprint

Number one in your life's blueprint
should be
a deep belief in your own dignity,
your own worth,
and your own somebodiness.
Don't allow anybody to make you feel
that you are nobody.
Always feel that you count.
Always feel that you have worth,
and always feel that
your life has ultimate significance.
—Martin Luther King Jr.

The next day dawned unusually bright and clear. Ellie sensed a change in the weather pattern. The warm summer days were soon to be gone for good. As students entered the room with their cherished objects, the classroom buzzed with energy. Moments before the starting bell rang, Quinn, an attentive and cerebral 6th grader came to her desk, blood gushing through the cracks in his fingers as he held his nose. "Uh, Ms. Gold?"

"Oh no. Hang on Quinn." She grabbed the tissue box and handed him about fifteen tissues. "Put pressure on the sides of your nose and put your head down into the tissue. Squeeze. That's good." Quinn obeyed, but Ellie saw that he had trailed blood across the room. "Class!" she yelled. "Please go to your desks and stay put! We've got a dangerous spill and I don't want anyone to get hurt." She grabbed her desk phone and called the office. "I've got a bleeder. I need a walk escort for a student to the nurse and a custodian for a blood spill."

Ellie put on latex gloves and gently guided Quinn to the hall. "How's the bleeding?"

"Better," Quinn said, his voice muffled through the Kleenex.

Ellie tried to wipe up the worst of the blood spills with paper towels as she waited for the custodian. The walk escort arrived and then the custodian shortly after. "Jim, I gotta wash my hands and dispose of these gloves. Can you take care of the dirty paper towels and keep a quick eye on them while I get cleaned up?"

"Sure Ellie, I got you covered."

"You're awesome. Thanks."

She walked down the hall to the custodian's closet and disposed of her gloves in a plastic bag which she tied and put in the trash and then scrubbed her hands in the utility sink. As she headed back to her classroom, she heard a commotion. When she returned, Jim was nowhere to be seen. He must have been called out on another emergency, Ellie thought. In the corner of the room Natalie was sobbing. "Give him back. Give him back!"

The other kids had formed a circle and Ellie could not see through their moving bodies. Through the corner of her eye, she could just make out Mason's jersey in the middle of the circle. He was holding a small bird by its leg and dangling it in front of the crowd. "I could kill it, you know. If I wanted to. Wouldn't you guys like some Chick-fil-A?" Cruel laughter filled the room.

Ellie surveyed the scene trying to process what she was seeing. Rae's face said it all. Her arms were shaking with rage, her skin beat red, and her posture so tense, Ellie could tell she was ready to fling herself at Mason at any moment.

"What are you guys doing?" Ellie said in her authoritative teacher voice. The students scattered to their seats and looked at her with wide eyed innocence. Gabe and Tyler were laughing so hard they could hardly contain themselves as they squirmed in their seats. She ignored them and trained her eyes on Mason. He began to shift uncomfortably under her gaze.

"Ms. Gold. Someone brought an animal to class," he said.

"Show me what you have." Mason pulled out the small and yellow ball of fluff from underneath his jersey, a baby chick.

Ellie moved quickly toward him and held out her hand. "Let me have it." He placed the bird roughly in her palm and she glared at him. "Have a seat."

"Ms. Gold, I was just trying to help you. Natalie broke the rules. You're not allowed to bring animals to school."

Ellie examined the chick gently. The feathers were ruffled, and the bird looked frazzled and traumatized. She stroked the feathers gently to put them back in place. "Mason, out in the hall now!"

"Ooooh" the kids hollered.

"Shh! Take your objects out and start sketching," Ellie barked. Mason stomped out of the room. She turned to Natalie who was now stifling her sobs. "Natalie, please put your bird back in the container you brought him in. We're going to talk in a little bit. She took deep breaths and tried to calm the rage that was brewing inside of her.

Once in the hallway, Mason attempted to speak,"Ms. Gold, I—"

"Mason, if you know what's good for you, you're just going to listen. There are school rules and there are life rules. Do you know the difference?"

"I think so, Ms. Gold." He stared at the floor and refused to look her in the eye.

"There's a school rule that we don't bring animals to school. Does that mean if a friend brought a puppy to school, you should kick the puppy and threaten to kill it?"

"No Ms. Gold, of course not," he coughed.

"Well, that's the logic you just tried to feed me, and you know what? It insults my intelligence as a teacher, and it insults you to give such a stupid excuse for your behavior. What you did in there makes me so angry, I want to go outside and scream. Do you understand me?"

"Yes Ms. Gold."

"Let me tell you what the life rule is. You never hurt an animal for your entertainment! Do you hear me? Not ever! What you held in your hand was a small and defenseless thing, a creature that needs your protection and kindness. You need to do some soul searching right now, Mason. You drop this tough guy act and learn what it means to be a decent person. Because at the end of the day, you have to live with yourself and right now you'd make anyone poor company. You owe Natalie an apology."

"But she broke the rule?"

"How do you know she broke the rule? How do you know she didn't get special permission to bring that chick for her art project?"

"I guess, I don't," Mason said. He stared at his shoelaces. The fight seemed to have left him.

"Mason, sometimes we have to be honest with ourselves. We can be mean and ugly and hurt things because it feels good, maybe because someone hurt us. You're better than that."

"Are you going to write me up?"

"I haven't decided yet, Mason. I'd like to not have to. I'd like to believe that it's enough of a punishment that you know that ugliness is in you and you're going to work on changing it. Do you understand what I'm saying?"

"Yeah, okay. Please don't call my dad Ms. Gold."

"You can go back to your seat and get to work on your letter of apology to Natalie." Mason at least appeared contrite as he walked back to his desk. "Natalie, please come out in the hall and bring the chick with you."

Natalie plodded forward with tears streaming down her face. "I'm sorry, Ms. Gold. I didn't mean to break the rule. I was so excited about the new chicks and I just wanted to paint one here at school. I couldn't think of anything else I wanted to paint."

"It's okay, Natalie. I told Mason I gave you permission to bring it."

"You did? But you didn't actually give me permission."

"I know, but if you asked me yesterday, I probably would have said yes."

"You would have?"

"Yes, but we would have made some very different arrangements. I would have had you bring the chick first thing in the morning and I would have kept it behind my desk to keep it safe. Do you know what the lesson is here?"

"I should have talked to you?" She said quietly.

"Yes. Natalie. I need you to find your voice. We can avoid a lot of trouble when we learn to speak up for ourselves. Your voice is important, Natalie." Ellie changed her tone. "Now, can I see it again?"

Natalie opened the brown cardboard box and lifted the chick out gently. She placed the bird in her curved palm. Ellie stroked the yellow feathers and held it to her cheek. "It's so soft, Natalie. So delicate. I can see why you wanted to bring him." Ellie handed the chick back to Natalie reluctantly. "Let's go back inside the classroom. I have a plan."

Ellie explained to the class that Natalie had special permission to bring the chick and lectured them all on how to properly treat animals and how to use hand sanitizer when handling them. The chick remained behind her desk in its cardboard crate all day and she invited small groups of two or three students to come up to see the chick or hold him with supervision. At the end of the school day, Natalie came to the classroom. "Thanks for keeping him for me."

Ellie stood up from her desk and handed the cardboard crate back to Natalie. "I have to say. I just love this little chick. He was so sweet," Ellie smiled. Suddenly Natalie rushed toward her and embraced her so hard it took her breath away. "Thank you, Ms. Gold."

"Well, you're welcome, Natalie."

* * *

Ellie took a deep breath and tried to decompress. Finally, the school day was over, and she could take a few moments to relax and not think about micromanaging 6th and 7th graders. The day had been crazy, but Ellie couldn't stop smiling when she thought about Natalie.

Melissa entered the room with her usual conspiratorial grin. "Oh my God, Ellie. This is so weird. She pulled from behind her back two jars of canned fruit. One looked like a jar of peaches and the other a jar of blackberry preserves. The jars were decorated with gingham lace trim. Both containers were adorned with an old-fashioned label and their contents identified with beautifully detailed handwritten calligraphy.

"Wow, those are gorgeous!" Ellie said.

"Yeah, I guess, but you know where I got them?"

Ellie was baffled. "I have no idea."

"Well, I was gone yesterday because I had a doctor's appointment, and I had a substitute teacher fill in for me. When I came back this morning, these jars were on my desk. Check it out."

Ellie took the note from Melissa which was handwritten on high quality peach colored stationary with the same distinctive calligraphy.

Dear Ms. Nielsen,

What a divine pleasure it was indeed to teach your class today. Your students were as lovely as could possibly be—just a dream really. Your classroom was just a delight. I love how you have posters of all the great scientists on your wall. How nice to put a face to their theories. Your students were respectful and full of joy. We had so much fun together learning about God's remarkable world and the mysterious process of negative and positive ions. I am appreciative of the wonderful way you are educating these children and helping them to learn about the world. As a token of my appreciation, I have a gift. I am a canning enthusiast, and these are from my most recent batches from this past summer. I hope you will enjoy them. Anytime you need someone to sub for you, I am happy to help.

God's Blessings,

Ruby L. Jones

"I'm confused, Melissa. This is a nice note, and you got a gift. What's the problem?"

Melissa eyes widened, "Are you kidding me, Ellie? This is weird. It's just really weird!"

"Oh, Melissa. I don't think it's that weird. It sounds like someone's just appreciating you. You just don't know what that looks like," Ellie laughed.

"Normal people don't write handwritten notes like this. They don't give gifts to people they don't even know."

"How was she as a sub?"

"Well, I guess she did the assignment on ions with them that I wanted her to do, but apparently for the last twenty minutes of class, she just told stories."

"Did the kids like her?"

"Most of them seemed to like her a lot."

"I don't think you have a problem then. In fact, if you don't want those jars, I'll take them."

"No, No. I'm going to keep them." Melissa put them protectively in her bag. She then drew up a student chair close to Ellie's desk and whispered, "I heard you had quite the day."

Ellie rolled her eyes. "Who told you?"

"Some of my sixth period kids were telling me about the chick you had in class and about quite a confrontation you had with bad boy Mason."

"Oh, Melissa, I was so mad I practically bit the kid's head off."

"It sounds like he deserved it. Did he really threaten to kill it?"

"I heard him. He said he would turn it into Chick-Fil-A."

"Oh my God! Did you write him up?"

"I haven't yet. I lectured him to death. I was hoping he could reflect on his actions and change."

"Do people really change? I don't know. You let him off easy, not that he'll be grateful for it. I have him in my 3rd period. He's an angry kid. Something's not right there."

* * *

Ellie waved from the porch as she watched the boys drive off with their dad. There was still about an hour left of sunlight. She returned to the empty house and settled on the couch with a fantasy novel. Friday night was her one night to herself. At first, she had dreaded each Friday evening with a passion. The house made strange noises at night and she found it difficult to sleep as a profound loneliness overwhelmed her. But over time, Ellie had adjusted to the new normal. Now she looked forward to a slice of time for herself. She could read a book, call Andrew or Brian, watch a romantic movie, or soak in the hot tub. Just as she was about to open her book, she heard a knock at the door.

Ellie opened the door cautiously to see Natalie standing on her front porch with a woman, Ellie presumed was her mother. Natalie's mother looked about the same age as Ellie. She was tall, sturdy, with long wavy blonde hair and a very attractive smile, "Hello?"

"I'm so sorry to bother you at your home. I'll try not to take too much of your time, but I'm Allison George, Natalie's mother. Sheriff Monroe mentioned he was your neighbor, so I knew where you lived."

Ellie remembered Melissa's warning about crazed parents and felt her heart skip a beat. "Can I help you?"

"I'm here with a gift for you actually. Natalie just loves you and I'm just so grateful. She's hated going to school every year since the third grade and now she can't wait to get on the school bus. I just wanted you to know the impact you're having on her life." Allison's eyes misted over as she spoke.

"Uh, Wow. I don't know what to say. That's really kind."

"You aren't going to believe what we got you!" Natalie gushed.

Ellie turned and smiled at her. "What did you do?" She teased.

"You'll see."

"Maybe, you should come out to the car with us and we'll show you," Allison suggested.

Ellie followed Allison to her large tan Suburban SUV praying that she wasn't going to appear on a Dateline mystery special. Allison pressed a button on her keyring and the trunk door lifted automatically. Inside was a huge white box."

Natalie's eyes brimmed with anticipation. "Aren't you excited, Ms. G?"

"Um, what is it?"

Allison laughed. "It's a chicken coop and a hen house set."

"What?" Ellie was floored. She had received a few gifts in her day, but this was a new one.

"You loved my chick so much and I thought you should have one of your own," Natalie reasoned.

Ellie was overwhelmed. "This is a very expensive gift. I mean, I don't really know much about chickens, but this seems a little extravagant."

"Ms. Gold…"

"You can call me Ellie, Allison."

"Ellie, what you have done for my daughter at school…I can't put it into words. It was just a joy to get this for you."

How could she argue with that? "I don't really know how to set it up."

Allison smiled. "We've thought of that. Levi is an old friend from our school days, and he owes me. He told me he'd set it up for you tomorrow morning if that works for you?"

Ellie felt a little pressure in her chest at the mention of Levi's name as the memory of their embarrassing encounter replayed in her head. "Well, it sounds like you have it all figured out."

"We'll bring the chicks down sometime tomorrow afternoon," Allison continued.

"The chicks?"

Natalie laughed. "Yes Ms. G. The hen house is for the chickens."

"Oh Natalie! Ellie knows that. I just got my chickens last year. I live in town, but we set up the hen house and coop right in the backyard and it's been so much fun. They're laying eggs now and that's saved me a bit on my groceries."

"How do I feed them?"

"Natalie can explain everything to you."

"Ms. Gold, I'll come and help you anytime."

Ellie was touched. "I'm just amazed. This might be the sweetest thing anyone's ever done for me."

Allison smiled. "We think the world of you."

The sun had almost completely disappeared behind the horizon as Ellie watched them drive away. She could not identify the powerful feeling that overwhelmed her, a mixture of incredible joy and pain.

* * *

As Saturday dawned, Ellie was determined to get the most out of her morning before she had to pick up the boys in the afternoon. The day was beautiful, and the sun was out. It was a rare blessing for a Saturday morning and Ellie needed to take advantage of the weather. Around 8:30 a.m. she began loading her Ford Explorer with her art supplies. She needed to get that stupid painting started if she was ever going to finish the piece in time for the auction. As she carried her easel, she noticed Levi crossing the property line with the calm easy stride that she had come to recognize since that fateful day by the river. He stopped by her car and nodded.

"Good morning, Ellie. I'm guessing Allison told you why I'm here."

"Uh, yeah. Sorry. I'm just on my way out the door, but the box is lying on the side of the house. Are you sure this is okay?"

Levi shrugged. "I don't mind. How are those boys of yours?"

"They're good. They're at their dad's now."

"Oh," Levi said. "Rae will be sad to hear that. I think she had plans to spend time with John today. Those kids spend a lot of time together."

"Yeah, they do. John can't say enough good things about Rae."

Levi grinned. "She doesn't say it, but I think she's pretty fond of that boy of yours herself."

Ellie smiled. "That sounds like Rae."

Levi locked eyes with her. She saw kindness in them. "You know. This is the happiest I've seen her in a long, long time. I can't help but wonder if your family has something to do with it."

"Oh, I don't know," Ellie teased. "It's probably just a coincidence."

Levi's tone became more serious. "I don't believe in coincidences."

Ellie smiled uncomfortably. "I guess, thank you? I wasn't expecting the hen house."

"Oh, I know. That's an Allison idea all the way."

"It sounds like you know her well."

"Yeah, she's married to my best friend from high school, so I guess you could say that. The four of us used to spend a lot of time together when my wife was still living."

"Oh," Ellie felt uncomfortable. "I guess in a small town that's not so unusual. I'm sorry about your wife."

Levi looked away. "Anyway, you go ahead and do what you were going to do. Have a good day." He nodded his goodbye.

"Okay. You too."

Ellie put the rest of the supplies in the car and watched Levi from the corner of her eye. She had never known a man so comfortable with tools and easy in his body, but she also sensed the pain brimming under the surface, a pain she shared.

Chapter 10

Foundation

People are like stained-glass windows.
They sparkle and shine when the sun is out,
but when the darkness sets in,
their true beauty is revealed
only if there is a light from within.
Elisabeth Kubler-Ross

She approached the church cautiously. The morning light filtered through the tall Douglas firs and pines. The church was painted white and boasted a tall steeple with a silver bell. The front entrance was adorned with a covered outside foyer where parishioners could sit on plain white benches as they gathered for Sunday services. On both sides of the church, spearhead shaped stained glass windows absorbed the sun's light and cast a colorful reflection on the pavement. According to the information that Lisa from the Veneta Historical Foundation had provided, the church was built around 1874. When she arrived, there were a few cars in the parking lot, and she could hear piano and voices as she set up her equipment. She hummed along to the melody of "What a Friend We Have in Jesus".

Ellie set to work. Tracing the structure was easy enough, but as she began to paint, boredom and lackluster followed. *Another building with a blue sky in the background. How generic. How uninspired.* As she gazed intently at the church in an effort to recreate the structure in all its historical grandeur, she was suddenly struck with a deep melancholy. For a moment she thought about Sally and Gary Pearson and all the people who had been so important in her life just over a year ago. How much had changed? She hoped Sally was okay now. Like herself, she was missing her mate, alone in the world.

In her old life, she had a church, a community, she went to Bible studies and led the youth group. Her marriage, she realized now, had not fulfilled her, but the community, the church had filled some of that empty space in her heart. But there had also been a dark side, the weight of the responsibility of ministry. Ellie had always felt the burden of leading, organizing, and pushing to keep programs alive in a dying church. She had advocated for ministries, made announcements, showed up for service projects and tried to lead through setting an example of active enthusiasm. She had done all of this while working full time as a teacher. Jesus' words from Luke 10:2 crossed her mind. *The harvest is plentiful, but the laborers are few.* Ellie always felt like she was carrying a heavy weight as a pastor's wife. She was burned out. *Why did God allow her to grow so weary and overburdened? She had been so invested, worked so hard.* And the deeper wound. *Why did he allow Davis to hurt her? To make her feel like she was worth so little?* She used to feel joy in her faith. Davis' betrayal colored her entire world and now she felt distant from God.

She stared at the canvas and knew the inspiration would not come. *God, if you want me back at church, living that life of faith, show me. I'm giving you a test, even though I know I'm not supposed to test God. I'm doing it anyway. You owe me one. If this terrible painting sells at the auction for a price that won't be a disappointment to Melissa and a disgrace to myself, I will go to this church and I will wait on your will. That's a promise.* It was a prayer, not a worshipful prayer or a respectful one, but a prayer, nevertheless. *I'm letting him know where I stand,* she thought. She computed the calculations in her head. The canvas, the supplies…She settled on a figure of about five hundred dollars. It was an exaggerated sum, but the number felt right in her mind. Melissa

116

told her five hundred dollars was a standard bid for lower end paintings at the charitable event. Ellie's painting was also mediocre at best. If someone bid five hundred or more dollars, it would be a miracle.

Her thoughts were interrupted by the deep chime of the church bell. She didn't realize that the bell still worked and rang at noon every day. People began to trickle out of the church into the parking lot. A small woman with dark hair was strolling toward her. Ellie was not in the mood to talk to anyone and tried to avoid eye contact by feigning deep concentration.

"Hi, are you painting the church?"

She glanced up at the stranger. The woman was stunning. Her build was slight, and she had smooth straight silky black hair with choppy bangs. She had dark almond shaped eyes and was dressed in a pristine white suit. "Uh, yeah. It's for the auction."

"Do you mind if I take a look?"

"Uh, I don't feel super proud of it, but I guess you can." She felt self-conscious as the woman moved behind her to scrutinize the painting.

"You've done a nice job with the dimensions."

"Thanks," Ellie said. "You seem to know something about art."

"I know a little. I'm a real estate agent, so I use some art to stage homes. I have some pieces in my own house that I love. Anyway, my name is Jewel, Jewel Peterson." She fished through her compact teal handbag and found a business card and handed it to Ellie.

Ellie took it. "Thank you." She glanced at the card and was impressed to see that half of it appeared to be written in an Asian script.

"Is this Korean?"

"Yes, it is." She sounded surprised. "I cater to Korean clients in Eugene, but I live here in Veneta. I'm half Korean myself. Do you speak Korean?"

"Oh no, not at all, but I know some middle school students that are quite in love with K-pop celebrities, so I've seen the writing before. Oh, sorry. I guess I should introduce myself too." She placed her paintbrush down and wiped her hands on her smock before extending her arm. "I'm Ellie Gold. I teach at the middle school and I'm also an artist when I have time."

"It's nice to meet you," Jewel said.

Ellie nodded. She glanced at the card again. "Well, if I need a real estate agent, I know who to call." She slid it into her pocket and smiled.

Jewel gave her painting another hard look. "What do you think of your painting?"

Ellie hesitated. "Well, honestly…, I hate it."

Jewel smiled. "I like your honesty."

"I usually go into a project with some inspiration, vision, or something, but I'm struggling with this one. It's out of my wheelhouse. I usually paint portraits, and this is as pastoral as you get."

"Hmmm," Jewel thought aloud. "I go to this church you know. I sing in the choir. We just finished Saturday choir rehearsal. There's so much history in a church. There are always stories."

"I suppose so," Ellie said.

"Do you see the stained-glass windows? Well of course you do, they're in your painting, but what I mean is, there's an interesting story behind them."

"Really?" Ellie wasn't sure she really wanted to hear the story, but she feigned polite interest.

"The church was built back in the 1870's, I think, and there was a fire around the depression era. They lost most of the original windows and the parishioners couldn't afford to buy new ones, so the ladies in the church went from house to house and collected colored glass. Some of the men in the church worked at the paper mill, which isn't here anymore, but they used that facility to melt the glass into different shapes and put them back together like puzzle pieces into the patterns that are there now. Some of the men knew how to solder the glass pieces together and taught the women. The project took several years, but they made these one-of-a-kind windows."

Ellie laughed, "I love that. It's like a community art project."

"Yeah" agreed Jewel. "That's exactly what it was. I just love those windows. I think they might be the whole reason I go to this church. If I get a little bored or distracted during the preaching, I find myself looking at the glass."

"I'd probably do the same thing," admitted Ellie as she thought of Davis. "Sermons aren't my thing."

Jewel nodded in agreement. "You know what I think when I look at them?"

"I have no idea."

"I think about all the people that worshipped in that building for over a century, the men, women, children who each had their own faith story. I feel overwhelmed by that thought. I think the history of a place matters, you know, because it's not history, it's people and their lives."

Ellie paused and thought about Jewel's observation. "I really like that. I think you might have given me an idea for this piece."

"Really? Do tell."

"Not yet, but if you're at the art auction, you might just get to see it."

"Well then, I'll make sure I'm there. I enjoyed talking with you Ellie. Unfortunately, I've got a one o'clock. Bye now."

Jewel strolled toward the street and got into a white Volvo. Ellie wondered if meeting her had been a dream.

She packed the Explorer and put her art supplies away. Before leaving she approached the church and scrutinized the windows. From far away, they looked professionally crafted, but close-up Ellie could see the uneven soldering and lumpy glass. Some of the windows consisted of simple mosaics like a dove with an olive branch and a wine glass with a loaf of bread. Others were complex, recreating scenes from Jesus' ministry including one mosaic depicting the baptism of Jesus. In the scene, John the Baptist was laying his hands on Jesus, while a white dove descended from the bright sky. Another window showed hands pulling a net filled with fish. It was Ellie's favorite. Each scale on each fish was a different colored piece of glass. The beauty nearly took her breath away when the sun hit the glass. Incredibly, the flaws in execution, somehow made the pieces more dazzling, more special. Ellie had never seen windows like these. She had studied iconography during her seminary days when she first met Davis. Her Master's thesis had been written on the subject and she had visited Catholic and Orthodox churches across the Eastern seaboard to study religious art, but this was exceptional. Jewel was right. Ellie could imagine the hands of the artists who had created these mosaics. They were raw and crude in a way but filled with passion and inspiration. They were forged during the Great Depression and these hands were most likely poor and not well educated and yet they had created art that rivaled the greatest in all the churches in the world. She vowed she would return to at least spend some more time with the windows.

* * *

When Ellie pulled into the driveway with the boys, Allison, Natalie, Rae, and Levi were all conversing in her driveway.

"Great timing. We just got here ourselves to drop off your surprise," Allison called.

"What's the surprise?" Miles asked as he jumped out of the car.

"I'll show you what I've been working on," Levi motioned with his arm for Miles to follow.

"My dad and I have been working all morning," Rae said to John. "You have to see this."

They all followed Levi to a spot of grass next to the barn where now a hen house sat.

"Wow! It's so cool!" Miles called back to them.

"Go ahead and take a look," Levi said. He opened the gate and Miles and John began to explore.

"These windows are awesome. They open and close," Miles yelled.

"It can get hot and cold in a hen house and if you can help create temperature variables for summer and winter, your chickens will be a lot happier," Levi told John. "It's getting cold and they're still babies, so they'll need the heat lamp."

"I did this part," Rae showed John a section of the gate.

Allison raised her eyebrows and a crooked smile played on her lips. "Levi, you've done some extra work. I don't remember the hen house I bought having an attic or skylights. You've also increased the size of the run and enforced it with more wire and a gate!"

Levi shifted uncomfortably and stared at the ground. "It wasn't a big deal. Rae helped me here and it was a fun father daughter project."

120

Natalie linked her arm into Ellie's and guided her through the structure and pointed out the important features. "This is where they'll eat and get water. This is where they'll usually lay their eggs and this is where they'll go when it gets too hot."

Ellie smiled. "I absolutely love it. I love the skylights, the trim on the windows. I mean if I were a chicken this is where I'd want to live."

Levi grinned. "I'm glad you like it."

"Levi, you better come back to my place and juice my hen house up like you did this one." Allison teased.

Levi shook his head. "You know you've got Mike and he's a pretty good craftsman if you get him off his rear end."

Allison laughed. "He has no interest in renovating my hen house. In any case, I don't want to forget the main event. I'll go get the chicks." She returned with a cardboard box with six excited, frantically moving chicks. They weren't as tiny as the one Natalie brought to class. They looked like the chicken version of gangly adolescents. "Okay, two of these are Orpingtons. They're the gold ones. This one here, that's got the red. It's a Rhode Island red."

Natalie passed a squirming ball of feathers to Ellie. "This one is called a Plymouth Rock. I guess it kind of looks like a rock cuz it's black and grey. There's two of those."

"They should all be females, but if you hear crowing, you're in trouble," Allison warned.

Ellie's mouth tightened into a grimace as she observed the sharp beak and beady amber eyes. She held the clucking Plymouth Rock away from her body before handing the creature back to Natalie.

Levi's eyes danced with amusement. "They better be hens. I need my beauty sleep. The hen house is practically on my doorstep."

"That's good. You'll be able to watch out for things," Allison said with the same knowing smile.

After about an hour of visiting with Allison and the children playing with the chickens, Ellie smiled as she waved goodbye to her guests. She realized that she really liked Allison. Maybe she had found a friend. While Allison had coffee with Ellie in the house, Levi stayed in the yard with the kids continuing his finishing touches on the hen house. Although she didn't know him well, Ellie had learned to read Levi's moods. She saw him almost every day at least from a distance. He worked constantly but made an effort to be there for Rae. He didn't smile much. Like her, he seemed intent on staying busy, not allowing himself too much time to think. But today, there was light in his eyes and easy laughter. Maybe Allison brought that out in him? Maybe he just came alive with a good project? Ellie was impressed with his carpentry skills, the way he worked on a project with his daughter and included Natalie and her boys. She also could not deny a feeling of kinship. If Levi could heal from losing his wife, perhaps she could heal from losing a husband.

* * *

The phone interrupted Ellie midstream while giving instructions to her third period class. "I'd like to have you try sketching the subject from a unique perspective. Maybe from a high vantage point or from a low vantage point, inside or... Oh, wait guys, hang on. Let me get that." Ellie dashed from the front of the room to her back corner desk and picked up the phone.

"Ms, Gold?"

"Yeah?"

"It's Twila from the front office. We're sending a sub down to your room to take over your class. Ms. Wallace wants you in the front office."

"Why? What's going on?"

"Your son is okay, but he got into a little trouble over break. Ms. Wallace is going to need to talk to you."

"Uh, alright. I'll be right down." Ellie felt fear churning in the pit of her stomach. "Class, I'm sorry. I have an emergency, a sub will be here any moment, so I can go take care of something."

The classroom was abuzz with voices. "Are you okay, Ms. Gold?"

She fought to calm her nerves. "Everything's okay and I'll be back soon. Don't worry, okay. For now, take out your sketchbooks and choose a subject from the classroom to draw from a unique point of view? Be good to the sub."

At that moment a striking African American woman came in through the door. She was not tall, but slightly heavy. She wore a side banana braid that descended all the way to her waist tied in a bright orange scarf. She wore a jean jacket, black T shirt, and long orange print skirt. "Ms. Ruby!" several of her students exclaimed in delight. Ellie couldn't think clearly but tried to organize instructions for Ruby. Before she could say anything, Ruby embraced her in a warm hug.

"Don't ya worry about anything Ms. Gold. I've got things here handled. Ya look a little frazzled, honey. Are ya okay?"

Ellie was overwhelmed by the deep southern accent and the physical intimacy she was not expecting. "Uh, I just gave them a sketch assignment. I'm not really sure why I've been called to the office, but it can't be good."

Ruby squeezed her arm. "It's alright, honey. Ya know, worry will do ya no good. It's like a rockin' chair. It might keep ya busy, but it ain't goin' nowhere. You're gonna be just fine. Ya just go down there and handle matters like the professional ya are."

"Uh, thanks Ruby. I appreciate it."

"It's no problem. Um Ellie, can I call ya Ellie?" Suddenly Ruby took her hand.

"Yeah, that's fine," she said with hesitation.

"Is it okay if I pray fer ya? I can do it real quick. I find that a few words to the Lord can help."

She was taken aback for a moment. "No, I don't mind."

Ruby closed her eyes and silently spoke her prayer while holding her hand in a firm grip. Ellie froze, wide eyed and then Ruby released her hand. A stranger grabbing her hand should have felt awkward, and it did, but for some reason Ellie also felt a sense of comfort. In a past life, she had prayed for many people in moments of need, but Ellie could not remember a time when someone had prayed for her.

There was no time to reflect on her odd encounter with the substitute teacher. She moved with purpose to the front office. As she opened the door, she almost collided with Levi who was on his way out.

"Whoops, sorry." Ellie cried in surprise.

"Woh! It's alright." His eyes brightened and he reached out an arm to steady her. He felt sturdy, solid. In contrast, Ellie wondered if her legs were strong enough to hold her. The stress over John was taking its toll.

"Levi? What are you doing here?" A terrible thought occurred to her. *Were the police involved with whatever happened with John?*

He seemed to read her mind. "I'm just here to take care of a little parental matter, which is why I assume you're here too." He gestured toward Rae who Ellie noticed now standing behind him with a sulky expression on her face. She was disheveled, dirty, and her jeans were ripped. *There must have been a fight*, Ellie realized by the look of her. Levi suddenly put his arm around her back and pulled her close so he could whisper in her ear. "We'll talk later." He gave her a knowing nod and left the office. Rae followed him, but she looked up at Ellie as she passed, her eyes expressing an emotion she could not read.

Twila nodded for her to take a seat. *Am I in trouble?* She wondered. Ellie waited till Ms. Wallace called her into the office. Her principal was a small woman with salt and pepper hair styled in a severe bob. She had a penchant for pant suits and practical shoes. Ellie felt uncomfortable around her because she had little humor and a deep passion for rules, even some that made little common sense.

"Ellie, John is in the detention room as we speak. He's been suspended for two days for fighting. You know we have a no tolerance policy, and this is the rule for any student that strikes another student."

Ellie took a deep breath. "Ms. Wallace, um Judy, I'm going to need you to tell me what happened. I'm sure you did an investigation and talked to the students involved. John, isn't really an aggressive kid and I'm having a hard time wrapping my head around this?"

Judy sighed as if Ellie's request for details made her tired. "Well, according to the witnesses we interviewed, your son was headed toward the student store when he was approached by three boys. One of those boys pushed your son against a locker, while the others said some unkind things. The incident would most likely have ended with that exchange, except another student got involved."

"Another student?"

"You know I can't share names with a parent regarding other students."

"Judy, you know full well that John will just tell me everything when we get home. I'm a teacher here. It would be helpful if you'd give me complete information. Who were these three boys?"

"Ellie, I can't tell you that and you know it."

"Okay, were they sixth graders, seventh graders?"

Ms. Wallace sighed, "The three boys were seventh graders."

Ellie felt her voice becoming more strident. "So, three seventh grade boys were harassing my sixth-grade son?"

"The situation escalated," Ms. Wallace continued, "when a female student intervened. She was the first to start throwing punches."

Rae, Ellie realized. Rae would not put up with her friend being bullied.

"Your son joined the female student in fighting. He punched one young man in the stomach and pushed two of the other boys, according to witnesses."

"What happened to the three older boys who were bullying my son?"

"They have been suspended as well."

"And the girl?"

"Also suspended."

"So, let me get this straight. A sixth-grade boy who was being bullied by three older students and the brave young lady who protected him by taking on three seventh grade boys have received the same punishment as the three seventh grade boys who targeted and bullied my sixth-grade son. Is that correct?"

Ms. Wallace shifted uncomfortably in her seat. "We don't tolerate violence from anyone. It's our no tolerance policy."

"It's a stupid policy." Ellie stood abruptly. "I'm going to step out and call John's father and then I'll take John home. Is the sub able to cover my classes for the rest of the day?"

"Twila did check with Ms. Jones, the sub, and it does seem she is available for the rest of the day."

Ellie's words were terse. "Thank you for your time, Ms. Wallace."

* * *

"John, I need to know what happened." Ellie was relieved to finally have John alone in the car. Despite the fact that he had been in a fight and was suspended from school, John seemed surprisingly cheerful.

"Mom, I was just going to buy something from the student store when Mason, this 7th grader I hardly know walks right in front of me and won't let me pass. Then some other boys grab me and shove me against a locker. Eric and Gabe, I think. Anyway, Mason's all like, *Is your mom Ms. Gold?* And I'm like *yeah* and then he says, *Your mom's the biggest bitch in the whole school.* Sorry about using that word, Mom."

She was stunned. The whole incident was because of her? Her son had been targeted because of her? "Oh, John. I'm so sorry."

"Oh Mom, it was awesome! Then, Rae comes out of nowhere and just pushes Mason so hard he falls on the ground. She's like, *Back off, you big jerk. Just back off!* Mason gets up and shoves her back and then she just punches him right in the nose. Then his friends all try to beat her up and that's when I shoved Eric and punched him in the gut. Mom, Rae and I totally won the fight. She kicked Gabe in the..., well you know, the place where guys don't like to be kicked. He was on the floor practically crying. Everyone was laughing. That's when Mr. Rudd stopped us and took us all to the office."

"Are you worried these boys will try to get revenge? Are you scared about going back to school?"

"Nah, not really. Rae's got my back and I got hers, plus, everyone knows about it including the teachers and the principal. Are you mad Mom?"

"I think we should go to Subway and get sandwiches. What do you say?"

"I like it."

* * *

126

When they arrived at the house, Ellie suggested John go inside and finish whatever homework he had. Ellie had asked Ruby if she could sub for her the next two days and she had agreed. Davis was busy with some odd job and was unable to take the time off to stay home with his son. Ellie figured she could use the break anyway. She was angry and it might not be a good idea to go to work tomorrow. She might say something to Judy that she'd regret later. Two days off would be good for her, even if it left her with no personal days for the rest of the year.

Ellie stared at the blue house next door and finally mustered the courage to cross the property line and knock. Rae answered the door. She looked surprised and a bit fearful to see Ellie.

"Hi Rae. Is it okay if I talk to you for a few minutes?"

"Uh, I guess so. Is John okay?"

"Yes. He's actually more than okay. Thanks to you." Rae's eyes widened. Ellie continued. "John told me what happened."

"Those boys were saying a lot of bad things about you." Her bottom lip quivered as her voice faltered.

"I know and I'm really sorry you guys were put in that situation. What I'm trying to say is...I don't think you should be in trouble at all. You were really brave. You protected a friend. If you were my daughter, I would be so proud of you." Rae's eyes were shiny with angry tears.

"They shouldn't have said those things about you. You were just trying to keep that chick safe and then they go and try to hurt John. Why are people such jerks?"

"That's a really good question. I wish I knew the answer." Ellie realized that Rae's question would not get resolved with adulthood. There were always jerks, always people intent on hurting others. "Life isn't really fair, but when you have friends that stand up for you... Well, it almost makes everything worth it. Don't you think? Thanks for being that kind of friend to John."

Rae nodded. "Ms. Gold?"

"Yeah Rae?"

"I think you're a good teacher, a really good teacher."

127

"Well, I think you're a good artist, and a really good person."

They smiled at each other. Ellie sensed the breakthrough with Rae she had been hoping for since the first day she had her in class. As Ellie turned to walk back to her house, she saw Levi pull up in his State issued Chevy Tahoe. He rolled down his window and called to her. "Can I talk to you for a sec? I see you got to talk to Rae," he said as he strode toward her.

"Yes. We had a good conversation. You've got a pretty incredible daughter, Levi. She's a loyal friend and she's brave."

"She's like her mother," Levi said. "I'm not too happy with the school's call to suspend her though."

"Me either. It's completely ridiculous. She stops a bullying situation, she protects a friend, and they get the same punishment. I just want to slap the principal!"

Levi chuckled "Really? I'd like to see that."

"Oh, I'm sure you would." Ellie couldn't help but laugh in return.

Levi shifted his tone. "I actually stopped by Mason's place. Not in a police capacity, but just to check in with his dad. I know him a little from grade school days."

"Wow. I didn't realize how connected everyone in this town is."

"Oh, you'd be amazed. It's a small town and most of us know each other in some way or the other. I talked to Clay, he's Mason's dad, about what happened with Rae and John today."

"And..."

"Mason's got it pretty rough, Ellie. His mom died last year in a DUI accident on Hamm Rd. It was not a pretty scene. Clay's been struggling raising Mason and the two younger boys on his own. He's got a bit of an addiction issue. He was taking something for back pain and never really got off the medication. I just wanted you to know about Mason, to see where he's coming from. I don't think Mason will try this again, but I let Clay know we weren't out to get him."

"I didn't know," Ellie said quietly. "I appreciate that you did that Levi, and it will help me when I'm teaching him. I was worried too, about John. I don't want him in danger at school just because he's my son."

Levi nodded. "I'm going to have to take a couple days from work while Rae's suspended. I don't want to leave her alone."

"Sounds familiar. Davis, my ex-husband is busy, so he won't be able to cover me. I'm going to be home for the next two days too. If you need to go get groceries or run an errand, you're welcome to leave Rae with me for a while."

"Oh, yeah. Same here. You can leave John with us, I mean...if you need to go out."

"Thanks," Ellie smiled. "Levi, you really are a good neighbor." She turned to walk back to her house.

"Ellie?"

"Yeah?"

"You know how I told you Rae was happier since your family arrived?"

"I do remember that."

"Well, it's not just John. It's you too. She really likes your class, and she likes you."

Ellie felt a rush of warmth. "Levi, it's mutual. I like her too." Levi met her eyes and Ellie felt an awkward lull. "Well, I've better go, but I'll see you." She turned but heard his voice in her ear.

"Okay. I'll see you around."

Ellie felt his eyes on her as she walked away. The warm sensation lingered long after their exchange.

Chapter 11

Framing

Until one has loved an animal,
a part of one's soul remains unawakened.
—Anatole France

She woke from a dead sleep and bolted upright in bed. The digital clock read 3:32 a.m. Ellie sat up and tried to identify what had disturbed her peace. The noise came again, a discordant squawking sound. *My God,* Ellie thought. *It sounds like some animal is getting strangled.* Dread filled her as she realized the sound came from the hen house. She wondered if a fox or coyote was threatening her chicks or something worse. Throwing on a sweater she hurried toward the front of the house and switched on the porch lights. She stared out the front window and scanned the yard for fleeing critters. Although the rain had returned, the evening was relatively clear, and she could even see stars in the night sky. She went to the hall closet and grabbed her broom, forced her sneakers on and headed into the chilly early morning air. In the daylight, her farmhouse property was idyllic, but at night, the landscape turned into the set of a horror movie. The barn cast strange shadows in the moonlight, bats flew, and owls hooted. She knew cougars and bears lived in the surrounding mountains and these creatures were nocturnal in their habits. Ellie proceeded to the hen house cautiously.

When she reached her chickens, nothing appeared to be disturbed or out of place.

"Everything okay?"

Ellie turned to see Levi heading her direction. Dressed in a T-shirt and jeans, he was hastily putting on a flannel shirt with one arm while he held a flashlight with the other.

"I'm not sure. Everything looks okay, but I woke up because I heard these weird squawking noises," Ellie replied.

"I heard them too." He approached her and shined the beam of his flashlight on the hen house. Ellie squinted as the light hit her eyes. Levi began to chuckle, "Is that your weapon?"

She realized she was grasping the broom with both hands. She rolled her eyes. "I try to be prepared. I thought there might be a raccoon or coyote."

"Most of us around here have a shotgun. Do you have one of those?"

"No. I thought about it, but I've never been trained, and I'd have to buy a safe if I had one."

He nodded. "Well, you shouldn't have a gun if you're not prepared to use it. Well, let's see what's going on here?" He approached the hen house and analyzed it carefully. Ellie breathed a sigh of relief. Levi always projected strength and confidence that put her at ease. Suddenly the squawking started again. Ellie jumped back in terror as Levi also stepped backward toward her. She grabbed his arm. He smiled.

"You're enjoying this aren't you?"

"Just a little." His voice was a deep whisper. Crouching, Levi circled the coop and knelt on one knee to examine the structure. "Well, we've definitely got some creature trying to get in and they're alerting us to the intruder. From the scratches, it looks like a fox, but we've got another problem." He shone the beam of his flashlight directly on the hens. "Take a look."

"I don't see anything."

"You see your Plymouth Rock there. She aint a she. She's a he. You've got the same problem with your Rhode Island Red there. She's a he too!"

"Are you saying two of my chickens are roosters?"

"Yes. That's exactly what I'm saying. They're trying to crow, but they're youngsters, so they sound like little monsters. That's not helping with the noise either."

"I don't want roosters!" Ellie wailed. "Their constant crowing will drive me crazy."

"Agreed. A good night's sleep is imperative for my job and this will not be a workable situation for me either," Levi grunted.

"Does this mean I have to twist their necks and chop off their heads? Because I can't do that. When I bought a farmhouse, I didn't sign up for that!"

Levi grinned, "You could do that, but I think I have a better idea. I'm going to need to make some phone calls. You're going to be around today, right?"

"Yeah."

"I'll be over in the morning."

Relief flooded her. "Thanks Levi. I really mean it."

"It's no problem, Ellie."

* * *

As she pulled into the driveway after dropping Miles off at school, she spotted Rae on her front porch.

"Hey Rae, you here to see John?" she asked as she approached the house.

"Dad wants to know if you and John can go to Carrey Farm with us in about an hour?"

"What's Carrey Farm?"

"It's this huge ranch outside of town. They've got horses and all kinds of animals."

"I think that sounds fun. We don't have other plans." Ellie smiled as she looked at Rae. This was the first time she had come over to play with John and had stopped to talk to her. "So, we have an hour? I was going to make John pancakes. Do you want some?"

"That sounds good," Rae said.

"Come on in then."

Ellie made pancakes, bacon, and eggs. Rae and John relived the highlights of their big fight from the previous day while they sat on stools around the kitchen island eating. Ellie listened to their animated conversation as she bustled around her kitchen. She heard a tap at the back door. She turned to see Levi. "You might as well come in too and have breakfast. It feels like lunch to me since I've been up since three in the morning."

"What you got?"

"The usual breakfast fare-bacon, eggs, pancakes and a pot full of coffee."

"Don't mind if I do." Levi took the stool next to Rae and began to dive into the pancakes.

"You must be hungry."

"I didn't think so until I smelled the bacon."

Ellie laughed. "Bacon will do that to you." She put two more slices on his plate. "So, tell me about Carrey Farm."

"Carrey Farm is run by Steve and Harmony Carrey. They run a ranch, board horses, do some rodeo stuff, and they also raise chickens. They actually need a few roosters. Do you have something to put those roosters in?"

Ellie poured him a cup of coffee as she thought about it, "We used to have a dog and I still have the dog crate. Would that work?"

"That would work just fine. We've found those roosters a new home."

* * *

John and Ellie joined Rae and Levi in the Chevy Tahoe after loading the roosters in the back. Unlike her Ford Explorer, which was only clean one month of the year, Levi's car was meticulous and orderly.

"Your car's spotless."

"It's my work vehicle so it's got to be," he said as he started the ignition and backed out of the driveway.

"It feels nice to be a passenger," Ellie said suddenly without thinking. "I've just been the one in the family driving and driving everywhere. I didn't think about how nice it is to just let someone else drive for a change."

"We don't always realize how much we rely on other people till they're gone," Levi said as he glanced sideways at her.

Ellie turned to check on John and Rae. They were busy looking through Rae's sketchbook while listening to music on their air pods. "Do you mind if I ask what happened with Rae's mom?"

"That's alright." Levi took a breath. "Melinda died three years ago from breast cancer. She was young and didn't have a family history of cancer. We didn't catch it till the disease had already metastasized throughout her lymph nodes and other organs. We tried chemo, surgery, and radiation and it was just too much for her body. She lost seventy pounds in just a few months."

"That's awful. It must have been so hard on Rae and you both?"

"If I'm being honest, Rae didn't really have a mother or father toward the end of it. I was just living on fumes dealing with my own grief and Melinda was so weak. Rae just went into that sketchbook of hers and hardly talked at all. I could see it happening, but I felt helpless to do much about it."

"Well, she's a strong girl. We're a lot stronger than we give ourselves credit for sometimes. It would be awesome if we could protect our kids from life though, but I don't think we get that option."

"Well, that's the truth." Levi pulled the Tahoe onto a gravel road and stopped at the head gate. *Carrey Farm* was branded at the top of the gate next to an icon of a large horseshoe. A metal gate blocked their path and Levi pressed a button on the intercom. A woman's voice piped through the speaker. "Levi? Is that you?"

"Yep Harmony. We're here with the roosters."

The gate automatically opened, and they continued their progress down the gravel driveway. The ranch was massive. Open fields mostly made up of clumps of soil surrounded them on both sides. The pastureland was filled with horses on one side of the road and cows on the other. A large red barn that looked to be about four times larger than the barn on Ellie's property dwarfed a new looking two-story craftsman home. The house was situated about a hundred yards from the massive barn. Behind the red barn was another large silver building that looked like a warehouse. The landscape was dotted with hills and mountains and lush forest.

Levi parked the Tahoe near the barn, and they got out immediately to stretch their legs.

"Can I show John the horses?" Rae asked Levi.

"Go ahead, but use your common sense okay? Make sure you fill John in on how to act around the horses. Don't walk behind them."

"Alright." Rae scampered toward the barn and John followed.

A woman emerged from the house to greet them. She was in her thirties, slim with long light brown curly hair. She wore a black and green flannel shirt with a jean jacket, bootcut jeans, and cowboy boots. She was an attractive woman with a quiet strength. "Hey Levi, you got some roosters for me?"

"I do and thanks for taking them. My hours aren't regular, and I need my sleep when I can get it."

Ellie went to the back of the Tahoe to help Levi with the crate. The crate was awkward for one person to carry, so she took the other side and helped him set the container down on the ground.

"Go ahead and let them out. Let's look at what we have here." Harmony sensed Ellie's hesitation. "Don't worry. They won't get far."

Ellie opened the latch, and the Rhode Island Red poked its beak out of the cage.

"He looks like a good one." The Plymouth Rock was not far behind. "He looks a little scrawny, but we'll fatten him up. He's going to have to bulk up to beat the competition around here. We'll carry them to the coop. You mind grabbing one?"

Ellie bent down and grabbed the Rhode Island Red. The kids had handled her birds so much they rarely gave much of a fight. Levi scooped up the Plymouth Rock and they followed Harmony to a large hen house surrounded by chicken wire.

She opened the chicken gate. "Set 'em down right here."

Levi and Ellie followed Harmony's orders and watched the birds acclimate to their new surroundings.

"They'll do just fine," Harmony assured her.

"I'm Harmony Carrey and you are?"

"Oh, I'm sorry. Ellie Gold. I'm Levi's neighbor and Rae's in my class at school. I'm a middle school art teacher. Anyway, it's nice to meet you." Ellie felt flustered under her gaze.

"Nice to meet you too, Ellie." *Was it her imagination or did this woman just give her a knowing wink?* "Well, Levi you are not going to like this, but Penelope had her litter nearly 10 weeks ago and I'm homing her puppies. I know you have allergies, but these are golden doodles, and they don't shed. I'm thinking it might be time for your Rae to have a puppy."

Levi sighed. "Harmony, you know the hours I keep as a sheriff. They're inconsistent at best and puppies need daily care. I just don't think it's a good idea."

"Well, I don't think it could hurt to at least look at the puppies." Ellie couldn't help herself. She was a sucker for cute fluffy creatures, and she wanted to see the puppies for herself and maybe hold one."

Before Levi could respond, Harmony was yelling across the farm. "Rae! Do you want to see Penelope's puppies?"

In less than a minute Rae and John emerged from the barn and ran toward them. "We're coming!"

"Oh, so you have a son," Harmony said.

"I have two actually. My nine-year-old is in school now. He's in the third grade."

"Oh really? I have two girls. They're both at school too. Isn't that where these two should be now?"

"It's a long story," Levi interrupted.

They followed Harmony to the back side of the house where a small kennel filled with pine shavings was located. Ellie couldn't contain the "Ahhhh" from escaping her mouth when she saw nine curly coated writhing puppies. "They look like little sheep."

Harmony laughed. "They'll need grooming. That hair doesn't shed. They'll just get thicker and thicker and very uncomfortable, but on the plus side you don't have hair shedding all over the house."

"Can we hold them?" John asked.

"I just cleaned out the kennel, so how 'bout we all go inside so I don't have to herd all nine of them out here."

"Yes!" said Rae.

Harmony opened the gate and Rae and John were the first inside. Ellie followed and then Levi reluctantly took the rear. The space was tight with all of them, so Harmony elected to stand outside and watch the puppies interact with new people. Ellie picked up the puppy closest to her feet and held it close to her cheek. "Oh, John. They're so soft. She snuggled the puppy close and he licked her nose.

"That's the big boy. We call him Hulk. Unfortunately, he's spoken for. All my pups have been tested for their compatibility for service dog training. Three of these puppies passed all the tests. Hulk there is the star student. I've already donated him to PAWS for veterans."

"Really? What's involved in the test?"

"A few things. They have to be able to retrieve, recover when they're startled, follow their human, be receptive to being held, and pain tolerance. Hulk there is a big old lump and very mild tempered." Hulk responded to his introduction by snuggling Ellie's neck and licking her cheek.

She laughed and handed Hulk, who was pure white in color to Levi who reluctantly took him from Ellie. She watched as Levi held the puppy and saw his resolve begin to waver. Even Levi could not resist a warm fluffy puppy. He smiled and lifted the pup so he could look him in the eyes. "You're a big guy."

Ellie smiled as she lifted another puppy that was near her feet. This one had a tri-colored coat and licked her cheek. She tried to snuggle with him, but the puppy refused. He wanted to run and play with the others.

"That's Patches. He's a squirmy one."

She set Patches down and took a moment to watch John and Rae as they interacted with the puppies.

John was holding a beautiful white puppy. The ball of fluff was lying in his arms almost like a baby while she licked his nose with a bright pink tongue. John was completely charmed. "This one just came right up to me and crawled into my lap. Mom, she's awesome. Look at her eyes."

"They'll do that," Harmony said. "If you'll let them, they'll choose who they want to go home with. Aurora there has her eye on your son. That's who she wants. I've had dozens of people look at these pups and she's never done that before to any of them. She doesn't want to go anywhere else. She's just happy to stay there with him."

"You think they really can bond that quickly?" Ellie asked.

"I've been doing this for ten years now and I have no doubt about it. Look Levi. Midnight there has his eyes on Rae."

Sure enough, Rae was trying to hold the little black pup. All the puppies were cream or white, except Patches and the all black pup. Unlike Aurora who sat calmly in John's lap, the black curly puppy was playing with Rae, pretending to growl and chew on her fingers.

"He just loves to play," laughed Rae.

Levi rolled his eyes. "Of course, that's the one for Rae. He's obviously the highest maintenance pup in the whole litter."

Harmony laughed. "You might be right, but he's also the one with the most personality and my most expensive pup next to Patches. He's one of my pups that passed the service dog testing."

"Of course, he is. How much?"

"Twelve hundred dollars."

"Twelve hundred dollars? For a puppy? Maybe we should just get a dog at the pound."

Harmony gave him a disapproving look. "That's actually my discounted price because you're a friend."

"Let me think about it," Levi grumbled.

"Dad, I'll take care of him. I really will," Rae begged.

Ellie moved and sat in the pine bedding next to John. "Can I hold her?" John reluctantly passed Aurora to her and she held the pup to her chest. The pup whined at first as she was taken from John, but then relaxed into Ellie's arms. "Hi little girl. How are you?" The puppy was different from the others because it had a heart shaped pink nose. The other puppies had black noses. She also had deep set amber eyes that made her look like an old wise soul. "She's just beautiful, John."

"Mom? Can we get her?"

"Harmony, did Aurora pass the service dog testing?"

"She came really close but failed one test."

"Which one?" Ellie asked.

"Pain tolerance. They pinch their toes to see how they react and Aurora there, did not like that."

"Who could blame her?" She held the pup protectively, closed her eyes and buried her face in her soft curly coat. She thought about all the pain and suffering her little family had endured over the past year. They had all been trying very hard to move toward the future, but they were broken. They missed their old family, their old church, the way things used to be. Miles woke up in the middle of the night crying when he missed his dad and John...? Like Ellie, he buried his pain because he felt he needed to be strong for her. He was the man of the house now. She couldn't make everything okay, but she could take this puppy home. This beautiful little girl could bring them comfort, and the hope that things would get better.

"Harmony, I'd like to get this puppy. How much does she cost?"

"Where did you find this woman?" Harmony asked Levi. "I love a woman who knows her own mind. Your price is eight hundred dollars."

"I could write you a check or do you need me to get a cashier's check?"

"I trust you," Harmony nodded. "And a regular check would be just fine."

"Dad, if John's going to get a puppy, don't you think I should get one too?"

Levi lifted his eyes heavenward and sighed. "Ellie, you are really not helping me out here."

"I don't want to help you," Ellie teased. "I'm on Rae's side. I for one, think she would do a great job taking care of that puppy. While you're at work, I think you would feel relieved that Rae has a companion." She gestured toward Rae and John. "Can you imagine the fun these two are going to have running around with these pups?"

Rae gave Ellie a bright smile. Harmony grinned, "If you like, we can make a trade on him. "I have some work you could help Steve and I with involving more shelves in the warehouse. We're trying to create a new space for storing more food and you're pretty handy with a saw."

Ellie could tell Levi's resolve was wearing down. She raised her eyes and leveled with him. "Levi, you know what I think? Maybe sometimes it's okay, not to be in control. We have to leave a little room for something good to happen, don't you think? Especially people like us."

Sadness traveled through his eyes for a brief moment. He nodded toward Rae. "I guess you're getting a puppy."

Rae and John were so excited, they could hardly contain themselves. John squeezed his puppy and Rae whooped and did a dance. Ellie laughed and Levi shrugged in defeat. After handing her check to Harmony, they got in the Tahoe to leave.

Harmony approached Ellie on the passenger side. "I find when you open your heart to a dog, you discover that your whole heart gets a little bigger. You have room for more love, and you have more love to give. It's one of life's strange things."

Ellie returned her smile. "For some reason this puppy seems like just what we need right now."

"I think it's just what Rae and Levi need too. Nice work convincing him," Harmony gave her a thumbs up.

Both Rae and John were holding their puppies in the backseat, their faces beaming with joy. "This is the best suspension ever!" Rae whooped.

Levi and Ellie both chuckled before Levi grew serious.

"Don't let those puppies pee in my car," Levi's voice was stern, but she could tell now that he was teasing.

"I guess we're not doing a good job with our parenting. Isn't suspension from school supposed to be a punishment?"

"It never made any sense to me. Getting to stay home from school was never a punishment in my book, but hey, life doesn't always make sense does it?"

"It sure doesn't. Roll with it, Levi. That's what I'm trying to do." They drove for a while without talking wrapped in their own thoughts and then Ellie thought aloud, "I don't have any of the things this puppy needs. I don't have a collar, a leash. We'll need a smaller crate to put by John or Mile's bed, chew toys, food?"

Levi smirked. "You're not really a planner are you? I was actually headed to the farm supply store downtown. I'm going to need a few things for our puppy too."

"Oh good. I guess we'll tag along with you, if that's okay? It's been fun."

Levi chuckled. "I think you're a little dangerous for me."

"Me?"

"The one and only."

Ellie sat back into her seat and smiled. "John? Rae? Have you thought about names for your puppies?"

"I thought we could call her Creamy or Snow White," John suggested.

Ellie nodded. "Those are good names. What about you Rae?"

"I think he looks like a Pax."

"Pax?" Ellie asked. "That's a unique name."

"I like that Rae," Levi said. "I think it's Latin actually. It means peace."

"That's right," Ellie said. "I remember studying about the Pax Romana in seminary.

"You went to seminary?" Levi asked.

"Uh, yeah. I did." Ellie suddenly felt tense. For some reason, she didn't want to share that part of her old life with Levi.

"Were you training to be a pastor?" he asked.

"Yes, and I was married to one," Ellie said hesitantly.

"I didn't know that. I'd like to hear more about you."

Ellie didn't respond. She didn't know what to say. "It's a part of a life that I've put behind me."

"Oh, I'm sorry, Ellie. I really didn't mean to pry." Levi could sense his trespass into uncomfortable terrain. He changed the subject. "The kids should probably stay in the car with the air on while we go in and get what we need. Does that sound okay Rae? You'll be in charge. The doors will need to be locked."

"You got it, Dad. I know the drill."

They pulled into the supply store and Levi surprised Ellie by jumping out of the car. He moved swiftly to her side and opened the door for her. "Well, thank you." Ellie said.

"No problem."

They walked together to the dog aisle that had every color of collar or leash known to man. Levi looked stumped. "Too many choices."

"Let me help you." She looked through the display of collars and leashes. "Red. You want red with that gorgeous black fur." She handed Levi a red collar and a red leash.

He held the leash in his strong calloused hands. "Red's okay. I think Rae will like it. What are you thinking? For Creamy?"

Ellie laughed. "You know that's not going to be her name, don't you?"

Levi raised an eyebrow. "Aren't you going to let the boys name her?"

"Are you kidding me? That's not really their area of expertise. Pax is a great name, but Creamy?"

"Okay then. What's her name?"

Ellie hesitated and then smiled thoughtfully. "When I look at her, I see the name Cordelia."

"Cordelia? Really? I'm thinking I like Creamy better?"

Ellie pretended to punch him in the shoulder. "If you must know, Cordelia is a character from Shakespeare."

"Oh, I do know," Levi said with a grin. "King Lear in fact."

"Wow. I'm impressed. You read Shakespeare?"

Levi's face was dry and expressionless. "Yes. I am literate. English was actually my favorite class back in high school. I also took a Shakespeare class in college. Cordelia was the youngest daughter of King Lear, the good daughter, right?"

"I didn't mean to imply you weren't well read. I just don't meet many people who know Shakespeare. In answer to your question, yes, she was the one that helped her father, the king, even when he rejected her. She took him in when he was completely destitute and practically out of his mind. The other two daughters, Regan and Goneril turned their backs on him. Now Cordelia, she knew how to love with her full heart. I admire that."

"I guess Cordelia is okay. More than okay. So, what color for Cordelia?"

"I've been the only girl in my house forever. Now there's another girl. I'm going pink all the way."

"Alright. Get your pink on," Levi teased.

"You really are the father of a teenager," Ellie laughed.

Chapter 12

Plumbing

I have great respect for the past.
If you don't know where you've come from,
you don't know where you're going.
—Maya Angelou

Ellie returned to school on Friday the last day before Thanksgiving break after a two-day hiatus. When she entered her classroom, she gasped in surprise. Lying on her desk were four mason jars filled with various canned fruit and vegetables with gingham bows and pristine white labels. She recognized the distinctive calligraphy on both the labels and the peach stationery on her desk. Ellie couldn't help but smile. Ruby had a signature style.

Dear Ms. Ellie,

I hope you don't mind me calling you Ellie. When I pray for a person, I feel like we're on a first name basis. I hope you feel the same. Last time we met, you were anxious, and we prayed together. Since then, I have felt assured from my own conversations with the Holy Spirit that your need was met. I want you to know your students were a joy even in your absence. Even a blind pig could see

the excitement and passion these young people are bringing to their work in your
class. I was truly privileged for the opportunity to substitute for you and I would
love to help you any time you have a need. I know most children like sweet things,
so I chose these jars especially for you and your two boys. I personally love the
peach preserves. I am happy to help you anytime, you just need to call.

God's Blessings,
Ruby L. Jones
541-376-9054

Ellie traced her fingers over the peach paper and admired the effort Ruby put into making the ordinary beautiful. She could recognize a fellow artisan from a mile away. Everything Ruby created took time and consideration. The effect made Ellie feel special and she carried that feeling through the rest of the school day.

* * *

Thanksgiving was fast approaching, and Ellie indulged herself on the Saturday before Turkey Day by sipping her coffee and enjoying the sound of rain pattering on the windows. She had two things on her mind. The first was the upcoming holiday auction. The painting took much longer than she anticipated, but now was almost ready. After the surprise encounter with Jewel, she had found inspiration for the piece and discovered that her joy and passion had returned for painting. Finding the time between teaching, parenting, and now taking care of a puppy had not been easy, but Ellie was beginning to feel like something lost was now found. When she thought about the painting, she experienced a nervous rippling in the pit of her stomach. Her artistic vision was not conventional. How would the people of Veneta respond at the unveiling?

Also pressing on her mind was Thanksgiving itself. Ellie had not spoken to her sister Nora in nearly a year. She called her parents weekly and spoke to Andrew and Brian on the phone, but she had kept physically distant from them. They knew too much. They cared about her. She didn't doubt their love, but she felt tragic and pathetic in their eyes. Her identity in the family would always be seen in light of the affair, Davis' betrayal. Ellie lived under a cloud of shame in their presence, one she wanted to escape.

Out of the blue, Andrew called the day before and suggested a visit. Ellie could never refuse Andrew. She was expecting him any minute but felt trepidation about what he wanted to talk to her about. Cordelia whined and alerted her to the sound of his arrival as tires hit the gravel in her driveway. "Good girl," Ellie said as she scratched her behind the ear. She smiled as she remembered Mile's delighted expression when he came home from school and found Cordelia. Fortunately, the boys had agreed on the name Ellie suggested without much fuss, but there was fighting over who would get to sleep with the dog. She finally caved and bought two dog crates, one to put in Mile's room and one for John so Cordelia could alternate between both bedrooms more easily. For the past week she rose at the crack of dawn to take the dog outside to relieve itself. Ellie claimed the quiet hours of the morning as her time to bond with the pup. Cordelia was, after all, the family's emotional support animal and like the boys she needed her own dose of puppy therapy. While her sons slept, Cordelia sat at her feet as she drank coffee. She would feed her, talk to her, and wind her fingers through her curly coat. Harmony said the pup might whine terribly at night as she adjusted to an unfamiliar setting, but Cordelia hardly made a whimper. She had a mild and even temperament and she loved the boys.

Levi and Rae likewise fell in love with Pax. In collaboration with Ellie and her boys, Levi put up a kennel not far from the hen house at the corner where their properties met. Before leaving for school, Rae and John put Pax and Cordelia together, so the pups were never alone even if the rest of the family were at school or Levi was working. According to Rae, Pax was also adjusting with flying colors, with one exception: he loved shoes. Any shoe left unattended would become his personal chew toy and Levi's good work boots had fallen prey to Pax's sharp puppy teeth. Ellie had laughed when Rae told her how angry he was, but when Cordelia chewed the leg of her favorite chair, Ellie got a taste of Levi's woes. The puppies certainly kept them busy. Rae could rarely be seen without Pax following closely at her heels and John and Miles rarely complained of boredom since Cordelia's introduction to the family.

Ellie was alerted to Andrew's arrival on the front porch when Cordelia barked. She was interrupted from her train of thought. "I'm coming." Andrew towered over her like a giant. He stood slightly damp under the covered porch as the rain poured behind him. His familiar form triggered an unexpected wave of emotion. "Andrew!" They hugged each other tight.

"Hey sis. Long time no see."

Her eyes filled with sudden tears. "I didn't realize I missed you so much," she said as she released him and wiped her eyes. Cordelia whined and rose on her hind feet to greet him.

Andrew's eyes creased as he smiled. "Missed you too, sis. Who's this?"

"This is our new puppy, Cordelia."

"Hi cutie." He scratched her head. "Cordelia huh? She's a pretty girl." His eyes scanned the space. "Where are the boys?"

"Miles is in the family room watching cartoons and John is at the neighbor's house with his best friend."

"Looks like I caught you in a good moment." Ellie gestured for him to step inside, which he did.

"Can I take your jacket?" He took his jacket off and she hung it on the coat rack near the door.

"Woh! What's happened to you?"

"What do you mean?" She was confused.

"You look really different. I don't want to sound rude, but you look like you've lost a lot of weight."

She registered his observation with surprise. Ellie's relationship with the scale was complex and since moving to Veneta she no longer even owned one. The priorities in her life no longer allowed her time to obsess over her weight. She was busy with work, the boys, and maintaining her little farm. When she was a pastor's wife, she was always worried about how the women at church would view her. As Davis withheld affection from her, Ellie had wondered if the extra pounds were to blame for his loss of interest and physical affection. But now? Without the scrutiny she experienced, real or imagined, her appearance did not seem as important to her. Her jeans felt loose, but she didn't realize other people would notice the weight loss. Andrew's words gave her a boost of confidence. "Thank you. I've been busy and I haven't had the time or energy to raid the refrigerator," she said lightly. "Do you want to sit down? Would you like coffee or anything?"

"You know I always love coffee." She went to the kitchen and poured two cups while Andrew walked through the house. "I really like the place. This looks like you. It feels right." She returned and set two cups on coasters and rested them on the coffee table.

"I'm glad you like it. I love it here. The boys get to run around and now with the dog, it feels like we're finally a family, which is funny because... you know..."

"I know." Andrew said. "Are you happier?"

"I think so. I'm busier. That's for sure." Ellie motioned for Andrew to sit on the sofa. "So, Andrew, what's up?" She sat down in the armchair across from the couch and sipped cautiously.

Andrew sat down and leaned forward with intensity. "Well, you know Mom and Dad want you to come to Thanksgiving dinner. I'm sure they've called you."

"Yes." Ellie sighed. "I'm thinking about going, but I haven't decided yet. Is that the reason you drove down from Salem to ask if I'm going to Thanksgiving?"

Andrew hesitated and then locked eyes with her. "No, not exactly. There's something I think you should know. It's Nora."

Ellie felt an uncomfortable tingling at the back of her neck. "Yeah?"

"No one from the family has seen her in several months. Mom and Dad didn't want to tell you and upset you."

"What?"

"Yeah Ellie. She's not answering her phone. Lee doesn't seem to have any idea where she is. She's left a few messages for Lee and Mariah so at least they know she's alive, but she won't tell anyone where she is."

"And Mariah?"

"Mom finally got her on the phone. She dropped out of U of O you know?

Apparently, she flunked out. She couldn't wake up and make it to her classes. She's moved back in with Lee in Bend and is taking care of him since Nora left."

Ellie sighed. She felt strangely numb, indifferent. "I guess I should say I'm sorry to hear that Mariah flunked out. You know I helped her with her application, but I think she got what she deserved."

Andrew's eyes darkened. "That doesn't really sound like you Ellie. My guess is her actions have caught up with her. She's a stupid kid. She's got to be swimming in guilt. Rumor has it that she's no longer seeing Davis. Is that true?"

Ellie stared blankly. "Andrew, I have no idea what Davis is doing or who he's seeing. I hope to God he's stopped seeing Mariah for our whole family's sake, but I honestly don't know. I haven't asked him. I talk to him about the children and that's it." Ellie felt her body tighten and she shrugged in an attempt to loosen her stiff shoulders. "As for the two of them. They both knew what they were doing was wrong and they did it anyway. You know that expression about making your own bed. Sometimes you get to lie in it."

Andrew raised his eyebrows. "Ell, I'm not telling you this to make you feel bad or responsible or anything. I wanted you to know because Lee said Nora's been upset since the conversation, she had with you last year. Apparently before she left, Nora had a big emotional spiral and Lee thinks she might try to contact you."

She felt the resentment in her throat. "Why? Does she need money?"

Andrew made a small involuntary gasp. "Ellie, it just sounds like she's in a bad place. I'm not sure, but I thought you should know in case she calls."

"Is she doing drugs?"

Andrew's eyes darkened. "No one seems to know, but we're all assuming she probably is based on her history."

"Andrew, thanks for telling me," Ellie tried to breathe evenly.

"What are you going to do if she calls?"

She hesitated. Cordelia seemed to sense her mood and jumped onto the armchair into her lap. She stroked the pup rhythmically. "Andrew, I really have no idea. The truth is when I think of Nora and Mariah, I just see two vultures, one picking off my money and the other picking off my husband. I know my feelings might not be reasonable, but I can't help it."

Andrew's eyes softened. "I totally get why you feel that way. You did so much to help Nora and Mariah. It wasn't just Davis who betrayed you was it?"

Ellie nodded. "I was there for all of them, you know? When they needed me, I was there? Davis, Nora, Mariah…they're the three people in this world who I invested the most time and energy to help and as soon as they got a chance, they turned on me. I just wonder if there's something wrong with me." Her voice was unsteady with emotion. "I guess I just was taught to believe that we would be rewarded for the good we try to do."

He nodded sympathetically. "What's that old saying—*No good deed goes unpunished.* No, Ellie. There's nothing wrong with you. They're all just deeply wounded people. I'm here for you, Brian is, and Dad and Mom. Do you really think you're alone in this?"

Ellie managed a small smile. "Oh, I don't mean to sound ungrateful. I know I'm blessed to have you and Brian, Mom and Dad. I know I'm blessed, really, I do. I guess I just feel like there's something defective in me."

"There's something defective in all of us, Ell. But you are worthy to be loved. Don't you know that? Don't you believe God loves you? That he's watching over you?"

Andrew's words triggered an attitude of indifference. She felt numb, maybe even angry. "I want to believe that."

Andrew stood up from the couch. "Come here, Ell." He put his arms out. "Someone needs a hug."

Ellie removed Cordelia from her lap and awkwardly rose to her feet. Her body moved mechanically toward Andrew and she allowed him to embrace her. "I'm pitiful. I hate people who feel sorry for themselves and here I am." She rested her head on Andrew's shoulder and breathed.

He patted her head. "It's okay sis. You have every right to be angry. I just wonder if maybe you need to let go of some of the responsibility, the pressure you put on yourself. People have to make their own decisions, even really bad ones." Ellie allowed his words to settle for a few moments.

"Sorry to interrupt," Levi stood at the front screen door, his face brooding and his clothes heavy from the rain. His eyes narrowed as they concentrated on Andrew's tall, lanky frame and followed the strong arms that were wrapped around Ellie. His face was tight, and his eyes burned. Ellie froze under his fixed stare. *He looks jealous,* she realized. Suddenly, Rae, John, and Pax approached from behind Levi, running to get out of the rain. Cordelia began to bark in excitement and Pax echoed her barks. John pushed in front of Levi and opened the screen door wide. Pax shot through the door and both dogs began to bark, wrestle, and prance around the living room causing complete chaos. John and Rae chased the dogs around the furniture and tried to grab their collars. Levi stood frozen in the doorway watching the unfolding pandemonium.

"Uncle Drew, grab him!" Andrew acted quickly. He knelt down and grabbed Pax by the collar just as he tried to shoot past him.

"Settle down, boy." He stroked his fur while restraining him. Rae was soon next to Pax and leashed him.

"Sorry," Rae said to Andrew, without processing his presence. She turned her head back to John who was now trying to leash Cordelia. "Let's take them both to my house."

"Let me say hi to Drew first." John insisted. Andrew stood again to his full height after releasing Pax into Rae's custody.

"This is your uncle?" Levi interrupted.

"Yeah, that's Uncle Drew," John said as he finally grasped Cordelia and was able to restrain her.

Miles, roused by the commotion, emerged from the family room where he had been watching cartoons. "Uncle Drew!"

Andrew kneeled and extended his arms. "My favorite nephews." They ran to him for quick hugs.

"We're going to go to Rae's to play with the puppies. You want to join us later, outside Uncle Drew? If the rain stops?"

"Sounds fun guys. Maybe you can show me the barn and the river."

"Okay," Miles said. The kids breezed through the back door with the dogs and peace returned to the house.

Levi's countenance changed. His face looked relaxed now, friendly, almost relieved. He took several steps forward and reached out his hand to Andrew. "You're Ellie's brother?"

He rose to his full height. "Yes, I'm Andrew. Nice to meet you." Andrew took Levi's outstretched hand.

Levi was a tall man, but he had to tilt his face upward to look Andrew in the eyes. "You're tall."

"6'4" laughed Andrew.

"Uh, I'm sorry. I'm Levi. I'm Ellie's neighbor and the town sheriff."

Andrew was perplexed. "Wow, really? Her neighbor and the sheriff? And it looks like you have a puppy too. Different color, but the same kind. A labradoodle?" Andrew's eyebrows were raised now, amused.

Levi shifted from one foot to the other. "They're golden doodles actually. The young lady you just met is my daughter, Rae. She and John are quite the buddies. The puppies are siblings from the same litter, Ellie and I just got roped into adopting them I'm afraid. You can ask Ellie about how that came to be."

Andrew nodded his head as he scrutinized Levi. "Oh, I see. Is it just you and your daughter or are you married?"

Ellie felt embarrassment burning her cheeks. "Stop the inquisition, Andrew. What are you doing?"

Levi smiled evenly. "No Ellie. That's alright. It's just me and Rae. It's been that way for a while now."

"I see," said Andrew. He gave Levi a knowing smile.

Ellie was mortified and looked to Levi desperate to change the subject. "I'm sorry Levi. What were you here for? With the dogs and everything, I got distracted."

Levi directed his eyes back to her. "I was at the vet yesterday and got flea tablets for Pax. I just thought I'd buy the value pack and share with you and the boys, you know, save money that way."

Ellie exhaled with relief. "Oh, good idea. Do you want me to write you a check?"

"Don't worry about it. I just thought I'd bring the tablets over." He reached into his pocket and pulled out a small packet and handed it to her.

"Thanks Levi. That was considerate."

"Yes, it was," agreed Andrew.

Ellie rolled her eyes. "Well, Levi. I'm sure you have a busy day planned. Thanks for stopping by. Let me see you out." She walked Levi to the back door leaving Andrew in the living room to fend for himself.

"I'm sorry, Levi, about him." Ellie shifted her eyes to indicate Andrew. "I don't know what he's insinuating and I'm sorry if you felt uncomfortable."

Levi smiled, his eyes bright. "It's okay, really Ellie. I don't mind. It's nice to meet your brother, you know, to discover more about you."

Ellie felt a nervous jitter in her chest. "He's ridiculous."

Levi laughed. "No, I like him. He's direct and I can tell he loves you. He's looking out for you. As a Law Enforcement Agent, I work with a lot of families. It's good when family members protect each other, really good."

"Well, thanks for understanding."

Ellie waited for him to leave, but he turned toward her, his eyes intense. "Ellie, I wanted to know if you're going to the auction Tuesday?"

A nervous chill ran through her spine as she felt his eyes on her face. "You know I am, Levi. I've got the unveiling of my painting and I'm hoping someone will buy it for a good cause. Are you going?"

"I already bought my ticket. I wouldn't miss it."

Ellie gave him a thankful smile and tried to lighten the mood. "Well at least there'll be one friendly face."

He grinned. "Okay. I guess I'll see you then." He made full eye contact as he nodded and then turned away. She watched him as he walked back to his house in the rain. Levi was a friend now. She should have thought to invite him herself. *Stupid Ellie,* she thought.

Chapter 13

Electrical

*Life beats down
and crushes the soul
and art reminds you
that you have one."
—Stella Adler*

Ellie rarely had an opportunity to dress up, but the Holiday Auction Dinner hosted by the Historical Society was the premier event in Veneta. The black sequin fabric felt snug, but miraculously she could wear the dress. When she looked in the mirror, she felt happy about her appearance for the first time in a long while. She was slimmer and her hair had grown long and thick. Her hairstylist suggested layers the last time she was in the salon and styled her hair to frame her jawline. The layers flattered her face and made her feel confident. The cocktail dress was last worn twelve years ago when Ellie celebrated her graduation from teacher's college. Knee length with a small slit, the dress managed to be both sexy and modest at the same time. Ellie twisted her hair up and secured it with a clip and reached for her dangly silver earrings. Melissa warned her that all the artists would be introduced to the audience and she wanted to feel as confident as possible when everyone's eyes were on her.

The evening promised some challenges. Davis and Ellie had agreed to share the boys over the holiday break and she half-heartedly consented to let the boys spend Thanksgiving with their father. Davis recently seemed more enthused about his fatherly duties and she viewed this as a positive opportunity for John and Miles. He wanted to pick up the boys the same night as the auction, but he was not able to arrive till after the dinner was already in progress. They had finally compromised and agreed that Davis would pick up the boys during the dinner at the Veneta Grange Hall.

Ellie placed the boys' backpacks in her trunk and made sure they looked presentable as they piled into the Explorer. When they arrived, the parking lot was already bustling with activity even though they were officially thirty minutes early.

Melissa met her at the door and waved at the boys. "Hey guys. Why don't you check out the refreshment table? There are gorgeous looking cupcakes and other goodies. Technically they're supposed to be for dessert, but I've pulled some strings for you two."

"Can we Mom?" Miles asked.

"Yes. That's okay, but remember we're at table seven, so meet me there once you've got your plates okay? And please don't run. Walk." The boys scampered toward the refreshment table.

Ellie's eyes opened wide as she absorbed her surroundings. "There's already a ton of people here."

Melissa motioned to her. "Here, let's move to the corner, so we're not blocking the door." Ellie followed.

"Wow, Melissa. They've made the grange hall look amazing. You guys went all out." Her eyes followed the multiple strings of soft white bulb lights draped from the ceiling to the floor and the silky black tablecloths. White lilies adorned every table. Lining each wall, three easels stood with white cloth draped over their canvases. They would all be unveiled when the auction officially began at 7:00 p.m.

"We're going to make so much money," Melissa laughed. "But yes. It's taken a ton of work. We've been decorating all day and the food is being catered by Mazzi's in Eugene, so hopefully no one's going to complain about the $40 per seat price tag.

"The money is for a good cause," Ellie said. "No one will complain."

Melissa grabbed Ellie's arms and pulled her closer, her eyes narrow with intensity. "So, Ellie. I have to ask." She paused for dramatic effect. "Who is Levi?"

Her pulse skipped several beats. "Um, he's my neighbor. Why do you ask?"

"Oh my God, Ellie. Are you kidding me? He stopped by my classroom on Friday and asked to buy a ticket from me for the auction. He requested to sit at your table."

Ellie took a breath. "We're good friends and he's here to support me. There's nothing weird about that." She tried to sound nonchalant.

"Ellie, you didn't tell me you had such a hot looking friend. He's gorgeous and he's your neighbor? Oh my God, I would be running out of eggs and sugar every day just as an excuse to chat him up."

"Oh, stop Melissa. It's not like that. You know Rachel Monroe?"

"Are you talking about one of our students?"

"She's his daughter. He's the sheriff here in town. He probably just happened to be at the school picking up Rae and decided to get a ticket. No big deal."

Melissa nodded. "Oh, I know Rae. I had her in science last year and this year. She's really made huge strides from where she was."

Ellie looked around carefully before speaking, "Her mom passed away just a few years ago. They've had a rough time."

Melissa grabbed Ellie's arm firmly and brought her face within inches of her own. She felt like one of Melissa's disobedient students. "Ellie, you need to hear this. People heal and they move on. I could be wrong, but Levi seemed hell and high water determined to sit near you tonight. Maybe you should just go with it. You deserve to be happy too." She smiled and allowed her words to sink in. "I love you girl, but you've got to live a little." She gave Ellie's arm a slightly painful squeeze. "Anyway, I've gotta get ready to emcee. By the way, I adore your painting." She released her arm and Ellie watched her hustle toward Lisa from the Historical Society. Her heart felt warm and hopeful. The feeling frightened her.

She headed to table seven where Miles and John were feasting on cupcakes. "Your dad should be here any moment. Don't eat too many of those. I don't want to send you off with stomach aches."

"Ellie?" She turned in surprise at Levi's voice. He stood holding his dinner ticket, his index finger highlighting table number seven. "Your friend, Melissa told me you'd be at this table. Hope you don't mind me joining you?"

"Of course not." She tried to smile at him despite her nerves.

His eyes lingered on her for a moment too long. "You clean up pretty good, Ellie."

She laughed nervously as she also noted how attractive he looked in the blazer and collared shirt he wore over dark jeans and dress shoes. "You don't look so bad either. I don't see you very often without your sheriff's jacket." She motioned to a seat near her. "You want to sit next to John? The boys won't be here too much longer. Their dad's actually picking them up any minute."

Levi nodded. "Sure." He took the seat and turned to John. "How are the cupcakes?"

"This one's got cherry in the middle and tastes really good."

"How about you Miles?"

"Mine's chocolate fudge." Miles had crumbs on the corner of his mouth and frosting on his shirt.

"I can tell," Levi chuckled. Your mom's not making you wait till dinner?"

John shook his head. "Nah. She's not strict on the days Dad picks us up. Is Rae with you?"

"Not tonight. She's at her grandma's house."

"I wish I could be at Grandma and Grandpas," Miles said. "Besides the cupcakes, this is so boring."

"A rare evening to yourself and you're here?" Ellie teased Levi.

Levi's eyes searched her face. "This is an important night for you. I wouldn't miss it." A wave of emotion suddenly overcame her. Levi had a way of expressing his deepest emotions like simple undeniable truths. Her voice caught in her throat and she couldn't respond. Levi saved her. "I've noticed you sneaking off constantly to the barn to work on that painting. I'm not going to lie. I'm curious."

Ellie managed a smile. "I hope I don't disappoint you."

"You could never disappoint me," he assured her.

"Ellie?" She turned to the voices of new arrivals.

"Jewel? Are you kidding me?"

Jewel laughed. "I told you I wanted to see the finished painting after we talked, but I didn't realize we'd be sitting at the same table. This is my husband, Frank." She gestured toward the man next to her. The adults all introduced themselves around the table. Frank was a distinguished looking man with glasses. He appeared older than Jewel who looked just as amazing as the first time Ellie met her in a burgundy velvet cocktail dress and matching burgundy heels. Jewel took the seat next to Miles and Frank sat across from Ellie.

"Do you like how your painting finally turned out?" Jewel asked once they were comfortably seated.

"Honestly, I'm not really sure, but you gave me an idea when we talked. What I can say is I enjoyed working on the piece. I wasn't able to say that for a long time so I'm grateful. That one conversation we had actually really helped me."

"I think the most important thing is how you feel about it, so good for you," Jewel said.

Ellie nodded. "I agree, but all the same, I hope you'll like what I've done."

Jewel smiled with understanding. "I know I will."

"How's my chicken girl?" Ellie turned to see Allison and a good-looking man following behind her that she presumed was her husband, Mike. "Can we join you?" Allison asked.

Levi addressed them immediately. "Well, if it isn't Mike and Allie? The more the merrier. You get the last two seats at our table," He stood to greet them both.

When they were seated, Ellie turned toward Allison. "It's so good to see you, Allison. Have you met Jewel Peterson?"

Jewel laughed. "Yes, I know the George's well. I sold them their house. Good to see you Allison. How's the house treating you?"

"Wonderful. We should clean it more, but the house is great. You're looking good." Ellie felt relieved that everyone was comfortable and at ease with each other.

As they were all settling into their seats, making the necessary small talk and catching up, Melissa appeared at Ellie's elbow. "It's almost time for the unveiling. You need to stand by your easel." Ellie excused herself and made her way to her painting. Levi gave her an encouraging nod.

Melissa took the stage with confidence and good humor. "Hello everyone. Hello?" She tapped the microphone. "Ladies and gentlemen. Can you all hear me? Oh good. I'm Melissa Nielson and I teach middle school science here in Veneta. You guys have come here to do the wonderful work of raising money for the district's science program. Can I get some applause for the science program?" The audience applauded politely. "Thank you so much. Funds tonight will allow students to explore their world in a hands-on way with the state-of-the-art equipment they need to be competitive with the best schools in the country. We have partnered with the Veneta Historical Society for tonight's fundraiser."

Ellie clapped and watched table seven from afar. She was relieved to see Levi chuckling as he spoke to Miles and John. There was a comfort in knowing he was looking out for her boys. Melissa continued. "Yes. Thank you. Can I get more applause please for the Veneta Historical Society?" The audience applauded politely again. "Thank you so much. In addition to your delicious meal tonight, our hope is that you will also bid on a one-of-a-kind painting by our local and very talented artists. Yes, more applause please."

Ellie observed as Allison cheered aloud for her and encouraged John to do the same. She couldn't help but smile and the warm feeling traveled from her lips all the way to her eyes. The feeling of having people in her corner was a new oddity. It felt good. Melissa hesitated for the applause before continuing. "You are all awesome. Thank you. I'm going to go around the room and introduce each artist and then they will unveil their painting.

Before we eat, there will be time for all of you to do your walk by and look at the paintings and make your private bids. Do you see the envelope I'm holding? There are envelopes like this at each station and slips of paper where you will write your name, phone number, and the amount you plan to bid. Lisa Lewellyn and the rest of the committee will sort through these and at the end of the evening we will share the winning bids. Alrighty then. Let's begin."

Ellie surveyed the eleven other artists around the room and listened attentively as Melissa introduced each one. Sue Mickelson painted the town hall in black and white, Jon Chang painted the library in what looked like an impressionistic style in pastels, Karinna Matthews made a mosaic of the fire station out of tile and Juan Ramirez made a tapestry of the Veneta Grange Hall. Each piece was well executed, detailed, and mostly realistic in style. The audience awarded each piece with mild oohing and aahing and polite applause.

"Now we have this year's depiction of Veneta Community Fellowship Church painted by Ellie Gold. Ellie is the art teacher at Fern Ridge Middle School and an accomplished portrait artist. Ellie, go ahead and remove the covering." She removed the white fabric with trembling hands. The hall went strangely quiet and Ellie stared anxiously at hundreds of blank faces. The guests seated at the tables closest in proximity to her canvas leaned forward to get a closer look.

She tried to read their faces. Spectators could recognize the structure of the church immediately, but the array of colors and the shapes inside the lines of the building were confusing to the eye at first. When scrutinized closely, the enigma of the painting revealed itself. The entire church was made up of tiny, intricate human beings of all ages, colors, and walks of life involved in various aspects of worship and daily living. They were praying, singing, weaving, building, laughing, reading, laboring, painting, writing, mourning, but all under one church. Each person was connected to another person like intricate puzzle pieces. From a distance the entire painting looked like a colorful mosaic, but the stained-glass windows provided a contrast to the intricacy of the tiny portraits. The windows in Ellie's painting very nearly modeled exactly to the windows in the actual church. They provided the only contrast to the hundreds of tiny expressive faces. There were two windows in the painting. The first depicted the fisherman's net filled almost to bursting with brightly scaled fish. The other illustrated the dove with the olive branch in its beak, flying peacefully amid the masses of humanity. The biblical images were much larger than the tiny people that made up the walls, the floor, the arches, and the bell tower. The painting was in fact two entirely different pictures depending on whether you viewed the piece from a distance or from a few feet away. The tables close to Ellie were the first to become cognizant of the two-dimensional nature of the piece.

"That's incredible. I see it now. There's maybe hundreds of faces and people in that painting," a woman said in amazement to the person seated next to her. Ellie's face flushed under the gaze of so many eyes. Once the unveilings were finished, she made her way back to table seven to the music of an acoustic band. People were now up and moving about to examine each painting and make their bids. Levi was still at the table with the boys. He smiled when she approached.

"That was quite the unveiling. Apparently, yours has the most buzz. Check it out." He pointed in the direction of her canvas. Ellie turned and saw that a nice crowd had formed around her painting. "I hope I'll get a chance to look at it more closely," Levi continued. Looks like I might have to show my badge to move them out of the way."

Ellie blushed. "Wow. I didn't expect that."

"Look, Dad's here!" Miles blurted. He got out of his seat and darted toward the front entrance where Davis emerged. Ellie observed that he also wore a suit jacket over khaki pants and loafers. He looked more put together than she had observed in a while. John waved from their table. Miles grabbed Davis' hand and led him toward table seven.

Ellie took a deep breath. "Hi Davis," she said evenly as he neared.

"Hey Ellie. This is a big event. I had a tough time finding a parking spot. Wow, Ellie," Davis said in surprise. "You look really good."

She ignored the remark. "The boys are ready, but their backpacks are still in my car. I did leave it unlocked for you."

"Well, we can stop by the Explorer before we go."

Davis' eyes narrowed on Levi. Ellie turned and saw Levi staring back at Davis, his eyes intense and focused, unflinching. "Um, Davis this is Levi. He's a friend of mine."

"Hi," Davis said. "John's told me a little about you." His voice sounded wooden and hollow.

Levi stood and reached out his hand to Davis. "Nice to meet you."

Davis took his hand. "Yeah, you too."

Miles yanked on Davis' arm. "Dad, have you seen Mom's painting? Look at the big crowd all around it."

"No, not yet. How about you take me on a quick look around before we go?"

Miles frowned. "It's kind of boring here, but if we stop by the cupcake table it would be alright."

"Come on Miles, the quicker we take Dad on a tour the sooner we can go." John stood up and the two boys flanked their father's side. Ellie watched the three of them move as a unit towards the displays.

"So that's your ex, huh?" Levi said once Davis and the boys were across the room.

Ellie looked at him plainly. "As far as I'm concerned, that man's as dead as your wife." The force of her words took her by surprise. "I'm sorry Levi. That was a little dark and I didn't mean disrespect to your wife. That was a very inconsiderate comment." She hoped he would accept her awkward apology.

Levi looked at her surprised. "It's okay. We can't check ourselves every moment. Sometimes the truth just spits out. So, it wasn't a good break up I'm assuming."

She realized this was not a can of worms she wanted to open. "You could say that Levi. In any case, I really am over it all now. We have to share the boys, so we make it work." As she spoke, she watched Davis from afar wave to her from the door indicating he was leaving and taking the boys. She nodded her understanding and watched as her two boys followed him out the door.

Levi studied her face and let the topic drop. Despite the awkward hand off with Davis, the rest of the evening was magic. The table conversation was fun and lighthearted. An acoustic band played music from their young adult days and made them feel like teenagers again. Ellie almost felt like she had stepped back in time into her old skin, the person she used to be. In John's absence, Levi moved to the seat beside her and she felt his presence and calm strength even when she wasn't looking at him directly. Levi too laughed and joked with Mike and seemed to have the time of his life. She was conscious for the first time of how aware she was of his presence, his every movement. She did not have to look at him to know exactly where he was. They were connected by electricity, hidden currents. She had known this for a while but had refused to acknowledge the truth. Levi terrified her, but tonight without the responsibility of caring for the boys, the food, the fellowship, the music, she felt free and alive. She allowed hope to grow in a small chamber in her heart

Desserts and coffee were served, and Melissa was back on stage. She smiled broadly at the audience. "The fateful hour has arrived. Lisa and the committee have deliberated, and we have the totals for the evening. Drumroll please." Melissa paused dramatically and waited as the drummer helped her build the suspense. "Our total for tonight is $18,700.00. I just want to add that his figure is well over $3000 the all-time record for this event." The hall thundered with applause. Melissa then began to name the paintings, the painter, the identity of the bidder, and the amount of the bid.

Melissa could hardly contain her enthusiasm as she announced the winning bids. Most of the art pieces were purchased between five hundred to a thousand dollars with the highest bid going to Karinna Matthew's mosaic for nearly one thousand eight hundred and fifty dollars. Karinna practically wept for joy when she discovered that her fiancée had purchased the piece. The crowd applauded wildly. Ellie waited in anticipation for Melissa to announce her painting. "Our final painting this evening is *The Church* by Ellie Gold. Folks, the bid on this one is unbelievable." Melissa paused for dramatic effect and Ellie could hardly contain her heart from beating out of her chest. "The painting goes to an anonymous buyer for five thousand dollars." Ellie, who was sipping ice water in an effort to look casual, spit out her beverage in surprise. Levi laughed and handed her a napkin. He patted her back gently as she recovered and table seven roared and hooted with applause.

"What? Are you kidding me?" Ellie said. Her face was flushed with surprise from the unbelievable bid and the gentle pressure of Levi's hand on her back. The success of her painting overwhelmed her. Melissa gave her two thumbs up from on stage. *Five thousand dollars? Who would have paid such an astronomical sum for a painting?* As she finally accepted the surreal unfolding of events, an anxiety overwhelmed her. *She was forgetting something. What was it?* Suddenly Ellie remembered her promise, the prayer, the deal she made with God. If the painting sold, she would go to the church, attend services. *This was no accident*, she thought.

Levi whispered into her ear, concern on his face. "Are you okay?"

She turned discreetly toward him and spoke softly. "I think I just lost a deal with God."

His expression was solemn. "That's never good."

Chapter 14

Insulation

> *A friend is one who overlooks*
> *Your broken fence*
> *and admires the flowers*
> *in your garden.*
> *—Unknown*

Thanksgiving arrived with gusty winds and nonstop rain. Despite her mom's shameless begging, Ellie decided against joining her family for the holiday. Standing up to her mother wasn't easy and the old Ellie would have caved to her pleading. The impulse to please was almost as powerful as breathing. Refusing her mother was a small act of courage, but also pride. Even a year since the incident with Nora, Ellie did not feel in control of her life or emotions. She did not want a repeat of last year. Going without the boys would leave her too vulnerable and unprepared if Nora arrived. She felt unsure of her place, her role in the family and Nora still remained a mystery. Except for occasional phone calls to a few in the family, she was off the grid. Ellie could only imagine why.

She spent Thanksgiving morning deep cleaning John and Miles' bedrooms and watching cheesy holiday movies. Instead of making a turkey, she roasted a small store-bought chicken and made a tossed salad. She glanced through the kitchen window and noted Levi and Rae's house standing vacant, the Tahoe conspicuously missing from their driveway. A longing tugged at her heart. She assumed they had traveled to Levi's mother's house in Sweet Home, a small town about an hour east of Veneta. At the auction he had asked her about her holiday plans in that deep steady voice of his and she had responded by telling him as little as possible. She could imagine him overreacting, fretting over her, perhaps even extending an awkward invitation to join them for Thanksgiving. Then again, the possibility that he wouldn't react or fret over her at all was even more distressing. Maybe she was flattering herself to believe he cared. Fear held her back. In truth, the holiday was lonely, and Ellie believed Andrew was probably right. She should have swallowed her pride and gone to her family gathering even without the boys, but finding the motivation to face them with her head held high was proving difficult. In the meantime, she needed to garner her courage to start attending church to fulfill the deal she made with God. Focus on one challenge at a time, she decided.

* * *

Ellie herded her boys to the door. Miles was excited about going to church, but John was dragging his feet. He enjoyed lazy weekends in his pajamas and spending time with Cordelia in the mornings. She bribed him with the promise they would go out to lunch at Lou's Diner and get burgers, fries, and milkshakes after church. He reluctantly agreed.

She arrived with only seconds to spare before the service and the parking lot was bustling with dozens of people. The Christmas season was in full swing and she could feel the holiday excitement in the air. Unlike South Hills, Veneta Christian Community Fellowship had many young families. As she pulled into the back of the mostly filled parking lot, she noticed small groups of people talking and laughing. They seemed in no rush to enter the building. She took a breath and tried to relax as she felt the tightening in her back and shoulders, her knuckles white from gripping the steering wheel. *Why was she so stressed about going back to church?* She realized her body was reacting to the raw force of her old life crashing into the new one. How could she reconcile these two worlds? Mixed emotions gripped her. In her marriage she had been a full partner with her husband and viewed the church through his eyes. Despite their separation, Davis lived in her head, his voice still resonated in her ears. Their whole life revolved around the ministry, but church became a painful obligation, their ministry together and their marriage, a lie. Davis was angry at the church and his feelings also colored her thinking with similar strokes. Returning to church now felt like an attempt to recapture a religion she no longer believed in, at least not in the same way as before. Her goal was to rediscover her own feelings and beliefs and that task included unpacking her own baggage when it came to her relationship with God and the church.

"Mom? Are we going in or what?" Miles asked.

"Yeah. I'm sorry. I was just thinking." She tapped the steering wheel.

"Well, can we just go inside and get it over with already so we can go to Lou's after?" John asked.

"That's the plan," Ellie sighed. "But neither of you take off anywhere. I need you to sit next to me in church so I'm not alone."

John rolled his eyes. "You don't even want to be here. Why are we here?"

Ellie closed her eyes as she considered how to respond to the same question, she was also asking herself. "John, sometimes we're resistant to what's good for us, even me, unfortunately."

"I thought you liked going to church?" Miles looked at her with surprise.

Ellie smiled. "I used to. This church is all new and sometimes it's kind of scary to try something you're not familiar with."

Miles nodded solemnly. "I felt that way about the first day of school, but now I've got friends and it's not so bad. It will be okay, Mom."

"Who made you so wise?" She smiled at him and then popped the car door open with determination. "Here we go."

They walked together as a family unit toward the very church that after weeks of painting and reinventing on canvas was now a part of her consciousness. Miles allowed Ellie to hold his hand and she felt grateful.

When they entered the foyer, the wooden double doors were wide open, and the inside of the church lay bare before their eyes. The rustic wooden pews were about three quarters full and most of the open seating was toward the front of the building. *Great,* Ellie thought. She wanted to avoid making a spectacle of herself in front of a hundred strangers. Her eyes scanned the assembly, and she spotted an empty pew in the front west corner. Although still in the front, the pew was off to the side and the least conspicuous of all the open seats. She made a beeline for the vacant pew and felt a myriad of eyes following her. Church goers always wanted to check out the new people during the service, whether at South Hills or Veneta Christian Community Fellowship, human nature was the same.

Once seated, Ellie scrutinized her surroundings carefully. The eastern morning light shone through the stained-glass windows and illuminated traces of colored light on the dais. The entire sanctuary was decorated with evergreen wreaths and gold ribbons. She inhaled the fresh fir scent that filled the spacious room. A large wooden cross towered above a manger carefully placed on a pile of straw. The furnishings took center stage. A pianist played *Angels We Have Heard on High* and she felt Miles already squirming next to her in the pew. She put her arm around his shoulders and gave him a squeeze. Suddenly a young woman appeared at the aisle closest to Ellie and spoke directly to her. "We have games and all kinds of fun activities downstairs for kids. Would your boys like to join us?"

Ellie felt her heart quicken in her chest. She didn't want to lose her boys and have to sit alone.

"Can we?" asked Miles.

"Yeah Mom. I think that would be more fun," John agreed.

Ellie sighed and raised her eyes to the young woman. "I guess they're going with you." She moved back into the pew and angled her knees to the side so John could scoot past her. Her eyes lingered on them as they followed the young woman down the stairs. She closed her eyes and tried to concentrate on the music and calm her pulse by breathing through her nose rather than focusing on the idea that she was sitting alone. Her shoulders felt tight and she could feel the tension moving down her back. Suddenly, she felt a gentle hand on her shoulder, and she turned.

"Ellie? Oh my gosh, so glad you're here. Can I sit next to you?"

She looked up to see Allison's smiling face and relief flooded her. "Allison. Yes. The boys just left me to go downstairs. I'd love to have the company."

Allison looked relieved. "Mike always works on Sundays, so he rarely makes it to church. I usually sit by myself because Natalie and Ryan are downstairs too and I usually don't get here on time." Ellie gave her a warm smile and shifted in her seat to make more room for her new friend.

At that moment, the worship team took the stage. She was immediately drawn to their faces. The first singer was a man in his eighties. He used a cane to maneuver across the stage, his body bent with age. Behind him a girl with a dark French braid and a navy blue sailor dress guided his elbow till they reached their spots on stage. *A family church*, Ellie thought. The worship leader was a petite blonde with a radiant smile. She led them in several worship songs and Christmas hymns with her guitar. The festive music and atmosphere did not remind her of South Hills at all, but her father's church in Stayton. As the voices of the singers rose upwards into the rafters, the sound surrounded her. Ellie felt a spark of something undefinable, authentic and real. She closed her eyes and let the music take her, remembering her childhood days when she loved church, especially hearing her lone voice made powerful by surrounding voices as they united in one message, one hope. As they sang, she gazed at the windows and felt the sun on her face. She allowed herself to feel the warmth on her cheeks and to believe that perhaps God's light was shining directly on her. With Allison's presence next to her, the mellifluous voices, and the spectrum of light and colors filling the sanctuary, she knew God was there. She simply felt Him, if only for the moment. She could believe that God loved her, and she was not forgotten.

When the congregation finished singing, the cheerful song leader asked them to take a seat.

Allison sat next to her and began to dig in her purse pulling out a white and green box. "Want some Junior Mints?"

"What are we? At a movie?" Ellie whispered as she tried to suppress her laughter.

"No, but I get really hungry around this time and I find a little sugar helps me pay attention," Allison whispered.

Ellie reached out her hand and waited for Allison to discreetly pour five chocolate mints into her palm. She smirked as she snuck one in her mouth. Alison made her feel like a little girl again misbehaving in church, but she didn't mind. In fact, she liked it.

Much like her father, the pastor was an older man in his sixties and his preaching was not exciting but centered in Scripture. Ellie found that she was grateful the pastor was older. If he had reminded her in any way of Davis, her heart and mind would have closed like a vault door. The preaching text was on Acts 2: 25-28.

I saw the Lord before me. Because he is at my right hand, I will not be shaken.
Therefore, my heart is glad, and my tongue rejoices; my body also will rest in hope,
because you will not abandon me to the realm of the dead, you will not let your Holy one see decay. You have made known to me the paths of life.
You will fill me with joy in your presence.

Ellie meditated on the words in her mind as the preacher spoke. This was the season of hope he insisted. Jesus was vulnerable and weak as a babe and every threat imaginable surrounded him in his fragile state, but God could transform the weak into the strong. His plans were not one with the world, but one with God's heavenly kingdom. The pastor reiterated the points several times in his message.

I will not be shaken. Ellie wished she could say the same. There were days when she felt stronger, but her strength was a veneer. The line between emotional stability and complete collapse was thin. Davis' betrayal was a deep angry pool always lurking beneath the surface, even behind her smiles and laughter. Even now, she was not sure that time would heal all wounds. The strength she had come to rely on was not the peace and good will Jesus promised, but a clawing and scratching of her sheer will, the determination to be strong for her boys.

My heart is glad, and my tongue rejoices; my body also will rest in hope. These

170

were qualities she wanted. She longed to rejoice in life again and to rest in hope. Her heart beat heavily in her chest as her mind touched on Levi and Rae. Levi's sudden appearance at the river, the way he saved Miles, his friendship and care. She was attracted to him. She allowed herself to admit the truth. In his quiet way, even in friendship, he watched over her like Davis never had. Yet, the idea of taking their relationship to the next step paralyzed her with fear. *Why?* She wanted to rejoice, to live in hope for a brighter future, but the baggage of the past overwhelmed her. She wanted to protect her boys, keep her family safe. Opening her heart to Levi might also mean opening herself once again to indescribable pain.

You will not abandon me to the realm of the dead, You will not let your Holy one see decay. You have made known to me the paths of life. Nestled in the sanctuary surrounded by other believers, Ellie could believe that God was there. Even in the moments where she felt completely abandoned, God had sent people into her life to encourage her, to keep her from falling into complete despair. She saw the pattern of His love in her parents, Andrew, Brian, Melissa, even her lawyer Lyle. Now that she was in Veneta, Levi and Rae were a significant part of her life, but Ellie needed more reassurance, a guarantee. *If God has a plan for my life, why am I the last to know about it?*

The sermon ended and the congregation sang the closing hymn, *Joy to the World.* The preacher dismissed them, and Allison grabbed her arm. "I have a proposition for you."

Her eyes widened with curiosity. "I'm listening."

"I have a small group of friends that meet at my house once a week, every Monday after work. Anyway, we pray for each other, talk about Scripture, and sometimes do a little Bible study and reflection. I really would like you to come, if you can?"

A wave of emotion hit Ellie. She was torn. On one level, she wanted to hang out with other women and develop friendships and a life separate from work and family, but on the other hand, did she really want to open herself up to the scrutiny of other women? Christian women who might look at her with judgement in their eyes? "Uh, I don't know. I've got the boys and they're still a little too young for me to leave home alone."

Allison shook her head sympathetically. "I remember those days. When you have young kids, your options can be pretty limited. Fortunately, I thought about that before inviting you. I've talked to Ryan and Natalie and they've agreed to watch the boys if you were to come. We have a game room downstairs with video games and air hockey. The boys would probably have the time of their lives and Ryan said he'd watch out for John and Natalie would watch Miles. We meet on Mondays from four to six."

She hesitated. "That's really sweet of your kids. I don't think I can give you an answer now. Can I think about it?"

"Of course." Allison was about to make her way out of the pew but turned around and touched her arm again. "This is going to sound weird, but I really want you to come. I've just seen you there with our group, almost like a vision in my mind. I can't shake the idea that you're supposed to join us. Does that sound weird?"

Ellie bit her lip. "Unfortunately, I'm not surprised by that at all." On the night of the auction, she felt the same pulling in her heart. Her father would call the sensation God's leading. Ellie could not help but remember Jonah in the Bible. God was calling her to Nineveh, she thought. Resistance was futile.

* * *

Ellie's nerves made her feel slightly nauseous as she stood on Allison's front porch. Multi-colored blinking lights and Christmas decorations adorned every fixture of Allison's home, which somehow seemed fitting to her friendly nature. John and Miles stood beside her, also anxious. John did not know Allison's son Ryan, who was in high school. He felt uneasy over the prospect of spending a couple hours with a boy he did not know. Miles was picking up on the anxious energy of both his mother and his brother and shuffled his feet. They did not have to wait long. Ryan opened the door. He was a good-looking young man, tall and manly for a tenth grader, much more confident than his sister Natalie. His smile instantly reminded Ellie of his mother's.

172

"Hi. I'm Ryan. Mom said to get the door. Come on in." He welcomed them inside and as they entered the great room, Ellie was overwhelmed by a sensory overload. A large Christmas tree adorned in red and white lights took center stage and dwarfed all other furnishings in the room. The space was filled with candles, wreathes, and red bows. The scent of apples and cinnamon hung in the air making her mouth water. Allison breezed into the great room from the kitchen. She looked beautiful, Ellie thought. She wore an honest to goodness navy blue printed apron with frilly straps and small apples all over the fabric. Underneath the apron, she wore a red flowing tunic over black leggings and apple shaped house slippers.

"Ellie! We're all in the kitchen drinking coffee and we're about to dig into an apple pie."

"It smells and looks amazing in here," Ellie said.

"Oh, thanks." Allison said casually. "It's that time of year. Ryan, have you met John and Miles?"

Ryan's smile was good natured. "I'm the one who let them into the house, Mom."

"I know, but have you been introduced?"

Ryan turned to the boys. "John, I have Smash Bros downstairs. Do you and Miles want to play?"

"That sounds cool," John said.

"Can I be Yoshi?" Miles asked. "I'm always Yoshi."

Ryan laughed. "Of course. I'm usually Snake. He's pretty cool."

At that moment, Natalie came into the room. "Ms. G!" She rushed forward and hugged her

Ellie returned the embrace. "Have you been working on your sketch journal, Natalie?"

"Totally. Do you want to see what I've been working on later?"

"I would love to see what you're up to after our study"

Natalie nodded and smiled as she looked at Miles. "I brought some cookies for us to take downstairs."

Miles furrowed his brow. "What kind are they?"

"I've got oatmeal and chocolate chip."

"The chocolate chip sounds okay. Are you going to play Smash Brothers with us?" he asked.

"Only if we get to play Mario Kart later," Natalie grinned.

"It's a deal."

"Well, if we get bored playing the Switch, we can also do some air hockey later," Ryan suggested. He gestured to them to follow and the boys and Natalie headed down the stairs to the game room.

Ellie turned to Allison. "How much are you paying your kids to watch my kids?"

Allison put her fingers to her lips. "Ssh! I'll never tell."

Ellie followed Allison to a spacious modern kitchen. A large island with several stools was centered in the middle of the room and around the island three women were seated holding decorative coffee mugs. Ellie shook her head with surprise when she realized she already knew every woman around the table. Dressed in a tailored black suit jacket with a while collared shirt, perfectly fitted jeans finished with polished black heels was no other than Jewel Peterson. Next to her, was Harmony Carrey. Her long curly hair was up in a loose bun. Strands curled down and framed the sides of her face. She wore a blue checked flannel shirt and bootcut jeans with cowboy boots. Finishing the group was Ruby Jones, who wore a long jean skirt with buttons up and down the front matched with a fitted teal blouse. Her beautiful hair was tied to the side in a banana braid with a tie-dyed scarf wrapped through the braid.

"Ellie!" the women all said at once as if greeting a long-lost friend.

She laughed. "I know you guys. All of you. Did you plan this?"

"Not exactly," laughed Jewel. "Allison and I started talking about inviting you after the auction dinner. We talked it over with Harmony and Ruby and guess what? Everyone knew you already."

"I don't know about you ladies, but the whole thing felt like God's will to me," Ruby added with her lush southern accent. Ruby patted the empty stool next to her. "Have a seat little darlin'. We're about to eat some pie."

Allison chuckled. "It's actually Ruby's recipe and her apples." She set a festive Christmas mug full of freshly brewed coffee in front of Ellie.

"We all helped a bit," Harmony added. "Ruby's got an orchard full of apple trees and we were out at her place picking apples, maybe two or three weekends back in September, right?"

"That's right." Ruby agreed. "They help me out with the pickin' and then they get enough applesauce to last three winters. Doesn't that sound like a deal made in heaven?"

"I think it does," Ellie agreed. "Ruby, those peach preserves were amazing and the way you put your mason jars together. Well, they're just quite impressive."

"Oh, I'm so glad you liked them. You are such a lovely teacher and a wonderful artist. I wanted to do ya a kind deed. That picture ya did of that church. Well, it just gave me chills, just all up and down my spine."

"I agree," Jewel added. "I watched that picture take shape from the very beginning and Ellie sure made some changes. Those little faces in the church. Each one looks and feels like a real person. That picture felt powerful."

"Each person a unique and livin' soul. I could live and breathe in that painting. It's just heavenly," added Ruby.

"Wow, I didn't realize everyone had seen my work."

"Well, I'll be," Ruby said. "It's the talk of the whole town."

"What I can't get over is the mystery of it all. Aren't you just dying to know who Mr. Anonymous is? Who would have spent $5000? Perhaps a dashing, handsome stranger. I just love a mystery." Jewel raised her eyebrows to suggest possible intrigue.

"And how in sweet tarnation do you know that Mr. Anonymous is a Mr.? Maybe it's a Mrs. Anonymous?" Ruby scolded.

"Oh Ruby, please don't take the excitement away. I think we can all agree that the story is much more exciting if it's a Mr.," Jewel smiled dreamily.

Harmony was determined to bring order to their conversation. "Hold the phone. Not to change the subject, but how's that puppy doing? Little Aurora?"

Ellie had to think for a moment before she realized Cordelia's former name. "Oh Harmony. She's just been perfect. The boys love her, and she hardly even whimpered when we brought her home. We call her Cordelia."

"Cor-de-li-a," Harmony tested each syllable aloud. "I like it. Definitely unique. And Levi? He's your neighbor right?"

"Oh, Levi and Rae are doing great with Pax too." Ellie felt uncomfortable under Harmony's insinuating gaze.

"I take it that Midnight is now called Pax," Harmony paused to choose her words carefully. "Levi's a close friend. I was friends with Melinda, you know his wife, before she passed as well. She would have hated to see him alone. He was a good husband. They had a strong marriage, a real marriage."

"What's a real marriage?" asked Ellie. "Aren't all marriages real?"

"Hmmm. I think no. Some people try to act like everything is perfect. That's not a real marriage," Harmony said thoughtfully.

"Lord, yes." Ruby agreed. "Ya gotta have some raised voices sometimes, some real anger. Clyde can tell ya all about a real marriage."

"Who's Clyde?"

"My husband," Ruby laughed. "He's a patient man, I tell ya."

Ellie joined in the laughter. "So, I take it, you're all married?"

Allison bit her lip and grimaced. Ellie assumed she did not want her to feel left out. "Yes. Most of us have been married for a while. Mike is actually my second husband. Now, that's a long story that I will share with you another time, but I hope you're okay with being our only single lady."

Ellie hesitated. "I was married for over fifteen years. I just got divorced over the summer. I still have no idea what it means to be a single lady."

Jewel put her fingers lightly on the top of Ellie's hand. "I'm a Korean American living in Veneta Oregon. I have no idea who I am supposed to be most of the time. I'm too busy, just being myself. Maybe we don't need to worry so much about labels. What do you say ladies?"

"Hear, hear," Ruby said and lifted her coffee cup like a wine glass. The ladies clinked their mugs to complete the toast.

Allison provided each woman with a piece of warm pie and then ushered them to her backyard. Winter had almost arrived, and the temperature hovered around forty-five degrees, but Allison's yard was equipped with a covered patio and a crackling outside fireplace. She had arranged two patio loveseats with throw blankets and a chair around the fire. "Sit down girls.

I'll be right back." Allison disappeared back into the house. Ellie found a seat next to Jewel and felt the warmth of the fire immediately, but even with her coat on her back and arms were exposed to the winter chill.

"Try this," Jewel said as she handed Ellie an orange throw. She wrapped herself in the velvety warmth and brought her coffee mug close to her chest.

"Allison always knows how to make a girl feel welcome," Ruby chimed as she settled next to Harmony on the other patio loveseat.

Allison breezed out of the house carrying flowers. She hurried over to them out of breath. "I went to the florist today and made each of you a bouquet of flowers," she said.

Harmony protested "Allison, you shouldn't have gone to the trouble..."

"Not a word," Allison warned "I wanted to. I had fun doing it."

"The girl's so generous she puts us all to shame," Ruby chuckled.

She set the flowers on the coffee table and grabbed a large bouquet of sunflowers. "These are for my dear friend Jewel, who always brightens my day. Her love is so great and so wide that only the largest and sunniest flower of them all would be fitting."

Jewel laughed. "Oh Allison. They're lovely. Thank you."

"My pleasure sweet JuJu," she winked playfully."My next bouquet is for a woman whose love for teaching and helping others blooms from every part of her, top to bottom. No other flower would do for our Ruby but the vibrant gladiolus." Allison handed her the bouquet of lavender, pink, and white gladiolus in radiant bloom.

The women cheered around the table. "It's not just love that's bloomin' from my top to bottom," Ruby joked.

"Oh stop. Don't be ridiculous Ruby," Harmony chided. "You are lovely just as you are."

"Indeed, you are, and I can't think of a more faithful friend," agreed Allison.

Ruby nestled her nose in the open blooms and smiled before looking up. "Well, I thank ya. It's jus' real special."

"Now this dear sister isn't afraid of a little hard work and can make anything grow, including my monetary investments. Did you know ladies, that the lovely iris can be cut from the root, replanted, and grow into a new plant? The iris is like my lovely Harmony who can take even two very small fish and multiply them to feed everyone. She is a wiz at what she does, and she always uses her gifts to serve others."

Allison handed Harmony the bouquet of purple irises and the ladies continued to cheer and hoot.

"You're trying to bribe me into doing your taxes for free aren't you?" Harmony kidded.

"Of course not," Allison said in mock surprise. Harmony flushed as she accepted the flowers. "It's the middle of winter and these are summer flowers. They must have cost you a pretty penny."

"Oh you never mind that," Allison said, waving Harmony's concern away like a pesky fly.

Ellie noted that Harmony didn't seem to like people making a fuss over her. Allison interrupted her thoughts. "My newest friend has already brought color and joy into my daughter's life and now is bringing that same joy into mine. She is strong, independent and remains beautiful even when holding a full-time job and raising two boys on her own. Dahlias are her flower because they bloom big and strong in the fall and late into the season even when the other flowers have long since lost their bloom." Allison handed the bouquet to Ellie. Her bouquet was more rustic filled with vibrant yellow, orange, and red dahlias that reminded her of fall. She stared at the blooms, transfixed, rubbing the cool firm texture of the petals against her cheek. A pool began to rise and overflow within her. Suddenly, without warning, she was crying.

Allison hesitated. The women turned to look at her, concern etched on their faces. Jewel placed her hand on her back. "Are you okay?"

Ellie felt ashamed and wiped her eyes. "I'm so sorry." Her voice choked as she spoke. "You just made me feel so special."

"Oh sweetie," Jewel said with sympathy and put her arm fully around her shoulders and squeezed. "It's Allison's fault. Going around and being all generous and taking us by surprise."

"And telling me I'm bloomin' all over," Ruby added with mock anger.

"And trying to get me to do her taxes for free." Harmony pretended to frown.

Ellie laughed as the tears flowed. "And destroying my makeup."

Allison played her part in the game. "Well, I just can't win, can I?"

Harmony's eyes narrowed in thought. "Hey girls. What flower would we get Allison?"

Ellie spoke without thinking. "A yellow rose."

"Why a yellow rose?" Jewel asked.

"They're the flower of pure joy, optimism, and friendship," Ellie said.

"Oh, I absolutely agree," Jewel cooed.

"Yes indeed. My mama just loved yellow roses. We had the loveliest yellow tea rose shrub back in Louisiana when I was a girl," Ruby reminisced.

Ellie raised her eyes and smiled at Allison through her tears. How could she express how moved she was? How special the personalized bouquet made her feel when she felt like no one had truly seen her in a long time.

"Thank you, Ellie, for that sweet thought. I love yellow roses. I had no idea you all thought I was so sunny."

"You're so generous." Jewel said. "You're our host after all and we appreciate you."

"Okay, enough." Allison's cheeks were flushed pink. "Harmony, I think you're up for the Bible lesson today." Allison turned to Ellie to explain. "You see, we take turns and share a story or Scripture that's meaningful to us and then we share with the group."

"We call ourselves the Prayin' Sisters," Ruby added. "Last year, Harmony wrote down every prayer request that we brought to the Lord and ya know what?" She paused for dramatic effect. "God answered every single one of 'em."

"It's true," Jewel asserted. "Harmony wrote every request we brought before God and wrote them down in her little brown leather notebook and then she started to put a check by the ones that got answered. Almost every single request has a little check now."

"Really? Is that true?" Ellie asked.

"Well, there's two that haven't been answered yet. Allison prayed that Mike would start going to church with her and that one hasn't happened yet," Harmony said.

"But we're still praying and he's definitely warming up to the idea," Allison said.

"What about the other one?"

"My mama got cancer and we prayed for her. I jus' wanted to have a little more time with her before she died, but God took her right quick in the night. But God's way wuz better than mine, you see. She wuz in a lot of pain, a lot of sufferin' and these women here bought me and Clyde tickets back to Louisiana so I could say my goodbyes. I made it two days before she went home to the Lord. She died with Jesus by her side. I also got to say what I needed to say to her, so I count that as an answered prayer."

Ellie's eyes softened as she looked at the women in the circle. Ruby's story illustrated what true friendship could look like in a group of Christian women.

Harmony pulled out her Bible. "Alright. I chose Luke 8:1-25. The Parable of the Sower."

Ellie reached into her purse and withdrew her weathered Bible. She ran her fingers across the worn leather and began to leaf through the smooth pages. Reading her Bible daily used to be a routine. She was out of practice. The notes in the margins seemed as if they were written by a different person. From the corner of her eye, she saw Jewel also leafing through her Bible and noted the dozens of careful handwritten notes in her margins. These were women like her. They liked to live in the Word meditating over its truths and mysteries. Ellie wanted to crawl back into her old skin to become the woman she once was, but then again, she didn't. The women here reminded her of the past, but there was also promise of a new beginning, a future where she could be loved for being the person she really was not the woman she pretended to be.

Chapter 15

Drywall

> *No winter lasts forever,*
> *No spring skips its turn.*
> —*Hal Borland*

"Ellie, it would mean so much if you would be with the family for Christmas." Her mom was pleading. "We just all really missed you at Thanksgiving and without knowing where Nora is right now, your dad and I would just really love you to join us."

"Mom, I appreciate that. I really do. You know I love you, but I'm going through a transition right now. I can't explain it, but I'm just trying to figure out who I am. I've been working like a maniac and I'm looking forward to some quiet time during the holidays. Davis is coming over Christmas Eve and I think I'm just going to be drained after that." Ellie could hardly take a breath, but she had to explain herself before her mother wore her down.

"What are you talking about? Of course, you know who you are. You're our daughter. I don't understand why you wouldn't feel relaxed and comfortable with your own family? It should be a nice break for you after having to spend time with Davis on Christmas Eve." Sandra spit out his name in the same way she would have spoken about a contagious disease.

Her mother was usually patient and understanding, but Sandra was now fully aware of the mortal damage Davis' actions had inflicted on her family unit. Enough was enough.

Ellie consciously relaxed her voice and tried to compromise. "I don't mind dropping the boys off for a couple of days, if you want to spend time with them. They love spending time with the both of you, but I need a little break this year, mom."

She could hear her frustrated sigh. "Well, I guess that's something. Oh wait, here's your dad."

She heard shuffling sounds as her mother handed off the phone. "Ellie? It's your dad here. We're just worried about you, but if you feel like you want to stay home, there will be other Christmases. Don't let your mom guilt you into coming. If you need to do this for yourself, you go ahead and do what's best for you. We'll understand. I'll make your mom understand, okay?"

"Dad, thank you. I don't think that Mom gets that since the divorce I just need some time to reassess. No one in our family gets divorced. I feel like I'm the odd person out and I just don't feel comfortable right now."

He chose his words carefully. "Ellie, I'm really sorry if your mother or I made you feel alone or more on the outside than you already feel. That's the complete opposite of what we want. Your mother and I want you to be happy and whole. We never want you to feel alone."

Her heart strained in her chest. "Dad, this isn't your fault or Mom's. You haven't done anything to make me feel bad. I know this is totally my own issue. I just feel a little depressed in a house full of happy marriages. That's all. I'm struggling to accept the failure of my marriage and I feel like I'm grasping at straws to find what God wants for me next. I know the separation was almost a year ago, but sometimes I feel like the effects are just hitting me now. I know that probably sounds weird."

"No. I understand. I really do," he said gently.

Her dad's patience encouraged her to continue. "All I know is that if I go to Christmas with the family I'm going to come home feeling like a failure, just as I'm beginning to gain some confidence back. I think it will make me feel resentful, even angry at God."

He was silent on the other end, but she could hear him breathe. "Sweetheart," he finally said. "You're going to have to work through this in your own way and in your own time and that's okay. Your mom and I just want you to know that we're here when you need us. Okay?"

"I know that, Dad. I always know that."

She sensed his hesitation again and then his carefully chosen words. "But honey, your mom and I never loved you because you were perfect. Do you understand that? We love you because you're Ellie. You're special just as you are. We miss you when you're gone because we feel the loss of not seeing one of the most special and beautiful people we know. You can't fault your mom for missing you."

Ellie smiled into the receiver. "Oh Dad. You always know exactly what to say."

"It's just the truth," he chuckled.

"Okay. Well, if it makes you and Mom feel any better, there's a part of me that really wants to be there with you. I know it's hard with Nora too."

His voice was soft again. "I think that's what's been difficult for your mom. We're used to Nora going silent on us, but you, Ellie, have always been steady. We've relied on you to feel like good parents. We've put too much pressure on you to make up the ground for your sister. You need room to be you."

Ellie was speechless. She realized the truth in what he said, the ingrained pressure she always felt around them to be a good daughter. "Dad, thank you. I love you. Merry Christmas.

"We love you. Merry Christmas, Sweetheart."

* * *

During the first two days of winter break, the boys stayed at her parent's house and when she came to pick them up, she had coffee with her mother. She did all she could to reassure Sandra that their mother daughter relationship was still as solid as always. They talked, gossiped, and bantered like the good old days when Ellie was still a respectable married woman. They were both teachers and could spend hours in shop talk discussing teaching methods and past students. She held so much respect and admiration for her mother, who had served God, her husband, her family, her church and her thousands of students with a selfless servant heart. Ellie loved her company, especially when they connected as friends rather than as mother and daughter. When she related to her as a friend, she didn't have to reflect on the burden of following in the footsteps of a woman who lived like a saint. She hoped the visit would serve as a peace offering for a missed Christmas, but also that Sandra could forgive her for not following through with the unspoken promise to carry on her legacy. They were both pastor's wives and teachers committed to their faith. As a divorced woman, Ellie felt only the disappointment of the unfulfilled promise of her life.

Christmas Eve arrived and the day with the boys was pleasant, even in its strangeness. She took them Christmas shopping at the Grocery Outlet and they bought humorous gifts, including secret presents for her and Davis with the forty-dollar budget she gave them. John bought Miles a packet of underwear and Miles bought John a toothbrush holder. She helped them wrap their gifts when they got home and placed them under the tree. They made sugar cookies and watched Christmas movies. Davis arrived that evening to add his gifts to the pile. He and Ellie agreed that she would have the boys for the first week of winter break and he would take them the following week for New Years, but they set aside Christmas Eve for joint family time. The boys deserved to have the whole family together once in a while.

She was surprised to see that Davis put a wrapped gift under the small tree for her as well as the boys. In their years of marriage, Christmas gifts from her husband always seemed like an afterthought, but this gift was professionally wrapped in shiny crimson paper and a lavish gold bow. Ellie felt unsettled.

For the holiday dinner, she prepared prime rib, mashed potatoes with all the fixings, yams, salad, green beans, and mushroom gravy. The table was set with her mother's hand me down fine china and a gold tablecloth with a

184

poinsettia patterned table runner. The boys chattered excitedly as they ate. Ellie focused the conversation on them and avoided Davis' eyes. Despite laboring over the meal, she squirmed in her seat and could not taste a single bite. As soon as the boys were finished, Ellie suggested they open presents.

"Can we, really?" Miles asked.

"Don't we usually open them Christmas morning?" John added.

"Yes, but this year Dad is with us tonight, so we thought it might be fun to open at least your dad's gifts tonight."

As they moved as a family unit into the living room, Davis' hand traveled to Ellie's back. Her body stiffened at his touch.

"Boys, your mom and I worked to get you something special."

"Should we open the big gifts first?" John asked.

"Maybe you should open your presents from each other first," Ellie suggested.

Miles' eyes widened in bewilderment as he removed the underwear from its packaging. He glared at his brother.

"I didn't want underwear for Christmas," he groaned.

Ellie grinned. "You're growing and you'll certainly need them."

John smirked as he removed the toothpaste holder from the wrapping paper. He raised his eyebrows at his brother in question.

"I thought you could put your pencils in it for school," Miles said defensively.

Ellie glanced sideways at Davis and smiled. Davis grunted aloud to suppress his laughter.

Together Ellie and Davis opened bags full of candy and chocolates from the boys. Davis grinned, "Guess I'm putting off my diet for the foreseeable future."

John and Miles tore the reindeer wrapping paper off a larger present, a gift that Ellie and Davis bought together.

"Thanks Mom and Dad. Thanks so much." The boys hugged and kissed them both when they opened their new Nintendo Switch Lite and the new games that came with the portable console. They also received new pajamas, sweatshirts, and winter coats.

"We scored, Miles!"

"Yeah!" Miles agreed as the two boys fist pumped.

"Good to see them on the same team once in a while," Davis smiled as he turned his face to her.

"So, they fight at your house too? It's good to know I'm not the only one."

Davis moved closer to whisper in her ear. "Well, are you going to open the gift from me?"

She sighed as she remembered her vow to always tell the truth. "Davis, it makes me feel a little weird. I mean I appreciate it, but I didn't get you anything."

"Oh. Yeah. Don't worry about that. I just figured you went to all this effort to make dinner tonight and I'm just appreciative you let me be here."

Ellie nodded. "Oh, okay. That seems reasonable." She opened the wrapping paper carefully and removed a box. Davis watched her intently. Inside the container she removed tissue until she could see a splash of teal. She ran her fingers along the plush smooth cashmere sweater. "Wow. Davis. This fabric feels extremely expensive. This is a bit lavish."

"Do you like it Mom?" John asked.

Ellie smiled at John. "Well, yeah. Who doesn't like cashmere? Davis, are you sure this is okay? I feel a little strange accepting a gift like this."

"Mom, are you going to wear it? You'll look pretty." Miles climbed next to her on the couch and looked up at her. His dark eyelashes framed his wide eyes.

Ellie's eyes moistened as she gave her son a strained smile. "Not tonight, Miles, but it's a very nice gift." She folded the sweater and returned it to the box.

"Look, Ellie. I'm not trying to pull anything here. I saw it and thought of you. I've put you through hell. It will never be a good enough sorry, but I want you to know I'm sorry."

Ellie felt a flash of anger rise in her gut. *He buys me a cashmere sweater?* She swallowed the anger and kept her voice steady. "Thanks Davis. The gift is really expensive."

At 10 pm Ellie glanced at her watch. "I think it's about time to call it a night." Davis took the hint. He hugged the boys and kissed them good night. Ellie walked him to the door.

"Thanks for tonight Ellie. You have no idea how much it meant. I hope you like the sweater."

She turned to make sure the boys were out of earshot. "Davis, the sweater was nice, but if you really want to say you're sorry, please just stop." She looked him directly in the eyes. "Are you and Mariah still seeing each other?"

Davis' face tightened. "We're divorced Ellie. It's not really your business anymore."

Ellie felt the anger flash hot in her chest. "No, you're right. It's not my business anymore. I mean, it's only my business because you bought me a sweater that probably cost two hundred dollars and you said you were sorry."

Davis stared at her blankly. "I am sorry, Ellie."

"People who are sorry, change their lives, Davis. They stop doing the actions that hurt their wife, their children… If they say sorry, but continue with the hurtful behavior, well then the sorry doesn't mean anything. It's worthless."

Davis' eyes darkened. "I'm breaking it off with her. I really am. Ellie, I miss you. I miss the boys, but you're not my wife anymore."

She rolled her eyes. "Okay Davis. We're divorced and you're right. It's not my business what you do or who you sleep with, but you made our boys hope that we would get back together tonight. When you gave me that gift, they were hoping their old family would magically reunite again. I saw the look in their eyes, the hope. It broke my heart. Let's just stick to the truth. You're still sleeping with my niece who broke up our marriage. Right?"

Davis's response was stony silence.

"Don't buy me sweaters and don't say you're sorry if you don't really mean it."

Davis nodded his head. "Ellie, I really want to break up with her but…"

She felt faint as she shook her head. "Davis, don't you see? The only thing that matters is what you do. Goodnight." She shut the door and locked it. From the corner of her eye she thought she had seen Levi standing on his front porch watching the entire scene.

* * *

On Christmas morning Ellie went to the front door to let Cordelia out. To her surprise she found Christmas presents at the door and a note on loose leaf paper. She grabbed the bundle of presents and brought them into the house and set them on the kitchen table. She picked up the note and read:

Merry Christmas to our favorite neighbors,
Rae, Pax and I left early this morning for Sweet Home, but we wanted to wish you a Merry Christmas from our family to yours.
Rae, Levi, and Pax

The gifts were wrapped in puppy inspired Christmas paper and Ellie couldn't help but smile. She set them aside to open later when the boys were ready.

Christmas morning was a quiet affair. She made a fancy breakfast with waffles, whipped cream, and Marion berries. She fried bacon and scrambled eggs while gulping down coffee to hide the lack of sleep from the previous night. After breakfast the boys opened a few more presents from Ellie which consisted mostly of clothes they needed. Then came Levi and Ray's presents. John got a new leash and collar for Cordelia and Miles received a box of Legos. There was another chew toy for Cordelia. Ellie's heart skipped erratically as she opened her gift. *They didn't have to get me a gift,* she thought. She felt nervous for some reason. There was no box or tissue paper and when she tore the wrapping, she pulled out a long navy-blue shirt. Printed on the front was a picture of paintbrushes dipped in various colors and a stick figure of a woman smiling in front of an easel. Underneath were the digitally printed words. *Ms. Gold, the World's Best Art Teacher.*

Ellie smiled and then noticed a small handwritten note on the floor. She knelt to retrieve it and read.

Ellie,

Just so you know. This was Rae's project from beginning to end. She designed the T-shirt and I helped her get it printed. She thinks a lot of you. Now she's doing her own art projects just for fun. She even lets me look at them, instead of always having her nose in her sketchbook. It's nice to see. I owe you one.

Levi

Ellie traced Levi's words on the paper with her index finger. She folded the note carefully and placed it in her jewelry box in her bedroom. She didn't know why.

* * *

The first week of winter break had passed and the boys were with their father. Bitter cold had enveloped the valley causing the temperature to dip into the teens at night. Levi came over early in the morning and helped her insulate the henhouse. Rae was spending the week at her grandmother's, so they were both on their own. Even Pax had left with Rae. Cordelia remained with Ellie since Davis lived in an apartment that did not allow dogs. She was grateful for the pup's company. The unexpected time with Levi allowed her the opportunity to thank him for their gifts.

"What do you think?" Ellie unzipped her winter coat and modeled her new T shirt from Rae.

Levi grinned. "It looks good."

"I'm just afraid the other teachers will get jealous."

"I think you'll be okay. You're the only art teacher at the middle school, right?"

"Oh you're right. Guess I don't need to worry. On a serious note though. I'm really sorry I didn't get you and Rae anything."

Levi chuckled, "Are you kidding? We feel indebted to you. Rae's at your house all the time and you feed her constantly. It's nothing."

"Well, I really love the T-shirt, and it's, well…, a thoughtful gift. Please thank Rae for me. I might not see her again till we're back in school. The boys love their presents too. John's using the leash with Cordelia all the time and Miles has probably played with those Legos as much as he plays his video games."

Levi smiled. "Rae really was the driving force, but I'll tell her." He looked toward the sky. "The weather's changing. There's a front coming in. We could get some snow."

"It's really going to feel like winter, a winter wonderland. That will be nice."

"Not for me," Levi sighed. "Snow in Oregon means traffic accidents and power outages. A perfect storm for chaos."

Ellie frowned as she considered the dangers of Levi's job. "I hope not."

* * *

The snow began to fall around 10 pm. The flakes were fat and heavy and since the weather had been so cold, they stuck quickly to the frozen ground and pavement. Ellie watched as her yard transformed into a sea of luminous white. Mesmerized by the beauty, she stroked Cordelia and sipped hot chocolate by the window. She glanced over at Levi's dark and empty house. He was out in this, helping stranded motorists and saving lives. She said a quiet prayer for his safety before she went to bed.

Ellie woke to the sound of Cordelia's whines. She rose abruptly to a black, cold house. She shivered and scrambled through the drawer of her bedside table to find her phone. When she pressed the power, she noted the time, 2:35 a.m. and then tapped the flashlight. The house was so icy, she could practically see her breath through the glow of her screen. The heavy snow must have downed a powerline, she realized. Even more disturbing was the sound of running water. Ellie moved quickly and threw on a pair of jeans, wooly socks, and boots. She opened the dog crate and Cordelia bolted to her side. She navigated her way through the forbidding house to the front door where she grabbed her winter coat. When she opened the door, the sound of running water intensified. The snow now looked about three feet deep and was still coming down, although not as heavily as before. She walked carefully through the snow and followed the sound of water to the back of the house. Cordelia trailed her and began to prance in the new fallen snow. Water was bursting forcefully out of a pipe and now a pool of water and ice filled the back corner behind the house.

"No!" she cried aloud. *What do I do?*

She thought carefully. *I need to turn off the water.* She looked around the house trying to locate the water main. *How can I find it, when it's buried in snow?* She thought she remembered seeing a ground panel for the water main toward the front of the house. She moved as quickly as she could through three feet of snow toward where she hoped the main might be. With her bare hands she scraped snow out of the way. In a matter of minutes her hands were aching with cold and her fingertips looked blue even under the light of her phone. She rose from the ground and went back into the house to search for gloves. With the help of her phone flashlight, she found a pair in a drawer. In horror she realized she only had ten percent of battery life remaining. Returning to the site where she hoped the main might be, she continued digging in the snow. She was wet, desperate and miserable. When she finally reached the ground with her gloved fingers, she could not find the ground panel. Glancing briefly at her phone, she saw now that the battery was at seven percent. Panic overwhelmed her. She was just about to dial Levi's number when the Tahoe pulled into the driveway next door. Despite the snow and the dark, Levi spotted Cordelia running and his eyes scanned the yard till he met her gaze. She could not read his face due to the distance between them but his eyebrows creased with worry under the dome light of the SUV. He immediately dashed out of the Tahoe and bounded toward her through the snow.

"What happened?" he said breathlessly when he was within voice range.

"I woke up to a dark house and the sound of water," Ellie said, her voice ragged.

"What are you doing? You're going to freeze out here." He looked at her under the beam of his flashlight. She was shivering and snow was caked to her long hair.

"There's a pool of ice water growing in my yard. I was trying to find the main to shut off the water."

Levi observed her shivering and suddenly pulled her to him, wrapping her in his arms in an effort to keep her warm. He looked down at her with concern. "I know where your main is. I'll turn it off. Look, you're freezing. Go into my house. You've got electricity, but my house runs on natural gas. I've got a generator. You can start the fireplace just by pressing a button and you'll be warm before you know it. I switched the fireplace to a battery starter before I went to work. I'll be there soon."

"No, I've got my house. I don't want to put you out."

"Stop being ridiculous. Here's my key. Go in."

Ellie did as instructed. Levi was sounding more like a police officer than her friend and she didn't dare disobey. He was right. The house was wonderfully warm. Cordelia followed her as she moved to the fireplace through the dark house and turned on the switch. Within seconds flames ignited cheerfully under the glass panel. Ellie took off her heavy wet coat and sat on the couch next to the front window made visible by the flickering light of the fireplace. Cordelia settled next to her and she pet her soft wet fur as she watched Levi. He was gathering tools from the Tahoe and moving toward a location a few feet away from where Ellie had been digging in the snow. He struggled and worked in the harsh elements for nearly half an hour. She watched as he put the tools back into the truck and then her eyes followed his deliberate gait as he moved back toward the house.

When he entered, Ellie wanted to bury her face in shame. He would think she was so stupid. She didn't even know where her own water main was, and she was a homeowner. Levi came in slightly out of breath. "I turned off the valve. The water's stopped. I guess you didn't winterize your pipes."

Ellie felt sheepish. "My dad told me I needed to do it, but I just forgot, and the Willamette Valley doesn't usually get the snow, so I guess I just made a bad bet."

Levi nodded. "I should have checked on it for you."

She shook her head. "No, Levi. I just didn't prioritize the house like I should have. You already do so much to help me out."

He took off his wet jacket and hung it in the closet. His pants were damp like hers. He moved toward her on the couch and gently coaxed Cordelia to move so he could sit next to her and warm up by the fire. She could see his handsome, strong face in the firelight, and she felt a sudden longing for him.

They sat in silence for a few moments looking at the fire. Levi finally spoke. "I'll go to the hardware store in the morning and see if I can replace the pipe. It looks like you've just got one cracked spot and fortunately it doesn't appear to be under the ground."

Ellie felt a strong desire to rest her head on his shoulder, but she restrained herself. She turned and looked at him instead. "Thanks Levi. I appreciate it. I don't know what I would have done if you hadn't pulled up."

His eyes searched her face. He grazed the side of her cheek gently with his rough hand. "I'm glad I was here. It was a crazy night. There were several accidents on Route 126 and some home emergencies."

Ellie closed her eyes and felt the nervous beating of her heart as Levi removed twigs and leaves from her hair. "Don't you get tired of being everyone's hero?"

He chuckled. "That's a little much, but I knew from a pretty young age that I wanted to help people."

She was so tired now, she felt almost drunk. "You really do help people. You don't just say it. You do it."

He shrugged, "Well, yes. That's the only way to help."

"I'm so tired," Ellie said. "The fire's warm and it's making me sleepy."

Levi's face was unreadable. "You'll sleep here. Take my bed if you want. I mean, I wouldn't mind sleeping on the couch," he said quickly.

"Oh no. I couldn't let you do that."

He hesitated. "Okay. Stay here then. I'll be right back." She watched him rise from the couch and head toward the back of the dark house. He came back after a few minutes carrying a flannel shirt and a toothbrush still in the box. "You're still wet from the snow. If I remember correctly, women like to sleep in oversized men's clothing, so I brought you one of my largest, softest flannels and I've got a toothbrush here that's brand new. I think you'll sleep a lot better if you're dry and comfortable."

"Thanks Levi," she said as she took the flannel and the toothbrush.

"The bathroom's the first door on the right in the hallway. There are fresh towels, and you can even take a hot shower. I've got a flashlight for you too."

"Levi?"

"Yes Ellie."

"Did you know it's almost four in the morning?"

"What a night," he grinned.

"When do you think the electricity will come back on?"

"That's anyone's guess, but usually it takes eight hours at least."

"Okay then. Goodnight."

"Goodnight Ellie."

She watched him walk past the kitchen and turn down the hallway toward his bedroom. Ellie followed a few minutes later to the bathroom and changed into the flannel and brushed her teeth. She ran her fingers through her tangled hair. Being in Levi's home put her nerves on edge and she tried to stay as quiet and unobtrusive as possible.

When Ellie returned to the couch, she saw that Levi had left several soft blankets and a pillow. Levi's flannel went down to her knees and was soft to the touch and warm. She did her best to settle into a comfortable position on the couch and Cordelia likewise curled on the floor next to her. She closed her eyes thinking of Levi.

She woke to the sound of birds chirping. Levi's house was still dark, and she could see a slim band of light filtering across the sky. She guessed the time to be around 7 am. The lights were still out and Ellie realized the fire and warmth of the house had made her desperately thirsty. She rose and tiptoed toward the bathroom and quickly brushed her teeth before heading back to the kitchen. Cordelia raised her head to watch Ellie's movements before dropping her head back onto her paws to sleep. *Rough night,* Ellie thought and smiled. She opened the cupboard door looking for a glass but could find only mugs. She grabbed a dark blue coffee mug and pressed the porcelain surface to the ice dispenser. The refrigerator must have been running on the generator because the ice rushed out noisily. She pressed the rim to the water dispenser and watched as her mug filled. She was so thirsty, she stood facing the refrigerator and sipped greedily.

From behind she heard the sound of bare feet on hardwood. She felt tense as she became aware of Levi's presence. He stood behind her and she sensed him move deliberately toward her. She felt his hand softly graze her shoulder and gather her long hair, which he placed to the side of her face exposing the back of her neck. He bent his head and brushed his lips gently on tender skin. "Ellie," he whispered into her ear.

The mug trembled in her hand as she turned to look at him. His eyes darkened with intensity. He took the mug gently from her hand and laid it on the kitchen island behind him. He placed his hands on her waist and pulled her to him. He brought his face to hers and kissed her with firm insistence. Ellie returned the kiss and brought her arms around his shoulders and neck. She allowed herself to melt into him as he repeatedly kissed her. For a moment she slipped into a realm of bliss she had never known before.

Levi shifted her around till her back was against the kitchen island. He lifted her gently till she was sitting on the counter. They were eye to eye now and he looked at her and brushed his fingers lightly across her lips. "I couldn't sleep," he whispered hoarsely. "I'm exhausted and I can't sleep because I know you're here in my house. You drive me crazy." He bent his head to hers and kissed her again.

Ellie kissed him back, but her mind was spinning. "Stop. Please stop," she cried as she broke away.

He was instantly concerned. "What is it?"

The emotions from the deeply concealed pool inside began to seep out of her. "I'm sorry. Levi, I'm sorry. I just can't. I don't know you." She jumped down from the island and bolted to the living room. Cordelia was up and wagging her tail. Ellie found her jeans and pulled them on and then her shoes.

"Where are you going?"

"I'll go to my house. Please don't try to stop me."

Levi looked at her stunned. "Ellie, I'm sorry. I wasn't trying to push you into anything. I just want to be with you."

The fountain burst inside of her. "Levi. I just don't trust myself."

His voice was gentle. "Can you trust me?"

Her breathing was heavy and ragged. "No. I can't."

"Okay," Levi's voice was calm. "Can we just sit down and talk about it for a sec before you go storming off?"

Ellie was pacing Levi's living room. "I don't want to sit down."

"Okay. You don't have to, but you need to talk to me. What's going on? Don't you realize we're made for each other?"

Ellie sighed. She found it painful to look him in the eye. "Don't you see ? I'm damaged goods Levi?"

"I don't believe that, Ellie."

"Well I am. Something happened over a year ago when I was married, before the divorce and I haven't been okay since."

Levi's voice was steady, his eyes trained on her. "What happened, Ellie?"

"I don't want to tell you. I don't want you to see me as some stupid, tragic victim."

"I'm not going to see you that way. That's not how I could ever see you."

Ellie let a rush of air escape her lips. "This wasn't supposed to be my life, Levi. I was supposed to be riding off into the sunset, posting my perfect family photos on Facebook. I'm from a ministry family and I went to seminary to be a minister. I wanted to do youth ministry or art ministry. I went all the way to North Carolina. Anyway, I met Davis there. I thought we were on the same page. I just thought my life would be a certain way."

Levi's eyes stayed with her and he listened. "You were married a long time, weren't you?"

She nodded. "Yeah, over fifteen years. He preached every Sunday. We visited people, prayed with them. We had two beautiful boys. I thought it was real."

"What happened?"

"I guess he fell out of love with me. He told me one night that he was having an affair and then I learned that he was sleeping with my nineteen-year-old niece."

Levi winced at her words. "Oh Ellie. I'm sorry," he said beneath his breath.

196

He moved toward her as if he wanted to comfort her, but she stopped him with her hand.

"Anyway, I thought that I had done everything right, you know? I loved him. I really did. I didn't hold anything back and I was rejected. My niece is beautiful. She's also the most selfish person I've ever encountered. I just have a lot of anger, I guess. I also don't have a lot of trust in my own judgement."

"Ellie, we all feel like damaged goods. When Melinda died, I was angry at myself, at her, at God. It's part of the grieving process. It's okay. You're going to come out of this even better. You're going to come out of this with me. We've both been through hell. Don't you think there might be a force up there that's rooting for us?"

"Levi. I can't. I just can't. I don't know how I feel about you. I don't know if I could ever really love anyone again. You deserve real love and I'm a shell of a person."

Levi's face was tight and controlled. "I don't believe that. You just need time. Don't you know me? Haven't I shown you who I am?"

Tears welled in her eyes. "I don't trust you. I don't trust myself." She grabbed her coat and walked out the door. Cordelia trailed behind her.

Chapter 16

Part III

Fixtures

> *Sometimes having coffee*
> *with your best friend is all the*
> *therapy you need.*
> *—Anonymous*

On the surface Ellie's life hardly seemed to change at all after the night with Levi, but she struggled to hide the seismic shift in her heart. There was now a chasm between them that neither knew how to cross. They waved at each other from across their yards and engaged in small talk in front of the kids. They skated around each other as though on thawing ice. Levi arrived that fateful morning and fixed her pipe as he said he would and then packed his tools. With determination in his gait, he walked back to his property and shut the door. The invisible barrier between them was an unspoken agreement where Levi consented to stay at bay and she battled the sea of her grieving heart a safe distance from each other. She longed for him, but also felt the heavy burden of her guilt, pain, and pride weighing her down like a millstone.

When Allison called her to see if she was ready to resume Bible study, Ellie could have kissed her. She found that she longed for the company of her female friends with a passion that caught her completely off guard. The epiphany that she needed them arrived with clarity one night in a vision.

Ellie found that she could no longer sleep. Nightmares visited her almost every night. The tidal wave dream returned with awful force. This time she searched endlessly and hopelessly for her two boys under volumes of murky, debris filled water. In another dream she was at a bus stop with Miles. He was grasping her hand and she was listening to his soft chatter when she was interrupted by a man with a newspaper asking for directions. When she turned back to Miles he was gone. She went inside to search the bus, she scoured the city streets and ran along both sides of the river. The possibilities of where Miles was hidden defied the logic of time and physics. She searched for him high and low but came up empty and in a breathless panic. Never had she felt so lost, so afraid. She woke up trembling and covered in sweat.

But sometimes with trials, comes the glimmer of hope, Ellie thought. When the nightmares first emerged, she tried to ease her anxious heart with prayers to God, but He was not there. When she tried to talk to Him about the fear, the anger, and her inability to forgive Davis' betrayal, her mind would go blank. One night she had a vivid night terror of a tornado whirling through her property. She saw herself clinging desperately to her sons as the wind's force separated and lifted them all into a black night. She awoke in a cold sweat, her body shaking. In that frightening moment she realized the battle she was fighting was a spiritual one. She closed her eyes and sifted through every comforting image she could imagine, and her mind finally rested on the Praying Sisters. The thought of them was so vivid and powerful, Ellie recognized the vision for what it was, a message from above. She remembered her father preaching about the power of visions when she was a girl. He used to say, "If you're ever visited by a vision from God, it's best to stop and pay attention." She could feel the presence of God directing her thoughts telling her to pay attention.

Jewel sat next to her. She felt her presence more than she saw her in the dream. Allison, Ruby, and Harmony completed the circle around the fire. The orange velvet throw was wrapped around her shoulders and the warmth from the fire traveled through her limbs into the marrow of her bones. Her eyes traveled to the faces around the circle and she felt the energy of each woman, the power of their different spiritual gifts.

Allison projected a warm and generous heart which Ellie felt from the heat of the orange throw, which in her mind was an extension of Allison herself. Ruby exuded strength and humor. Her warm brown eyes were filled with experience and pain, like an old soul whose pains and struggles only made her stronger. From Harmony, Ellie felt the strength of a truth teller, a problem solver, wise beyond her years, a woman unafraid to be herself. She finally turned her head to look at Jewel and her eyes rested on her features almost like she was seeing her for the first time. Under Jewel's gaze, Ellie felt covered in interested compassion. Her eyes were wise enough to see through the surface of things and zero in on the true pain a person was trying to hide. Jewel was a healer. Ellie soaked in their gifts like a porous sponge. Acceptance was the one word that encompassed the entire vision, and she knew God had finally given her the direction she had been longing for. In the middle of that dark night, she wanted to see the Praying Sisters as desperately as a penitent sinner longs to see a priest. She needed to unburden herself, to confess. She longed to tell them everything about Davis, about Levi, everything she could not let go. She prayed for their wisdom. She could no longer live without peace.

* * *

Allison embraced her at the door. "I hope your holidays were amazing."

She shook her head and the tears welled up before she could stop them. "It was pretty terrible. Levi hates me now."

Allison raised her eyebrows. "Levi could never hate you. Come in. You need coffee, pie, and maybe just a smidge of prayer."

She followed Allison to the kitchen where the Praying Sisters sat laughing joyously around the kitchen island. Outside the rain poured, but around the kitchen table were the comforts of food, coffee and friendship. She felt their joy and knew she had arrived at the place she needed to be.

Each woman embraced her in turn. They saw her tears and waited patiently for her to unburden her troubles.

Ruby patted the stool next to her. "Ellie, spill the tea. We're listenin'."

She laughed in spite of herself. "Well, I hope you don't mind getting sloshed with the tea I'm about to spill."

Harmony looked her in the eye. "There's nothing you could say that would change our affection for you."

"Here, here," Jewel agreed. She took her pink blazer off and hung it on the back of the barstool settling in to hear Ellie's story.

Allison set coffee and pecan pie in front of her before claiming the spot across the table.

Ellie took a deep breath and then told them everything. She told them the truth about Davis, her marriage, Mariah, and Nora. Her friends did not interrupt her but listened with empathy. Ruby could not contain her reactions and did break in with an occasional, "Oh Lord Jesus" or "Heavenly Father." After Ellie covered the backstory of her marriage, the betrayal, and her broken relationship with her sister, she confessed her growing affection for Levi and her inability to move forward with him the night the power went out. "I just can't seem to let the past go. I want to see where things could go with Levi, but everything feels wrong." When she finished, her friends surrounded her with love.

"Oh Ellie," Allison said. "I'm so sorry. Some men really know where to hit us where we're the most vulnerable. You've been so strong." She put her arm around her and squeezed.

Harmony was shaking her head in disbelief, her blood boiling unable to comment.

Jewel placed her hand on Ellie's. "I'm so glad you told us. I'm going to pray for you every night. You're intuitive Ellie. If you can't move forward with Levi, there's a reason why. We've got to find out what it is."

Ruby nodded. "Forgiveness is messy business. They don't tell us women that in the movies, but it is."

Allison pulled out her Bible. "You know, it's funny. The scripture I was going to share with you all today is Colossians chapter three. Let me read some verses to you. *Therefore, as God's chosen people, holy and dearly loved, clothe yourselves with compassion, kindness, humility, gentleness and patience. Bear with each other and forgive one another if any of you has a grievance against someone. Forgive as the Lord forgave you. And over all these virtues put on love, which binds them all together in perfect unity.* What do you ladies think? Is God telling us something here?"

Ellie frowned and shook her head. "I know if I'm going to be the better person that I'm supposed to forgive. I am trying. I do a pretty good job of forgiving on the surface. Davis comes over, he picks up the kids. We can engage in small talk. It's just in here." Ellie placed her hand over her heart. "I haven't really forgiven him, and I can't get past the hurt."

"Don't be so hard on yourself," Harmony insisted. "These things take time and isn't there such a thing as righteous anger?"

Ellie nodded, but then shook her head again. "Yes, but I know now the anger is getting in my way. It's destroying my peace. I have horrible nightmares where I'm trying to find my children and we're all scattered apart and just lost."

"Oh Ellie," Jewel sighed. "I know that pressure of having to be responsible for everyone else. That's a very difficult position if you're not being fed yourself."

Ruby nodded thoughtfully. "I only tell this story because I think it might help ya. I've had so much anger in my life that sometimes it just felt like I was marinatin' in a mixture of bitterness and resentment. I've always believed that there are energies out there. There's God's energy, goodness, light, everything wonderful and then there's darkness, evil, despair, the thangs of Satan. I was born in a cloud of negative energy in Choctaw Louisiana, a sawmill town if there ever wuz one. That town wuz so poor the children had tumbleweeds for pets. My daddy died before I knew him in an accident at the sawmill. My mama was the kind of woman that could not be alone, not even for a few weeks. She had to have a man around, even if he wuz a bad one. My brother Dean and me went from one abuse to the next,

Lord, I'm telling ya, all because of the company she was keepin'. I think our lives woulda pretty much have been a one-way ticket to the grave if it wasn't for Ms. Emma Ray Langston. She wuz an eighty-two-year-old retired schoolteacher, a widow livin' on social security. That woman took my brother and I into her home when we had no other place to go. She's the one who taught me how to cook, can every scrap of food from the garden, and clean like there wuz no tomorruh. She also kept my head screwed on right and made me study and focus on the future. I loved that woman. I spent a good deal of my young days just survivin' and the anger toward my mama and all her boyfriends began to eat me to the bone. Ms. Emma asked me not long before she died, *When ya gonna stop being a member of the walking wounded and get busy doin' the thangs the Lord has planned for you?* I can't say that I understood that right away, but I began to realize that I could take steps. Maybe baby steps, but steps nevertheless to healin' muhself, with the Lord's help. My first step was to go to teachin' school and change my perspective, focus a bit on somethin' positive rather than my hate."

Ellie nodded. "You're amazing Ruby. You've been through so much. You probably think I should just get over myself."

"Lord, not at all. There are few thangs worse than betrayal, but when a mama betrays her own children, I don't think it's too different than a husband betrayin' his wife. I'm just saying you're not alone in it."

"So, what's my first step?"

Ruby laughed, "Oh Lord, wouldn't it be a summer day in heaven if someone could just tell us? Yer first step is between you and the Lord. I believe when a person listens, God speaks."

"Ellie, you're not the only person struggling with forgiveness. It's not easy. Maybe a lifetime pursuit," Jewel added.

As her time with the Sisters drew to a close, Ruby pulled Ellie aside. "I'd like to ask a favor?"

"Uh, maybe. What's the favor?" Ellie responded cautiously.

"Every Saturday mornin', I teach some students. I was hopin' you might be willin' to do an art lesson for about twelve to fifteen students? Nothin' complicated, but fun for kids between five and twelve. Do ya think ya could?"

"Uh, yeah. I think I could. Davis has the boys most Saturdays so I think it would work."

"Alrighty then. I'll be at yer house around seven a.m."

"Seven a.m. on a Saturday!" Ellie groaned. "That's my one day to sleep in."

"Oh sweetie, it'll be worth it. I promise."

* * *

She woke up that first weekend in February with no idea what to expect. She dressed hastily and put her hair in a bun. By six am she was gulping coffee while traveling from the barn to the front of the house preparing art supplies including a small class set of easels, smocks, and paints for a small art class. Ellie shivered under her winter coat. Ruby pulled up not long after in an older model Honda Odyssey. A man was driving, and Ellie assumed he was Clyde, Ruby's husband. Both Ruby and Clyde got out of the minivan, while keeping the engine running. Clyde was tall and thin. The corners of his eyes drooped down slightly giving him a tired look.

"Clyde's gonna help ya put yer thangs in the back. He helps me every Saturday. He's as sweet as my mama's iced tea."

Clyde waved his hand dismissively, but he smiled, and the smile transformed his face. "Hello Ellie. I've heard a lot about you." Clyde's accent was not as thick as Ruby's. Ellie wondered if he was an Oregon native and perhaps the reason Ruby had moved from Louisiana.

"Hi Clyde. It's nice to meet you too. Thanks for helping me with my gear."

Clyde nodded and began loading the car. Ellie and Ruby helped squeeze the materials into an already packed cargo space. Once they were in the van, the sky began to spit out icy rain.

Ruby turned to her husband. "Be careful on the road there Clyde honey."

He did not answer but rather grunted his response. Ellie's impression was Clyde was a taciturn man and Ruby most likely dominated the conversations in their house.

"Ellie this is gonna be a treat. Yer gonna meet some of my favorite little students."

"Where are we going exactly? And why are you being so mysterious?"

"I don't like to ruin surprises," Ruby insisted.

They left Veneta behind them and began to climb an old mountain road. As they gained elevation the ice turned to snow. Clyde was a slow and cautious driver. When they reached the ten-mile post Clyde pulled off the main road and drove into the woods. An inch of snow now coated the ground and she saw tents and campers on both sides of them and people walking around.

"What is this place?" Ellie asked.

"This is none other than the campground. These people here are off the grid. This is no official campground. We're on loggin' land, but a little camp sprung up here 'bout four years ago. Most of the people here wanna be left alone. They're homeless or evadin' the law, wrestlin' their pain or addiction."

"Um, Ruby. What are we doing here?"

"Teachin'," Ruby said. "There's kids here, you see. Some of us women in the community decided we'd set up a Saturday schoolhouse. It's been over a year now. And now I can't imagine not comin'."

Ellie zipped her coat and put on her orange knitted cap. She was glad she was wearing boots. Ruby and Ellie took an armful of teaching supplies and headed through the layer of snow toward a large white tent set up toward the middle of the campground. As Ellie walked in she was almost ploughed over by Levi on his way out.

Ellie almost lost her balance and her grasp on the box she was carrying, but Levi grabbed her elbow and steadied her. He supported the box with his other hand. "I'm sorry," he said instinctually and then studied her with his eyes, "Ellie," he almost whispered.

"Levi, I'm sorry. I don't know where I'm going. I was just following Ruby."

"She's over there," Levi indicated with his eyes. "You alright?" he asked.

"Yeah. I got it. Thanks."

"Alright then." He proceeded out of the tent.

Ellie took a deep breath and consciously shifted her thoughts away from

Levi. Her eyes searched the space with awe. "You could fit fifty people in here."

"And we do on occasion," Ruby chuckled.

The wide frame tent had been decorated to feel cozy and welcoming. Colorful rugs were placed in the central learning space, desks, a chalkboard, bean bags, and even a few computer stations. "Wow, who's funding this?"

A few of the churches in town and believe it or not Harmony and her husband Steve are a big help. They don't just breed dogs you know?"

Ellie's eyes widened. "No, I don't know. Tell me."

Ruby was unpacking teaching supplies and placing them on a large desk positioned in front of the smaller desks. "Harmony and Steve run a food program through their farm. Well it started as a food program. Now, Carrey Farms has become a charitable organization and they've helped to gather funding for programs like this one and a few others."

Ellie shook her head in surprise. "I had no idea."

"Harmony is the last person in the world to brag about her accomplishments, so there's no way to know these thangs unless someone tells ya."

"I saw Levi."

Ruby nodded and smiled. "Oh yes. He helps out a couple times a month here. Someones gotta set up the tent, keep the generator runnin', and the kids love him."

"They do?"

"Sweet Ellie. That's a good man there, but I think ya know that." Ruby smiled knowingly.

She ignored the comment. At that moment Clyde and Levi came into the room carrying easels. "Where you want these Ellie?" Clyde asked.

"Oh, thank you Clyde, Levi. If you could set them up in rows about four feet apart. That would be great." She noticed that Levi seemed to avoid her eyes. She busied herself setting up each station and placing protective smocks at each desk. Volunteers began to filter into the tent. Ellie subtly tracked Levi's movements in and out feeling her heart quicken every time he entered the space. Suddenly she heard a chorus of voices.

"Miss Ruby, Miss Ruby!" Ruby spread her arms out wide as a group of three children who looked to be about five to six years old came into the tent. She hugged and greeted them each.

"It's so warm in here," a little girl said.

"Levi and Clyde have been workin' all mornin' to get it just right for y'all. You know why?"

She shook her head.

"Cuz you're important."

Ellie saw the flash of joy on the small girl's face and it melted her heart. A few minutes later about fifteen children filled the space and sat crisscross applesauce on the various rugs. Ruby read the children a story and they listened with rapt attention. She was a natural storyteller and Ellie couldn't help but smile at the different voices and expressions she used when reading. *No wonder the kids love her,* Ellie thought.

When story time was over, Ruby instructed the children to choose a book from a special shelf she had brought just for today and to find a spot on a rug or a bean bag to sit on and read. A little boy with long stringy hair in a threadbare T-shirt and jeans much too small for him approached Ellie with a Scooby Doo book. "Will you read to me?"

"Of course." She followed him to a shag orange carpet and sat down crisscross applesauce. To her surprise the little boy crawled right into her lap.

"What's your name?" he asked.

"Uh, I'm Miss Ellie," she said. "What's your name?"

"Luke," he said in a barely audible voice.

"Hi Luke." He settled into her lap and Ellie began to read. "Scooby and Shaggy had always been best friends and they loved chocolate sundaes." As she read, Luke relaxed in her lap. He reached his little hand up and gently grabbed a lock of her hair. While she read, he twirled her hair in his fingers. Ellie thought he might suck his thumb with his other hand. He was so small and vulnerable, and Ellie felt a little emotionally overwhelmed, but she continued to read and focused on keeping her voice steady. She remembered reading to John and Miles and the memories flooded her. The tent was warm and around her she felt happiness and joy in the space as volunteers read with children. All she wanted to do was to keep little Luke safe and to protect him from harm.

Ellie glanced upward and saw that Levi had entered the tent again. He was looking at her mesmerized, his face unreadable. Ellie flushed under his gaze. Fifteen minutes later, she was at the front of the makeshift classroom, showing the students how to use watercolors and to draw whatever they thought was the most beautiful thing in the world. "It doesn't matter if your watercolors don't look exactly like what you're trying to paint. What's more important is the colors you choose and what they say. Do you see trees, water, flowers, mountains? Each color communicates and reminds us of this beautiful world." Little Luke had refused to leave her side, so she simply placed him beside her at the teacher's easel and they worked together. He was enjoying blending all the colors together.

Ellie smiled. He painted in a similar way to Miles. "See how all the colors end up looking gray. I think what you're creating looks like rocks. That's awesome," Ellie encouraged. Luke looked up at her and smiled before dipping his brush into the red. Levi appeared suddenly. "Sheriff Levi!" Luke said with awe.

Levi tipped his sheriff's hat to the little boy. "Hello Mr. Luke. I'd like to see what you're painting." He turned subtly to Ellie. "I'll give you a little break so you can check in with the other kids."

"Good idea. Thanks." Ellie walked the room and checked in with each of the children and the volunteers. Ruby was helping a group of children in the back.

"Great lesson," Ruby said when Ellie reached her. "I'm gonna strong arm ya into comin' more often."

Ellie laughed. "I'm enjoying it, Ruby."

* * *

Ruby and Ellie were both out of breath by the time the children left and their supplies packed up and ready to go. Ellie had hugged little Luke goodbye. He had begged her to come back. She was careful not to make promises she couldn't keep. With boys of her own who often suffered disappointment at the hands of a father who sometimes broke promises, Ellie treaded carefully. The truth was, she wanted to come back. She wanted to see Luke again and encourage and love him. In that room working with other volunteers, she felt a high, a feeling of pure joy and purposefulness. Once a person has a taste of joy like that, they begin to crave it, that feeling that life can mean so much more.

Clyde was his taciturn self as they drove home, but Ruby talked a mile a minute. "Girl, you just did so good! You're a teacher already, so I knew you'd just be a natural, but that Luke, the way he just crawled into your lap. That was just precious."

"Yes." Ellie agreed. "Do you know much about him?"

"Well, just about every story in that tent is a sad one. Little Luke lost his mama to drugs. I don't mean she's dead or nuthin'. She's just lost. No one knows where she is. I don't think Luke even knows his daddy. He lives with his grand daddy. He calls him papa. When his papa was still workin' he did construction and his body's gone to hell in a handbasket. He takes prescription drugs for the pain, but he abuses 'em and he's raisin' that little boy at the same time."

"Is he a mean man?"

"Nah, but neglectful. Little Luke just runs around that camp gettin' underfoot."

They sat in silence for just a moment before Ruby broke the quiet. "Ellie? You thought at all about the first step?"

"The first step?"

"Yes, what we were talkin' about with the Prayin' Sisters? We were discussin' healin' and findin' that first step. You found it yet?"

Ellie thought for a moment before an epiphany overwhelmed her. "Ruby! You know what? I got it. I know the first step."

"Well, praise the Lord. I knew you would."

* * *

Ellie wrapped her sweater more tightly around her chest as she watched the intent expressions of her seventh and eighth graders as they tried to master the art of making an origami crane. She walked the room and encouraged several students and gave others pointers as she observed their work. She gave Natalie a quick nod from across the room and Rae a big thumbs up. That girl was so talented with her hands and had natural dexterity like her father. She was a wizard with origami. She finally made the journey to the back corner where Mason sat. His origami crane was a certified disaster and he had about five other crumpled attempts on his desk. Ellie bent down and spoke quietly. "Mason, do you think we could talk out in the hall for just a few minutes."

Mason rolled his eyes and looked at her with such a hostile expression that Ellie felt her confidence almost disappear. She tried again, "You're not in trouble I promise. I just realized there's something important I need to speak with you about. You can go out in the hall first and I'll meet you in a minute." She was trying hard to make sure the conversation with Mason wasn't attracting attention from the other students.

Ellie walked back toward the front of the class and through her peripheral vision saw Mason stand and move toward the door as she requested. She continued to supervise the class for a couple more minutes and then darted out into the hall. Mason was leaning against the lockers, his arms crossed over his chest. She recognized the defensive posture. Ellie said a quick prayer in her head, asking God for the right words. "Mason, thanks for agreeing to talk to me. I appreciate it."

Mason's expression betrayed nothing, and he kept his hostile stance and refused to look her in the eye.

"I wanted to apologize to you," she continued. "I know the incident with the chick happened a while ago, but I've had some time to reflect on it and what I said to you and I think I did some things wrong."

Mason's posture changed. His arms were still crossed around his chest, but his eyes were wide with curiosity.

"Anyway, I think what I missed is that you've been going through a really hard time and you've kind of done an amazing job hiding it and doing the things you need to do. You've been coming to school every day, trying to stay up on your classes, socializing with your friends. I know you help your brothers too. You've taken a lot on yourself. I just want you to know that I see that about you and I admire it. I think you're a good kid. Actually, kind of an amazing one."

Mason dropped his arms and turned his face from Ellie, his eyes tracking the ceiling. She did not want to embarrass him. "I had a really hard time a year ago myself. Someone I loved left me. It was really hard. I didn't do well with that at all. I only bring it up because I want you to know that I see you and that you have a friend."

Mason rubbed his eyes with the back of his sleeve. "You know about my mom?"

"Yeah. I do. It's a small town," Ellie said quietly.

Mason stared back up at the ceiling. "She used to make us lunches. Sometimes I'd open my lunch and there'd be a PB and J sandwich. She'd put a smiley face in it by pressing M&Ms into the bread. She was funny like that."

"I like that," Ellie said with a smile.

"She liked art. She used to paint too," Mason said.

"Well, I hope we can learn some ideas on how to remember her in this class. Art can be pretty awesome for that."

Mason took a ragged breath. "I think we better go back inside."

"You're right, but thanks for letting me talk to you." Ellie returned to class and directed her students through the cleanup process. Before the bell rang, she traveled to her lunch box and took out the homemade PB and J sandwich she had made for lunch. She wrote a quick message on a sticky note and placed it on the Ziploc bag.

I know this won't be as good as you mom's, but sometimes something homemade is nice. This is a truce.

Ms. Gold.

Ellie stood by the door when the bell rang and said goodbye to her students. Without speaking she handed the Ziploc bag to Mason as he went through the door. His eyebrows furrowed as he stared back at her, but then took the bag. Ellie thought she might have seen just a hint of a smile.

Chapter 17

Floors

Everyone who drinks this water
Will be thirsty again,
But whoever drinks the water
I give them
Will never thirst.
Indeed, the water I give them
will become in them
a spring of water
welling up to eternal life.
—John 4:13-14

"So, ya gonna tell us about the first step?" Ruby asked Ellie.

"What first step? What are you talking about?" Harmony interjected.

They were around the table again with apple pie this time, courtesy of Ruby's orchards and Allison's baking prowess. The pie was the perfect blend of tart and sweet with a blast of cinnamon. Ellie was savoring every bite while basking in the glow of her coterie of friends.

"Let me bring ya up to speed. Last week we were talking about healin' and the steps ya take to get there. Ellie told me she found her first step,"

Ruby continued.

"You did?" Jewel turned her head to scrutinize her. "Spill it Ellie. I want to hear everything." She pulled her chair closer in a conspiratorial fashion.

Ellie tried to find words. "You know. I don't think I should talk about it. All I can say is God pointed me in the right direction. I made a mistake in how I treated someone. Ruby got me to think clearly is all. I realized you might not be able to face the biggest monster in your life even if it's staring you in the face, but you might be able to pick off a smaller, less fierce one."

Allison smiled and nodded. "Good for you. That's not an easy thing you know. I hate admitting I'm wrong about anything."

"That's true," Harmony teased.

"Oh, stop or I'm taking that pie away from you."

Harmony pulled her plate protectively to her. "Those are fighting words." She held up her fork like a mock weapon.

"Ladies, Ladies," Ruby interrupted as the referee. "This is supposed to be a Christian Bible Study, not a fight club."

Jewel's eyes creased with mischief. "How about a Christian fight club?"

"Oh Lord, Jesus," Ruby turned her eyes heavenward and groaned.

Jewel laughed and gave Ellie a knowing glance. "It's just too easy to press her buttons."

The women moved from the kitchen to Allison's living room and settled around her coffee table. "So, you want to share this week, Ellie, a verse that's inspired you?" Allison asked.

Ellie remembered that she agreed to share a verse for today's session, but she hesitated. Her voice sounded unsure in her head as she spoke out loud. "I've been praying this week about my life and the steps I need to take. I do feel like the Holy Spirit is guiding me, but I think what I'm hearing from God right now is that I need to be a student, not a teacher. Does that sound strange? I'm not trying to cop out, but I just feel like I should be listening to what one of you brings to the table rather than my own voice blowing hot air."

Jewel nodded thoughtfully along with the other women. "Then you should listen. Follow your gut." She looked around the circle. "Anyone feel like they have something to say this week? Come on Allison, you're our fearless leader. What about you?"

Allison shook her head. "Yes, I know I'm the host, but my mind's drawing a blank. Ruby you're rarely at a loss for words?"

"Aint that the truth, but I'm feelin' a peace in my spirit. I know it's not me who needs to be speakin' today."

Harmony groaned out loud. "Okay. I wasn't going to say anything or bring it up, but God's not going to let me off the hook I can already tell. I had a fight with Steve last night and it was a doozy."

"Oh no, honey. What happened?" Ruby asked gently.

"Well, you know we've been doing the kid's food program for a few years now and running it out of the warehouse, right?" The women all nodded their heads. "Well, Steve apparently met the minister of the Baptist Church when he was at the library last Tuesday and after talking to him, he agreed to take on a community clothing closet as a part of Carrey Farms. He said we would make room in the warehouse for the clothes that would be coming in. Piles of clothes. Mountains of clothes. Apparently, we're going to be clothing the entire State. Get this. He says, we're already doing the food program, so why not clothe people too?"

Jewel laughed sympathetically. "That sounds like Steve."

"Well, I just about murdered him. The warehouse is packed with food and there's no room. We're going to have to reorganize everything and it's going to be so much work. We just got Carrey Farms financially solvent last year as a charitable organization and now he's adding more wrinkles."

Allison furrowed her brows in sympathy. "Oh, I'm sorry Harmony. He's not a detail person, is he?"

"No, he's not and he agreed without even telling me. And you know what? I'm always the bad guy because I'm the one who lacks the faith and doesn't have the vision. Do you know why that is? Because I can balance a checkbook. I wouldn't have agreed because it makes our whole organization vulnerable."

Ruby nodded her head. "You and Steve are about as different as night from day. Ya know that's the reason Carrey Farms even exists at all don't ya? His generosity, your business savvy…"

"I know you're right, but I'm still angry at him and I still have to do the work."

Ruby wrinkled her nose. "Well, is Steve plannin' to sit on his behind and make ya do all the work by yer lonesome?"

"No. He'll help of course, but I'm going to have to come up with a plan for how we're going to store everything. Jobs like that are not in Steve's wheelhouse. We're talking about a large expenditure to make the space and the time involved also is costly. It's just stressful."

"You're the brains, he's the labor. You'll make it work," Allison encouraged.

Ellie set her coffee cup down and spoke quietly. "I'm sorry Harmony about the work and the stress. I used to get that stress all the time in my past life when I was a minister's wife. I'll help if you need it on a Saturday or Sunday afternoon."

"Yes, me too," Jewel offered.

Allison joined in. "I think we would all help you, Harmony in any way we can."

As Harmony looked around the circle the tightness in her lips began to soften. "Thank you. That does make me feel better. Although, we've still got a month before the clothes start arriving."

"Do ya think in your heart Steve is right?" Ruby asked. "I mean, do ya believe it's what God wants?"

Harmony grimaced. "Yes. I do think it is the right thing to do in my heart, but I worry that we'll get exhausted, burned out from taking on more than we can handle and compromise our whole ministry. You know Steve doesn't have the greatest track record in that area. He'd give the shirt off his back. He doesn't always think about consequences."

"Yeah, sounds like Steve," Jewel agreed. "But Harmony, it's also what you love about him."

"True," she laughed. She pulled out her black leather Bible and began to turn through the pages. "Well, I have my verse," Harmony continued. "Romans 12:3: 'For by grace given me I say to every one of you: Do not think of yourself more highly than you ought, but rather think of yourself with sober judgment, in accordance with the faith God has distributed to each of you.'"

"Ah, a good one. Paul's meditation on being a living sacrifice," Allison said.

"The very one," Harmony agreed.

"So why did you choose this verse?" Jewel asked.

"I'm struggling with the part of myself that wants to live for God and the other part that wants to live for me," Harmony admitted. "I sometimes worry that Steve's going to give every piece of himself and our belongings to God and there won't be anything left for us. Does that sound selfish?"

Ruby laughed. "Oh Lord. Here ya are, two of the most generous people in Veneta that anyone would ever be fortunate enough to meet and yer still worried about bein' selfish?"

Harmony shook her head. "Ruby, if you saw my dark mean old heart, you wouldn't think I was so generous."

Ruby waved her hand dismissively. "Nah, ya just human, that's all. Jus' give yerself a moment to breathe. We have doubts when we act out on our faith. Ya wouldn't be a real person if you didn't feel that way."

Allison nodded thoughtfully. "I think you're right to be concerned. We're supposed to be living sacrifices, not just sacrifices. Steve needs you to balance him, so you don't go bankrupt. What good would you be to anyone if you extended your resources to the place where you couldn't help the children and all those other people you feed?"

"I know it must be stressful," Ellie added. "But how wonderful to have a husband who loves the Lord the way Steve does and the way the two of you work together. I think it's really beautiful." Ellie could not take the dreamy quality out of her voice.

Allison's eyes focused on her. "You'll find someone like that too. I know it."

Harmony spoke softly. "Thank you, Ellie. You put that into perspective for me. You're right. I need to be like Steve sometimes and focus on the bigger picture."

"But that don't excuse him from makin' arrangements without talkin' to ya first," Ruby chimed.

Harmony nodded in agreement. "I think I can forgive him for that. After a good scolding first."

"Atta girl!" Jewel laughed. "The two of you are going to be just fine."

Before leaving, the women embraced each other as they gathered their belongings. Harmony hung back and approached Ellie as she gathered her purse. "Ell? I've been thinking about you this week and was wondering if you were busy Saturday?"

"I was going to go with Ruby to the campground schoolhouse next weekend but I'm free this coming Saturday. Why?"

"Well, it's a few weeks before the mountain of clothes come, and the weather has been warm and drier than usual. Do you like horseback riding?"

Ellie laughed, "horseback riding? Um, I've never really been, except when I was a kid, and I rode a pony at a friend's birthday party. It was around a circle and the pony had a leash that this man held as he walked us around the ring."

Harmony laughed. "I think you mean a lead line. Well, you live in Veneta now. I think you should do the real thing."

"With you?"

"Yes, with me. Why the hesitancy?"

"Well, I think Jewel told me that back in your high school days you were the equestrian team's star barrel racer."

Harmony raised her eyebrow with amusement. "Oh, I was. Is that a problem?"

"Um, no. But you're a star barrel racer and I call a lead line a leash. I just don't want you to have unrealistic expectations of my riding ability and frankly, I'm a little scared."

Harmony laughed. "I got you. I got your back. You don't have to worry, and I think it would be fun."

"Well, I'm going to put my trust in you and say yes, but please be kind and gentle with me," Ellie pleaded.

* * *

218

When the following Saturday arrived, she pulled up to Carrey farms around 7:30 am. The valley was blanketed in fog, but the air was certainly warmer than usual. Harmony left the gate open allowing Ellie to drive up all the way to the barn. As she got out of the Explorer, several golden doodles surrounded and greeted her with enthusiastic barking. Harmony came out the front door of her Craftsman house and smiled. "They recognize family."

"What?" Ellie asked.

"They recognize family. They know you've adopted one of them."

"You think?"

"Nah," Harmony laughed. "But I do think they recognize a kind soul when they see one."

Ellie flushed with pleasure. "That's sweet, Harmony. Thank you!"

"Just stating the obvious. Come on then. Let's go to the warehouse. I'll show you around." Ellie followed Harmony to the large grey structure that was situated directly behind the red barn. Although, very slim, she moved with an agile strength and she watched as Harmony muscled the large sliding door to the warehouse open. Ellie stood wide eyed as she absorbed what seemed like miles of shelving. Boxed food, canned food, and dry goods of copious quantities filled the shelves. In the front were several cafeteria tables covered with fresh produce.

"Harmony, this is just amazing. Where did it all come from?"

She leaned against one of the more solid cafeteria tables and sighed. "That's a long story. We started everything about a decade ago in the red barn next door, but soon were overwhelmed with all the food we were getting. We had the warehouse built just four years ago. It's 5000 square feet of space, if you can believe it? Our food bank started with just small community organizations and local churches, but we just began to grow. Now we take cast off supplies from several grocery stores, a bakery, and a dairy. Carrey Farms has fifteen employees. We get funds from all over the place, even a few donations from overseas."

"It's impressive." Ellie said as her eyes scanned the room again.

"Well, it's all God, because I can't even tell you how it came together. But you can see I have quite a job ahead of me, but I've already got some ideas and I'm gathering a little work crew together in my head made up of some our employees, my daughters of course, and volunteers including Levi."

Ellie shifted uncomfortably. "Oh."

"He and Melinda were a big support to Steve and me when we were getting this off the ground. Mike and Levi probably built half these shelves. Melinda helped me with my food organization system, which we still use today. It's the reason I gave him quite the discount on Pax." Harmony's eyes twinkled slightly with mischief.

"Did you really charge him $1200 for Pax? I guess it's none of my business. You don't have to tell me."

Harmony shook her head and smiled. "I don't care who knows. He tried to pay me, but I wouldn't take his money. Steve and I owe him too much. Plus, I really wanted him to have that puppy for Rae. They've been through so much."

Ellie smiled. "Oh, you should see Rae with Pax? Well, the four of them. John and Rae and the golden doodles. They're kind of inseparable."

Harmony looked directly at Ellie, her eyes focused. "Kind of like a family it seems."

Ellie's heart beat rapidly. "Are we going to ride?"

Harmony locked up the warehouse and they crossed to the barn. The sky was brightening, and Ellie allowed the fresh air into her lungs. Her eyes lingered on the beauty of the evergreen covered foothills. A landscape that had been dark and eerie almost moments before was transforming before her eyes. Sunlight pierced through the glimmering haze of mist and her body shivered as she tasted the promise of hope. She shuddered involuntarily as she caught her breath.

Steve was already in the barn. He was slightly shorter than Harmony, but had a handsome face and wore glasses which made him look slightly bookish despite his jean jacket and cowboy boots. "So, this is the famous Ellie?" Steve reached out his hand.

Ellie took it. "Hi and yes. Nice to meet you Steve. Harmony's been showing me around and this place is just, well..., just awesome."

Steve laughed. "Thank you. We aim to please. I'm getting the horses ready for your ride." He pointed an accusing finger at Harmony. "Don't do anything reckless or crazy, honey. I mean it. No galloping down ravines or trick riding."

Harmony laughed. "I won't. Ellie's a newbie and she made me promise to go easy on her."

"Okay, Ell, meet Annabelle. She's your ride," Harmony said as she guided a chestnut-colored horse by its bridle out of its stall and led the animal into the corridor of the barn.

The warm, gentle eyes made Ellie fall immediately in love, but she smiled mischievously as she turned to Harmony. "Isn't Annabelle the name of a deranged, murderous doll? Is this one of those horses that looks as gentle as a dove and then the second you try to ride her turns into a raging demon?"

Harmony feigned mock disbelief and covered the horses long pointed ears with her hands. "Don't say such things in front of Annabelle. She might get ideas."

Steve laughed. "Ellie, Annabelle is as gentle as they come. I promise you. She's eighteen years old and she just wants to please."

"Okay Ellie. It's time to get on." Harmony nodded toward Steve. He knelt with one knee to the ground and showed Ellie the stirrup.

"Put your foot here and use some momentum to climb up."

She felt awkward but managed to mount the horse, but not at all gracefully. Harmony laughed. "You'll get better with practice."

Steve handed her the reins and demonstrated how to hold them in true Western fashion. "Good luck," he said with a wink.

"I'm going to need it," she whispered.

"Don't worry," Steve whispered back. "Harmony will take care of you. She knows what she's doing."

Harmony had disappeared into the neighboring stall and then emerged on top of a jet-black horse. The gelding towered over Annabelle and reminded Ellie of the stories of Black Beauty. Her friend rode with her back straight, but somehow looked completely relaxed and at ease.

"That horse is gorgeous." Ellie couldn't hide her awe.

"Ellie, meet Duke. He's my first love, even before Steve."

Steve laughed and shook his head. "That's the truth."

"Okay Ellie. Just follow my lead. Kick just lightly on her sides to get her moving. Annabelle will usually just follow whatever Duke is doing, so you shouldn't have to worry about much at all."

"Okay, if you say so." Ellie kicked her legs gently into the horse's side and sure enough, Annabelle plodded forward.

They rode out into the open field. The sun was now shimmering through the last remains of fog and Ellie felt a touch of its warmth on her nose and cheeks. "Where are we going?"

"We have over a hundred acres. There's a path that cuts into the foothills and does a nice loop through the woods. I want to take you somewhere."

"Really? Where?"

Harmony laughed. "I want to surprise you."

They rode together side by side now and Ellie watched as the landscape awakened from the fog to become fully brilliant with sunlight. Her eyes traveled past the foothills to the mountains behind them. "This isn't really a farm is it? You've got a ranch here."

Harmony nodded. "Yes, Steve inherited the property from his father and his father from his grandfather. He came razor thin close to losing the whole place. Before we married, he hired me to do his accounting. What a mess."

"How did you manage to keep the place?"

"Well, Steve had to accept he just wasn't a rancher. He's not an entrepreneur or a businessman. The man's just not built for it. You see, Steve just wants to help people and he enjoys working with them, a humanitarian so to speak. He's also a pretty good fundraiser. Although, I didn't know that at the time. The thought occurred to me as I was pouring through his financials that if we turned the ranch into some kind of charity, he could save thousands in taxes. Steve was going to have to restructure or repurpose the ranch if he was going to keep it. It was tough. He had to sell off some pieces of land and do some of what I call restructuring of assets. He was fortunate enough to get permission from the county to section off and sell about twenty acres and then we were able to save the rest. The sale got Steve mostly out of debt and then the charitable organization status changed us from a profit to a non-profit."

"Wow, smart."

Harmony smiled. "That's just the half of it. For me, the charitable organization was a smart business move to avoid taxes, but Steve, well, he just ran with it. Turns out the idea was an answer to something he was searching for in his soul. Veneta has a lot of poverty and a lot of kids and families going hungry. We also have a lot of good people who want to help. God used us to bring the two together. He just had this vision that we could feed whoever was hungry. When Steve's passionate about something, he can sell the idea to practically anyone and that's what he did. He just got people on board, people you wouldn't even expect. He's like the energizer bunny and you can't help but get pulled in. Just as an example, one day, he's at the Tractor Supply and he starts chatting with another man looking at riding lawn mowers and they start talking about farming, the weather, whatever and then he tells him about the food program. The next week we get a check for $10,000 from Mr. Walter Byron, the owner of the chicken farm five miles out of town."

"Wow. Really? After just one conversation? That's crazy. What did you think about all of it? Accomplishing something like this is a leap of faith?"

"Don't I know it? This was over a decade ago about a year before we got married. I saw this land as the perfect ranch property, and I agreed to help Steve with his finances because he promised me that I could keep Duke at his ranch. Boarding other people's animals was something Steve had done for a while sometimes even absorbing the cost. When I first met Steve, I just thought he was an idiot for putting this beautiful piece of property in jeopardy and being charitable even when it cost him money. I didn't get it. He was trying to make the farm profitable, so he could keep his family legacy, but he was bleeding money. He tried ranching, even growing Christmas trees, but nothing seemed to grow or prosper because he was going against his calling, you see? Or at least that's what I think now. My dream at the time was to have a horse ranch, but when I saw the charity come to life, the people that came together to help, and I don't know, just the feeling of being a part of taking care of other people, I realized his dream was better than mine. I just fell in love with Steve, this life, you know?"

Ellie smiled and nodded. "It's romantic. You may not have started on the same page, but you eventually settled there. Davis and I were never on the same page. I guess he pretended we were, but I don't think in his heart we ever were."

Harmony patted Duke's neck and cooed to him till he slowed to keep an even pace with Annabelle. "So, Ellie, what about you and Levi? Is there potential that you two might be on the same page?"

The heat came to her cheeks and Ellie turned her face to look at the mountains to the east, so Harmony would not read the expression on her face. Her directness always frightened her, but she also loved her friend's ability to cut to the very heart of a matter. "Harmony, I think I really blew it there. I just think Levi deserves something, someone better than me."

"You are a silly goose, aren't you? Levi only has eyes for you. It's as clear as day to anyone observing."

Her heart felt a moment of lightness as she heard those words, but then doubt and fear assailed her. "If he had feelings for me, I think he's realizing now that he was suffering from a form of derangement syndrome. I'm sure he thinks I'm a complete idiot now."

The terrain was changing around them and now Ellie rode behind Harmony as they began to follow a winding mountain trail that traveled upward into the foothills. The conversation ceased as the riding became more arduous and distance was needed between the horses. Ellie shifted uncomfortably in the saddle as her muscles began to ache from the pressure on her thighs. They climbed for about thirty minutes before Ellie heard rushing water. They were on the ridge now of one of the foothills and Harmony led her through a copse of trees toward the sound. What Ellie saw took her breath away. In the middle of the forest was a hidden pond surrounded by trees and light. The water bubbled because its source was an underground spring. From the pool a tributary had formed, and the excess water cascaded down the mountain in a small waterfall toward the valley below. Above the trees, sunlight filtered through the leaves and created green patches of light on the grass and rocks. "Wow," Ellie said.

"Yes. It's beautiful isn't it? Our own little slice of heaven. I come here to pray sometimes or just to be alone and think."

The two women dismounted, and Harmony took both Duke and Annabelle's reigns and strapped them loosely to a nearby tree.

Ellie nodded in agreement. "I can see why. This is where you wanted to bring me?"

"Yes."

"Why?"

"You're an artist. I knew you'd appreciate the visual. This spring bubbled up only last year, you know. Before then, this was just the top of the ridge, nothing special, but now it's a haven for wildlife. I've seen every kind of creature imaginable taking a drink up here from deer, raccoons, even a black bear, especially in the summer when water gets scarce. This little stream waters all our horses and animals and it's the most beautiful spot on our entire property."

"Well, it's gorgeous. I'm just surprised and touched that you'd want to share this with me."

"Well, we've been talking about taking steps to change our lives and I just wanted to encourage you that you can do it. You're the stream Ellie and you can transform your life just like this landscape when you allow God's goodness to flow out of you."

Ellie closed her eyes to allow Harmony's words to sink in. "I've felt that," Ellie agreed. "I just need courage. I just feel so scared and I don't even know why."

"Courage comes from faith. At least that's what I think. I'm going to walk a bit to a spot I know and get some time with the Lord. Are you alright if I leave you here for about fifteen minutes? It's a great spot to pray."

Ellie nodded her assent.

"By the way Ellie, I know Levi. I know him well and I promise you, he hasn't said a word to me, but there's no way he sees his affection for you as a derangement syndrome. You know, he understands in his own way what you're suffering. He's suffered too and he's gone through his own hell to come out on the other side. Two years ago, you would have never recognized him. He was so angry after Melinda died. I didn't think he'd ever find his way out of the pit of grief, but he did. I think he's just waiting for you to find your way through your own pain. I think he's going to be waiting for you on the other side."

Before she could respond Harmony walked away and left Ellie to ponder her meaning. The idea that Levi could love her filled her with indescribable joy, but for some reason the fear that he might love her was equally paralyzing. She found a large rock to sit on near the pool and closed her eyes to listen to the sound of rushing water. She tried to imagine God's love coursing through her and to envision what complete joy in the spirit would look like. A verse from 1 John came to her suddenly. *There is no fear in love. Perfect love drives out fear, because fear has to do with punishment. The one who fears is not made perfect in love.* Ellie heard her father's voice again in her mind speaking over the rush of water. *How long will you punish yourself, Ellie, because you are afraid to see that you are valuable and important to God? Why are you hiding in shame? Come out into the light.*

* * *

The house looked the same. Sally Pearson had not neglected the garden that grew strong and lush around the home she once shared with her husband. The plants grew as eclectic and magical as ever. Gary was gone, but she could feel his presence, his love for Sally in the garden that was just beginning to show signs of spring. As she approached the entrance, her eyes rested on the white door and the intricate glass mosaic featuring a white dove. How similar it looked to the dove in the stained-glass window of the church, the dove in her painting that soared above the people leading them to God's peace. She hesitated and in the silent and broken voice of her yearning asked God for faith and courage.

The quiet air filled with the hollow sound of her fist knocking on wood. From inside the house, she could hear movement. Sally opened the door and stared at Ellie. Her eyes opened as wide as saucers. "Ellie? Is that really you?"

"Sally, yes. It's me. I'm sorry it's taken me so long to check on you."

The older woman's sharp features missed nothing. "Ellie! Better late than never. Come in. I'm getting the coffee ready."

Ellie released the air she was holding and allowed herself to breathe. She followed Sally and made her way to the Dutch inspired kitchen. Sally's hair had grown longer and was now cut in a fashionable bob. A wave of guilt washed over her as she realized how much time had passed since Gary's death. "Sally, I'm just really sorry. I should have come to see you so much earlier."

"Nonsense. I was taken care of very well. I knew that when you and Davis left you must have your reasons. I hear you're divorced now."

Ellie stood in Sally's kitchen feeling heavy and awkward. "Yes..." Ellie clamored for words. The fear and anxiety forced her to look desperately around the kitchen for a place to flee. Sally put her hand gently on her shoulder. "Sounds like we both suffered a life changing loss." The small woman took Ellie in her arms and embraced her. "I am so sorry," she whispered hoarsely. "I miss Gary all the time, but God has given me strength enough for each day. I hope He has done the same for you."

Her breath caught in her throat. "Yes, He has..." she faltered.

"Well, sit down. Coffee is ready." Sally gestured toward the kitchen table and she sat awkwardly as Sally set a cup of coffee in front of her. Ellie stared for a moment at the steam rising from the cup and she was taken just for a moment in her mind to Allison's kitchen and she saw the beautiful faces of her friends. She felt a small piece of courage rise in her chest. She picked up her spoon and placed a cube of sugar into the brown liquid and watched the crystals dissolve. She would do the same to her fear.

"When we left, we didn't tell anyone why. I don't feel like I have to tell everyone why, but I think I've always felt guilty that I didn't come and tell you."

Sally reached out and touched Ellie's hand. Her sharp eyes were trained on her face, the lines around her eyes creased in worldly knowledge. "My dear, what happens in a woman's marriage is private. You don't have to tell me or anyone. Even Gary and I had our secrets."

Ellie laughed awkwardly. "I guess I know that, but what I'm trying to say is that I want to tell you. Not telling the truth has made me feel like a liar, especially when Davis and I ministered at the church together. I feel the weight of sin and I need to release it to someone who knew Davis and me when we were together. I need you to forgive me, Sally, for my part in hiding the truth."

"Did he have an affair?" Sally asked bluntly. "It certainly would not be the first time a pastor has fallen."

Ellie nodded. "He was sleeping with my nineteen-year-old niece. I knew about it for a few months before the marriage fell apart. We tried to see if there was a path to healing and reconciling the marriage, but there wasn't."

Sally shuddered and shook her head. "I'm sorry Ellie. I'm so sorry. In your shoes, I would probably do the same thing. The church sadly is often the last place you should go to confess. There's a lot more judgement than forgiveness, unfortunately."

"Well, I agree with you. I'm not going to confess to the whole church, nor do I feel the need to, but someone from South Hills needed to know. Someone else who's lived in that place of pain. I knew it was you."

Sally smiled. "Davis was an incredible preacher, but you were always my favorite. You know that?"

Ellie shook her head at this revelation. "No."

"Did you know everyone at South Hills called Davis Preacher?"

Ellie's forehead creased in confusion. "They always called him Davis around me, so I guess I never noticed."

"Preacher Davis this and Preacher Davis that. Our Bible study group used to pour over his sermons. They were that good, but do you know what we called you?"

Ellie shook her head. "No. What?"

"Pastor Ellie. Pastor Ellie this and Pastor Ellie that. Do you understand what I'm telling you?"

"I think so," she said slowly.

"Ellie, you love God, and you want to serve others. When I needed someone desperately you were there for me and you were a great comfort. That's your calling. To be a minister to others. It doesn't mean you have to be a minister at church, but you're called to minister. Do you understand me? Don't let your pain rob that calling from you, okay?"

She felt Sally's words rise into her chest from her gut and wash over her. "I won't," she choked.

* * *

The phone rang and Ellie picked up. "Hi Mom."

"Ellie, I'm inviting you to Easter Sunday and brunch up here in Salem. Please say you're coming. All the family will be there, your brothers and…"

"I'm coming."

"We're going to have a ham dinner and all the fixings. Wait… You're coming? Oh Ellie, praise the Lord."

"Yes Mom. The boys will be with me too. I'll be there a little early to help you with the meal."

"Oh Ellie. You've made me so happy."

Chapter 18

Exterior:

The True Church can
never fail. For it is
based upon a rock.
—*T.S. Eliot*

Ellie's head was pounding. When the seventh period bell finally rang, she was relieved beyond measure. She waved goodbye to her students and ran to her desk to fish for her bottle of ibuprofen. With the help of her now warm bottled water, she gulped down four pills and waited for the pain relief to take effect. Her cell phone suddenly rang. "Hello?"

"Hello Ellie?" said a timid and birdlike voice.

"Nora?" Ellie tried to hide her shock.

"Yes, it's me. Um, are you okay to talk for a bit?"

Ellie studied her classroom for possible interruptions. "Just a sec." She grabbed her keys and moved to the classroom door. She peered into the empty hall and locked it from the inside with her key. "Okay. Yes. Go ahead, Nora." She walked slowly back to her desk, anticipation and fear building in her gut.

The line was silent for a moment, heavy with the awkwardness between them. "Ellie, I'm at a facility in Bend. I've been working on getting myself better. Next Tuesday, we have a special visitor's day and I'd like you to be my visitor. We have things to talk about, to clear the air. Do you think you could drive up to Bend and see me?"

Ellie sank into her desk chair and took a breath through her nose. "I'll have to take a couple days off from work, but yes, Nora, of course. What's the address?"

* * *

Harmony had insisted they meet outside for Bible Study. The sun was shining, but an icy wind undercut any warmth from its rays. Allison was desperately trying to start the fire and Ruby was complaining. "Lord, sometimes I wonder if we're not livin' in Siberia. Jesus have mercy on us. I can't think of any place in the entire country, but Oregon that can go through all four seasons in one day."

"That's definitely true," agreed Jewel. She handed Ruby another blanket and Ruby wrapped it around her head.

"Now you're just plain exaggerating. It's not that cold," Harmony scolded.

"Honey, it's so cold politicians are walkin' around with their hands in their own pockets."

Ellie laughed. "Oh Ruby. You have the best expressions."

The fire was finally crackling, and the friends brought their chairs as close as they could to its flames without getting scorched.

"So, ladies, I need your prayers," Ellie said softly through her chattering teeth.

"What's going on?" Jewel asked.

"My sister called me and wants to see me."

"Is this the same sister who is mother to the niece who is, well you know, "with" your husband?" Allison said softly.

"Ex-husband and oh yeah. The very one."

"We're listenin, honey.'" Ruby encouraged.

"Where do I begin?" Ellie lifted her eyes heavenward. "There's just some baggage there. When we were in elementary school, even middle school, I used to look up to her so much. Nora was so beautiful, and she could be really fun too. We shared a bedroom growing up and I felt so close to her, but everything changed when she went into ninth grade. It was like one morning we were best friends playing with Barbies together and the next day she was like a complete stranger. She would shut the door and lock me out of my own room, sneak out of the window at night. I don't know. She just went into this full-scale rebellion. My parents were worried sick about her. We were this happy harmonious home and then Nora blew up our world like a hurricane."

Ellie allowed the memories to wash over her as she felt the warmth of the fire on her face. "For four years our house was a nightmare, and it was because of her. Every week there was a new drama. I remember my parents rushing over to the school because she was caught with weed in the bathroom. Then a month later, the call from the police station because she was arrested for public indecency. Apparently, she was having sex with her boyfriend in a public park and they got caught by the police. I didn't find out the whole story till years later. Anyway, shortly after that she just ran away. She was gone for over a month. You can't imagine the torment our whole family experienced. My parents called the police. My mom was a complete train wreck. She took a month off work and cried every day. My dad walked around like a ghost. The rest of us, Andrew, and Brian, well, we just tiptoed around on eggshells. None of us got any attention because Nora had sucked up all the oxygen. There were only fumes left in our house. The tension, it was just off the charts."

"What on earth was going through her mind?" Harmony interrupted.

"I have no idea. I didn't understand how she could hurt them, my mom and dad, wound them right at the core. Hurt me, my little brothers. The whole situation was inexcusable, and I learned to hate her. She was already so pretty, talented, but nothing was enough for her. I just never understood the reason why. We had a good life, good parents."

Jewel furrowed her brow in thought, "hmmm." She took a dainty sip of her chamomile tea and then met Ellie's eyes. "That's awful Ellie, but something was wrong. Why would she just go crazy like that?"

"Some kids just go rebellious." Harmony said. "They're wild, untamed."

"I wish I knew her reasons. My dad was a Christian minister, my mom a teacher. They were so embarrassed by her behavior and she seemed to take perverse pleasure in publicly humiliating them. My mother yelled at her, screamed at her. I remember them arguing till she was blue in the face and Nora a shrieking mess, but my dad never raised his voice. He was always so gentle, never judgmental, but his eyes were just so deeply sad. I just felt like she destroyed our entire home, my sense of safety, my brothers, all of us, our happiness sacrificed for what?"

Jewel uncrossed her legs and leaned forward. "Ell, you have your reasons to be angry, but my guess is your sister must have been deeply angry too, maybe she still is. I just wonder why. I don't think it would hurt to ask her to find out her story, you know? It might help you at least understand. Maybe this is a chance to clear the air?"

As Jewel spoke, Ellie saw the next step forming before her eyes and the revelation terrified her, the call from God to face her biggest fears and discover the truth, to walk through a dark tunnel with only faith to guide her. The biggest challenge in Ellie's quest lay before her and she questioned whether or not she had enough strength. "I guess you're right," she sighed. "It's just, she's had over twenty years to tell her story. I'm not sure I have the patience to hear what she has to say."

Allison suddenly shrieked and grabbed Ellie's hand. "Ellie? I think we should go with you! All of us."

"Oh no, Allison!" She cried. "That's too much. I would never ask you guys to do that."

"Oh Lord," Ruby said. "The five of us ladies on a road trip. We haven't done anything like that since the age of dinosaurs. It just so happens that I don't have a single job lined up next week, so I'm free as a bird. I'm all in." Ruby nudged Harmony. "Harmony honey? What about you?"

"Well, you know… I'm always busy, but the truth is…I need a break, a breather." A wicked smile spread across her face. "I'm rather excited about the idea of leaving Steve with both the girls and that mess of a warehouse.

Let him manage it for a couple of days."

"That's one good way to get yer man to appreciate a woman," Ruby chuckled.

I'm pretty sure Steve could watch the fort and the kids while I'm gone. You know what? It's one night. I'll make it work."

"Yay!" Allison clapped her hands and smiled from ear to ear. "Jewel, come on Ju Ju what about you?"

Jewel rolled her eyes. "Don't call me that." The corners of her mouth turned into a smile even as she sighed. "This week my client finished the signing process on the house we've been negotiating and truthfully I have a small window, but Frank and I were going to celebrate, and he'll be disappointed."

"Frank will live," Harmony barked.

"Yes. He will and when I'm gone and come back, he's actually at his most pleasant, so I'm going to tentatively say yes."

"Well that's good. It just wouldn't be the same without our Jewel. Oh ladies, this is gonna be a road trip to remember, but I do need to warn ya. I require a very soft bed to sleep in and I am not a dainty sleeper," Ruby confided.

Ellie's cheeks flushed. The love of her friends surrounded her. "That's okay Ruby. No one's perfect. Are you really sure you have time just to drive with me to see my sister? To spend the night at a hotel? I feel like it's asking too much. You really don't have to."

Jewel took her hands. "Don't you see Ellie? We want to."

* * *

Ellie cinched the sash of her trench coat more tightly around her waist as she walked from Allison's front door to her car. The boys were at their dads for the evening and Ellie wondered how she should spend the rest of the evening alone. She had stayed a bit later than the other ladies to dish with Allison on how well the hens were laying eggs and to talk about the possibility of acquiring a few more birds in late spring to join her little flock.

The other women were long gone, but Jewel was in her white Volvo visibly upset. Ellie approached her car with concern and tapped on the window. "Everything okay?"

Jewel rolled down her window an exasperated look on her face. "My car's refusing to start," she whined not without humor.

"Oh no. You need a ride?"

"I was just going to call Frank, but I think he's in transit from work on his way home and he doesn't usually pick up the phone when he's driving."

"Jewel, I can drive you no problem. The boys are at their dad's and I've got nothing going on. Where do you live?"

"Off Territorial Highway. That's not too far is it?"

"Yeah. Definitely too far. Forget it then." Ellie pretended to walk away and then turned back with a sly smile. "You know I'm kidding."

Jewel laughed. "Well, I'm freezing. Your heater better work."

"You bet it does and between you, me, and the fencepost I've been freezing the entire night. Harmony's idea to meet outside was a bust."

Jewel smiled. "Agreed. I'll call the towing company tomorrow and text Allison in case she's wondering why my car's still in front of her house." She opened the car door and followed Ellie to the Explorer. As Ellie had left Allison's house, she had started her engine with a touch of a button on her keyring and the car was already warm.

The women climbed into the SUV and for a moment sat silently absorbing the heat from the vents. "Oh, thank the Lord. This feels so good," Jewel laughed. "I thought I would never be warm again." Ellie nodded in agreement and after a few moments finally released the brake and began to drive.

As the rhythm of the road set in, Ellie noticed that Jewel did not seem like her cheerful self. Her brow was furrowed as she stared down at her phone. "Ellie? Do you mind if we make a quick stop on the way?"

"Yeah sure. What's going on?"

Jewel hesitated. "My mom lives a couple miles from us and she's texting me. She's upset about something."

"Oh, I didn't realize your mom lived nearby."

Jewel audibly sighed. "Yes, and she drives me to drink. Frank too." As they drove up Territorial highway into the hills Jewel pointed to an obscure gravel road. "Okay turn here."

"Here?"

"Yes, here," Jewel repeated.

Ellie turned quickly. The gravel road was narrow and wound its way up the hill like a coiled rattlesnake. She stepped hard on the accelerator to create the momentum needed to reach the top of the hill and push through the dozens of potholes in the road. Nestled on the ridge was a grey, single wide trailer that had seen better days. "You should stay in the car. I won't be long," Jewel promised.

Ellie watched her friend leave the car. She wore tailored jeans, a trim and fitted black blazer and a white silk blouse with silver pumps. She looked like a living ad for Ann Taylor. Ellie would never have imagined Jewel's mother lived in a rundown trailer.

Ellie opened her Spotify app and listened to a folk station while she waited. As she stared out the window, she spotted the blinds in the trailer moving erratically from her peripheral vision. Concerned, she turned the radio down and felt her heart rate quicken when she heard screaming from inside the trailer. Ellie bolted out of the SUV and ran up the walkway toward the trailer door. She approached the door cautiously but could not make out the screamer's words. The voice did not belong to Jewel.

Ellie opened the door and as she did so, saw an object spinning toward her. She ducked just in time as a cup went whirling past her head and shattered a few feet outside the door she had just opened. "You bitch! You're just a little bitch!" Ellie heard a stream of words in a foreign language that she assumed was Korean and then in clear English, "And who is this?" A small woman was curled up in the corner of the trailer screaming. She reminded Ellie of a trapped and cornered animal. Spittle rested in the corner of her mouth and her eyes were bloodshot, her face contorted in monstrous rage. Her finger was pointed accusingly at Ellie and for a moment she froze in complete bewilderment. Forcing herself to recover from the shock, Ellie remembered her ministerial training and moved deliberately away from the door to Jewel's side. She spoke quietly and kept her tone as calm and measured as she could manage.

"Hi. I'm Ellie and a friend of Jewel's. I was just giving her a ride and thought maybe I could help. Can I get you anything?"

The angry woman gave Ellie a piercing stare. Ellie allowed the awkward silence to sit for several moments as the out-of-control woman scrutinized her. Finally, after what seemed like an agonizing eternity, she seemed to determine Ellie was no real threat and changed tactics. "My daughter is abusing me. She won't fill this prescription I need, and she doesn't care if her old mother lives or dies. I gave her everything and she's just a little bitch!" Ellie's ears were then assailed by angrier Korean that she could not understand.

Ellie kept her cool, but the idea of anyone calling a person as lovely as Jewel a bitch floored her. Ellie squeezed Jewel's arm and gave her a reassuring look. "What's your mom's name?" she whispered.

"Daisy," Jewel whispered back. "She abuses her meds and other things. I'm sorry you had to see this," Jewel said under her breath. Ellie now saw that there were several shattered items across the floor. Jewel moved stealthily to a supply closet and took out a broom and dustpan and began to sweep and pick-up glass, strangely graceful and feminine in her silver heels even amid shattered debris. Ellie turned to the sink and filled a glass of water and moved to the side of the woman's bed and sat down next to her in a plain wooden chair. "Hi Daisy. I'm sorry you're having a rough day. Would you like a glass of water?"

Daisy glared at her. "I want my meds. That's what I need, not a glass of water."

"I understand that," Ellie said gently. "We don't have them now, but we'll see what we can do."

Daisy slumped back in her bed and grimaced. "Everything hurts," she groaned. "Well, you can get me some Vodka then. There's some in the cabinet over there." She pointed to the corner cabinet above the tiny refrigerator. Ellie looked to Jewel for guidance, but she just shrugged and continued to sweep glass and debris into the dustpan.

"Okay coming up," She found another glass, a small one and began to fill it with the half empty bottle of Vodka.

"Don't you dilute that with water," Daisy said. Her voice sounded tired and edgy now.

Ellie poured and brought the glass to Daisy who now seemed calmer. "Here you go." She watched her gulp the Vodka greedily and then shut her eyes. Now that Ellie sat next to her, the smell of the woman overcame her. She tried to breathe through her mouth rather than her nose hoping it would help. "Jewel just wanted to check on you, Daisy. She was worried about you." Ellie said gently. Daisy said nothing now. She looked like she was quietly dozing into Neverland. Ellie rose and joined Jewel in straightening up the trailer. "So, what do we do? Leave her here?"

"Unfortunately, yes. I'll call her case worker."

They left the trailer quietly after Jewel locked up. "I really have tried everything Ellie. We're in transition now. She's going to be placed in a group home, but services are taking their sweet time. Sometimes I'm afraid I'm going to walk in there and she's going to be unconscious or something worse."

The scene with Daisy stirred emotions within Ellie that made her feel unsettled. "Jewel? Has she always been like this?"

Jewel turned her face away. "Yes. Since I was about twelve years old. She's a bottomless pit, Ellie. No matter what I do, or how I try, it's never enough. She never gets better, but I think she's getting worse."

"Your dad? Where was he?"

"He died when I was about fourteen," Jewel said softly.

"Did you live with your mom?" Ellie asked in shock.

"Yes. I took care of her for a long time, most of high school."

"How on earth are you the person sitting next to me today? How did you overcome THAT? Did she always talk to you like that? I mean scream that you're a bitch and such."

Jewel sighed and then laughed. "Yes. That and a lot more. She called me every name in the book in English and Korean. She wasn't in her right head then and she's not now," Jewel said.

Ellie was stunned. "Why are you laughing?"

"I'm not laughing because it's funny. Sometimes it just helps somehow."

"What's wrong with her exactly? I mean medically speaking?"

She has bi-polar, depression...you name it. Every doctor she sees seems to give her a new diagnosis. She's a hopeless addict now. She's not able to care for herself really, but every time she gets in a group home situation she gets kicked out. Frank and I help out as much as we are able. You know, try to balance caring for her without destroying our own lives."

"How did you get out of that home and well..., I don't know become you? The successful, amazing Jewel that I know?"

Well, I didn't grow up in that trailer. Dad was a military man, and we had a nice home. When Dad got diagnosed with cancer, we started going to church together. It was what he wanted. He knew I was going to be left alone and that Mom was losing her grasp on her sanity. He wanted me to have faith, a center. He tried to pour a lot of love into me during that time. He wanted me to know that I could pilot my own life with God's help. He told me Mom had a disease. I wasn't responsible for her choices."

"Did that work?" Ellie asked.

"Don't get me wrong. The verbal abuse was terrible, but deep inside I knew I was worth something. The church was a big support to me. Several of the ladies came down to check on Mom. I was sort of the adopted kid at everyone's house, but I don't know...The people there, especially the elderly people made me feel like I was something special. I went to church every Sunday like clockwork. There were usually programs and events throughout the week. I practically lived there. It was an escape to say the least. The people there, they didn't let me stew in the pain and suffering. When it got real bad, the youth pastor and a group of leaders helped me contact the state and get social workers involved. I started living with an elderly couple at the church the last half of senior year while Mom got treatment. They've been like my parents ever since. I wouldn't have been able to do that stuff on my own. I'm not saying it wasn't terribly hard and awful. It was, but I guess, I just had hope."

Ellie started the engine and shook her head. "Amazing."

Jewel smiled thoughtfully "It's where my faith journey began. You can't really recognize the light if you don't know what the darkness looks like. God sent people into my life to help me right when I needed them."

Ellie smiled and nodded thoughtfully. "That's the truth." She looked carefully at her beautiful, accomplished friend with new eyes. "You went to college?"

"I went to the local Christian college in Eugene. The church paid most of my tuition through a scholarship. I wouldn't have been able to go if it wasn't for the church community. You don't really need a college degree to be a realtor but going to college got me out of Veneta. It was the chance I needed, and I took it. I was encouraged to take it. That's where I met Frank."

"That's what the church is supposed to do," Ellie said quietly. "People that are there for you when you most need them."

Jewel placed her hand gently on Ellie's shoulder. "We have to do that for each other."

* * *

Although she was only planning on staying in a hotel for one night, Ellie struggled with packing her overnight bag. What to bring? Part of her felt like she was going to a slumber party and she couldn't suppress the smile that rose to her cheeks when she thought of her friends. She sighed however as she realized the one last detail that needed to be taken care of before she left with her crew. She walked slowly and purposefully to Levi's door and knocked.

Half of her hoped to see Rae open the door, but the other part of her knew she wanted to see him and to see him close up. How many times had she gone to sleep seeing his face? How many times did he appear in her dreams? Too many times to count now. She felt her heart quicken as she waited. Her heart was not disappointed when Levi opened the door. He was dressed for work, wearing his Sheriff's jacket. The sight of him reminded her of the first time she had laid eyes on him, how he had scooped Miles from the river and saved the day. His eyebrows rose in surprise, "Ellie?"

Her voice was slow to come to her. "Uh, Levi. Hi." Her voice sounded breathy in her ears. "I'm sorry to bother you. I have a favor to ask." Ellie hesitated and felt the heaviness of Levi's eyes on her. She froze suddenly with fear and then spoke again. "Is it inappropriate to ask for a favor?"

Levi's eyes lingered on her, his face unreadable as he leaned against the door. "Ellie, of course not. I've wanted to talk to you, but also give you the space you need. Look, I'm here for you. No matter what. Do you understand me?"

Warmth filled her body as Ellie realized Levi was not angry with her, that he missed their friendship and camaraderie just as she did. "Levi, thank you. I want that. I want us to be comfortable with each other like before."

"Me too. Agreed. What can I do for you?"

"I have to go and visit my sister. She's in Bend in a rehabilitation center and it's a bit of an impromptu visit. The boys are going to Davis', I need someone to watch over Cordelia. I could even pay Rae if that would make the deal more enticing."

Levi dismissed the idea with his hand. "Rae would never take your money and I wouldn't let her. Of course. We'll take Cordelia as long as you need. Is everything okay?"

Ellie allowed herself to process the question. "I'm not sure. I don't have a good relationship with my sister, honestly, but I'm hopeful. I feel a leading, Levi."

Levi smiled at her gently. "Hope is good. Wait here a second, Ellie, would you?" His eyes were insistent. She shifted her balance from hip to hip uneasily as she waited at the door. Levi did not make her wait long. He returned holding a book with a worn brown leather jacket.

"What is it?" she asked.

"It's my Bible," Levi said. "I want you to have it."

"You want me to have your Bible? Why?" Ellie was confused.

"Ell, I went through a very dark time after Melinda passed. I was very angry, quite frankly I drank too much, and truthfully, I didn't do right by Rae. This is what I read when I was in the tunnel of grief. I kept reading when I couldn't find my way out and well...eventually I found a ray of light. I've highlighted all the good passages." He winked playfully for a second and then his face turned more serious as he opened the Bible carefully. Ellie's eyes widened as she saw underlined sections and notes in the margin. Levi scrambled to find words. "This was my grief Bible and it helped me. I was in the middle of the storm, but I just kept a little piece of myself open, you know?"

"Open to what?"

"Open to hear what God might be trying to tell me or how he might be trying to lead me. I think maybe this Bible is the only thing I can offer you right now."

"I don't think I'm in the storm anymore?"

Levi's eyes cut through her. "There are all kinds of storms."

Ellie took the Bible with both hands. She felt strange emotions churning in her chest as she processed the thoughtful and intimate gift. "Won't you miss it? It looks like you read it a lot."

Levi smiled. "I bought a new Bible a couple months ago. The new Bible is a Hope Bible. I'm through the tunnel now. It's time, you know, to start a new chapter with a new Bible, for me anyway, but I think this one might help you."

Ellie returned his smile. "I hope I'll be able to buy a Hope Bible too someday."

"Me too, Ell," Levi said.

She ran her fingers over the worn leather. "Can I bring Cordie over this afternoon?"

"You got it. I'll let Rae know to expect her." She heard Levi's door shut gently behind her as she walked back to her house. Somehow with Levi's Bible in her hands she felt stronger.

Chapter 19

Finishings

Real spiritual friendship is
Eagerly helping one another
Know, serve, love, and
Resemble God in
deeper and deeper ways.
—Tim Keller

Ellie watched Davis drive away with the boys. Miles waved to her from the car window and made a goofy face. Ellie couldn't help but smile at his antics. Even now, watching them leave with Davis still brought a jolt of pain to her heart, the feeling that she had failed to provide her boys with the childhood they deserved, the childhood that came with a complete, nuclear family. About fifteen minutes later, Allison pulled up in her Suburban which was packed to the gills with middle aged women and their belongings. Ruby rolled down the passenger window and called to her. "We got room for just one more, so hurry your little hiney and climb aboard."

"Hold your horses," Ellie teased. She grabbed her overnight bag and Allison got out from the driver's seat to open the back. Ellie raised her eyebrows as she looked at the packed cargo space. "Woh! You know we're just going to be away for one night."

"You can blame Ruby for about a quarter of the luggage and all those designer bags, see there? They belong to Jewel. The smallest person here has the most stuff." The corner of Allison's lips rose just slightly in a wry smile.

"I heard that. It's important to travel in style." Jewel insisted.

Harmony whirled her head around from the front passenger seat. "Come on ladies. We're on a schedule here."

"What schedule is that?" Ruby snapped. "We don't have any scheduled engagements tonight that I'm aware of."

"Ruby dear, I love you to death, but I've traveled with you before and you have about a three-hour span before you have to use the bathroom. It's taken us so long to get going that according to my watch, we've got only about an hour and a half of driving time before we're going to have to take a bathroom break, maybe less. At this rate we won't arrive at the hotel till after midnight."

"Oh Lord Jesus! It's like takin' a trip with yer vice principal," Ruby groaned. "Relax Harmony. It's called a vacation, a getaway. If I have to use the bathroom, I have to use the bathroom. There's no need to make the workin's of my bladder a case for the federal courts."

Allison laughed. "Ruby, remember that for Harmony this is the way she likes to vacation. She likes a schedule, order, and we love that about her don't we ladies?"

Ruby rolled her eyes. "Well..., Jesus our savior loves her. I'm not so sure about my own feelin's at the moment."

"Sure, we do," Jewel agreed. "Come on Ell, you're sitting next to me." Jewel patted the seat next to her. Allison was the driver and Harmony sat next to her in the front passenger seat ready to offer driving advice at a moment's notice. Ellie and Jewel took the center of the SUV, and Ruby claimed the entire back seat for herself. She already had her feet up and had arranged a series of pillows behind her to support her back.

"Ruby's a diva and doesn't know it," Jewel mouthed silently as Ellie took a deep breath and climbed in.

As Allison drove, Ellie listened to the women chatter as they each shared a little piece of themselves with each other. Harmony reported that the clothes were beginning to arrive now at the farm, but there was a system in place to handle the load. She now realized that she had worried too much. She needed to trust God more and worry less. Allison was concerned for Mike because he had terrible back pain after straining himself at work. The pain made him cranky and hard to deal with. Jewel wanted help guessing what Frank might have planned for their upcoming anniversary. He surprised her with a special date every year and the women entertained themselves by guessing what he might try this year. Ruby was worried about one of the students she had subbed for at the High School who she felt might have an eating disorder and needed prayer. Ellie found that she enjoyed sharing her life with these women and being allowed to share in their lives. With their love around her and Levi's Bible in her overnight bag, she felt calm even as she knew she was about to confront Nora.

Harmony was right. A little after two hours of driving Ruby announced that she needed to use the little girl's room. Harmony groaned. Jewel giggled and Ellie stifled a smile. Allison diverted their attention. "There's a McDonald's up here before the town of Sisters. We can stop there."

"A Big Mac sounds kind of good," Ellie admitted.

"A Big Mac sounds more than good," Ruby agreed.

"Women our age shouldn't be eating Big Macs," Jewel teased.

"Come on Jewel! Don't be that way," Allison pleaded. "You're the one person here who could probably eat five Big Macs and not even gain a pound."

"What I wouldn't give for that girl's metabolism," Ruby wailed.

"It also wouldn't hurt to get gas either," Allison added as she pulled into the busy parking lot. Next to the McDonald's was a Chevron station. "I'll drop you off at McDonalds, get the gas real quick and then join you inside."

Ellie opened the door and stretched her legs. The sun was almost finished setting now and the golden light of dusk was beginning to fade. For a moment, Ellie shivered as she felt the darkness falling. Ruby patted her shoulder, "Come on Gurl!" The first stop was the bathroom and then

Ellie and Ruby headed towards McDonalds leaving Harmony and Jewel in the convenience store next door after Harmony admitted she forgot her toothbrush at home. They ordered and found a booth by the window. "Oh my," Ruby sighed as she stared out the paned glass. Ellie followed her stare and saw a disheveled man sitting on the curb.

She had noticed him when they first pulled up. He had the look of the walking dead, the same identifying features she saw in the faces of the homeless in Eugene. They were forgotten people suffering from indescribable pain dulled only by the comfort of addiction. His face was covered in grime and he had long, greasy hair. He was barefoot and his feet were cracked and bloody. He was covered in so much dirt and hair, his age was impossible to determine. In no way did he look like a savory or safe character. Sitting next to him was Jewel. The visual offered an odd juxtaposition. Jewel wore a gold sequin jacket with a black blouse and designer jeans. Her black and gold tiger heels made her look like she was ready to walk a runway in Paris. "What is she doin'?"Ruby exclaimed.

Harmony arrived with her tray and sat next to Ellie. "Is Jewel out there talking to that homeless man?"

"Take a look fer yerself?" Ruby nodded toward the window. Jewel was sitting across from the man on the pavement crisscross applesauce like she had no care in the world. She was laughing now and so was the man. In fact, Ellie noticed a light in his eyes, almost a changed man. "What on earth could she be talkin' to him about?" Ruby wondered aloud.

"I'm not sure that's the safest choice," Harmony said. Stress lines appeared on her forehead as she wrinkled her nose.

Allison sat down next to Ruby with her tray of large McDonald's fries. "Oh, she's alright. This is classic Jewel behavior. She'll strike up a conversation with anyone."

Ellie remembered how Jewel had once approached her in a parking lot when they were strangers and realized the truth in Allison's words.

"We'll keep an eye on her," Ruby added.

"If he does anything aggressive, I'm going out there. I have my conceal and carry license," Harmony insisted.

"What?" Ellie asked. "You do? You have a gun right now?"

"I don't like to draw attention to it, but of course. I'm always ready to protect myself and my friends. Steve won't let me travel alone without one."

"I have a taser," Ruby added. "Right here on my keychain." Ruby showed Ellie what looked like a pink flashlight with a pink feathery strap. I know… ," she nodded. "It looks like a flashlight, but it will zap you, if you're not careful!" She lunged toward Ellie suddenly and she jumped back startled. Allison laughed.

Taking a deep breath, she recovered herself. "I will keep that in mind. Don't mess with Harmony or Ruby. Note taken,"

"Oh, I wouldn't mess with either of them," Allison said, a sparkle in her eye. "They can both be scary."

Concern for Jewel and her safety made them finish their food quickly and then walk outside in the dark to check on her. "I've got my taser ready," Ruby whispered.

"Hey Ladies! Meet my new friend, Jack," Jewel said as they approached. There were awkward hellos around the circle and then Jewel continued. "Jack's been traveling all across the Pacific Northwest. He walked here from Redding, California. It's like two hundred and fifty miles. Isn't that amazing?"

They all nodded, and Jack smiled. "The weather was pretty crazy too, sometimes especially as you hit the mountains, snow, sleet, hail, ice, you name it."

"I can only imagine," Ellie said as she positioned herself protectively next to Jewel.

"His shoes gave out and he's stranded here till he can get another pair," Jewel continued. She then turned to look Jack in the eyes. "Your feet look like they're in pretty bad shape. I've got a first aid kit in the car. Would you mind if I cleaned up your feet, bandaged them and gave you some socks? I've got these awesome winter socks. They're so soft it feels like your feet are surrounded by feathers. I'd give you the shoes if I had them, but I don't think the ones I'm wearing would do you much good."

Jack gave Jewel's tiger heels a once over and wrinkled his nose in confusion before laughing. "They look a bit small for me and not ideal for hiking."

"That, they are not," Jewel agreed. "Jack, I don't want your feet to get infected. I know you're going to want to continue your adventure."

"I wouldn't want to put you out, but if you have it in your mind to do it, I won't stand in the way. I can't really imagine your socks would fit me." His voice was gruff, but his eyes twinkled.

"Oh, they're the stretchy kind. My husband Frank can wear them so there's no reason they wouldn't fit you."

Harmony's eyes narrowed warily, but she said, "I'll go get the first aid kit." Allison handed her the keys.

"Can you bring my smallest bag too? I think that bag is the one I packed my socks in. Also, Harmony I've got a little basin. I stowed it away in my big suitcase. Can you get that?"

Harmony frowned but did as Jewel asked and returned with both the kit, the bag and the plastic wash basin. "Who on earth brings a plastic wash basin on an overnight trip?" Harmony asked as she handed it to Jewel.

"I do. You'd be surprised how many times I've ended up using it to wash dishes in a hotel room." Harmony rolled her eyes. "What size shoe do you wear?" Jewel asked.

"I'm a size ten," Jack said, his voice like crushed gravel.

Jewel gave a covert nod to Allison who gave Jewel a wink in return. "Ruby and I have to run and get a few supplies at the store. Are you, Ellie, and Harmony okay to wait here for a bit?" Allison asked.

The question was directed to Jewel, but she was distracted. "Yes. We're okay," Ellie said. Harmony nodded her agreement and watched as Ruby and Allison headed toward the Suburban. Jewel was already busy fishing through the first aid kit. Ellie bit her bottom lip as she eyeballed Jack's feet. Determining the severity of his injuries was difficult because both feet were caked in dirt, grease, and grime. Ellie could see dried blood and what looked like crusted pus around his heels. His toenails were long, yellow, and grotesquely twisted. His feet were covered in blisters and the odor reminded Ellie of what she imagined rotting flesh must smell like. Ellie felt her stomach lurch as she realized she was suppressing the urge to vomit.

She took a step back and breathed through her mouth. "Jewel, I think we should probably soak his feet first and then wash them. We can put the antiseptic on after that." Jewel handed Ellie several clean washcloths from her designer bag and the wash basin.

"We should fill the wash basin with warm water and let his feet soak for a bit with some Epsom salt," Jewel suggested.

"I'll go," Ellie said, anxious to relieve her nostrils from the horrible smell of Jack's feet. She went to the bathroom in the convenience store and filled the tub. As she poured the warm water, she wondered what Jewel had gotten them mixed up in. She felt self-conscious as she returned to the front of the store. Harmony was tapping her foot with her arms crossed and looked relieved when she spotted Ellie. Jack was sitting on the sidewalk and Harmony helped Ellie place the wash basin beneath his feet on the road beneath the curb where he sat.

"Alright, Jack. Put those suckers in there and let 'em soak," Jewel said. Jack laughed and eased his feet into the water. He winced. Ellie gave one washcloth to Jewel and then handed the other to Harmony. She shook her head vehemently.

"Nope. I'll take care of the wash basin. You and Jewel can do the washing," her voice was strong, matter of fact. Jewel handed Ellie and Harmony two pairs of latex gloves.

"Wow, you really are prepared for anything," Ellie said with awe.

"I've never regretted packing too much," Jewel laughed. "Life is full of surprises and I like to be prepared." After allowing his feet to soak for several minutes, Jewel began to clean Jack's left foot and Ellie took his right. She felt incredibly awkward, but Jack was beaming. "I think I might have just met two angels today," he said. Harmony coughed and Jack turned his face toward her. "Okay, two angels and a half angel." He laughed heartily at his own joke. Harmony tried to conceal the edge of a smile that surfaced at the corner of her mouth.

Jewel laughed. "You're not going to think any of us are angels when we pour the antiseptic on your cut feet. You might call us devils then."

Jack chuckled. "There's no joy without pain. Life has taught me that one."

Ellie soon realized they could not continue their job without more water. In just a few seconds of soaking, the clear water had turned almost completely black. Unceremoniously, Harmony took the basin and walked toward the field behind the service station and dumped the water. As she walked back, she noticed an outdoor faucet on the side of the restaurant and was pleased to find that there were spigots for both hot and cold water. She rinsed the basin, refilled it, and set the tub once again on the ground before his feet. They soaked them again and once the water turned black repeated the process several times.

After the caked dirt and body fluids had been removed, Ellie was able to see the extent of the damage to the man's feet. The cracks in his heels were wide and deep, the major source for the dried blood. The cracks were somewhat infected because his feet were obviously swollen and the skin around the wounds red and irritated. Smaller cracks covered the entire area even the arches. Protective calluses, the size of quarters were prominent on the pads of his feet and his toes were misshapen and deformed. The smell had improved after several soakings in the wash basin. Jewel had added lavender scented Epsom salt, which also helped with the smell. Ellie could hardly believe anyone could walk on feet so damaged. Washing his feet was an arduous job and Ellie was conscious now of the dozens of onlookers staring at them in confusion from inside McDonalds or peering at them from the gas station. Jewel seemed completely unaware of the attention they were attracting. She spoke in her usual conversational voice. "I don't know, Jack. You may want to lay off your feet for a while and let these suckers heal. Maybe even see a doctor."

Jack chuckled. "Can't remember a time in recent history that my feet didn't look like this." Harmony gave Ellie an alarmed look that she pretended not to notice.

"I see," Jewel nodded without judgement.

The old washcloths now lay discarded next to the wash basin. Harmony busied herself by taking them to the trash can, because they were now too filthy to be used again. "Okay Jack. Forgive me!" Jewel took the antiseptic and poured the liquid lightly on clean cotton balls and dabbed gingerly on Jack's wounds. She then poured more liquid on his wounds. The fluid bubbled over his cracked feet and he erupted in a strident howl. His face contorted into rage and he screamed out several expletives as the pain hit him. Ellie and Jewel hastily backed away. After a few moments his shoulders eased as he recovered from the pain He tossed his head back and laughed heartily like a crazed maniac.

"Okay," he said. "The pain has passed."

"Are you sure?" Ellie asked, feeling slightly timid by the violence of his outburst.

"I won't bite. I promise."

Jewel dabbed ointment over his wounds and Harmony handed them both gauze and first aid tape. As they were finishing the bandaging process, a young man came out of the McDonalds with four cups of coffee in a beverage holder. "Hi," he said awkwardly. "My mom saw you guys out here and wanted to buy you all some coffee."

"Oh, what a sweetie," Jewel cooed. "Please tell your mother thank you for us. That was very thoughtful."

"And from me too," Jack added. He extended his newly acquired cup of coffee outward in a mock toast and took a gulp.

Ellie took a tiny sip and smiled at the young man. "That was kind of your mom. We appreciate it."

He whispered to Ellie. "It's cool what you're doing. If you need anything else from McDonalds, my mom and I would be happy to buy it for you. Just let us know." He walked back into the restaurant. *This is all Jewel*, Ellie thought.

Harmony watched the boy leave and looked to Ellie. "That was nice of them."

"People can be very thoughtful sometimes," Ellie said.

Harmony nodded. "Sometimes you can even surprise yourself."

"Wow, these really do feel like feathers," Jack said. He now held the winter fleece socks that Jewel had given him. He placed the socks against his grimy cheek and then began to put them on. The Suburban pulled up in front of them and Ruby and Allison appeared. Allison was holding a box as she walked toward them. "We got something for you, Jack," she said as she handed him the box.

Jack guffawed. "It feels like my birthday."

Ellie couldn't help but gasp when he opened the box and a pair of brand-new hiking boots emerged. Jack's eyes widened and filled with light. Ellie knew the troubles in his life were probably vast and overwhelming, the depth of his pain was more than a foot washing and a new pair of shoes could heal, but for the moment he looked like a child at Christmas time.

"Five angels," he said as his eyes brimmed with tears. "I always felt like I'd be lucky to meet just one angel, but I've met five."

Ruby shook her head. "Oh no. We're just ordinary women I assure ya. Ya just caught us on a good day."

Jack looked Ruby directly in the eye. "There's nothing ordinary about this, mam."

Harmony interrupted. "Ladies, I think it's time to hit the road."

"Jack, you need something to eat before we leave?" Jewel asked.

"Oh no. My heart is full. Thanks to you ladies," Jack said.

"Try to stay off those feet for a while. Let them heal," Jewel replied.

"Will do," Jack promised.

As they climbed in the Suburban and Ellie looked at her beautiful friends, she could not help but echo his thoughts. Her heart was also full.

They didn't arrive at the Comfort Inn till nearly 11 pm. Harmony had been right of course. Several stops were made on the way to accommodate Ruby's bladder, but they all had been affected by the incident with Jack and there was a sense of excitement and joy. Harmony could not resist giving Jewel a mild scolding in the car. "That man could have been a psycho murderer!"

"We were in a public place!" Jewel countered. "You were all with me. I felt perfectly safe."

Allison interjected in her gentle way. "But Harmony, you saw the light in that man's eyes when Jewel talked to him. We were able to do something special for him. Jewel opened the door and we all got to come out of it more compassionate and generous and it was fun picking out those hiking boots.

Don't you think?"

Harmony nodded, but grimaced as she turned to Jewel. "I can't believe you and Ellie cleaned his feet."

Jewel laughed. "It was a little gross, but you emptied that tub. Honestly, that was the most disgusting job."

"You were both actually touching his feet."

Ellie laughed as she looked back on the event with some disbelief. "I refuse to even talk about it. I had a frozen smile on my face the entire time."

"Nah," Jewel said. "You handled it like a pro."

* * *

Allison parked the car, and the women began to unload their belongings. "Ellie, come with me and we'll check in." They walked side by side into the lobby and Allison whispered into her ear. "We have two rooms booked. Ruby and Harmony cannot share a room. You get that right? They'll kill each other."

Ellie laughed. "Yes. They are not meant to be bunk mates. So what's the plan?"

"I think Jewel and Harmony take one room and you, me, and Ruby the other. Do you think that's good? We're separating the two packrats."

"Sounds good," agreed Ellie.

They waited in the lobby semi patiently as Allison handed out the room cards. "Okay, Jewel and Harmony you're roomies and the rest of us in the other room. The doors are adjoining, so we can still hang out altogether if we want."

"Yay! Slumber party," Jewel whooped.

Ruby glared. "I am worn slap out. You've caused enough excitement fer a month. I plan to get some shut eye."

"Alright, Alright. Fair enough," Jewel retreated. "Someone gets grumpy late at night."

They parted company with Jewel and Harmony at the doors to their rooms. "So, who's sleeping where?" Ruby asked when they were inside.

253

Allison gave Ellie a knowing look. "Ruby, you get the queen by the window. Ellie and I will take the bed near the bathroom."

"Oh, you are just saints! Thank ya kindly," Ruby gushed.

"No problem. You don't mind sleeping in the same bed, do you?" Allison asked Ellie.

"I think we'll survive one night."

Ruby took a long time in the bathroom. When she came out, she was dressed head to toe in satin lavender pajamas that included a lavender hair wrap and lavender satin slippers. "Wow!" Ellie said. "You don't mess around with bedtime."

Allison snuck into the bathroom. "I won't take long, Ell."

Ruby smiled. "If ya don't treat yerself well, no one else will." She climbed into bed and removed a matching lavender eye mask from her night bag as well as a pair of earplugs.

"You come prepared."

Ruby nodded. "I've found that gettin' good rest opens the door to a good tomorrow. The best intentions won't amount to a hill of beans if yer not well rested. That's what I've learned teachin' anyway. Now, goodnight. You and Allison oughta get yer rest too and not stay up all night. You have a big day tomorrow. I'm praying for ya, ya hear?"

"I know you are. Thank you, Ruby. You make me feel strong."

"That's cuz ya are strong. Always remember that." Ruby settled into her bed and adjusted her eye mask. "Goodnight Ellie. You've got this," she winked and then pulled the mask over her eyes.

"Goodnight Ruby."

Allison came out of the bathroom and Ellie went to brush her teeth, wash her face, and brush her hair. As she prepared for bed, the thoughts of Nora began to catch up with her. Tomorrow there would be no more hiding. She would be confronted directly with her childhood scars and she would be forced to make choices, choices that would reveal who she really was. She felt anxiety building in her stomach. When she came out Ruby looked like she had already succumbed to the throes of deep sleep. Allison was in bed already reading. She nodded toward Ruby, placed a finger to her lips and smiled.

Ellie went to her night bag and pulled out Levi's Bible and her reading glasses. The leather felt soft, but the bulk of the Bible reminded her of his masculine strength, the way he made her feel safe, cared for, and protected. Ellie crawled into bed next to Allison and propped several pillows behind her back. She ran her fingers through the creases and opened randomly to a page. Ellie's eyes widened as she absorbed the highlighted text and various notes in the margins. She had opened to Philippians 3 and her eyes focused immediately on Levi's blocky handwriting. He had written these words:

Look forward. Leave behind the past. Have faith in God's plan for your future. God's plan for you is always good, always better than imagined even when it doesn't feel like it in the moment.

Her eyes scanned the highlighted verses 12-14.

Not that I have already reached the goal or am already perfect, but I make every effort to take hold of it because I also have been taken hold of by Christ Jesus. Brothers and sisters, I do not consider myself to have taken hold of it. But one thing I do: Forgetting what is behind and reaching forward to what is ahead, I pursue as my goal the prize promised by God's heavenly call in Christ Jesus.

The power of the words filled her. Levi was right, a person only had the choice to move forward. The time had come for Ellie to walk strong rather than grasping and clinging to the past. She had to walk into her meeting with Nora tomorrow with faith. If she could just trust God, she would have peace or at least she needed to believe that.

Allison said goodnight and turned off the bedside lamp beside her. She set Levi's Bible gently on the bed stand and turned off her light. She closed her eyes and said a prayer in her head.

Lord, help me to trust you. I give myself to you, my life, my future, my everything. Give me the strength I need tomorrow to face Nora. Help me to forgive her for past wrongs, to look forward and put the past behind me. Help me to understand Nora, to see her through your eyes. Help her to forgive me for all the wrongs I have held against her, my refusal to forgive and let go of hurt. Thank you for my praying sisters, for Levi, for my boys, my family. Help me to live in the knowledge that I am blessed. No matter what happens, help me to know that you love me and that you are in control of all things.

She closed her eyes and felt peace descend on her like a soft veil.

* * *

Ellie jolted upright in bed. She was startled as she took in her strange surroundings before recognizing that she was still in the motel room. She gazed at the bedside alarm clock and registered the time, 3:02 a.m. A sonorous sound filled the room that reminded Ellie of thunder. The noise began soft but began to grow till it reached a grating crescendo and then a diminuendo of what sounded like snorting noises. The realization dawned on her that Ruby was snoring. Allison rolled over next to her. Through the dim light of the alarm clock, Ellie could see her pressing her pillow to her ears and groaning. "Allison," Ellie whispered as she tapped her shoulder.

Allison's body began to shake followed by the sound of uncontrollable giggling. "Lord help us. Ruby said she snored, but it's like she's going for a world record or something."

Allison's giggling sparked her own laughter. "Right? I woke up and thought we were in the middle of a thunderstorm."

"Seriously. I mean, I bet Jewel and Harmony can hear her from the next room. She sounds like a buzz saw." Allison now spoke through laughter so intense tears glistened in her eyes.

"Allison, I don't think I can sleep with that noise," Ellie confessed.

"Should we head over to Jewel and Harmony's room?"

"It's 3:00 in the morning. I don't want to wake them up."

"How about we go to the lobby and just hang out?"

"I'm in my pajamas."

"Yes, and you look so cute," laughed Allison. "Who cares? We're dressed, enough. No one knows us here. We have nothing to prove. Let's live a little bit."

Ellie thought for a moment and then shrugged, "okay."

The absurdity of the situation had the effect of a time machine. Ellie and

Allison felt like adolescents at a slumber party as they tiptoed past a sleeping Ruby, out of the room, and into the hallway in their pajamas. They carried blankets with them and scurried through the halls of the motel toward the lobby giggling like schoolgirls. The hotel desk clerk looked about ready to chastise them, but then seemed to register their age and focused his attention back on his computer as they settled on the couches in the lobby.

"How often do you think he sees women our age in their pajamas in the middle of the night?" Allison asked.

"Probably more than we think," Ellie sniggered. "You know what?"

"What?"

"I'm kind of hungry. Do you think we can get anything to eat?"

"You had a Big Mac today."

"I know, but those burgers are empty calories and now my stomach's grumbling."

Allison looked around the lobby. The motel store is closed, and I know the dining room is closed. Should I ask the clerk what our dining options are at three in the morning? He loves us, I can tell."

Ellie joined Allison in her scan of the room. "Let's not make his life any harder, shall we? I got it! Vending machines—Look—over there." Ellie pointed to the far corner of the room. "You got any quarters?"

"I didn't bring my wallet?"

"I did. Let's see what they got."

Holding their blankets, they darted toward the vending machines and scrutinized the selection of candy and junk food. "Peanut M&Ms and Reese's Peanut Butter Cups. I think I'm in heaven," Ellie laughed.

"Any Junior Mints?"

"Nope, but they got Raisinets."

"That will work," Allison clapped in delight. "Hey look! This vending machine has instant coffee. You game?"

"Absolutely. Yes. Here's a $5 bill. I'll get the chocolate. You get the coffees. Deal?"

"Deal."

Heavy laden with coffee cups and junk food, the two walked back to the lounge and sat in the sofas. Ellie dumped a pile of candy on the coffee table and grabbed a bag of peanut M&M's. "I'm going to have the worst heartburn," she groaned.

"Well, the vending machine where I got this coffee was also selling Tums, so you're covered," Allison chortled.

"Am I sabotaging my visit tomorrow with Nora by not getting my sleep and eating heaps of junk food?"

Allison attempted to toss a Raisinet into her mouth and missed. "Nah. We weren't going to get any sleep anyway considering how Ruby was snoring."

"I suppose you're right."

Allison sat back into the sofa and brought her coffee to her chest and sipped daintily. "So, tell me how you're feeling about tomorrow. Oh wait. I guess we're talking about today now."

Ellie sighed deeply. "I think I'm feeling okay. I have to tell you something." She watched as her friend's eyes widened. "What?"

"You know the book I was reading before I went to bed?"

Allison shrugged. "I didn't really notice, but I saw that you were reading before you went to bed."

"Well, it was a Bible."

"Okay?"

"Well, not just any Bible. Levi's Bible. He gave it to me before I left. He told me it was his grief Bible and that it helped him get over losing Melinda. He wanted me to have it. He said he thought I could use it, that reading the scriptures that he read, underlined, and took notes on might help me."

Allison's eyes widened as she gave her a full on cheshire cat grin. "Ellie! Seriously? Oh my God and I'm not saying that to swear. That's like the most incredible gift I've ever heard of anyone receiving. You gotta know he's in love with you."

Ellie's face turned crimson. She shifted her position on the sofa and brought her knees to her chest. "I don't know about that, Allison, but I know how it made me feel?"

"And how was that? I'm dying to know."

"In my relationship with Davis, I never really felt like he loved me or had my back. This whole day knowing that I had that Bible tucked away in my night bag, I've just felt strong, you know? Almost like I had a secret weapon. I feel like I'm covered, like someone's got my back."

Allison smiled gently. "Ellie, that's what it feels like to be loved. Don't you know that?"

"I read some of it. I mean Levi's Bible. I landed on a chapter in Philippians about looking toward the future, focusing on God's promise. He has notes and everything. It's almost like I'm hearing his voice."

"Is that a good thing?" Allison asked.

"Yes. I think it is," Ellie admitted.

Allison emptied the last of her Raisinets into her palm and shoved them into her mouth. Ellie enjoyed watching her behave uncharacteristically graceless. Allison was usually the poster girl for good manners.

Her friend's brow furrowed in concentration as she ate. "That's what you're supposed to do then. I hope you're listening to Levi and you're moving forward and putting the past behind you. Did you know I was married before?"

Ellie tore the wrapper of the Reese's Peanut Butter Cups. "You've mentioned that fact, but you've never told me the details."

"That's because the details aren't pretty, but I know something about moving forward. When I was a kid, we didn't have much fun at my house. My parents were Jehovah Witnesses, and they were just so strict. Jehovah Witnesses are known for taking their faith pretty seriously. We don't celebrate birthdays, holidays, no fourth of July if you can imagine. There was a lot of time at Kingdom Hall, but not a lot of joy in our household. I guess I was just looking for an escape, a little fun. I wanted to feel like it was okay to be a healthy teenage girl with wants and desires. Anyway, I met this guy when I was working my first high school job at a gas station. Seriously, it was such a stereotype. He pulled up to the station in his Harley Davison. His name was Chad and he was a bad boy, dangerous, incredibly good looking, and several years older than me. Basically, he was the entire recipe for tragedy and heartbreak, and I was a goner the second I laid eyes on him."

"Really? How old were you?" Ellie asked.

"All of seventeen. But I was so confident at the time that he was the one."

"So young. What happened?"

Allison leaned back into the sofa and thought. "Well, we started hanging out and he was quite the sweet talker. He told me I was beautiful, special, the most amazing woman he had ever encountered, you know the usual nonsense, but it just worked like a charm on me. No one had ever told me I was beautiful or special, you know?"

Ellie nodded sympathetically as the themes of her story and Allison's seemed to intertwine in her head. "I get it, Allison."

"In our home, we were always made to feel like we were being prideful or vain if we complimented each other. I was taught that most celebrations like Easter and Christmas were pagan holidays and that God wouldn't want us to celebrate them, but really, I think my parents believed that celebrating something like a birthday was just downright prideful, you know, sinful. Like somehow, we were trying to put focus on ourselves rather than God. I just always thought that if God loved us why would he look down on us for celebrating a birthday or a party? I mean Jesus celebrated with wine, went to weddings, and hung out with people from all walks of life. He tried to connect with people. Our religion always seemed to set us apart and create divides. I felt very alone, and those circumstances made me very vulnerable to Chad's manipulation."

Ellie's eyes widened. "What happened?"

"We got married, eloped. I got on the back of his bike and we drove all the way to South Dakota where Chad had a job lined up with his cousin at an oil refinery."

"Wow, you were a brave girl."

Allison chortled. "Brave and stupid. I had no idea who I had married. The oil refinery job was real, and it was a good job. Chad was making lots of money, working all the time and coming home drunk with friends. He wanted sex. He wanted me to cook and clean for him and his friends and sometimes when he got real drunk, these "friends" wanted me to serve them in other ways too."

"Oh my God! What did you do?"

"Oh Ellie! I hardly knew a single person there, but next door was a kindly neighbor who was also a wife of one of the oil refinery men, but her man wasn't like Chad. He was a Christian man, a true Christian and he loved his wife. He didn't do the heavy drinking and partying that most of the guys were doing. Her name was Lindsey and I think his name was Scott. I ran over to her house and just stayed there till the drunken parties bled themselves dry. She let me stay in their spare room."

"Very glad, you had Lindsey."

"Oh, me too. That was God. He's always there even in the worst storm."

"How long did the marriage last?"

"I stayed in it a whole year. I wanted to go home after three months, but you know what got in my way?"

"What?"

"Pride. The idea of telling my parents I was wrong. Having to go home penniless with my tail between my legs. I stayed in that mess for nine more months because of my pride."

"And then..."

"Then I knew I had had enough. Chad hit me and I finally realized there was nothing in the marriage I could salvage. My cheek was bruised, and I had a black eye. I didn't even do anything. He just hit me because he was drunk, and he could, and I knew I had to get out."

"How did you do it? How did you leave?"

"Chad gave me an allowance for groceries, and I began saving some back. Lindsey and Scott gave me two hundred dollars and bought me a Greyhound bus ticket back to Eugene. He went to work, and they took me to the bus station. I didn't look back. That was quite a bus ride—longest four days of my life."

Ellie smiled. "And now you're with Mike."

Allison looked thoughtful and took a deep breath. "Mike may not go to church and he may be quiet about matters of faith, but I've never met a man who could love me with more devotion, gentleness and faithfulness than Mike. Honestly, if it wasn't for the nightmare with Chad, I don't know

261

if I would have had the eyes to see what a wonderful man Mike was and is—how perfect he is for me. At the end of the day, it's a man's actions that matter, not his words."

Ellie wrapped her blanket around her shoulders and leaned back into the sofa. "I couldn't agree more."

"Ellie, women need to be treated like special jewels, rubies of great price. If you meet a man who treats you that way, he's a keeper."

"So that's the lesson of the story, I take it?"

Allison laughed. "Why yes. That and well..., also this. When you meet your sister tomorrow, just remember that God's already made you whole. You don't need your sister to act a certain way to make you okay. Does that make sense?"

"I think so, Allie. Thanks."

Chapter 20

Walkway

*You gain strength,
courage and confidence by
every experience in which
you really stop to look fear
in the face. You are able to
say to yourself, 'I have
lived through this horror, I
can take the next thing
that comes along.' You
must do the thing you
think you cannot do.*
—*Eleanor Roosevelt*

Ellie felt someone shaking her. She opened her eyes and then shut them tightly again. A pitiful groan escaped her lips. The sun was streaming through the motel window. Allison was shaking her. "Come on beautiful. Today is the day."

"What time is it?" she said through clenched teeth.

"8:00 am."

Ellie sat up in bed and rubbed her eyes. She squinted as the harsh sunlight filtered through the blinds. Even through the glare, Allison looked gorgeous. She was wearing a fitted purple blouse and skinny blue jeans tucked into a pair of knee-high boots. "You're dressed already?"

"I've been up since 7:00 am. I wanted to take a shower. I felt sticky because I still had candy residue all over my pajamas and even in my hair. Ruby's been up since 6:00 am and I thought it would be best to try to give you a couple hours of sleep. We managed to sneak in without her even knowing we were gone."

Ellie tried to clear her muddled brain. "What time did we get back to the motel room?"

"5:30 am." Allison looked at her with concern. "Are you having heartburn?"

"A little," Ellie admitted. Allison handed her two small pills.

"These are hospital grade antacids. I think they might help you and they take only about ten minutes to take effect. Hey, but on the positive side, you did get more than a couple hours of sleep."

"Do I have time for a shower? I'm supposed to meet Nora at ten."

"I think you have time for a quick one. The rehab center is only about ten minutes away. I'm going downstairs to the lobby to get our continental breakfast. Everyone else is down there already. Meet us when you're ready."

Ellie used her time in the shower to clear her head, to think about her approach to confronting her sister. She needed to enter a room with her sister without the baggage of the past, an open heart. The Praying Sisters had enlightened her perspective on Nora. Jewel's words stayed with her. *Why would she go crazy like that? Something must have happened.* Nora had a story and Ellie had never taken the time to listen. She realized that her anger toward her sister was like a powerful storm. When she was with Nora, the force of the storm was so intense that she was never able to get past her own emotions, much less understand her sister's. Was it possible that Nora and Ellie were both victims of their own pain, lashing out at each other like wounded animals? Perhaps it was time to change the pattern, to try something new.

Chapter 20

* * *

The breakfast room consisted of one long buffet table and about five large tables near the great window overlooking the motel parking lot. An older couple were eating breakfast at the table closest to the lobby. The Praying Sisters were seated closest to the window and despite the early morning hour engaged in animated conversation. "The lady of the day," Ruby said as Ellie approached the table. She scrutinized her plate. "What?Justt one boiled egg and a slice of toast?"

"My stomach was a bit upset this morning, Ruby. I think this is about all I can handle, but thanks for the concern."

"Well, I hope ya slept okay. Clyde tells me I have a bit of a problem with snorin'. I hope it didn't bother y'all none."

Ellie hesitated, but Allison interrupted, "Oh no. Ellie and I didn't notice a thing. We slept like babies."

"Really?" Harmony asked. "Someone in this hotel was snoring. We could hear it in our room, couldn't we Jewel? It sounded sort of like a power tool. I thought the hotel was doing maintenance in the middle of the night at first. I almost called the front desk before I recognized the sound for what it was."

Jewel caught Allison's warning look from the corner of her eye and nodded. "Oh, it wasn't so bad. I hardly noticed any noise."

"Really?" Harmony said incredulously. "That's not what you said last night." Harmony grimaced as Allison subtly kicked her under the table.

Jewel gracefully changed the subject. "Ellie, I hope you don't mind, but the four of us wanted to really be here for you today. I mean it's the reason we're here. We don't want you to read them now, but we've each written you a note of encouragement."

Allison pulled a small silk change purse out of her bag, opened the metal clasp and removed four pieces of colored paper. "Ruby came up with the idea and she brought her beautiful note paper. We each got to write our message to you on a different color of her special stationery. Ruby's is the

265

peach one, mine is the yellow, Jewel's is pink, and Harmony's is the blue one."

"Oh, nevermind givin' me credit," Ruby insisted. "We've all just been tryin' to think of the best way to support our Ellie."

Allison passed the folded paper notes to Ellie. Each slip of paper was cool and smooth to the touch and she traced each note gently with her fingertips. She placed the notes in her jacket pocket and zipped the closure for safe keeping. Her cheeks felt flushed. "You know ladies. I may not have been lucky in romantic love, but I think I may have just hit the jackpot in finding the most wonderful and best friends this world has to offer."

Ruby smiled. "Ya know what I think?"

"I don't even dare to imagine," Ellie laughed.

"I think you bring out the best in us Ellie. Everyone of us just wants good things fer ya. When you see someone suffer and struggle, but keep the faith, well that's an inspiration."

"I'm an inspiration? Ha ha. That's a good one," Ellie sniggered.

"Well, we're not here for no reason," Harmony said. "You're family, plain and simple."

Ellie was touched. "When you guys are with me, I always feel like anything is possible."

"Anything is possible," Jewel said.

* * *

The rehab center was a simple grey industrial building with large glass doors in the front. Allison parked the SUV, but Ellie hesitated to get out. Her gut was churning. She was always surprised by the overwhelming sense of helplessness that descended on her the moment she was in the proximity of Nora. Ruby placed a hand squarely between Ellie's shoulder blades. She felt the power of her touch and then her silent prayer. Closing her eyes, she felt the power of the prayer in the pressure of Ruby's steady hand on her back. The other Praying Sisters sat silently allowing her to take her own time. Ellie reached into her purse and touched the spine of Levi's Bible and drew courage from the softbound leather. She opened the door and let her boots hit the pavement.

Her friends surrounded her, and they walked toward the front entrance together. The sun was shining brilliantly, and Ellie felt the warmth of its rays on her face. God had graced them with a beautiful, unseasonably warm spring day. Next to the front door was a garden area with roses, which weren't yet in bloom and several awnings with tables and chairs. Allison stopped by the front entrance. "What do you say we wait out here for you? We're here if you need us, but you got the space you need. It's a gorgeous day and we'll be just fine gabbing out here. You know us. Is that okay or do you want us to all go to your sister's room?"

Ellie laughed at the thought. "She might think I brought a posse to beat her up. Perhaps not the best approach since I've come in peace. I shouldn't need a gang just to have a conversation with my sister."

"Just so you know, Ellie, I'm not above beating her up if you think that would help you," Harmony dead panned.

Ellie laughed and the tightness in her shoulders eased. "Thank you, Harmony. I do love my sister, but I appreciate that offer. In fact, in a weird way knowing you would beat someone up for me makes me feel really good."

"Come here," Jewel said as she embraced her with a quick hug.

Jewel released her and Ellie took a moment to meet her eyes and then the eyes of all her friends. "Thank you, ladies. I still can't believe you came up here with me."

Ruby frowned and looked at her watch. "It's past 10:00 Ellie. Go!"

A middle-aged brunette woman in glasses and a blue blouse greeted her at the reception area. "I'm here to see Nora Brown. She's expecting me."

"Sign in here," the woman said. "When you're finished visiting, you will need to sign out."

Ellie signed her name and then froze. The last signature recorded belonged to Mariah Brown. She had checked in at 9:32 and had not yet signed out. Ellie looked desperately to the glass doors and wondered if she should flee. Were Nora and Mariah planning a surprise confrontation?

What kind of set up was she walking into?

Levi's words came to her as she took a deep breath, *Look forward. Leave behind the past. Have faith in God's plan for your future. God's plan for you is always good, always better than imagined even when it doesn't feel like it in the moment.*

Okay Levi, Ellie thought. *Let's see if you're right. I'm not running. Here goes nothing.*

"Nora Brown is on the third floor, room 322. There's an elevator. You just take a right at the cafeteria. Okay?"

Ellie nodded. "Thank you." As she walked toward the elevator, she subconsciously unzipped her pocket. Her fingers traced the soft paper messages of encouragement from her friends. She pulled out one of the notes—the yellow one, Allison's note. The elevator opened and Ellie stepped inside the empty space, but she focused on Allison's handwriting.

Hi Sweet Girl!

I had such fun last night. It's been years since I've raided a vending machine and eaten junk food in the middle of the night in a motel lobby. Okay, busted! I've actually never done that before—LOL. That's the kind of thing you can only do with a special person, the best kind of friend. That is how I've learned to think of you. Words of encouragement? Well, here it is. You are special and amazing. We all need to hear that, but in your case, I really do believe it. I will never forget the love you showed my Natalie and how you helped her build confidence in herself and her abilities. I want you to also have that confidence in yourself. God does not forget those who love him, and he won't forget you. He sees you. He really does. You can face today in all confidence. I promise.

Much Love,

Allison

In her mind, Ellie saw Allison's beautiful smile and remembered how their paths had crossed not so long ago when her friend came to her door with a chicken coop. *I am blessed,* Ellie thought.

The elevator opened into a hallway with grey linoleum and white walls.

Ellie took a deep breath and tried to project the confidence of Allison's blessing. When Ellie reached room number 322, the door was open and Nora was visible sitting sideways in a chair with her feet wrapped over the arm frame, a book on her lap. She was next to the window and the sun poured into the room. Half of her face was in shadow. Ellie knocked cautiously on the door. "Nora?"

Nora's face turned to the door and now her features were entirely in shadow with the bright sun behind her. "Ellie, hey. Come on in."

Cautiously she entered the space and surveyed the room looking for evidence of Mariah's presence, but Nora was alone.

The room was clean and cozy, but a little antiseptic. Grey carpet covered the floors. There was a small kitchenette and a tiny living space. In the corner was a single bed and then a large window with a compact blue loveseat and two high back chairs. Ellie wondered how Nora could afford such a place. When she greeted her, Nora rose to her feet. "Hi Nora. You look good." Ellie wasn't lying. Her sister had gained a little weight, which in her case was a good thing. Her cheeks no longer looked hollow and there was even some color in them. The circles under her eyes were less pronounced.

Nora gave her an awkward smile, but Ellie noticed a strange calmness in her demeanor. That was new. In her experience, Nora always seemed jittery and on edge, just a little out of control, but in this moment, she seemed peaceful and rested. "Hey Ellie," why don't you have a seat here. The loveseat or the chair, either one."

She did as instructed and settled on the loveseat. Nora sat next to her on one of the blue high back chairs. "This is a nice place, Nora."

"Yes, it is. I know what you're thinking. How on earth did I get in a rehab facility? How am I affording it? Right?" Nora's voice was not accusatory, just matter of fact. She shifted in her seat and centered her body, placing both feet firmly on the carpet.

"The thought might have crossed my mind," Ellie admitted gently.

"It's quite a story and it involves you."

"Really? I want to hear it, Nora. I want to listen." Ellie hoped her tone suggested invitation, not judgement.

"Well, it's been over a year since we last talked…"

"I'm sorry about that Nora. I didn't mean half those things I said that Thanksgiving. I was in pain." She hesitated. "Oh shoot. I'm sorry, Nora. I'll let you talk. I told myself I would try to hear you better than I have." Ellie took a breath and tried to focus on listening.

Nora surprised Ellie with a smile that went all the way to her eyes. "It's okay, Ellie. I'm sorry too. I was in a lot of pain myself. The affair with Mariah and Davis brought up a lot of baggage for me. Garbage in my life that you don't know about, but that I've been trying to deal with for over twenty years. I haven't dealt with it well and I know it."

"Tell me," Ellie said gently. "I'm not your spoiled sister with the perfect life anymore. I think I'll understand better now."

Nora looked at her quizzically. "I think you're right. We're not the same people we were, not either of us."

Ellie laughed lightly. "You know Nora, I'm hoping that maybe that'll be a good thing."

"I think so too. So, I guess, I'll start first by telling you why I'm here." Nora looked Ellie in the eye for a moment and then focused her gaze on her white tennis shoes. "After the bomb detonated a year ago and we all found out about Mariah and Davis, I spiraled bad. You know my whole life I've gone back and forth between sobriety and using. Lee never judged me because he couldn't kick alcohol, but I was doing quite a bit of heroin, a heavier drug than what I've done in the past, my attempt to self-medicate, I guess. A friend of mine, and I say that ironically, introduced it to me a few years ago. At the time I thought it helped me function. You know it made me feel euphoric, safe and happy. Unfortunately, the drug wears off and then the depression, anxiety, mood swings are even worse than before. The habit gets expensive besides. Anyway, I got into a pretty bad fix. Life took a very bad turn when I got into a car with some guys I met at another friend's party and went to New Mexico with them. I ended up in a hotel in Albuquerque sick to death from withdrawal. Those guys took my money and stranded me. The hotel owner was knocking on the door constantly trying to get me out of the room while I was puking and sick as hell. I can't say it was the first time I was in a bind like that one, but I'm over forty years old now. I was being swallowed alive by choice. The reality dawned on me that no one had to threaten to send me to hell, I was already there."

"I'm sorry, Nora. What happened?" Ellie said gently. Nora grabbed a glass of water and sipped.

"I called Lee. He called the motel and paid for my room for a couple of days and drove all the way down to get me. He was so mad, but...well, he's always been my person, you know?"

Ellie nodded. "I'm glad he was there for you."

"We drove back up to Oregon and well, I made a list of things I was going to change in my life. One of the first things on my list was I was going to go to church. This was a bigger deal than you know, because church is really the reason, I became an addict to begin with."

Ellie opened her eyes in surprise. "What do you mean?"

"Do you remember Pastor Calvin?"

Wow, that's a name from the past. You mean that youth minister who was at our church for about a year when I was in the fifth grade? I remember him. He was good looking."

"Yes, that's the one. He worked under Dad. Anyway, I started having sex with him the summer after my eighth-grade year." Nora's words were matter of fact, but the reality of what she said rushed over Ellie like a cold wave.

"Oh Nora! He had a wife and two small kids. He had sex with you?"

Nora nodded solemnly. "I don't think I was the only girl either in the youth group. The relationship, if you can call it that, lasted for about four months."

Ellie shook her head in disbelief. "Did Dad know? Mom?"

Nora took a deep breath. "Mom never knew. Dad? Well, I never told him, but I've always thought he suspected the truth. Pastor Calvin was fired when another church member brought some accusations forward. I remember Dad asking me if he had ever touched me inappropriately, but I thought I loved him. I denied everything. At the end of the day, I think Dad

271

didn't really want to know what happened. I think it would have killed him. But honestly I never felt like he looked at me the same way after that."

Ellie's eyes welled with tears. She felt a burning sensation in the back of her throat. "You were fourteen years old! Of course, you felt like you were in love. Nora, it wasn't your fault."

"Well, eventually, Calvin dropped me like a hot potato. He left town and I was left feeling like I was so dirty I could never be made clean. I didn't feel like I belonged in the family anymore. I guess I just believed if anyone knew the truth, they would just never be able to love me. Beyond redemption so they say."

"Nora, I'm so sorry. It's not true, you know? You're not beyond redemption. Not at all," Ellie whispered.

"I'm not like you, Ellie. You're a very centered person, but I've always had intense mood swings. Even before Calvin, I think I was showing signs of bi-polar which is probably why I was so susceptible to his advances. I tended to get really hard on myself, you know? To not have any confidence. When some authoritative man, a spiritual leader who people respect, comes in and tells you you're all that and a bag of chips, you just feel so good in that moment. Of course, I was fourteen and incredibly stupid and my hormones a mess on top of everything else."

"And Mariah…Oh Nora." The epiphany descended on her as she now realized the motive for her sister's anger. "I get it. I'm sorry. I'm so sorry."

"I really thought life was going to be different for her. I saw this bright future where she achieved everything I couldn't. My hopes for her just went up in flames when I found out about Davis. I blamed you. Honestly, it wasn't logical. I knew you couldn't control him, but I was eaten up with envy. You had the childhood, you went to college, you were the one who made something of your life."

Ellie reached out and put her hand gently on Nora's arm. "Oh Nora, life is so funny. I've envied you."

Nora laughed. "You envy your drug addict mess of a sister? How could you envy me?"

Ellie's cheeks burned as the confession rolled to the surface. "I envy you because men love you. Heads turn for you. Look how Lee has stuck with you through everything, even when you've tested his love. I feel like you know some secret about romantic love that I don't. I gave everything to Davis. I made life easy for him, cooked for him, cared for our children, supported him in his work, and it was like he couldn't wait to sleep with someone else. That rocked my confidence, Nora. It's made me feel like at my core, I'm not really worthy of love."

Nora laughed in surprise. "That's the stupidest thing I've ever heard. Davis is sick, Ellie. For every Lee, I've met ten other men who were awful. You didn't find the right person that's all. It's not you. Ellie, you're beautiful and that's on the outside and the inside. I mean that. I remember plenty of young boys from our childhood days who were plenty in love with you. Maybe it's time to stop looking for someone you can help and let someone help you."

Ellie sat back in the loveseat and realized that she finally felt at ease with her sister, almost like the old days. "So, you started going to church?"

"I did. I have a friend in recovery who recommended I go to a group therapy Bible class for addicts at Central Bend Community Church. Getting the nerve to go was terrifying, but Lee said he was going to leave me this time for real if I didn't follow through after the Albuquerque fiasco. I met a woman named Maryanne Phillips there. She and her husband run this rehab center. Maryanne was my mentor in the Bible Study, and she fought to get me a place here. My insurance is covering some of the cost, but where it falls short the Church and the Phillips are covering my expenses. They fought for me—hard. Maryanne really believes in me. I'm not going to blow it this time, Ellie. God's given me this chance."

Ellie took Nora's hands into her own. "I'm learning that it's almost impossible to accomplish anything difficult on our own. I did everything I knew how to do to save my marriage and it didn't work. Maybe it's okay to need help. Maybe it's the whole point. I'm not sure we ever learn anything if we can't find that place of humility. I respect what you're doing, Nora, the courage it takes to let yourself rely on God's help. You can do it." Her sister's eyes filled with genuine surprise and then her face flushed in embarrassment.

"It's about time isn't it?" she laughed almost apologetically. "I've been running so long; I hardly know what to do when I'm sitting still."

Ellie nodded her head in empathy. "You're telling me? I'm the fixer, remember? I guess God's been telling me recently that He's the fixer and I'm pretty broken. I can't go around fixing other people, you know?"

"Well, welcome to the club," Nora chuckled. Her eyebrows furrowed and she looked at Ellie with a frightening intensity. "I'm so glad, we found some common ground, but there's another issue I need to talk to you about."

Ellie nodded. "Mariah's here, isn't she?"

Nora's eyes widened. "How did you know?"

"Her name was in the log in when I signed in."

Nora nodded in realization. "It wasn't my intent to blind side you. I want our family to find healing somehow. I think the three of us could talk it out. I could at least mediate, so you can have a conversation with Mariah. She's still my daughter."

Ellie hesitated and met Nora's gaze. "I understand that. Of course, she's your daughter. I want healing too. Does Mariah know I'm here?"

Nora bit her lip and Ellie could see the strain in her jaw as she tried to choose her words carefully. "Ellie, she wants to talk to you. She actually approached me about a week ago."

"Really? When I last saw her, she made it pretty clear she never wanted to see me again."

Nora sighed. "Things change I guess." Her face tightened and Ellie saw all of her forty plus years etched in the drawn lines around her eyes and mouth. "She's still with him, you know?" Nora whispered. "She's drinking—too much, she's depressed all the time, the relationship makes her miserable, but... it's like she's obsessed with him. I can't get her to see clearly."

Ellie's mind was invaded by dark memories. *He doesn't love you.* Mariah's cruel words were vivid. Her thoughts flooded with images of her niece's tear-stained eyes and the raccoon like smeared mascara, the strident threats of suicide. They were all tools to accomplish her main objective: to have Davis for her own. "Do you think I'll have any better luck than you talking to her?"

Nora smiled, but her eyes betrayed her despair. "You know the expression, a wing and a prayer. Ellie, honestly, it's the only thing left I can think of to do."

Without thinking, Ellie reached for her sister's hand and gave her palm a gentle squeeze and nodded her consent. Nora picked up her phone and sent a quick text. "I told her I would text her when we were ready to have the conversation. I'm not sure where she is, but she's nearby somewhere."

Ellie took a deep breath and rose from the sofa and walked toward the kitchenette. "Is it okay if I get a quick glass of water?"

"Help yourself."

Several cheap plastic cups were stacked next to the sink and Ellie removed the top one from the stack and turned on the tap. After she filled the cup, she leaned against the counter and sipped her water while watching the door for Mariah. Her fingers were in her pocket and she felt the edges of one of the Praying Sister's notes. She pulled out the piece of paper and immediately associated the peach stationery with Ruby. She unfolded the paper slowly and was greeted by Ruby's graceful penmanship.

Sweet Ellie,

I find that when we put our best wishes in writing, they have a new power, a lasting power. I hope you feel the same way. I want you to know that I believe you are a beautiful soul, the kind of person who will sit with a child with no mama and read to them, the kind of woman who has the bravery to face kids every day struggling with their own losses and pain and offer them a piece of hope. You help them unlock a little beauty inside themselves. That's true faith sister and I assure you, you have it!

My encouragement is just to remind you that today is about your own healing. God is working. Your sister may not act as you hope she will. We can offer our love, our forgiveness, but it doesn't mean they will be accepted. The benefit of love and forgiveness is not just what they do for others, but also what they do for our own souls. Today, focus on your own growth. Give your sister to the Lord. Let God hold Nora in His hands. I do believe that you are strong, especially with God helping you. You've also got four women who love you to pieces. Don't you ever forget that!

Forever Your Praying Sister,
Ruby

Ruby's words were indeed like precious jewels. Ellie almost felt like her friend was next to her speaking in her ear. She felt Ruby's love and a bit of her strength. *Thank you, Ruby*, Ellie thought. *I need your strength.* A minute later, when Mariah entered her mother's room, Ellie hardly recognized the young girl who once had been a regular fixture in her home. Her niece had bleached her hair almost a white blonde. Layers of make-up covered her face like thick powdery armor, too light for her complexion. Her eyeliner was so dark and thick that Ellie could hardly recognize the eyes of the young woman underneath. She had gained weight. The lithe figure of her youth had been replaced by the figure of a larger, much heartier woman, the figure of a woman who regularly finds solace in a bottle.

Mariah's eyes hardened into a glare as she stared with hostility at Ellie. Nora did her best to soften the energy of the room. "Mariah, why don't you have a seat next to me on the loveseat. Ellie, you want to take the other chair?"

Mariah walked with a determined gait, the chip on her shoulder unmistakable. A grey tunic covered her ample form, and she wore black leggings and black boots with silver chains that clinked when she walked. She slouched into the chair and stared at Ellie with open hostility. The look in her eye was not so different from the look she remembered in Daisy's eyes in the moment after she had thrown a cup at her face. Mariah's expression held rage, fear, envy and as Ellie stood in the path of her glare, she felt almost hopeless. Unsure of what to do in the face of such open hatred, Ellie put her hand in her purse and touched the leather binding of Levi's Bible, drawing on his strength. She focused her mind on Ruby's note of encouragement. Ruby, Harmony, Jewel, and Allison were with her. Ellie spoke without thinking, "Those who wait on the Lord will renew their strength, they will soar on wings like eagles. They will run and not grow weary; they will walk and not be faint."

"What did you say?" Mariah asked. Her voice seemed almost mocking.

"I'm sorry," Ellie said. "Did I say that aloud?" She turned to Nora. "Do you remember that verse, Nora?"

"Oh yeah. Isaiah 40:31. Who could forget it? Dad used to recite those words all the time and made us all memorize that verse," Nora groaned. "What made you think of it now?"

"I'm not sure exactly," The verse came to her as she thought of her friends who had traveled by her side so she could stand firm and strong in this very moment. What about Mariah? Who did she have to support her? Davis? Where was he? Nora? She was trying to help Mariah but battling her own addictions tooth and nail. Ellie saw Mariah vividly. She was alone without the wings of an eagle lifting her above the storm. Her niece did not have a Ruby, a Jewel, a Harmony, or an Allison to stand beside her. She did not have a Levi, the kind of man who would give you a grief Bible and encourage you to seek God's grace in the middle of the storm. Mariah was an animal fighting in the thick of the struggle, scratching and scraping to survive. Ellie could not hate her. She was blessed with wings, but Mariah was trapped in a pit of despair. "Nora says you wanted to talk to me."

"Yeah. I do." Mariah leaned forward, her posture in the chair aggressive. "Why won't you let him go? Why do you keep clinging to him? Isn't it clear, he doesn't love you anymore!"

She was genuinely confused. "Mariah, I'm not sure that I understand what you're asking."

The words burst forth with violence. Her body shook as she spoke. "Davis says you're threatening to take the kids from him if he marries me. He says you're holding them over him, so we can't be happy. You're not happy so you don't want anyone else to be."

She waited for Mariah's anger to subside staying quiet as long as the moment would allow. Mariah suddenly burst into tears. Nora reached over and rhythmically patted her back as she sobbed. "Mariah," her mother said gently. "Can you listen to what your Aunt Ellie has to say?" Mariah rested her head on her mother's shoulder like a child, not a woman, Ellie thought.

She prayed silently for the right words. "Mariah, you've known me since you were born. I need to ask you honestly if you think I've ever lied to you?"

Mariah glared at her through her tear-filled eyes. "No," she finally admitted. "But why would you tell me the truth? You have every reason to hate me. So, why would I believe anything you have to say?"

Ellie found herself transfixed by the chains on Mariah's boots and she focused on the silver links as she spoke. "I was very angry about the affair when it happened, but I can say now, that I haven't allowed my anger over Davis' betrayal to change who I am. I'm not the kind of person who would lie or be vengeful, not then and not now. I hope you can believe me."

Ellie consciously lifted her eyes to look at Mariah directly. "I need to tell you the truth, but the truth can be hard. I don't want to hurt you, but we both deserve the truth. At least, I think we do." Ellie sat tall in her seat and considered each word carefully. "Davis and I divorced last summer. I think it's been nearly eight months. I need you to understand that I don't have any claim on him at all. I don't want him back. We share two amazing boys and I want John and Miles, your cousins, to have the best father they can possibly have, but I don't foresee a future where Davis and I will ever be together, not ever. If Davis wants to marry you, or move across the country with you, or whatever, I wouldn't have any claim or say on his decision. My hope is that he would not move too far away from the boys. My opinion is that the relationship between you and Davis isn't healthy and I think—harmful. I don't think my sons should have their cousin as their stepmother. I think it would be devastating to our entire family, but Mariah, Davis is a grown man who makes his own decisions and I'm not seeking to be a voice in his ear or influence him. If he's failing to commit to you or give you what you want and need from a man, then you have only him to blame for that. I don't have a part in any of this and if Davis says that I do, he isn't telling you the truth."

"Do you still love him?" Mariah's eyes blazed with fire. The words formed an accusation, not a question.

"No." Her voice was firm and then gentle. "There's someone else. I love someone else." She said the words before she could think them through and yet they rang as true as her own blood. She loved Levi. The knowledge flooded her, and she accepted the truth.

Mariah shot back. "You're trying to make me doubt Davis, to doubt his love for me."

Her eyes were filled with paranoia and fear. Ellie was not sure the truth mattered, but she tried.

"I am not standing in your way, Mariah. I promise."

Mariah continued to sob as Nora stroked her back the way she had comforted her when she was a small child. Ellie faced her sister directly. "Nora, I enjoyed our visit. I'm happy for you. I hope you'll call me again soon. Maybe we can rebuild what's been broken."

Nora nodded, her eyes still sad. "I'd like that, Ellie," she whispered.

Ellie turned her attention to her niece. "Mariah, since you were a little girl, I loved you. I know what I'm about to say may seem hard for you to believe, but I really do want good things for you. I hope you do find that love you're looking for. I've been looking for it too. I know how awful it feels to be loved by someone who can only love you with half their heart. I probably understand what you're going through better than anyone. You deserve better, sweetie. In fact, we both do."

Mariah's voice was so soft, Ellie could barely hear her words. "Why doesn't he love me? Why doesn't he want to stay with me?"

Ellie's heart flooded with emotion as she remembered her own pain and for a moment saw herself in Mariah's despair. "Mariah," Ellie said gently. "Do you think Davis can make you happy? Do you think he's capable of loving you the way you need to be loved? Your Grandpa told me once that all of us have difficulty seeing clearly, but some people can only look through a glass darkly. They are so focused on bitterness and envy that they can't see the good things anymore. True love should bring joy. It should make you happy. The right person will love you the way you need to be loved."

Mariah looked up at her and her eyes flashed with anger. "You just don't love him the way I do. You weren't enough of a woman."

Ellie felt a flash of anger rise from her gut and the heat rose to her face.

Nora looked ready to defend Mariah, but she surprised them both with a throaty laugh. "Yeah, I guess you're right." She thought for a moment. "Sometimes you have to be the kind of woman that just knows when to let go." Ellie stood slowly and grabbed her purse. "Well, I have to go. I have work tomorrow and I have to get over the mountain pass. Goodbye Nora. Goodbye Mariah."

Mariah was silent and brooding, but Nora rose from her chair and hugged Ellie briefly. "Bye Sis."

Ellie thought of Ruby as she left the room. For a moment she had borrowed her friend's unwavering strength and she voiced a silent thankful prayer.

Chapter 21

Inspection

...And you will know the truth
And the truth will set you free.
—John 8:32

The Praying Sisters eyed her anxiously as they all piled into Allison's Suburban for the return trip home. Ellie knew they were desperate for news and she enjoyed building the anticipation, teasing them with her silence for a few moments longer. Harmony finally broke the tension. "Well...?"

"Well..." Ellie replied with a laugh. "I didn't just meet with Nora, but Mariah too."

"Oh, Lord have mercy!" Ruby bellowed. "You had a confrontation with the other woman? Two hens and one nest. That's never good."

"No, it's not, Ruby, but you know what? I don't want that nest anymore. She can have it."

Jewel's eyebrows arched upward to her hairline. "You're laughing?"

"Yes. I'm laughing. I feel so unbelievably free."

Allison laughed with her. "You go girl. You must have let her have it."

"Nah, you guys have taught me better than that. I saw Mariah clearly for the first time."

"Okay, we want details," Jewel exclaimed.

Ellie gave her friends a play-by-play of the meeting with Nora and then the confrontation with Mariah.

"Well, there's some drama right there," Ruby's eyes filled with light. "Ellie, I'm just so proud of you."

"I've had enough drama for a lifetime," Ellie admitted. "I couldn't have done it without you guys. I just felt like you were there with me lifting me up. Now, I feel good, like the chapter is finally closing and maybe I can start a new one."

"Closure," Harmony nodded thoughtfully. "That's what you needed. Maybe you're ready now to let something or SOMEONE good in your life."

"I get the hint, Harmony." Ellie rolled her eyes playfully. "I'm not going to lie. I see a place for Levi in my future. I'm getting close to believing that maybe, just maybe, I could put myself out there again."

"Hallelujah!" Ruby exclaimed. "We've all been prayin' to hear you say jus' those words."

"What's still left to do?" Jewel asked.

Ellie was thoughtful. "There's still one more thing I have to do."

"The last step. Are you going to let us know what it is or are you going to be mysterious?"

"I'm going to be mysterious, but I promise when I've made the last step, I'll let you know."

"Well, okay then," Jewel said in resignation. "I'm waiting on pins and needles."

Ellie reverted to listening mode for the rest of the trip. Ruby, in usual form, forced the traveling party to stop twice to use the restroom. As they climbed the mountain pass, the weather began to turn. Evening was approaching, but the sky was unusually dark under ominous thick clouds.

"Ruby, we're not stopping for any more bathroom breaks. We've got a surprise spring storm to outrun," Harmony's tone was decisive, and Ellie could trace worry.

Allison echoed her concerns. "I don't like the look of that sky. I've got my chains in case it snows. I've got some experience driving in snow, but I always prefer to avoid it if we can. The roads have been nice and clear, so we need to cover as many miles as we can before the snow hits."

"I'm callin' Clyde right now. I'm gonna let him know what elements we're drivin' home through just in case we don't get to our destination as expected."

"Good idea, Ruby. I would call Frank, but I don't have any bars. I tried to leave him a text."

"Ruby, do you have any bars on your phone up here?" Ellie asked. "Because I don't."

"I got jus' one bar, so I'm gonna make this call right quick." Clyde didn't pick up, but Ruby was able to leave a hasty message.

Finally, they reached the mountain's summit. Ellie stared at the snow-banks on both sides of the road. They were over ten feet high and created the illusion of driving through a great white fortress.

"Are you going to pull over and put on those chains? I think it's going to start snowing at any moment," Harmony said.

Allison nodded. "I'm going to keep driving till it does. The more distance we can cover the better."

Twenty minutes later, the snow hit and hit hard. Allison slowed and made the winding turns carefully. Within ten minutes of the first flakes, there was an inch of snow on the road. The ladies watched mesmerized as the dark night turned bright. Snow covered the ground and coated the fir trees reflecting what little light remained from the day. Butterflies began to flutter in Ellie's chest. There was little to no traffic on the road. "Seriously, it feels like we're the only people in the world. Where is everyone?"

"Apparently they all got the memo that today was not a good driving day," Harmony said dryly. She turned her head to Allison. "How are we on gas?"

"We're okay. We've got maybe three quarters of a tank."

"That's good at least."

Allison pulled over when the Suburban began to slip on the turns. "Time for chains," she called.

I'll help," Harmony said.

"I'll watch you two and learn," Ellie echoed. She found her coat, hat, and gloves and bundled herself up to face the elements.

"I'm stayin' in the car and Jewel's keeping me company. I don't think the two of us would be much help in this situation I'm afraid," Ruby confessed.

"I didn't bring any shoes except my heels," Jewel said mournfully.

"You're kidding?" Harmony exclaimed. "You brought five suitcases and not one pair of boots or even tennis shoes?" She shook her head. "Unbelievable."

Jewel snapped her fingers and pointed at Harmony. "No judgement needed."

Allison chuckled. "You're fine Jewel. We have all the help we need." She playfully punched Harmony in the shoulder. "You, stop!"

The snow was falling in fat flakes and Ellie caught a few on her tongue as she opened the door to the harsh winter storm. Miles and John would be in heaven. As thoughts of her boys filled her mind, she realized she missed them terribly. She wanted to hold Miles in her arms and listen to John as he shared about his day. The need to be home with her sons overwhelmed her.

Allison and Harmony knew what they were doing. They unraveled the chains from the trunk and adjusted them around each tire and latched the chains together like pros, neither woman afraid to get their hands dirty or knees wet. Allison handed her two flashlights and Ellie managed to shine one beam on Allison's work and the other on Harmony's. They were finished in about twenty minutes, but the snow continued to accumulate on the road. "We're just going to have to move real slow till we get out of this," Allison said.

"What's a road trip without a little adventure?" Harmony said. "We'll make it."

"Not if we wait here too long," Allison warned.

Harmony frowned. "What's the ground clearance on your snow beast?"

"I've never driven in more than half a foot and I didn't think it was great," Allison confessed.

They piled back in the SUV and Allison drove with new focus and intensity. Visibility was terrible in the white out. "These are downright blizzard conditions," Ruby moaned.

"If we can just lower our elevation enough, this snow will turn to rain," Allison assured them. As she spoke a creature shot out in front of them. Allison stunned, slammed on the brakes and the Suburban began to spin. Ellie felt disconnected from reality as she saw the deer they had swerved to avoid, dart back into the woods. They were spinning like a out of control merry-go-round. She could hear Ruby praying and Jewel whimpering in a ten second interval that lasted a lifetime. The SUV halted with a thud as the side of the vehicle slammed into a snowbank. Ellie immediately realized their good fortune. They weren't on the edge of a cliff. The SUV could have been careening down a ravine.

"Everyone okay?" Harmony asked.

"I'm okay," Allison said.

"I'm good," Ellie grunted.

"Uh huh," Jewel managed.

"I am not alright. Not at all!" Ruby said. "I saw my whole life flash before ma eyes."

"She's fine," Jewel said as she found her voice.

Allison sighed. "Well, I guess we need to check the damage, but I'm stuck on this side." The SUV was angled in a ditch and the driver's side of the vehicle was wedged into the snowbank. The passenger side was elevated, and Harmony had to fight gravity using her legs to open the door. Ellie did the same on her side and they both awkwardly made their way out of the Suburban, sweating from the exertion. Ellie held the door open for Jewel and Ruby who were bundling up the best they could. Ellie and Jewel both worked to help Ruby out of the rear of the Suburban and out the door. Allison grabbed flashlights and handed them to Harmony before grabbing the passenger seat and pulling herself upward toward the door.

Jewel shivered and pulled her wool coat around her as the snow coated her black hair. She was wearing her trademark Tiger heels and looked conspicuous amid an Oregon blizzard. Ruby was covered head to toe in scarves and stood shivering next to Jewel, looking miserable, but biting her tongue. The women surveyed the damage. Harmony narrowed her eyes and finally spoke aloud. "We're wedged pretty good in that ditch."

"Yeah," Allison agreed. "We're going to need a tow."

"No one has phone service, do they?" Ellie asked. The women affirmed her fears as they checked their phones for bars. "What do we do?"

Harmony spoke with confidence. "This is a major road and there will be snowplows and traffic coming, but we'll have to wait. They have stranded motorists all the time in these surprise storms."

Allison nodded. "The good thing is that we have plenty of gas and other than being wedged the Suburban is not mechanically damaged from what I can tell. The tail pipe is clear. We can keep the heat on till help comes."

Ellie nodded as the reality of the situation hit her. "I guess I won't be at work tomorrow and I can't call the school to tell them. I hope I don't get fired," she joked.

Harmony shook her head. "I don't think we'll be here all night. I highly doubt it, but I guess it's possible."

"I'm freezing," Jewel shivered. "Can I get back in the Suburban?"

Allison nodded. "Yep, go ahead." She pulled a large stick looking object out of her coat pocket.

"What is that?" Ellie asked.

"A road flare. Bless Mike, he always keeps a few in the car. I'm going to set them ablaze around the Suburban and into the road a bit so help won't miss us when it comes."

Harmony smiled. "Smart girl. I'll help you." Allison handed two of the flares to Harmony.

Ellie watched as Allison twisted the cap off and then struck the flare against the cap to light it. Harmony followed suit and soon there was a soft orange glow surrounding the Suburban. Allison poked her head through the passenger window. "Jewel? Ruby? Could you turn on our hazard lights?"

"I got you," Jewel said and soon the flashing of lights joined the orange glow of the flares.

The women piled carefully back in the car and Allison restarted the engine. Warmth soon filled the cabin.

"So, what do five self-sufficient, independent, capable women do when stranded in the snow in the Oregon wilderness?" Ellie asked.

"Well, have a Bible study of course," Ruby said. Laughter filled the cabin despite the grim circumstances.

"I can't think of a better time for prayer," Allison agreed.

* * *

Ellie rested her head on Jewel's shoulder. Despite the intensity of the storm, she felt sleepy. They had prayed together, sung a few hymns, and then shared struggles and secrets.

"What time is it?" Jewel asked Allison.

"It's a little past eleven."

"It very well might be my imagination, but I do believe the snow's lettin' up just a bit," Ruby said.

"You know. I think you're right," Harmony agreed as she peered out of the foggy glass. "There's lights headed this way. Should I get out and flag them down?"

"Couldn't hurt," Allison said. "You better hurry."

Harmony used the strength in her legs to open the door from the downward angle of the Suburban and then twisted around so her back took the brunt of its weight. Holding the door open while also finessing her way outside took all her strength and agility, but Harmony finally managed to struggle free of the Suburban. Gravity forced the door shut with a bang. The women still inside the SUV could see the bright flash of car lights, but the fogged-up windows did not allow them to make out the vehicles that stopped or even see Harmony. A few minutes passed as they listened to the running engines of halted vehicles and then Ellie could hear a dog barking. She jumped back startled when paws hit the window and a dog whined. The sound was familiar, and she used her jacket sleeve to clear the fog from the window. She could just make out the outline of a curly haired white face and soft brown eyes. "Cordelia?" she cried.

Ellie struggled to open the middle passenger door of the Suburban. As soon as there was a crack open, Cordelia jumped into the SUV and fell into her arms. The door slammed behind her. Cordelia covered her face in dog kisses and whined with such joy Ellie thought she might faint. After the dog greeted her, she moved throughout the cabin to greet them all, dirtying their jackets with her wet paws and hitting their faces with her wagging tail. No one seemed to mind. The door opened again. Levi poked his face into the vehicle. Relief flooded his face as his eyes rested on her. "You okay?" He forced his gaze from Ellie and nodded toward Allison, Jewel, and Ruby.

"We are now," Ellie laughed.

Clyde poked his head into the cabin next to Levi. Ruby let out a gasp. "Clyde honey?" Her voice sounded like she was on the verge of tears.

"I'm here, Ruby," Clyde said. "I got your message, and I was watching the clock. When you didn't come home or contact me, I knew something went wrong. I called Levi here and we made our way up intent on finding you."

"Oh, I'm so glad you did," Ruby gushed. "I just wanna hug ya!"

"We better help make that hug happen," Ellie nodded to Levi. He reached his hand to her and helped pull her out of the cabin. Ellie felt the electricity as he took her hand in his. Cordelia bolted after her, tail wagging. Jewel followed Ellie and Allison crawled from the front seat to the back so Levi could offer her a hand. Levi pulled the middle row of seats forward and both Levi and Clyde offered a hand to Ruby and pulled her out of the rear of the Suburban. As soon as she was out the door she fell into Clyde's arms and sobbed. Clyde held her.

"You didn't think I'd let you freeze out here, did you? I know how much you hate the cold."

She laughed through her tears. "I do hate the cold! I hate it so much! I've never missed Louisiana so much in ma life." They kissed and held each other a bit longer.

Levi was hunched over his radio talking to someone on the other end. Harmony walked toward them. "He's talking to Mike and Steve. They left before they could call them, but they've been in radio contact since they started tracking us. Sorry it took so long after I got out. I was talking to Steve on the radio."

Levi handed the radio to Allison so she could talk to Mike. Clyde was driving a large blue Ford F150. He rigged a towing cable to Allison's Suburban and worked with Levi to drag the vehicle out of the snowbank. The men spent about a half hour scrutinizing Allison's vehicle for damage before proclaiming it safe to drive. "You okay Allison, to drive the Suburban home?"

"If I'm following you? No problem," Allison beamed.

"I'll do you one better. I'll be in front and Clyde will drive behind you. At least you got chains on. How did you slide off the road anyway?"

"A stupid deer. There's ice underneath this snow, which didn't help either."

"Ah. That would do it. Alright, well I think we're ready to head home. Ruby's already moved her bags, all fifty of them, into Clyde's truck. Ellie, I assume you're going to ride with me and Cordelia? Let's get your bags out of Allison's vehicle and put them in my Tahoe."

"Right." Ellie said. "We're neighbors. That makes sense." Ellie felt her stomach flip with girlish excitement, but she tried to stay cool.

"Once we get to Veneta, are you okay to drop off Jewel and Harmony?" Levi asked Allison.

"Of course," Allison nodded. "We started this trip together at least some of us should end it together."

"If you're feeling too stressed to get behind the wheel, we can figure something else out. We could always get your car tomorrow."

"No, Levi. I'm okay. As Harmony always tells me, it's always best to get back on the horse once you fall down."

Levi nodded. "I would agree with her."

* * *

The Tahoe smelled like Levi, an earthy mixture of fir, rain, and soil. When they were alone and driving, silence filled the cab. Ellie looked out the window at the snow that was now lightly falling and stroked Cordelia's soft curly fur. "I was worried," Levi said softly.

"Thank you," Ellie said. "For coming for us."

"I didn't even think about it. I wasn't even off the phone with Clyde before

I was in the Tahoe driving. If anything happened to you..."

"I'm sorry to have made you worry."

"I don't want you to be sorry. I just want you to be safe." Ellie did not know how to respond.

"You make me feel safe, Levi."

He looked at her sideways while he drove, his expression difficult to read. "Really?"

"Your Bible meant more to me than I can say. I know it might seem strange, but today I met with my sister and my niece. You know, the one I told you about that night."

Levi was silent as he processed her words. "How did that go?"

"God gave me the strength I needed. You know, wings like eagles. I had those wings because of you and Allison, Ruby, Jewel and Harmony. When we started spinning on the road and we were stuck in the snow, I wasn't really afraid. I mean, I was a little afraid, but not really, you know? God already led me through the shadow of death. Why would I be afraid of a little deer or a snowy cliff on the side of a mountain road? I read your notes about trusting that God has a better future for you. I'm beginning to believe maybe for the first time."

Levi grinned. "For the record, you should be afraid of a deer that bolts in front of your car on a snowy cliff, but point taken. I'm really glad to hear that the Bible helped."

"Yeah. Sometimes when I was reading your notes, I felt like you were there talking to me, steadying me. I liked hearing your voice in my head."

Levi grinned. "Not everyone feels that way about my voice in their head."

Ellie returned his smile. "Well, I do. I'm really glad we're friends again."

Levi's face turned serious, "Is that what we are? Friends?"

"You are a true friend, Levi." Ellie heard a sigh escape his lips. "Levi, that's no small thing for me. It's the best compliment I could give anyone." *He didn't understand her, but she couldn't tell him, not yet. I am so close, Levi. Don't give up on me yet.*

Levi nodded. "Well, it's something."

Chapter 22

The Garden

> *Extreme fear*
> *Can neither*
> *Fight or fly.*
> —*William Shakespeare*

The next evening Ellie savored making dinner in her own kitchen. Miles helped her with the cooking while John set the table. Cordelia was lying on the kitchen floor determined to be in the way. After her adventure in the snow, Ellie wanted no more interruptions from time spent with her boys.

"How long do I let the butter cook?" Miles asked.

"You should add the cream now." Miles slopped the heavy cream into the pan. "Poor it in slow and stir." Ellie watched as he followed her instructions with care. "Nice," Ellie encouraged.

He beamed."I'm going to be one of those kids on MasterChef Junior."

Ellie smiled. "You'd win for sure, especially with this Fettuccine Alfredo recipe." She focused on peppering the grilled chicken. "John, how's it going with the table?"

He groaned. "I was finished with setting the table in like two seconds."

Ellie glanced over and saw the plates and cups had been arranged in a helter-skelter fashion. "John, you can do better than that." He sighed heavily but returned to the table and set the dishes more carefully. "Don't forget the silverware."

"I got it. I got it!"

Soon they were sitting around the table. "Miles, this looks so good."

"I have a special stirring technique that makes the Alfredo sauce perfectly smooth and creamy," Miles said with pride.

"Well, it worked," Ellie grinned. They began to eat, and she allowed the boys a few minutes to devour their food before starting conversation. "So, boys I wanted to ask you something. Um, what do you think if I were to start seeing Levi?"

"What do you mean see Levi?" Miles asked. "Don't you see him every day?"

Ellie grinned as she remembered the need for direct and clear language when talking to Miles. John poked his brother in the arm. "She means date Levi. You know like boyfriend and girlfriend."

"Oh. Gross," Miles said as he wrinkled his nose in distaste.

John looked at her skeptically. "Mom, Rae and I kind of thought you guys were boyfriend and girlfriend already."

The heat rose to her cheeks. "No, John. I'd want to talk to you about a decision like that before I went ahead and brought someone into our lives."

Miles eyes widened. "Levi's kind of already in our lives, right? And Rae and Pax? We talk to all of them like every day. I mean I don't talk to Pax, but you know what I mean? They're kind of like our family."

"They are, aren't they?" Ellie agreed.

"Rae and I talked about it a long time ago. We think it's alright. I like Levi and I think you should be happy, Mom." John sounded so mature.

Ellie flushed as she looked at their sincere faces. "I love you boys. You come first, you got it?"

"We know, Mom," Miles said as he wrinkled his nose again.

John was already on his phone, probably texting Rae.

* * *

There was preparation before the final step. Ellie made an appointment with Lyle after school on Wednesday. Allison agreed to watch the boys.

"Are you sure this is what you want to do?" Lyle seemed skeptical. His eyebrows were knitted together in concern like she had lost her mind.

"Come on Lyle," she laughed. "You know my Dad. What choice do I have really?"

Lyle smiled. "You've been listening to too many sermons or reading your Bible too much, but as your lawyer I can't advise you that this decision is in your best interest."

"Six months ago, I would have agreed with you," Ellie laughed nervously. "I really appreciate your work on this even thought my request goes against your counsel."

Lyle chuckled. "In truth, clients go against my counsel all the time, but usually because they are asking for more than I think the law will provide. For the record, I think the world needs more people like you, but I'd probably be out of a job if that were the case."

"Please, Lyle. Don't give me too much credit here. I'm doing this for me, really I am."

He nodded. "Good luck, Ellie."

"I don't need it. I have a good lawyer." She stood up and walked to the door, but turned at the last minute and said, "Thank you, Lyle. For all your talk of being a rogue church member, I know as my Dad would say, you're the cream of the crop."

Lyle waved her off. "Aw, shucks, Ellie. Just don't tell anyone."

"It's our secret, Lyle."

As she left his office, she stopped at the coffee shop below, the one with the yellow awning. She ordered a vanilla latte with half the syrup. She sat by the window and watched the people walk by, wondering what each of their stories might be. Her hands were in her pockets and she traced the corners of one of the unopened notes from the Praying Sisters. Harmony's blue note lay in her palm and she unfolded the message carefully.

Ellie,

As you probably guessed writing these notes of encouragement was not my idea. I'm not really the kind of person who writes notes to people, but I'll do my best. I love animals because they make sense to me. You feed a dog and treat them with kindness, and they are loyal to you. They never betray you, not ever, the same with horses. People? Not so much. You can invest everything you have in a person and you don't necessarily get the return you're expecting. I know your marriage taught you that, so you don't need to hear this from me.

You're probably wondering what my point is? I'm kind of wondering myself. Well, in accounting terms, everyone invests their money, their time, their resources into different things. We have choices on how we invest. God is a different kind of investment. Whatever we invest in God, He will give us a spiritual return beyond what we can imagine. Okay, so back to my point about animals. I guess what I'm saying is, animals sometimes know more than humans. They know who feeds them and who to invest their time and energy. They know where they feel complete. God is the one who feeds us and makes us whole, but most of us people are still pretty ignorant. We run around like chickens with our heads cut off. Do you remember when we went horseback riding, the spring I showed you on my property? As you face your sister or whatever your fear, remember that God is inside of you, that spring is inside of you. Ellie, if your center is in God, you can face anything. You are complete just as you are. Okay, I went longer than I wanted. Remember we are standing strong with you today. You're never alone, not really.

Your sister,
Harmony

Ellie folded the note and closed her eyes. Harmony's writing style was simple, but her words were wise, reminding her to stay centered on God, as her final task loomed before her. She would need God's strength, the spring of life inside of her in order to face Davis. *Thank you, Harmony*, Ellie thought. *You're never one to mince words and that's just what I needed.*

As she pulled into Davis' complex, she began to second guess herself. *Was she being stupid? Naïve?* She stopped the car in the guest parking area and pulled Levi's Bible from her purse. She said a silent prayer. *God, help me.*

294

Please let me know I'm on the right path. She closed her eyes and opened the Bible randomly. The heading at the top of the page read Philippians and there was a folded letter on the page with Levi's printed handwriting which probably explained why the Bible had readily opened to this spot. Ellie read the verses that were highlighted— Philippians 4:4-9 first before turning to Levi's letter.

Rejoice in the Lord always. I will say it again: Rejoice! Let your gentleness be evident to all. The Lord is near. Do not be anxious about anything, but in every situation, by prayer and petition, with thanksgiving, present your requests to God. And the peace of God, which transcends all understanding, will guard your hearts and your minds in Christ Jesus. Finally, brothers and sisters, whatever is true, whatever is noble, whatever is right, whatever is pure, whatever is lovely, whatever is admirable—if anything is excellent or praiseworthy—think about such things. Whatever you have learned or received or heard from me or seen in me—put into practice. And the God of peace will be with you.

Ellie felt peace as she read the words. Harmony was right. She needed to be centered in God, to rejoice and focus on the blessings in her life that brought her joy. This was the spring of life. Only by abiding in her blessings would she be able to let go of the hurt, pain, and bitterness. She needed God's help to let go of the past and embrace the future.

Thanks to the Praying Sisters, she knew now how to truly put faith into practice. Ruby had modeled faith to her when she brought her to a schoolhouse in the middle of the woods where she gave forgotten children all the love she had to give. Harmony liked to complain, but she always searched for the most efficient way to feed and clothe the poorest of the poor. Jewel cared for her abusive mother and sat at the feet of a homeless man and cleansed his wounds. Allison possessed an uncanny awareness of the people around her. She had seen Ellie and encouraged her and poured generosity on her when no one else did. Because Allison valued her, Ellie learned she could value herself. Davis had betrayed her, but these women had restored her faith. They had taught her that weaknesses could become your strength. She ran her fingers gently over Levi's handwriting hesitant as the thought occurred to her that she might be invading his privacy, but

Levi had made himself vulnerable. He had given her the Bible.

Melinda,

There have been days when I'm so angry, I can only think about drowning myself in booze. I wasn't much of a drinker when you were alive, but now I understand its appeal—a poor replacement for what I've lost, but an easy fix. I keep hoping that if I drink myself into a stupor the pain will stop, but it doesn't, at least not for long. Then there's Rae. I'm not being the father she needs. I know I'm not being the man I need to be. I'm not making you proud that's for sure. Living in shame and disappointment offers no relief from pain. I guess I'm realizing that now.

These verses about joy and peace are a slap in the face telling me something I know I need to hear. Melinda, you are with God. You are at peace. I'm hanging onto a past that can never be again and I'm destroying my own life with drinking and Rae's in the process. I got to wake up—drag myself out of the pit. I just don't think I can do it by myself. I guess that's where God enters the picture. At least that's what I hear you saying in my head.

Faith is belief against everything your eyes are telling you, that all will be made right someday. Today, I cleared the house of every drop of beer, wine, liquor, everything. I took Rae to the park and tried to talk to her. That wasn't easy. She lives in her sketchbook and will hardly look at me. It's a small start, but knowing you'd be proud of me made it easier.

Melinda, you were, still are, the light of my life. These verses ask us to take notice of what is praiseworthy and what is admirable. You always had faith, always believed the world could be better. You tried to make the world better and that's what I learned from you. You always put Rae and me first. Scripture tells us to put those worthy things we've learned to practice. I know the best thing I can do to honor you is live your example. Rae must come first. I'm going to try to be the father she needs.

Yours Always,

Levi

Yes, Levi, Ellie thought. *I'm just as tired of clinging to my grief. The time has come to let it go to open the door to hope, to act.* As Ellie walked toward Davis' apartment, she found comfort knowing that Levi had already walked this road or at least a similar one. She tapped on the door. From within she heard muffled movement and suddenly the door opened. Davis stood wide eyed his T shirt half tucked into his jeans in the doorway. "Ellie?" He could not contain his surprise.

"Sorry for the surprise visit. Is this a bad time?"

"Uh, no. It's okay. The apartment's on the messy side, but would you like to come in?" She followed him into the small entryway. "Are the kids okay?"

"Yeah. They're okay. That's not why I'm here. I need to talk to you about something else."

Davis raised his eyebrows. "Wow, you haven't talked to me about anything but the kids since...I don't know December when we had Christmas Eve dinner."

Ellie nodded. "I guess you're right." She followed him into the living room and then stopped in her tracks. "Oh, Davis."

Davis followed her eyes. "Oh, that." He glanced down at his feet.

A thousand little faces stared at her from the painting, her painting. In all the months since they had separated and then divorced Ellie had never been to his apartment. The boys had never said a word. "You bought it? Why?"

His face was flushed. "I saw the painting that night at the auction when I went to pick up the boys. The moment I looked at your piece, I felt a powerful emotion. I remembered those days back in North Carolina when I first saw your paintings. The dove, the fish, the church—I don't know. I guess they made me remember what it felt like to have the promise of your life before you rather than disappointments behind you. I made a bid for the painting. I knew I wanted it."

"You paid $5000," Ellie whispered.

"I wanted to make sure I bid high enough to guarantee I'd get it."

A melancholy washed over Ellie as she saw the shame and despair in his eyes. "Davis, the promise of your life doesn't have to be behind you."

He sighed. "When you've made the kind of decisions I have, when you've done the things I've done, there is no future, Ellie. The only thing waiting for me on the other side is hell. That's the one thing I feel sure of."

"Is that where you think you're going?" She asked slowly. "I didn't know you believed in hell?"

"I believe in hell more than I believe in heaven," Davis said quietly.

"I see," Ellie stared at her painting again like she was viewing it for the first time. "I still don't understand why you bought it?"

He shook his head."Ellie, I'm not sure I understand why myself. It's just… your painting is the way the church should be, the way I wanted the church to be, but I've never felt that peace. God, how I'd love to have peace, even a second of it."

Ellie saw Davis clearly. He was a man stuck between his past and present. A creature motivated by a bottomless pit of cravings that could never be filled. He wanted everything without surrendering anything. Most of all she felt his powerful anger towards God. In the almost two years since they'd separated, Ellie had experienced God's grace and mercy; Davis was still waiting on His wrath. She pitied him."Life isn't easy is it? I've been hit hard myself with my own struggles, Davis. But I think when you look at the painting, you're not seeing the whole picture."

He followed her gaze with his eyes. "I was wondering about the fish and the net?"

"Yeah. What do you see there?"

Davis shrugged, "Jesus' apostles, fishers of men, I suppose."

"Uh, huh," Ellie said. "When we're lost there's always the hope that we can be found. God's always trying to draw us from our sea of hurt and pain, casting His net for us. Even for you, Davis. I hope someday you'll let Him pull you out of your sea of torments, but you'll have to let go of the sin that's destroying your life."

"You mean Mariah?" His voice was heavy.

"Yes. You know it's wrong and you know it's brought nothing but pain to you, Mariah, me, the boys, my family. We need God to change what's broken and make us whole. That's when we can move past our sins and moral failings to the good part."

"What's the good part?" Davis said almost in a whisper.

"Forgiveness," Ellie said softly. "And then full acceptance."

His face was hopeful. "Are you saying you would take me back? That everything I've lost could be restored?"

Ellie shook her head. "No. Davis. I think you know the time for that passed a long time ago. You fight to win someone's trust back after there's been a betrayal as deep as what happened between us. You never fought for me. I'm not what you really want, maybe I never was, and I've learned to accept that. You're still in a destructive relationship with Mariah. You can't skip over the hard part. That's where you have to start."

He was nearly eight years her senior, but Ellie observed a childlike and vulnerable quality in his expression. "If I knew you would take me back, I'd have the courage to cut all ties with her. I just need something to hold onto. Otherwise, it's just too damn hard."

"No Davis. Even if Mariah wasn't in the picture, we could never go back to our marriage. I'm not the same person anymore. I don't want to be that person anymore. God has other plans for me."

His jaw tightened and his eyes grew even wearier. "I can't Ellie. I just can't seem to change my story."

"Davis, the church is just people. We're not perfect. The life you're living now doesn't have to be your story. I mean, it's a part of your story, but you still get to decide where the story is going to go."

"I've gone through it a thousand times in my head, every scenario, Ellie. There's no happy ending for me. It doesn't matter what I do."

"Davis, God doesn't save us from pain, but He helps us grow and learn through it. There's an opportunity here for you to make things right, to feel God's peace, but you'll have to go through the tunnel."

His eyes flashed with anger. "Why does God make it so hard? Why don't I ever get what I want. Even when I get what I want, I don't get what I want."

She studied his face trying to understand his erratic changes in mood, his vacillation between raw anger and vulnerability. "Because we don't want the right things, Davis.

They stood in silence looking at each other for a few moments."I saw

Mariah a few days ago," Ellie said softly. She looked at his features closely intent on reading his reaction.

He shifted nervously. "How did that happen?"

"I went up to see Nora. She asked to see me, and I got blindsided by Mariah. Nora tried to mediate a conversation between us."

Davis continued to shift his weight from foot to foot. "What do you want to say Ellie?" His voice sounded irritated.

"She thinks she loves you. For some reason, she's under the impression that I'm standing in the way of you two being together. Why would she think that Davis?"

His eyes darkened as his mouth tightened in a grimace. "I have no idea what to do with her. If I stay with her, Ellie, there's only going to be pain and suffering. If I leave her, it's the same story. She'll be miserable and I'll be completely alone. I'll have nothing left, no one. There's no way out."

Ellie nodded thoughtfully. "Neither of you are happy. Davis, I wish I could change your story and help you find that peace, but I can't. I think in your heart you know exactly what you need to do. You know hanging on to Mariah just so you're not alone is selfish and will hurt both of you in the long run. It will continue to hurt your relationship with your boys. But Davis, I can't help you any more than I can help Mariah. I came here because I have business with you."

His eyes drooped with fatigue as he turned toward her and sighed. "What is it then?"

She opened her purse and pulled out the piece of paper. "When I asked for the divorce last summer, I wanted you to pay for how much you hurt me, for making me feel so helpless and for hurting our boys, our family. You destroyed me where I was most vulnerable, my self-confidence, my worth as a person. I didn't believe at the time that I could heal from that kind of wound. The settlement we agreed on was about my hurt and your guilt. I thought the money would make me feel better."

Davis shook his head. "Ellie, I agreed to the settlement. I did hurt you and I accepted the agreement because I acknowledged my actions. Besides, my mom would have wanted you and the boys to have the money."

She struggled for the words. "Davis, do you remember when you bought me those Williams Sonoma plates right before I found out that you didn't end the affair with Mariah?"

He turned his face away from her and said under his breath, "What's the use, Ellie, of opening old wounds?"

"I'm not trying to open old wounds. I just want you to understand me. Do you remember?"

"Yes. I remember." His voice was clipped.

"That night, I went outside, and I launched every single one of those plates into the backyard. I watched them fly through the air and listened to them shatter."

"They were five-hundred-dollar plates. That was money well spent." His words were doused in sarcasm.

"You know why I did that?"

"Because you hate me. I get the picture, Ellie."

She sighed with frustration. "No, Davis. Not because I hate you, but because my pain and suffering can't be bought. Even though I was a total mess, I realized something that night. I'm worth more than plates and I'm worth more than the settlement."

Davis rolled his eyes and his shoulders stiffened. "Ellie let's be realistic. You got nearly a million dollars from that settlement. That's more money than you'd see in a whole career of teaching. Are you going to tell me that you think your personal value is more than a million dollars? Because most people would disagree. Do you think you should have received more money, because I didn't peg you as being that greedy?"

"You're not getting me." She handed him the slip of paper. His mouth opened as he stared at the figure. "There should be $789,234.00 there. Maybe some change. I asked Lyle to dissolve the trust he set up for me and give the money back to you. It's not quite the full amount because I put some of the cash settlement toward the house and renovations when I first received the funds. I thought that was fair because we share our boys and the house has been a safe place for them, but other than that, all the money from the cash settlement should be there."

"Ellie, what are you doing? We agreed on that figure." His eyes were now wide and his voice animated.

"I hope you'll still continue to pay monthly child support for the boys and to help them if they need you."

"Of course, I will. Why are you doing this? I don't understand what you're doing."

"This is me doing my best to forgive you, Davis, and to let you go. I'm doing it as much for myself as for you. That was Madeline's money. It never belonged to me. I think the settlement made you feel a little better like you had paid for your sin so to speak, but that's not how it works, at least not for me. If you really want to make things right, do the right thing by Mariah. Do the right thing for yourself. Find your faith again. If you really believe the path, you're walking on leads to hell, why are you on that path? Be courageous. Change your direction."

"I can't Ellie. I've made my choices." Davis stared at the check in his hands and bit his lip.

She shook her head. "I'm sorry Davis. I'm just sorry. I want that peace for you. I don't want the father of my children in hell, even one of his own making."

Davis' voice choked. "Thanks Ellie. I'm not really sure what to say."

"I do have a favor to ask."

He tightened his fingers around the check and his shoulders tensed. "Okay?"

"I want the painting back."

Davis looked up from the check and frowned. "Why?"

"I don't want this piece hanging in your apartment where it will never see the light of day. I think I would like to donate it to my church in honor of four women who have been a spiritual friends and mentors to me. I need the painting to be in a place where it will encourage people. That's what I want. Is that okay?"

Davis' eyes narrowed with understanding. "I see. You're right. I'm hanging onto the past. Take it then."

"Davis?"

"Yeah, Ellie?"

"Remember what I said about the net?"

"Yeah."

"It's only too late if you decide you're not going to try."

* * *

Ellie picked up the boys from Allison's. She would tell the Praying Sisters everything at their next meeting, but for now she sat still in the moment. The boys chattered in her ear as they talked about Ryan and Natalie and the adventures they had at Allison's. Her sweet friend rarely allowed them to leave her house without gifts. Allison had purchased them a new game for the Nintendo Switch and the boys were desperate to get home to play on their console. Rain began to sprinkle on the car window as they drove away, and Ellie switched on her windshield wipers. By the time they arrived home, the wipers were moving as rapidly as possible struggling to keep up with the torrential downpour.

She parked as close to the house as she could, and the boys darted toward the covered porch with their new game in tow. Ellie followed them with her jacket pulled over her canvas to protect the painting. Once inside Cordelia whined from the kennel and Ellie released her to run around the house. She removed her jacket and was relieved to see that her canvas was safe from rain damage, but the ten seconds of exposure to the elements had left her soaked to the bone. She placed the canvas in her study and made her way to her bedroom carrying her jacket. She took a shower and changed into a pair of flannel pajamas. As she ran a brush through her hair, she spotted a piece of paper on the floor. The folded pink paper had fallen out of her jacket. *Jewel's note*, Ellie realized.

She picked up the note gingerly and sat on her bed to read her friend's message.

Ellie,

I never got a chance to thank you for that night with my mom. You proved to be a caring friend and you also have pretty good reflexes. You did a nice job dodging that cup. My mom's got good aim. In all seriousness, thank you. There was no judgement. You just wanted to help and instead of focusing on my mom and her issues, you encouraged me. Now, it's my turn to encourage you.

You asked me how I survived growing up with my mom. I told you how the church helped me. People were there for me when I needed them like Ruby, Allison, and Harmony. Frank has been the most generous and supportive partner a girl could have. I've survived maybe even thrived because I didn't have to carry my burdens alone. Likewise, I'm happy that we can be here for you now, so you don't have to face a meeting with your sister alone.

Okay Ell, so let's talk about you and what's really important. I'm just going to say it. If you find a person out there who truly loves you and wants to carry those burdens with you, a person who brings out the best in you, recognize them for who they are: A gift from God. From one friend to another, stop messing around! It's time to live your life. Levi won't wait forever. You have so much to give. Start living.

Love,

Jewel (P.S. Please Don't Hate Me for telling you the truth!)

Jewel's words resonated. Ellie smiled. *Jewel, I could never hate you,* she thought. The truth was she had been running away from Levi when she should have been running toward him. She knew this, had always known it. *Was there really any other man on the face of the earth crafted more perfectly for her than Levi? God had placed him in her path and yet she had been too fearful to embrace the gift. She had taken so many positive steps towards faith and healing, but she was still hiding from God. I should run over to his house right now and tell him the truth, but I'm terrified. What if he realizes that I'm not worth the effort? What if he tells me he doesn't want me?* The thoughts crowded her mind and heightened her fear.

I've been afraid before, she realized. She was afraid before she confronted Mason, afraid to tell Sally the truth about her marriage, afraid to confront Nora, to face Mariah, to stand in front of Davis and give him his money back and yet...She had accomplished those feats with God's help and now she was stronger for it. *Why did confessing her true feelings for Levi seem even harder than all those fears she had already overcome?* A small voice inside of her offered the answer. *You still don't believe you have any worth. You don't believe you're worthy to be truly loved.* Jewel's words slapped her back to reality. *Levi won't wait forever.*

She threw on her tennis shoes and bolted out into the rain. She felt free, awake, and alive as the cold raindrops hit her face and pelted her jacket. She almost lost her footing as she slipped through the mud. She reached Levi's porch without practicing what she would say and pounded on his door forcefully. Levi opened the door suddenly while Ellie was in mid knock. She stood back awkwardly as Levi's eyes widened with surprise.

"Ellie? Are you okay?"

"Yes," she said.

Levi looked her up and down. "You're in your pajamas and you're soaked."

"I ran over here...because I realized something." Ellie needed a moment to catch her breath.

A bemused smile played on the corner of his mouth. "I'm listening."

"Levi, I'm in love with you. I've been in love with you for months. I was just too damaged and insecure to believe that you would really want me."

Levi's smile widened. He moved forward and grabbed her around the waist and brought her toward him. "I want you." He kissed her roughly at first and then he traced his thumb across her lips. "Let me try that again." He kissed her gently this time. "I love you, Ellie."

Ellie heard giggling and saw Rae staring at them from the window. "Oh," she said embarrassed.

Levi turned around and smiled at Rae and gave her a wink. She gave Levi a thumbs up and disappeared into the house.

"Rae's on our side," Levi grinned.

"So are John and Miles," Ellie confessed. "I guess I was the last one to figure it out."

"Better late than never." Levi kissed her again. He released her gently and looked at her with a playful light in his eye. "So, to what occasion do I owe the pleasure of this late-night visit?"

"So formal," Ellie teased. "I wanted to invite you to go shopping with me tomorrow. Do you think you can get away for an hour or two?"

Levi smiled. "I think I can manage that. What are we shopping for?"

Ellie pulled out Levi's Bible from underneath her flannel pajama top. "I'd like to buy a new Bible." She handed Levi's old one back to him.

"Something wrong with this one?"

"Oh, no. This was the most wonderful Bible I've ever had. In fact, if it wasn't for this Bible, I wouldn't be shopping for a new one. But it's time for a new one, a Hope Bible."

Levi pulled her close to him again and whispered in her ear. "I'm so glad to hear you say that."

The End

About the Author

Debby Handman writes novels and blogs to inspire women who have survived divorce. Her characters journey from the heart of pain to ultimate healing and joy. Debby is a missionary kid, pastor, musician and teacher who lives in Oregon. She finds joy in raising her two sons, teaching and writing. Photo by Alesha Culp photography.

You can connect with me on:
- https://www.debbyhandmanauthor.com
- https://www.facebook.com/Debby-Handman-146956512016632

Made in the USA
Monee, IL
12 February 2022